HOPE RUIZ

Promises of Forever

Drops of Forever Book One

First published by Hopeful Hearts Publishing 2021

Copyright © 2021 by Hope Ruiz

This novel is entirely a work of fiction. The names, characters and incidents portrayed in it are the work of the author's imagination. Any resemblance to actual persons, living or dead, events or localities is entirely coincidental.

Hope Ruiz asserts the moral right to be identified as the author of this work.

Hope Ruiz has no responsibility for the persistence or accuracy of URLs for external or third-party Internet Websites referred to in this publication and does not guarantee that any content on such Websites is, or will remain, accurate or appropriate.

Designations used by companies to distinguish their products are often claimed as trademarks. All brand names and product names used in this book and on its cover are trade names, service marks, trademarks and registered trademarks of their respective owners. The publishers and the book are not associated with any product or vendor mentioned in this book. None of the companies referenced within the book have endorsed the book.

First edition

ISBN: 9798571042628

This book was professionally typeset on Reedsy.
Find out more at reedsy.com

STACY!! You da real MVP. I'd be so lost if it wasn't for you. You read and read and read over my stories constantly. You must get tired of reading the same thing over again, but you do it with no complaints. You helped me build this world, and I really don't think it would have been half as good without you. You saw all the stories when they were separate and you saw them together. You gave me feedback on the stories themselves and the covers. You're just so ridiculously helpful.

Thank you!

Contents

Acknowledgement

My family is always so helpful when I write. My sisters let me read my stuff to them and they give me feedback. My mom listens when I lay out the plots of everything. They give me honest feedback about the book covers. My dad is always there wishing he was a reader to read my books but is so proud of me, anyway. Both my grandmas read my books and tell me nice things. My husband, Javier, may never read my books because he's not a reader either, but he's always there as a silent supporter. He gives me shit when I need stuff to make this work, but he gets it for me, anyway. Stacy, as well as my sisters, are a vital part of my story writing process. I couldn't do it without them. My best friend, Alyssa, too. Thirteen years of friendship and experiences together give me so much to work with. I would never be able to do this alone, and I'm so thankful for everyone who's so supportive and willing to help me make something substantial out of the random ideas that pop into my head. Couldn't do this without you guys. Thanks for always being there for me.

One

Evan

Yesterday, my father asked me to come for a meeting with him at our family's mansion where I grew up. It must be serious for him to ask me to his study. The only time he allowed me in there was when specifically called in, usually for a lecture or to discipline me for typical teenage shenanigans… or as typical as a billionaire teen in a private school with other wealthy kids can get. Needless to say, I haven't been in some years since entering adulthood.

I walk into the drab office. It's huge, with dark wood floor-to-ceiling bookcases on three of the four walls. They're all filled with first additions that probably cost a small fortune by themselves. I mean, this place has freaking ladders to get to the top. How uppity it must seem, but to me it's normal.

"Sit down, son," my father says, barely looking up from the papers he has in front of him.

I sit in the black leather chair straight across from him. It's large, and I used to feel so small sitting in them, which I'm sure was on purpose. Now I'm a grown man big enough to fill out the chair.

"What's up, Dad?" I ask, making myself comfortable despite not knowing what the hell I'm here for. Never show weakness. That's what dad always says.

"I want to speak to you about the future of my company."

I sit up straighter. This is an unusual meeting. I've wanted to take over my family's company since I was old enough to understand what it meant. I thought it was always assumed I'd take over one day. My father never specifically said, but he's big on keeping things in the family. He also never objected to me working in his various companies. Surely, he knew why I did.

"As you know, our family owns several businesses as well as being silent partners in dozens of others. The Van Holsten Conglomerate is vast and profitable, so I need to start thinking about a successor for myself when it's time for me to step down. I need to be able to train them to keep this company up to my impeccable standards," Dad explains.

This is it! This is the moment I've been waiting for. Dad is officially going to recognize me as his successor for the company, and all my hard work will have paid off. I'm pretty much sitting on the edge of my seat. Then his next words hit me like a ton of bricks.

"Now, Tyler Dean has been working with me for quite some time and I think he would make a fine choice to take over when I step down. You've known him most of your life so I want to get your opinion of him, his character, that sort of thing."

Are you fucking kidding me? He wants Tyler to be his successor? The guy's like two years older than me. What would make him the better option to take over the company?

Anger thrums through my veins the more I think about my father's words. Why am I always so invisible to him? I've always been interested in the company and his work and here he is, passing me over just like he always does.

"You're kidding, right?" I ask. I'm surprised I keep a level of professionalism to my tone because all I want to do is scream at him.

"Not at all. I know you knew Tyler in school and I need to know if he's the kind of person I can have taking over," Dad replies oblivious, or so it seems. My dad is a cunning businessman. Perhaps he knows exactly what he's doing and what my reaction would be.

2

"Tyler would be an okay choice. Sure, he's worked for the company and he knows the ins and outs, but is he really going to care about it beyond how much money it makes him?" I start. Dad is silent, waiting for me to go on. "See, I've been dreaming of taking over your company for as long as I can remember. I've worked at every level, at every little business. I've gotten to know the employees and the board. No one will care more about this company as much as I do. It's been my entire life, and every action I've taken has been with the intention that I would one day take it over. This company has been in our family for generations, and you've grown it bigger and better than ever. I deserve to have my chance to do the same. Why give it to someone else when you've got a perfectly willing and capable son to succeed you?" I finish my speech, waiting for a reaction.

Dad is staring at me hard with his hands steepled in front of him as if he's thinking. It's silent for a long time, or it feels like it, as I wait for my father to pretty much decide my future right here, right now. If I can't do this, I don't know what I'll do. Everything I've ever done has led me right to this moment.

"The problem, Evan, is you're young and you don't seem stable, at least to the people who matter. You have no family beyond your mother and me, which is what this company was founded on, and it's a deep ideal we hold fast to. There's no one in your life to share this with and to help you. All you've got is a series of women that don't last longer than a few weeks, and none of them from the right family or background to help you run this conglomerate. Having someone by your side the way I have your mother is a big reason I've been so successful. Tyler is married with a baby on the way. There's no one even on your radar for you to marry, and certainly not someone appropriate. This is why I didn't think of you first," Dad explains, and... really?

I don't have a series of women. At least, not the way he's thinking. They're just dates that never go anywhere because they aren't who I want them to be. He wants me to be married to take over the company? Fine. It shouldn't be hard to find a wife. I'm pretty well known and I'm good-looking, but my dad said she needs to be from the right family. I know plenty of people who come from the right background. Allie Stinfield comes to my mind, or Kristie Cleaston. They live in L.A. now, but no. Kristie and I didn't work as anything more than friends in high school, so it wouldn't work now. Allie... she's only ever been one of my best friends. She'd probably do it if I asked, but I can't do that to her. She deserves to find her happily ever after.

Another pops into my mind. The person I really want. She's someone I went to high school with, someone from the right background, but I haven't seen her since we graduated high school and besides, she dislikes me... a lot. I know why and it's my biggest regret because I was head over heels for her since junior high. She's the one that got away and the one I'll love my whole life.

I let the thought exit my mind as fast as it entered because having her marry me at all, especially like this, would be nothing short of a fantasy. And like all fantasies, this one won't come true.

"I have someone in mind for you to marry if you're serious about taking over the company. You'll need to marry before your twenty-fifth birthday or I'm picking Tyler," my dad says, breaking me out of my thoughts. I stare at him. He's really going there. My twenty-fifth birthday is only a few months from now.

"Who is it?" I ask, cautiously.

"The daughter of a business associate of mine. He needs my help to bail out his company, and his oldest is about your age. I'll make her marrying you a condition for my help, then you'll have an appropriate wife by your side and I'll have a successor."

4

Two

Brooke

~⚬⚬⚬~

Three Months Later

Today's my wedding day. Weddings are supposed to be one of the happiest days in someone's life. I can tell you right now, it won't be mine. For me, it's like my world is ending. I only ever imagined marrying one person, and that's just never going to happen.

I'm sitting here with my arms crossed and a resting bitch face as I look in the mirror while someone twists and pulls my pale blonde hair into some elaborate up-do fit for a queen.

The women doing my hair and the others doing my makeup irritate me. Everything about today is irritating me. My mother is nowhere to be seen and in the room with me are my "bridesmaids" twiddling on their phones paying me no mind. I don't even know the women. My mom and some wedding planner I've yet to see picked them.

This entire stupid affair is someone else's perfect wedding, not mine. Why would I get any say in this wedding, anyway? I didn't get to pick the dress, the venue, the food, or the colors. Hell, I didn't even get to pick the groom.

Dear old mother and father picked the man I'm marrying today. 'He's a good man for you', they said. 'He was looking for a bride and his parents

5

agree that you're a suitable match,' they said. Obviously, they're getting something out of this arranged marriage, but I don't know what that is.

Perhaps my groom will tell me. Who knows what kind of man he is because I sure as hell don't. I have no fucking clue what he's like because I've never met him. I've never even so much as seen a picture of him.

I guess I'll see who my future husband is when I walk down the aisle. Gah! The thought makes me seethe with anger at my stupid parents for getting me into this fucking mess.

When the torturers doing my hair and makeup finish, they step back to let me admire their work. I'll give them this, the makeup is subtle and works well for me. It gives me a natural look that I'm totally digging and will probably try to recreate on my own. My hair is all pulled up with little diamonds sprinkled in there. I'm not entirely sure they're fake. And the tiara! Oh my God, it's insane. The freaking tiara boasts hundreds of diamonds I'm positive are real. My parents are well off, but this? This is ridiculous. They don't have the kind of money for this. I can think of one family that does. But no! I won't go there. I can't. I'll relent that it looks pretty fitted snugly in my hair, completing the up-do, though.

As much as I loathe this day is happening at all, I'll admit I look good. Gorgeous, even. Will Mr. Groom agree? An unexpected part of me hopes he does. Even though I don't know him, being rejected is not something I'm down with.

I've spent the last few months trying to fight this stupid marriage, but my parents had me by the balls, metaphorically speaking, of course. My father owns several businesses doing I don't even know what, and my family is pretty well off as I said earlier. This wedding is a marriage of convenience and nothing more. Some business associate of my dad's has a son my age who needs to marry before his twenty-fifth birthday to inherit whatever business his dad owns.

My dad gave me little choice in the matter. Marry this guy or be disowned. I would have been fine with the disowning because I don't need the money or the extravagant lifestyle. I'd be fine with making my own way, but I'm the oldest of three girls. I love my sisters fiercely and I'd do anything to protect them. The next one younger than me is barely eighteen. If I had said no to this sham of a marriage, Rebekah surely would have been next.

Since I know nothing about this man, there's no way I would subject Rebekah to it. She just graduated high school and is starting college later this year. She's going places, and I can't derail that by being selfish. Almost surely she wouldn't have been able to go live out her dream while married to some rich dude who's probably expecting a trophy wife that stays home.

I'm definitely not that kind of person either. I finished college this year with a degree in teaching and I'm supposed to start at a local elementary school this fall, but I don't think that's happening anymore given what I said about being a trophy wife and all.

My mother chooses this moment to walk into the bride's room of this lavish hotel they picked out for the wedding. The bridesmaids drop their phones and rush over to me, acting like they've been attentive all along, all for my mom's benefit. I roll my eyes. Why couldn't my sisters be my bridesmaids again, or my best friend, Willa? Mom still hasn't given me a straight answer to that question, though I've probably asked it a million times.

I stand from the chair and turn to face my mother, who's unzipping the dress from the garment bag. I haven't seen the dress yet out of principle, but I'm a tiny bit curious about what it looks like. I hope it's not too foofy. Princessy is just not me. Then again, most of this wedding isn't, so it's not looking good.

The bridesmaids help me out of my white silk robe as my mother walks over with the dress. I lift my arms so the four of them can get it over my head without ruining my hair or makeup. They pull and yank to get the corset back tight before Mother turns me to the full-length mirror. After placing my veil just behind the gaudy tiara, my mom says,

"Look in the mirror, Brooke. You look stunning."

I open my eyes to get a good look at myself. For once, my mom is right. I look damn good. The dress they picked out is pretty fitted and strapless. It hugs all my curves and flares out at the bottom with a short train. I approve of this one piece of the wedding.

"Thanks, Mom," I deadpan.

"Oh, don't be like that, Brooke. It's a happy day. You should be more excited," Mom replies as she fusses with my veil.

I bite back all my responses because none of them are kind and I don't have the energy to argue with her anymore. It's all I've been doing for months and it's not like anything is going to change. Definitely not now that we're at zero hour.

Grudgingly, I'm going to try to make the most of this stupid wedding and marriage. Might as well win where I can. Maybe I'll even like my husband. It could happen, right?

My dad knocks on the door, and Mom lets him in. My dad looks at me and his eyes fill with tears. Those tears do nothing but annoy the shit out of me. I would cry with him if this were a wedding I actually wanted.

I say nothing as my father pulls himself together. He takes my arm, then my mom hands me my bouquet. She leaves the room, followed by the bridesmaids, leaving me and Dad.

Dad and I exit and we stand waiting just outside the ballroom while one by one my bridesmaids make their way down the aisle with some Abercrombie model groomsmen.

This is it, my last moment as a free, unmarried woman. I take a deep breath. Here. We. Go.

Three

Evan

I'm standing at the altar waiting for my bride. My hands are sweating and I feel so hot I might pass out. It's like they have this church set at a million degrees, or maybe Hell is just coming to get me for agreeing to this medieval shit. I'll be a pile of sweat before my bride even starts her descent down the aisle.

I have absolutely no idea who this woman is other than the fact she's the daughter of some business associate of my father's. He never bothered to tell me her name, and I didn't ask. It was never going to be who I wanted, so fuck it, right?

The closer it gets to the beginning of the ceremony, the harder my heart beats out of my chest. Why did I agree to this again? Just to take over a business? My father seriously arranged a marriage? How fucking pretentious is that?

The room fills with people, though there are few here for me. It's only immediate family for me and my bride, business partners, and other important people. My groomsmen aren't even my friends. I don't know them at all.

I know damn well my friends, Noah, Allie, and Kristie, are going to be livid when they find out. And they will find out. No doubt, it will be splashed all over the newspapers and magazines by morning. A Van Holsten getting married is a big deal. A Van Holsten getting married when there was no official engagement announcement or wedding plans is an even bigger deal. It's been torture trying to keep it from them for the last three months.

Dad was very adamant that no one knows this is an arranged marriage. He said the optics would look bad. If that's the case, why enforce this as a condition at all? My bride's father agreed to the clause in their contract pretty quickly. Not sure how he got his daughter to agree to this wedding, but it's probably because I'm apparently the number one most eligible bachelor and anyone would think themselves lucky to be tied down to a child of the "Big Four". That's seriously what the media calls me, Noah, Kristie, and Allie. Our fathers are the four richest men in America, so the four oldest children of the four are America's "sweethearts".

Anyone who knows about this arrangement had to sign an NDA. That's probably also why none of my friends are groomsmen and none of hers are bridesmaids. The fewer people knowing what a sham this all is, the better.

Some piano music starts, causing me to look up sharply. Bridesmaids and groomsmen walk in pairs down the aisle, telling me my bride will come soon. I'm not ready. I'm not fucking ready to meet the woman I'm going to be stuck with for the rest of my life. Oh God, what am I doing? I can't fucking do this. Did my dad know I would have a panic attack at the altar? Is that why he put in the twenty-fifth birthday stipulation so I couldn't just be engaged until he named me successor? So I couldn't back out of this when the panic threatened to drown me?

Nerves are running rampant through my chest, causing difficulty breathing. Is taking over the business so important to me to be stuck with someone I might hate for the rest of my life? I hesitate with the answer. It should be no. Nothing is worth tethering me to some stranger, but when I'm not panicking, the answer is yes. Hey, if I can't get happiness out of my marriage, at least I'll have the business to run.

I attempt to drag in deep breaths while simultaneously trying to appear like the love of my life is walking down that aisle when the *Wedding March* comes on. I see her dad first and recognize him instantly as Harold Jacobs. If

I was paying more attention to the people in the pews, I would have noticed her mother and sisters.

I see her then, next to Mr. Jacobs, and my heartbeat steadies. Every live wire nerve I have calms down, leaving a pleasant buzzing in my body. She's got a veil over her face, but I can imagine what she might look like. I haven't seen her in almost seven years, but she can't look that much different, can she?

Her face is angled at the floor. She's afraid to look up and see who she's marrying. I can guarantee they didn't tell her because she wouldn't be going through with it if they had. Assuming she doesn't run out of here like a bat out of hell the moment she realizes it's me she's marrying, this could be my second chance.

I let her go once, but I will not let the ridiculously unattainable Brooke Jacobs get away from me now. Maybe dreams really do come true because I've loved her for almost fifteen years.

Four

Brooke

When the *Wedding March* starts playing on something ostentatious like a harp, my dad walks while I follow grudgingly. Everyone stands to watch as we walk down, and I'm glad the veil covers my face. I'm pissed off this is happening and also nervous to see my groom.

I'm too scared to look at the altar and the man waiting for me, so I keep my eyes angled down the entire walk. I only look up slightly when my dad places my hand in a warm, calloused one. I'm not expecting callouses on the hand of the son of some faceless business associate of Dads. Most of them are snooty, entitled types who wouldn't lift a finger for manual work. Who is this man?

I still can't make myself look further up than the black tie knotted at his neck. I hand back my bouquet and hold on to both his hands tightly because I feel faint. God, this is actually happening. I'm marrying a stranger. He could be an ax murderer for all I know. I could be his next victim, buried under the concrete in our basement by our first anniversary.

I'm snapped out of my panic when my hands are released so he can pull back my veil. I'm going to be exposed in just a few seconds. I take a deep breath to steady myself though my legs still tremble under my dress. Perhaps I should have hoped for a puffy one with a hoop skirt to hide my shaking.

As my groom pulls my veil up, I look at his face. My light blue eyes meet his blue/green hazel ones that I recognize in an instant. I haven't seen him in person since graduating from high school. All I've seen is his face splashed on the front of the tabloids and trashy gossip websites. In every picture, he had a different woman on his arm. You know, tall model types.

We went to the same private schools pretty much since middle school, and I've loved him nearly as long. I haven't liked him for much of that time, but my heart used to beat for him. He was the golden boy who could do no wrong because his family's basically American royalty. He played lacrosse and was Prom King our junior and senior years.

I wasn't unpopular, but I wasn't in Evan Van Holsten's caliber of popular either. I rode the middle ground with one good friend and stayed out of the way, especially after what happened just as we were headed into ninth grade.

* * *

It's summer and ninth grade starts in just a few weeks. Evan's hosting a party in his pool house to celebrate. He invites me because we've been somewhat friends since elementary school and I know I've loved him since I was ten. My friends tell me I don't know what love is since I've barely talked to him, but the feelings haven't subsided in three years, so maybe they don't know what they're talking about.

I decide to go since I've never been to a party before and also because it's my chance to really talk to Evan Van Holsten. I'm fourteen and officially a teenager. It feels like the in thing to do. Evan's the most popular person in school and he's going to dominate the high school. I feel honored to be invited to something only the most popular people will attend.

My mom drops me off at the front gate, and I follow the signs towards the pool house. I've never been to Evan's house before, and I'm very excited. As I get closer to the pool, I hear music thumping from the speakers and there are already a ton of kids here.

I'm looking for Evan because I really don't know that many people. The girls I was friends with in junior high moved and I haven't had a chance to make more. I'm pretty shy and, at the insistence of my parents, I'm trying to get out there more. Hence the reason I'm here at this party now.

The first two people to greet me are Kendra Berretti and Zack Lochlan. They're friends with Evan, so I figure I'm in good company.

"I'm so glad you could come. Evan has not stopped talking about you since you accepted his invitation," Kendra says as she loops her arm through mine.

I smile, thrilled Evan's as excited about me being here as I am. Zack smiles at me. His smile is similar to Evan's so I feel safe. I return the smile while they walk me into the pool house. It's filled with people, kids I've gone to school with forever but don't really know. I scan the room, but I don't see Evan anywhere.

"I could have sworn Evan was in here just a minute ago. Maybe he's looking for you," Kendra says, releasing me.

"I'll go look for him," Zack says, leaving me alone with Kendra.

We sit on some plastic chairs and Kendra chats me up. It feels so great to be making friends already. Kendra's friends with Noah Whittier, who is Evan's best friend. I'm with the right person. Zack comes back and sits next to me, shrugging when I look up expectantly.

"Sorry, can't find him."

"Oh, okay," I say, thoroughly disappointed.

"Let's go swimming," Kendra says, standing to take off her dress.

Underneath is a neon pink bikini. Zack pulls off his shirt too, and he's pretty muscular from playing lacrosse even though he's only fourteen. Hesitantly, I pull off my sundress to reveal my own bikini that my mom just bought for me.

It's the first time I've ever worn one, but my mom said I was old enough now and that I didn't need to wear a one-piece anymore unless I absolutely wanted to. I decided since I was going to a pool party with all the popular kids, I would let her buy me one.

The bikini is black with white polka dots and strings holding the top and bottoms together. My boobs are growing faster than most of the other girls, so they already fill out the bikini pretty well. I'm getting curvier in the hips and Mom assures me it's all part of puberty.

Zack appraises me, and I think he appreciates what he sees. I blush at the *attention I'm not used to. I follow Kendra to the pool and we sit on the side, dipping our feet into the warm water. Zack cannonballs straight into the middle of the pool, splashing us both.*

"Zack!" Kendra squeals and I laugh.

I spend probably an hour sitting poolside talking with Kendra, and I never see Evan. I see Noah and his other friend, Allie Stinfield, with him, but never Evan.

Eventually, I get up and leave Kendra to find the bathroom and something to drink. I search around, hoping the pool house has a bathroom. I don't want to go inside the house. Evan's dad scares me.

I find a door and push it open, but it's not a bathroom. It's a supply closet filled with pool cleaning things. Also inside is a boy and a girl making out. I gasp and I'm about to give them their privacy when the boy turns around and reveals himself to be Evan. The girl behind him is his other friend, Kristie Cleaston. I stand there frozen, unsure of what to do. My heart is cracking and I turn to go.

"Brooke, wait!" Evan calls after me, but I'm already almost back to the pool.

There are tears in my eyes when I get back to Kendra. She must see them because her smile falls, and she looks at me with concern.

"Hey, what's wrong?" she asks.

"I just saw Evan and Kristie making out in a closet," I say, trying to stem my tears. It's all embarrassing enough without the crying.

"That's where he got off to," Zack says, coming up behind Kendra.

"I think I'm going to go home," I say.

"Oh, no, don't. Not yet. At least go swimming with me once before you go," Kendra pleads and because I think we're becoming friends, I give in even when every fiber of my being is telling me to get the hell out of here.

Together, Kendra and I jump into the pool. I'm still underwater with her when I feel a tugging on the back of my swimming suit top. I think little of it, and I surface in the shallow end of the pool near the stairs so I can leave.

As soon as my body breaks the water, my bathing suit top floats away and my boobs are free. Everything is quiet for a millisecond before everyone in the place laughs hysterically. Every sound echoes off the walls of the pool house, making the laughter seem ten times louder than it is.

Everything sounds far away when, for a second, all I can hear is my own heartbeat. Then the laughter comes back full force, so loud it's making my head pound. My body heats with embarrassment.

I spin trying to cover myself with my hands and Evan is staring straight down at me with a surprised expression. I'm horrified, and I can't help the cascade of tears down my face. I walk out of the pool and everyone just moves away, all the while laughing at my misfortune.

I glance at Evan again and he's not laughing, but he's not making any move towards me or to silence his friends. As soon as I'm out of the pool, a girl I don't recognize runs towards me and wraps me in a towel.

"Hey, it's going to be okay. I'll get you out of here," she whispers, leading me out of the laughter-filled pool house after grabbing my dress and shoes.

"I'm Willa, by the way. I just moved here," Willa tells me once we're outside.

"Brooke. Thank you," I whisper, and that's the start of our friendship.

I do not doubt for a minute that Kendra was responsible for pulling my top off and Zack was an accomplice. They're both two-faced assholes making me think they were my friends and that Evan actually liked me. They preyed on my weaknesses and insecurities to get a laugh.

I'm also positive Evan and anyone else who is a part of their group is the same, so though I'm sure I love him, even at only fourteen years old, I no longer want anything to do with him. I left that party embarrassed with a brand new reputation heading into high school. I left that party broken with walls so high around me only those with permission could enter.

✳ ✳ ✳

I shake myself out of the painful memory when I see someone behind Evan hand him rings out of the corner of my eye. I have to focus on him to stop my panic. He may not have been the mastermind of my greatest embarrassment and the thing that set the tone for the rest of my high school experience, but he didn't help me, he didn't reprimand anyone. He was still friends with the people who did it to me, and for that reason, I haven't liked him since that party. He embodied everything bad about high school, popular people, and the rich and entitled. That's what I've told myself over and over every time

16

those stupid feelings try to creep back up enough for me to want to act on them. I'm happy to love him from afar but never put myself out there for him to crush again.

A bridesmaid nudges my shoulder and I realize she's trying to hand me Evan's ring. My hand shakes as I take it from her. I don't want to go through with this. I can't be married to someone like him, but I can't stop this wedding either, not without major blowback from the Van Holstens.

Instead of running away like I want to, and also kinda don't want to, I nervously repeat the vows the priest is saying. I stumble over the words and given no one is supposed to know this is an arranged marriage; I hope it just sounds like I'm overcome with emotion.

I slide the simple white gold band on Evan's finger, paying attention only to his strong tanned hands. I just can't look into his eyes. He must think he's the unluckiest guy in the world to get stuck in this marriage with me, of all people. A stranger might have been better for him. For me, I'm debating whether an ax murderer would be better than Evan freaking Van Holsten. Gah, what am I even saying?

I'm jarred into looking up when Evan's velvety deep voice repeats the vows. In his eyes is such intensity that you wouldn't know we haven't seen or spoken to each other in seven years.

He slides the ring on my finger. It's a solitaire round stone that's not as big as I expected. It's still big but not in an 'in your face, I've got money' kind of way. The band on the engagement ring is actually two thin bands braided together. The wedding band is plain but has the same braided design. I wasn't expecting anything other than a simple band, but this ring is gorgeous and exactly my sorta thing.

I look up, surprised, only to be met with a smirk. I give him a disapproving frown so he knows his "charms" won't work so easily on me. The high walls I erected that night at his house do not have so much as a crack, even after all these years. Evan Van Holsten will not be the reason they crumble. Hopefully.

"You may now kiss the bride," the officiant says.

My expression changes to panic when Evan grabs me around my waist and brings me toward him. I expect a quick peck out of him, but instead, I'm surprised by the most dazzling first kiss I've ever experienced. Without thinking, my arms wind around Evan's neck during this passionate kiss, and anyone who didn't know better might think we are in love — or that it's not one-sided, at least.

I'm breathless when Evan finally pulls away from me. He looks almost as surprised as I am. He grabs my hand when they announce us as husband and wife.

"For the first time ladies and gentlemen, Mr. and Mrs. Van Holsten."

Five

Brooke

Evan and I walk back down the aisle together and out of the ballroom with loud cheering behind us. I wonder where we're going when Evan leads me to an elevator where he presses the button for the penthouse. What the hell is he expecting here? There's no way I'm sleeping with Evan today or ever.

The elevator opens to the nicest-looking penthouse I've ever seen. The couch is stark white and there's a bottle of champagne on ice next to it. Behind us are two separate rooms, and a full-sized kitchen. There's even a freaking fireplace. Is Evan trying to impress me with his money? Because it's not going to work. I've grown up around these rich assholes. Wealth doesn't impress me.

I'm staring at it all when Evan steps around me and sits heavily on the couch. He loosens the tie around his neck and lays his head against the back of the couch. God, he looks sexy.

I don't move for a few minutes and Evan opens one eye to look at me.

"You can sit. I don't bite," he says with a half-smile.

I have so many questions that I don't even know where to start. I just stand here in this ridiculous wedding dress looking at my *husband* wondering where we go from here. I'm married to Evan Van Holsten? I still can't fucking believe it.

"Are you just going to stare at me?" Evan asks, an eyebrow raised. I shake myself and narrow my eyes at him.

"Why did you agree to this?" I ask, but I still don't move.

"I didn't know who I was marrying. My father didn't tell me," he replies, and I'm more shocked than I should be. I didn't know who I was marrying. Why should he?

"I barely know you, Evan. We haven't seen each other in seven years and even before then..." I say, letting the rest of the sentence suspend there.

"I know, Brooke," Evan responds and I can tell he remembers that night in the pool house as well as I do.

Evan sighs when I don't say anything or make a move to the couch. I still don't know what I'm feeling or what I'm going to do. I can't stay married to this man. It'll be the unhappiest marriage in the world. I was fine with unrequited love when it wasn't staring me in the face every God damn day. I'll be a trophy for him while he gallivants with his mistress models.

"Jesus, Brooke, will you sit? I'm not going to attack you," Evan says.

I scowl but stalk forward and fall onto the couch. I'll give him this; he had the right idea. The couch is comfortable and I'm exhausted already. The reception hasn't even started.

"Why did you bring me up here?" I ask as I kick off my shoes.

"I'm tired and they have to rearrange the ballroom for the reception so we have time. Besides, we barely know anything about each other and already we're married. I thought we could get to know one another, you know, catch up while we wait and we could do it alone instead of with a thousand eyes on us," Evan replies.

I turn towards Evan and relax on the couch. I hold out my hand for him. He eyes it for a second before smiling and taking it in his large one.

"Well, Evan Van Holsten, I'm pleased to see you again. I'm Brooke Jacobs," I reintroduce myself.

"Nice to meet you, Brooke Van Holsten," Evan replies with a devilish grin.

God, nothing good is going to come from being married to his man. I won't be able to stop myself from falling deeper in love with him, and it'll break my heart irreparably. I need to harden myself against him. I might love him, but I certainly don't like him very much.

"Is it too early to start drinking?" I ask, nodding towards the bottle on ice. I'm trying to grasp onto anything to distract me from the feelings that are annoyingly popping up again. It was easy to put them in the back of my mind when I haven't seen him in years, though my heart ached at every glance at a magazine cover.

Evan laughs for the first time since we married and it's just as beautifully velvet as his speaking voice. It leaves a warm, gooey feeling in my chest. No, no, no! I need to stamp it down.

He reaches behind him to grab the bottle of champagne and goes to work on the cork.

"What are we celebrating? Our marriage?" Evan asks with a smirk. It sets me on edge. Why is he so ridiculously confident and self-assured? It's annoying.

"What else is there to toast?" I ask, blandly. "At least my husband isn't an ogre."

"Are you calling me good-looking?"

"Your words, not mine," I say, even though Evan *is* panty-dropping gorgeous.

"Well, I'm glad my wife is such a knockout. You look beautiful, by the way. I'm a terrible husband for not telling you sooner," he replies with a smile and I laugh, though not from amusement.

"Now I know my husband is a liar. I've seen the kind of women you parade around with. I'm nothing like them," I say with some acid in my voice. I'm jealous. Damn it!

I realize I'm being pretty bitchy, but Evan's presence brings out the worst in me. He doesn't say anything to my comment, and he doesn't make eye contact either as he works the cork. Did I hurt his feelings?

He finally gets the cork to go, and it pops off the ceiling, narrowly missing us before landing somewhere behind the couch.

Evan gracefully puts his mouth over the opening so he doesn't get champagne all over his suit. Once the stuff isn't fountaining out of the bottle, Evan passes it to me.

"No glasses?" I ask before taking a long drink.

"Nah. Glasses are for losers. Have you never had a drink straight from the bottle?" Evan asks.

"I don't drink much and when I do, it's usually at some function or another," I admit.

"Parties weren't your scene in high school," Evan says, and it's not a question. He knows the only party I went to was an utter disaster.

"No, but they were definitely yours," I reply. He just shrugs, then closes his eyes and lays his head back against the couch.

"I'm not ready for this reception," Evan comments.

"Why?" I ask though I'm sure it's for the same reasons I'm dreading it.

"We're going to have to go out and pretend with all our guests that we're madly in love when you can't stand me. It's draining, mentally and emotionally."

I notice he doesn't mention his feelings toward me, and I wonder if I'm being unfair. It's been seven years since high school. He could be a totally different man now.

"I don't hate you," I whisper, looking down at my hands. I can feel rather than see when Evan lifts his head. I can imagine the curious look he's boring into my forehead.

It's the truth. I wanted to hate him throughout school, but you can't hate someone you've loved since you first laid eyes on them. Besides, he didn't laugh. That has to count for something, right? I don't hate him, but I don't like him and I don't think he's the kind of person I want to be associated with.

"You don't?" he asks and seems surprised.

"No," I start and I want to tell him why, but I don't want him giving me the look of pity he gave me that night. "I just don't like you on principle," I finish instead.

Evan sighs and grabs my hand. I look up into his hazel eyes and all I see is some annoyance and maybe some hurt?

"What principle is that?" he asks tightly.

"You grew up the prince of the Upper West Side. Everything was handed to you. You never had to work a day in your life for anything. Everyone dropped to their knees at the chance to talk to you or to be friends with you, and you soaked up the unwarranted praise. Girls fought their way to get close to you only to be given a small taste of you then rejected. Half the people want to be you and the other half hate you for having what they don't," I explain.

"And what half are you?"

"Well, I don't want to be you, but I don't hate you. I guess, like always, I ride the middle ground and feel dislike for you generally."

"You grew up the same as me. Your family has money. We went to the same private schools most of our lives. Why are you so high on your horse?" he asks.

"My parents wanted to hand me things, but I don't think that's right. I worked for every good grade I got. I got into an Ivy League on my own merits without my parents flinging money at them. I never wanted to go to a private school, but it was expected. Can you honestly say the same?"

"Can you do me a favor?" he asks with a sigh. He looks even more hurt from my words than he did when I started. I can't form thoughts when he's looking at me like that, so I just nod.

"Can you please give me the benefit of the doubt? I don't know who you think I am, but I can probably guarantee you it's wrong. We're stuck together for better or worse, and I'd like more days to be good than bad. Just get to know me, the real me, before making a decision that you're going to be miserable married to me. You don't have to fall in love with me, but friends would be a decent place to be," Evan finishes and I'm speechless once again.

Evan's phone buzzes. He sighs as he reaches into his pocket.

"Yeah? Okay, we'll be down in a sec."

"Are they summoning us back to the wedding?" I ask breathlessly. I still haven't replied to his proposal.

"Yes, we are summoned."

Evan gets up and helps me. He holds my hand as I slip my shoes back on, then follows me to the elevator. We stand in awkward silence all the way back down to the ballroom.

"Hold my hand and act like this is the happiest day of your life," Evan directs and I do as we exit the elevator and head into the ballroom to the throng of guests.

My parents and Evan's stare at us as we enter the reception area. Evan's tie is still loosened and his hair is messy from running his hands through it. Honestly, he looks pretty damn sexy and possibly like we just had sex. The thought of that causes an unexpected and unwanted thrill to run through my body.

The rest of the guests cheer as we enter as husband and wife, then we center on the dance floor for our first dance. I struggle to hold up my short train with the loop provided. Whoever got my dress apparently didn't think a bustle was necessary. They should try holding several pounds of fabric on their wrist a whole night and tell me it's unnecessary.

Evan notices and loops it around his wrist for me before placing the hand on my waist. I give him a look and some random song comes on that we move to. Evan is a superb dancer. Figures.

"What?" he asks when he lifts me back up from a dip.

"You keep surprising me," I reply as I scrutinize him.

"Well, we have an entire lifetime together to get to know one another, so I expect we'll both be surprising each other often," Evan whispers into my ear.

I shiver as much from his words as from his warm breath against my neck and ear. Evan kisses my head and I can feel his smile against my hair. I know we need to look in love and happy, but that seemed sincere.

Clapping is the only sign for me that the song and dance are over. Evan leads me away so we can mingle. He keeps a hand on my lower back as people congratulate us.

"I'll be right back," Evan whispers into my ear, then the warmth of his hand on my back is gone, and it feels oddly cold. I shake my head. I think the champagne and the general atmosphere are getting to me.

Mom and Dad, followed by Rebekah and my baby sister, Natalie, pull me off to the side.

"See, it's not so bad. He's gorgeous," my mom says, smiling in Evan's direction. He's talking to his parents, I think. I follow her gaze and he's looking at me. He gives me a small smile.

"So, you're basing the wellbeing of my marriage on the fact that he's good-looking? I went to high school with him, Mom. Why didn't you guys tell me who it was?" I reply, annoyed and a little whiny.

It bothers me how much nothing else matters to her. He's basically American royalty, and now he's family. That is what they care about.

"Don't be dramatic, Brooke. Evan Van Holsten is a gentleman, and I'm sure he'll treat you as such. Count yourself lucky. Plenty of young women would kill to be in your shoes right now," Mom replies, not even looking at me.

"He is pretty good-looking," Natalie whispers and nudges my shoulder with hers. I roll my eyes. That's all anyone ever said when they found out I went to school with him, though Natalie wasn't old enough to think it at the time.

"Be sure and act normal, Brooke. You don't need to scare Evan off with your ridiculous interests. He can always annul or divorce you if he finds you too… different," Mom says.

I would be offended if anything Mom said offended me anymore, but it's pretty normal. Natalie is the golden child and they leave Rebekah alone mostly, probably because she's the middle child.

I do kinda feel like crying though and I swallow a few times determined not to do that here in front of them. I won't let them win. A hand positions itself on the small of my back and I know it's Evan. Relief floods me just by his simple touch, which surprises the fuck out of me.

"If you don't mind, I'm going to steal my beautiful bride so we can cut the cake," Evan says to my parents and we move toward the ridiculous six-tiered wedding cake all done up in fondant and royal icing. I hope it tastes as good as it looks.

"Thank you," I say, and Evan pulls me closer to his side. He's warm, and he smells delectable.

"I will always be here to get you out of awkward situations," Evan replies before kissing my temple.

I smile briefly, then drop it. I would not normally feel better at Evan's presence or his touch. The sooner this day can end, the happier I will be.

Evan and I position ourselves in front of the cake for pictures. We cut the cake and Evan unceremoniously shoves a small piece in my mouth, smearing as much of the white frosting on my face as he can before licking the remaining bits off his fingers in such a sexy fashion.

"You've got something on your face. Just there," Evan says, laughing as he motions to his mouth. I roll my eyes, but I can't help a smile.

"Payback's a bitch, you know," I reply as I shove my piece in his face. He laughs as he tries to take some of it off with the small napkins on the table.

I'm surprised when Evan pulls me towards him by the waist and gazes at me. I think for a second that he's going to kiss me when he lowers his face. Instead, he licks frosting off my cheek and I squeal.

"Evan!" I shout, but instead of anger, I giggle. I fucking giggle! What the hell is going on?

Evan looks at me again pretty intensely, and this time, he definitely will kiss me. In the seconds I have to decide if I'm going to let him or not, I panic. I don't want him to kiss me again, do I?

I spend too long going back and forth so before I know it, Evan's soft, perfect lips are on mine again. I don't think I want to, but my arms wind around his shoulders while people cheer. The smile I see when he finally pulls back is enough to make me question everything. He asked me to give him the benefit of the doubt. Perhaps I should...

I try to relax in Evan's presence when we take our formal pictures after we're cleaned up. Curiously, finding my smile isn't as hard as I thought it would be. Evan often whispers in my ear making jokes about the people here causing me to laugh. The photographer is not amused and keeps giving us dirty looks.

I have my dance with my dad, and he's all teary again. I don't have the patience for it, and so we don't speak. Before walking away once the song ends, Dad kisses my forehead like he used to when I was younger.

"I know this isn't what you wanted, but I love you, Brooke. We need this and I hope one day you won't be angry with your mother and me," Dad says.

I want to ask him what he means, but I can't before he walks away and Mr. Van Holsten takes his place. He gracefully grabs my hand and we fly across the dance floor.

"Hello, Mr. Van Holsten. It's nice to meet you," I say, trying to be polite.

Evan's father is a serious-looking man, and even though his only son is getting married today, he has not once cracked a smile. He gave Evan a severe handshake and a pat on the shoulder earlier. Perhaps there's a reason Evan is the way he is…

Mr. Van Holsten looks like Evan—or I should say—Evan looks like him. He's older, but his facial features are strong and he's good-looking. He's got a George Clooney kind of older man hotness. I imagine this is what Evan will look like when he's in his fifties.

Mr. Van Holsten looks severe most of the time, but Evan wears an easy smile that puts people at ease. I've always thought so, but where it used to annoy the shit out of me, tonight I've been welcoming it.

"Mrs. Van Holsten, I'd like to welcome you into the family."

His words are nice and hearing his last name attached to me is off-putting when not coming from Evan, but there is something in his tone to suggest that he's not such a welcoming guy. I put a smile on my face and bob my head genially.

"I expect you to make this marriage work. You don't have to love my son, or even like him, but he is the heir to the biggest fortune of the western hemisphere. He must conduct himself a certain way therefore you must conduct yourself a certain way. There will be no mischief from you. You will not embarrass this family with infidelity or anything else unbecoming of the name Van Holsten. Do I make myself clear?"

I sort of expected Evan's dad to be this way, but hearing these unkind words towards me throws me off a bit. I don't know what to say, so I just nod meekly. Richard Van Holsten is not someone to mess with. He's a very powerful man and to be honest, he scares me. He always has.

"Perfectly," I reply after swallowing the lump in my throat, trying to sound more confident than I feel. I will not let this bully of a man know he

27

intimidates me.

"Wonderful. I'm glad we understand each other. Be a good and obedient wife to Evan and we'll all get on swimmingly."

Mr. Van Holsten drops his hands from mine the minute the song ends. I stare after him, wide-eyed. Obedient? Is he for real? Whatever kind of asshole his dad is, I'm getting the sense that Evan is nothing like him. Evan might have had an entitled air about him in school, but I never saw him as vindictive.

Evan comes back up to me and sweeps me into his arms. After my nerve-wracking conversation with his dad, his approachableness makes my nerves fizzle out. I relax into his arms.

"I saw you and my dad were having a pretty intense conversation. Is everything okay?" Evan asks, looking concerned.

"He was just welcoming me to the family," I half-lie. I don't want to burden him with his dad's attitude towards me right now.

Evan gives me a look that tells me he doesn't totally believe me, but he doesn't pursue the conversation any further. When the dance is finished, he deposits me at the head table, then leaves to mingle with the guests. I suppose he's good at that, and I wonder if I'll be good at it too. I'm sure his dad expects me to support him with business dealings and whatnot.

Rebekah and Natalie slide into the seats on either side of me with stupid grins. I shoot a stern look at them.

"What?" I ask.

"How's married life, Mrs. Van Holsten?" Rebekah asks me with a laugh. I scowl.

"Well, so far, it's been fine. Evan is not quite what I remember but I've already been threatened by his dad, apologized to by ours, and told I'm lucky by Mom. So, I guess, all in all, I've hit the parent trifecta," I gripe, but then I sigh. It could be worse. Is that what my life is reduced to? Oh, it's not so bad because it could be worse.

"Well, you could have said no. I wouldn't have minded being shacked up with Mr. Hottypants," Rebekah says fanning herself as she watches Evan speaking with some people. I roll my eyes.

Natalie, who's sixteen, also appreciates how hot my husband is. She laughs at what Rebekah said. I still don't think I would have wanted to subject Rebekah to whatever Mr. Van Holsten's got going on. It could be bad news for me if I step a toe out of line. I'm pretty reserved compared to Rebekah, and I think she would have a harder time walking the straight and narrow. Besides, I would die if my sister got to marry Evan given my feelings for him.

"Mr. Hottypants asked me to give him the benefit of the doubt. I think I'm going to give it to him," I say with a sigh. I should be nicer to him. I would have been nicer to a stranger.

"Does that mean you guys had sex up in that penthouse? He totally had sex hair when you came back down," Rebekah asks, and Natalie snickers.

"God, Rebekah! No, we did not have sex. We've literally been married for a few hours. I'm not sure I even want to sleep with him. He's been with so many women. What if he has some kind of venereal disease?" I reply, my voice pitched an octave higher.

"There's always the honeymoon," Natalie says with a shrug.

"You're too young to be thinking about that," I reprimand.

"Oh, Mr. Hottypants is coming over," Rebekah says, and she and Natalie share a laugh. I scowl at them again when Evan stops in front of me with a smile.

"Are you ready to go?" Evan asks, holding out his hand for me to take.

"God, yes," I reply, throwing my sisters a dirty look. They laugh again, ogling my husband.

Evan grabs my hand and guides me towards the doors. I turn around and stick my tongue out at them. They laugh and I smile before giving them a small wave.

We take the elevator back up to the penthouse, and it still elicits nerves. I think maybe I could be wrong about what kind of man Evan is now. I'm different than I was in high school, so maybe he is too. I shouldn't judge him based on the family he was born into. I wouldn't want someone doing that to me. For my sake, and his, I hope he's a better man than those he associated himself with.

Six

Evan leads me to one of the bedrooms in the penthouse and another dress bag is hanging in the closet. He pulls it out for me and lays it on the bed. I give him a questioning look.

"I didn't think you'd want to be on a plane in your wedding dress. My mother's personal shopper picked this out. I hope it fits. Let me warn you, you're probably going to get one of your own," Evan says.

"One of my own what?" I ask.

"Personal shopper," he replies and laughs a little as my eyebrows shoot to my hairline. Evan moves to leave the room so I can change, but I stop him.

"Evan?"

"Yes?"

"I need help," I say, jutting a thumb to the corset back of the dress. I cringe that I even have to ask.

Evan flashes me a steamy smile and I roll my eyes. How many times did that work for him with the ladies? He slowly unties the bow from the laces. I look over my shoulder at him as he methodically loosens the corset back until I have to hold the front of the dress to maintain my modesty.

"Thank you," I whisper breathlessly.

"No problem at all," he rasps, then leaves the room, clicking the door shut

30

behind him.

I let out a breath, and the dress drops to my feet. I kick it off, then fight tooth and nail with the stupid petticoat thing. That leaves me in my strapless bra and white lacy undies. I open the dress bag to find a light pink dress with a black belt. It looks like something my mother would wear, but it's actually pretty nice. It's got a high neckline, and it's sleeveless. It's the uniform of the wealthy, elite woman.

I put it on quickly, and it falls to my knees. I zip the dress as far as I can and buckle the belt. I step into black pumps and leave the room. Evan is coming out of the other bedroom in gray slacks and a dark blue dress shirt. He's rolling the sleeves up to his elbows, showcasing his ridiculously attractive forearms, when he catches sight of me.

"You look nice."

He looks damn good too. His clothes fit like they were made for him. Ugh, they probably were.

"Thank you. Can you zip me the rest of the way?" I ask, turning around.

I feel Evan's presence behind me rather than see him. He zips it up quickly before putting his arms around my waist. I freeze, waiting for him to do something. What do I want him to do? Let go? Pull me closer? This is all too confusing.

There was a point where I wanted nothing more than for Evan Van Holsten to hold me and kiss me. For him to be my boyfriend. I tell myself all those desires died when I found him in the closet kissing Kristie Cleaston, but they didn't. Besides, it was never going to be me. We ran in the same circles, but his circle was still too high for me to reach. That much was revealed when his friends violated me with no repercussions.

"I hope our marriage turns out to be a happy one," Evan whispers, then kisses the top of my head, letting me go, and grabbing my hand. I don't take it away.

What? Did Evan Van Holsten really just say that to me? I'm having the hardest time reconciling the man next to me with the jerk I went to high school with. It's all throwing me through a loop.

We walk out of the elevator holding hands to see a line of people a mile long. They stand on either side of the aisle we walk through to get to the car that's waiting to take us to the airport.

I have no idea where we're going, but apparently, Mrs. Van Holsten's personal shopper bought me everything I need for the honeymoon, and both our bags are packed and already in the car. I slide into the black town car, and Evan gets in after me. We're sitting with a modest space in between us. We're going away by ourselves for I don't even know how long. I wonder how that's going to go.

"Where are we going?" I ask as the car heads into traffic. It's late and I'm so tired I could fall asleep right here.

"Since I knew nothing about you, I just picked where I'd like to go for a honeymoon. I figured it would be indicative of who I am so we can learn about each other," Evan replies.

"Okay. Where is your perfect honeymoon?" I ask, intrigued.

"We're going to the Bahamas. They have this magnificent resort there I've always wanted to go to. It's got all sorts of things to do and a water park. I've never been to one before. As you can imagine, dear old dad thought it wasn't appropriate for us to go somewhere so… normal," Evan explains.

I sit stunned because I've always wanted to go to the Bahamas. Also, because I never thought of Evan or his family as people who would want for anything, but that doesn't seem to be true. Evan wants to go do this normal family vacation thing for our honeymoon, and it sounds magical.

Despite the money, my parents let us do normal kid things. We went on family vacations to Hawaii and the Cayman Islands. I've been to a water park and Disney World. Evan never had, even though money was not an issue. And that's very sad to me.

"Is that okay? We can go to Europe or anywhere you want. We can change our flight plan," Evan asks nervously when I don't answer right away.

"No, the Bahamas are perfect. I love the beach," I reply with a small smile.

"We've got like a month, you know?"

"Really? A whole month?" I ask, surprised. An entire month alone with Evan? God help me.

"Yeah, I think my dad wants us to take the time to get to know each other.

We don't have to take the whole month if you don't want to," Evan replies.

It's summer, so I don't really have much going on. Since I'm not quite sure what's going to happen, my teaching job will be on hold too. Besides, a month away from my family and all the expectations sounds lovely, even if I have to spend that time with Evan.

"Let's take the entire month," I reply as the car slows down. Evan smiles at me when the door opens out onto a tarmac.

"I should have known you'd have a private plane," I say.

"It belongs to my father's company, but we get to use it. There's also a yacht anchored in the Bahamas so we don't have to stay in a hotel," Evan replies while pulling me along to the plane.

Rich Boy Evan's finally made his appearance. I roll my eyes at the back of his head but let myself be dragged. At the top of the stairs, Evan picks me up, and I squeak at the unexpected gesture.

"What are you doing!" I shriek.

"Carrying you over the threshold," Evan replies matter-of-factly.

We walk through the plane door and he carries me to the light-colored leather seats where he sets me on my feet. The seats look like they have recliners with footrests, and I long to lie in one and fall asleep.

Evan sits next to me and makes a grab for my hand. He must think better of it because he pulls his hand back at the last second and folds it into his lap. I find myself a little sad he didn't grab it.

"Next stop, Bahamas."

"Sounds good," I say, feeling sleepier than ever.

After we're safely in the air, I kick off my shoes and put up the recliner. I snuggle into the seat as far away from Evan as I can get and drift off. I need space.

I'm awakened as the plane dips in descent. Evan's asleep next to me with his head back against the headrest. A fuzzy white blanket had been put over me while I was sleeping, and I wonder if the kind gesture came from Evan or the plane staff.

When I put down the recliner and sit up, the noise or motion wakes Evan. He gazes at me with bleary eyes and a small smile appears on his face.

"We could have slept in the bed. It would have been more comfortable," Evan complains as he rubs his neck.

"There's a bed on the plane?" I ask.

"Of course."

"You say that like it's normal for planes to have beds," I reply, rolling my eyes.

"For me, it is," Evan says without a hint of joking or superiority. I'm confused. Where's the cockiness about the money he has? Where's the entitlement?

"Well, I would have passed anyway. I don't want to share a bed with you," I remark, turning towards the window.

"Yet."

"Excuse me?" I ask, whipping my head around to see a cocky ass grin on Evan's face.

"You don't want to share a bed with me yet. Give it some time. I'm an extremely charming man," Evan says.

"Did your mommy tell you that?" I snap. Evan smirks and his eyes twinkle with playfulness.

"She did, in fact. She always tells me what a special, charming boy I am."

"Well, don't hold your breath. You might die," I retort and look back out the window.

"I think we're in the Bahamas," I say after a few silent minutes. It's the middle of the night, but there's another town car waiting on the tarmac for us.

The captain comes out speaking with Evan and shaking his hand. The flight attendants open the door and we walk down the stairs straight to the car. We're taken directly to a marina and I stand there staring up at the ridiculously large yacht.

"Seriously?" I say, gaping at the monstrosity.

"Seriously," Evan confirms.

He takes my hand again and leads me up the gangway and to the bedrooms. I'm still dead tired and I just want to sleep. The room Evan leads me to is ginormous with a canopy bed and a freaking couch… on a boat. A guy comes in with my bags and sets them on the floor. A minute later, a woman comes in and heads to the closet. I guess she's putting away my stuff?

"Well, I'll leave you to it," Evan says.

"You're leaving?" I ask, surprised. He's not trying to share a room with me? After those comments on the plane?

"I thought you'd be more comfortable having separate rooms for now. I don't want to push you into anything you're not ready for," he replies with a small smile.

"Thank you."

Evan's been so sincere and sweet since the wedding. It's disconcerting and I feel cracks in the walls I've erected. Nope, that can't be happening. I need to repair those cracks right fucking now. They've protected me from everything else Evan's posse did to me. I can't let him in, even if parts of me want to. It will only end in pain, embarrassment, and heartbreak if I do. Evan's the only person who's ever had the capacity to break my heart, and he's already done it once. I won't give him another chance, even if the first time was just my fragile fourteen-year-old heart.

"I'll be in the room next door if you need anything," Evan says, grabbing my hand and squeezing before letting go and leaving the room.

The woman leaves my closet and the room pretty quickly. I go in after her to see what kind of shit this personal shopper bought me. There are tons of dresses; summer, casual, and gowns. There are so many bathing suits, I could probably wear one a day and never have to wear the same one twice for the next six months. There's an overabundance of different types of shoes. I'm happy to find some simpler clothes including jeans and t-shirts.

I find some silk pajama shorts with a matching tank top. I slip them on in the closet and head to bed. I'm asleep the minute my head hits the ridiculously fluffy pillow.

* * *

The sway of the ship wakes me up. It's still dark outside, but I know the sun will rise soon. That'll be something to see on a yacht in the middle of the ocean.

I walk out of my room and stumble around barefoot, trying to find a door to lead me to the upper decks. I've never been on a boat bigger than a pontoon before, and this is just crazy. I finally find my way up to an area that has a fire pit and several couches. The air is warm, which is good because I only put a silk bathrobe over my skimpy pajamas.

I walk closer to the seating area and I find someone is already lying on a couch taking up one whole section. Evan's lying there shirtless, wearing nothing but some gray board shorts. He's got his arm across his eyes and I think he's asleep.

I eye those tanned washboard abs a little too long before taking a seat on the couch across from him. I sit quietly, watching as the sun breaks the horizon, and the sky turns in a flurry of pinks, purples, and oranges. I'm admiring the view when I feel someone watching me. I look over to see Evan staring at me.

"Good morning," I say politely.

"Morning."

"Did you come out to see the sunrise?" I ask, looking back at the sky.

"I couldn't sleep, so I came out here to look at the stars. I figured I'd stay for the sunrise, but then I guess I fell asleep. Looks like I missed it," Evan replies with a lop-sided smile as he sits up.

The sky is just a pale pink now as it's rapidly turning brilliant Bahama blue. We both look up at the gorgeous sky.

"How are you holding up?" he asks thoughtfully. I blow out my breath, wondering if I should tell him all my crazy jumbled thoughts.

"Honestly?" I ask.

"Always."

"I'm okay. It's been a lot. I was thrown into this and I've spent months trying to figure out what kind of man my husband would be. I never in a million years thought it would be you. I haven't thought of you in seven years." Lie. I think about him every day. "And then the most popular guy in our high school, star lacrosse player, prom king is my husband. I want to dislike you because you were a jerk in high school, but I realize that's

36

probably not fair to you," I say.

"I wasn't a jerk in high school," Evan hisses. I scoff, and it sounds very unladylike.

"You were the biggest player and entitled jerk I've ever met," I say.

"I wasn't a player and I don't know what I ever did to make you think I was a jerk," he replies.

I stare at him incredulously. I know he remembers the pool house incident. He alluded to it at the wedding. Does he really think he didn't do anything? I mean he didn't exactly, but it was his party and his stupid friends that he continued friendship with. That showed me he thought there was nothing wrong with their "joke". Instead of all that, I say,

"You always had girls hanging on your every word. You left broken hearts in your wake." Including mine, but I can't tell him that. I can't give him that power.

"That wasn't my fault. I only dated one girl. I wasn't interested in most of the girls from school. The one I really wanted to be with never gave me the time of day."

"Who was that?" I ask, my breath leaving me. Could he be talking about me? No, that's ridiculous. That would be too fairytale-like, and it's not how real life works. Wouldn't matter, anyway.

"Just a girl," Evan says, tight-lipped. Yeah, not me then.

"What did my dad say to you?" Evan asks, changing the subject after a beat of silence.

"You know, he welcomed me to the family. Told me there's a certain expectation of how I need to act and I should behave accordingly in all aspects of our marriage. I can't have... dalliances, as if I would do that to you," I reply, uncertain.

"You wouldn't think of having an affair? Even though you can't stand me?" Evan asks.

"I may not like you very much, but I still made promises to you when I said the vows. This marriage might be a sham, but those vows mean something to me," I say then in a tiny voice because I need to know, I continue, "Will you have a mistress?"

"No, though my dad didn't give me the same riot act. He just told me to be discreet."

I scowl at the double standards. His dad's an ass. Though I'm surprised Evan won't be parading women around like he did before. How gentlemanly of him.

"Don't worry. I will take my vows to you just as seriously. I like you even though you don't care for me. I've never not liked you. You're kind and you've got a great sense of humor from what I can remember. Most girls in my social circle these days don't have one to speak of. They aren't smart like you and all they've got going for them is their looks. You've got the whole package," he says with a shy smile.

This conversation and seeing Evan like this is making me second guess everything I thought I knew about this boy. But he's not a boy anymore. He's a man who's had years to change who he is.

Seven

Evan

I'm not sure what I was expecting when Brooke found out she was marrying me, but I sure as hell didn't expect so much loathing. She says she doesn't hate me, but sometimes it feels like she does. Other times, when I catch her off guard, it feels like I'm slowly thawing that cold front she puts up. I just can't get a read on her, not that I ever could.

I'm sitting at the table with the breakfast spread in front of me. Brooke went to her room to change out of the silk robe and skimpy shorts she was wearing. That's probably a good thing because she looked spectacular. Her skin is creamy and perfect. It was soft in the few places she allowed me to touch yesterday.

While I'm waiting for her to come back, I'm trying to think back to high school. The only thing that comes to mind is that stupid pool party I had before ninth grade. I'd invited her because I liked her, but then I dropped the ball when she found me making out with Kristie in the closet.

I didn't intend to do that to her. I liked her for a few years, loved her even, and we were sorta friends, but Zack fucking Lochlan convinced me Brooke would never go for me. Kristie was there, and she liked me. We'd been best friends for our entire lives. Very few people knew me the way Kristie did—does. I guess I just got caught up in the moment, but I knew I

39

fucked up the second I saw Brooke's hurt expression.

Everything solidified when her top got pulled off by someone at the party and she was exposed to the whole ninth-grade class. I could see the humiliation, embarrassment, and hurt on her face and I just stood there, staring.

That was the first time I'd seen boobs in real life and they were perfect, but I should have overcome my stupid puberty hormones to cover her the way Willa did. I could have been the one to come to her rescue, but I didn't, and that's one of my biggest regrets in life.

After Willa escorted Brooke out of the pool house, I was furious. I yelled so loud, everyone stopped laughing and the music screeched to a halt. I wanted to know who pulled the sick joke, but everyone stayed quiet. I had an idea who it might have been, but I didn't have any proof, so what could I do? I was only fourteen, anyway.

Brooke was different after that night. She was no longer the carefree girl I liked, but a closed-off person too afraid to let anyone in again. We broke her. Even though she must have known I wasn't involved, she must have felt anyone at the party was culpable. That none of us could be trusted again. Maybe she was right.

I always liked/loved Brooke, but she never gave me the time of day, not after that night. She never talked to anyone else besides Willa because Willa was the only person she felt she could trust.

I watched her in school, and I knew she was sweet and kind. She had a wicked sense of humor, and she was also fiery when it was warranted. Maybe that was something that developed after that night at the pool house. I don't know. All I know is that I wished more than anything she'd let me in again, but I ruined my chance when I kissed Kristie. Seeing how that ended up, it wasn't worth it.

And she called me a fucking playboy! I only ever really dated Kristie for two years before she broke up with me. I didn't sleep around, but maybe she assumed I did after finding me in a closet. Girls hung off me a lot, and I was too nice to tell them to fuck off, though I really fucking wanted to. That was mostly because of my family name and money rather than any of them actually liking me. It's still true to this day. All those women Brooke saw me with on the magazines were only dates. I didn't sleep with hardly any of them. They just wanted my money. They didn't know *me*.

I'm still trying to figure it all out when Brooke comes back in a red and white polka-dot sundress with a red swimming suit poking through. Her blonde hair is wet from a shower, making it look darker than it is. It's flowing freely down her back as it air dries. She has minimal makeup on. Just mascara from what I can see. She. Is. Stunning.

I realize I'm staring when Brooke clears her throat lightly and sits delicately across from me, very careful not to let me see anything. I focus on my breakfast, but when I look back up, I catch her staring at my uncovered body.

Brooke quickly looks away, and I smile a little. Not completely immune to me, then. That gives me hope that at some point during this marriage, I can convince her to be *with* me, not just married to me.

We eat in silence; me eating my eggs and bacon, Brooke eating her banana. Watching her mindlessly eat it while staring off in space is kind of erotic. I shift uncomfortably in my chair when her eyes focus on me.

"So what's the plan for today?" Brooke asks before sipping at her coffee, which I note she takes with ridiculous amounts of sugar and cream.

"Well, we could lounge around the pool or we could go explore the resort. We could go snorkeling. There really isn't a set itinerary for when we have to do stuff," I reply, hoping she'll want to go do something with me. Brooke is silently sipping her coffee, mulling over her options.

"Let's go to the resort," she finally says. I smile, ridiculously excited.

"We can head there after breakfast," I reply as someone hands me today's paper. I look at the front page and my eyes go wide.

"Fuck," I mutter, but Brooke hears, and her head jerks up.

"What?" she asks, then gets up to walk behind me when I just sit there staring at us splashed across the front.

There's a picture of Brooke and me walking hand in hand down the aisle after the ceremony. We look happy, so at least it doesn't look fake. The headline is in big block letters glaring at me.

41

Promises of Forever

PRODIGAL SON AND PLAYBOY PRINCE HAS FINALLY FOUND HIS PRINCESS

Notorious playboy and heir to Van Holsten Conglomerate, Evan Van Holsten, tied the knot yesterday afternoon in a decently sized ceremony to the relatively unknown Brooke Jacobs. According to sources, the wedding was fast as no one knew they were engaged. Reports say that his best friend, Noah Whittier, son of hotelier Clarence Whittier, was not in attendance. The other children of the "Big Four", Allie Stinfield and Kristie Cleaston, daughters of Dr. George Stinfield and famous attorney, Joshua Cleaston, were also nowhere in sight. This leads many to wonder if there's something in the oven leading to the hasty nuptials.

"You've got to be kidding me," Brooke says over my shoulder. I glance back, afraid she's going to be pissed, but her expression is more amused than irritated.

"What?" I ask, unable to guess what she's thinking.

"You have the shittiest journalists writing about you. They couldn't think of any other reason for a quick marriage than an unplanned pregnancy?" she replies.

"They're writing about you now, too. Our every move is going to be up for scrutiny. We need to be careful in public, just in case. We need to look happy and in love. I don't want my dad coming back saying we aren't playing our parts," I remind her.

Brooke nods as she takes her seat opposite me again. She picks at a muffin and that's the only way I know she's bothered by the article. I'm about to ask her what she thinks or if she's okay when my phone buzzes. I look at the caller ID and see the names. Fuck.

"I need to take this. I'll meet you in an hour so we can go," I tell Brooke before getting up and heading to my room.

I answer the video call, and as soon as I do, two different boxes pop up.

"What the fuck, bro?" Noah, my best friend my whole life, says before I can even say hello.

"Seriously! How could you not tell us you were getting married? Is it true? Is she pregnant?" Kristie asks sharing her camera with Allie, Kristie's best friend, and my other really great one. For most of our lives, it was the four of us.

"We would have come to support you even though you married Brooke Jacobs of all people," Allie chimes in.

I roll my eyes. There's probably a reason Dad didn't let them know. They would be able to tell none of this was real, and it was arranged in a second. I know it even now, so I decide to tell them the truth.

"My dad arranged the wedding. I didn't even know who I was marrying until I saw her dad," I answer with a sigh. There's a collective gasp from the three of them.

"Why did you agree to marry a stranger?" Allie asks quietly. She's always been soft-spoken.

"My dad said if I wanted to take over the business, I needed to marry someone "appropriate" before my twenty-fifth birthday," I say, inserting air quotes with my free hand.

"That's such bullshit. You've been working towards taking over that company basically your whole life. You're the most qualified person with or without a wife," Kristie defends me. I smile at her fierce loyalty.

"He wanted a family man. Someone settled with a woman backing him. He was going to choose Tyler fucking Dean. That was not going to happen, so I agreed to the marriage," I reply.

"That asshole? No wonder you went with it. Brooke Jacobs, though? She was such an ice queen in school. How is she now?" Noah asks.

I peer at him through the camera. He's a buff dude with tattoos covering both his arms and piercings on his face. I think he's going for sleeves, trying to rebel against the lifestyle we grew up in. He flips his brown hair up and his brown/green hazel eyes bore into mine.

"She's got all these thoughts about me from high school that are wrong, but she's holding onto them so tightly that it's making her unsure. She's stuck with me and she's civil, but she's not all that impressed," I reply.

"What did she think you were like in high school?" Allie asks, her blue eyes gazing kindly at me. Her fiery red hair is in a messy bun on the top of her head, a smaller rebellion than Noah's, but a rebellion just the same. Helen Stinfield is prim and proper at all times and expects Allie to be as well.

"She thought I was a jerk player who had different girls on my arm every week," I answer to which Kristie snorts and busts out into loud laughter. Allie's nose scrunches, trying to subdue her own because she has a kind heart and doesn't want to bask in my misfortune.

"You never dated anyone in high school besides me. When we weren't together, you were pining for the ice queen herself. Why did she ever think you were a player? You have absolutely no game," Kristie says through her wheezing, her dark hair falling into her face. I scowl and her green eyes twinkle in a way that makes me smile.

"Ha-ha. You're hilarious, Kris. She doesn't know I liked her in school when I wasn't dating you," I reply glaring at Kristie.

"That's part of the reason we broke up. You've always had a thing for her," Kristie says.

"I thought we broke up because we were better as friends," I retort.

"We did, and also because you had the hots for Brooke. I always noticed."

"I'm sorry, Kris," I say, suddenly guilty.

"It's no big thing, Evan. I love you, but I was never in love with you. We had our fun, but it wasn't right because your heart always belonged to her. Seems like it still might," Kristie says with a softness she doesn't let out often.

"She changed after the incident at the pool house," Allie says, and I nod in agreement.

"I think she's got all these negative feelings towards me because of what happened there. Even though I didn't do it, she probably thinks we're all to blame. Maybe we are," I reply, sighing.

"None of us did shit to her. I know she was hurt when she saw us in the closet, but we definitely didn't pull her bathing suit top off. None of us were in the water. I can guess who did though," Kristie says, and if we were all here in person, she'd be eyeing Noah.

"Kendra and Zack said they had nothing to do with it," Noah says defensively, guessing what her look meant.

"Sure," Kristie replies, rolling her eyes.

"So, what are you going to do?" Noah asks, glaring at the camera. I know the glare is for Kristie for bad-mouthing his girlfriend and friend.

"Well, we're on our honeymoon. I guess I'll try to make my wife fall in love with me… or at least not hate me so much. Maybe if I can explain myself about that night, she'll change her mind," I reply, shrugging.

"Aren't you quite the romantic?" Allie chuckles.

"Where are you?" Noah asks.

"Bahamas. We're going to the Atlantis resort," I say, feeling excited about it again.

"Oh, you've always wanted to go there," Allie says with a kind smile.

"Come visit me before you go home," Noah says.

"Are you sure Kendra won't mind?" I ask, eyeing him.

"She'll get over it," Noah replies with a shrug.

"Fine, we'll come to see you."

As soon as I say the words, I wonder if Brooke will even want to. She probably dislikes Noah as much as she does me, and if everyone's suspicions about Kendra are true, Brooke definitely won't want to see her. Noah's the only one in denial about what a bitch Kendra is.

"Get back to your wife and make her fall madly in love with you. All you gotta do is thaw that ice queen's heart and you'll be set. What's not to love about you?" Kristie says, trying to hype me up. I smile at my best friends.

"Yeah, easy peasy. Thanks. I'll call you guys later," I say.

"Keep us in the loop. Love you, Evan," Allie says before we exchange our goodbyes.

I sigh and throw my phone on the bed. I feel better after talking with them. They are the only three people in the world who truly know and understand me.

I get up and go to my closet. I look in the full-body mirror. We're going to a water park so I might as well just keep my board shorts on. I grab a black t-shirt and flip-flops before making my way back out to the table.

Brooke is sitting there in her cute sundress, one foot on the floor, the other underneath her. She has on some white sandals with flowers covering the straps.

"Ready?" I ask, excitement filling my body. She gives me a small smile and gets up from the table. After a slight pause, she takes my outstretched hand and I lead her to the speedboat that will take us to the resort.

Eight

Evan

We don't speak during the boat ride to the island, but that's mostly because it's loud as fuck and doesn't allow for conversation. Once we get there, we walk side by side, but she's careful not to touch me.

"Was that business you were attending to?" Brooke asks, trying to sound nonchalant. I hide my small smile, secretly thrilled she's wondering.

"No. Noah, Allie, and Kristie called me," I respond. Brooke's eyes dart to me, wide.

"You still talk to Kristie?" she asks.

"The three of them are my best friends. Noah moved to Florida after we graduated from college, and Allie and Kristie moved to L.A. during our senior year. We still try to talk every few days and see each other a few times a year. Noah actually wants us to visit before we go home," I reply.

"You still talk to your ex and your jerk friend wants us to visit? They hated me in school." Brooke is still incredulous.

"Kristie and I broke up sophomore year. We decided we were better as friends. Besides, she knew my heart belonged to someone else," I say, and Brooke stiffens beside me. Does she realize I'm speaking of her?

"Noah's never been a jerk, and none of them hate you. Do you not realize how you were in school?" I ask, honestly wondering if she didn't recognize

47

the cold front she put up for everyone, even now.

"I don't know what you mean," Brooke says, and not defensively. She really doesn't know.

"You pushed everyone away from you. They called you an ice queen because you were so cold to anyone who tried to get close to you, except Willa," I explain. Brooke bristles.

"I had a good reason!" she cries. My shoulders slump and I nod.

"I know you did. No one realized what that party did to you until later, but then you iced everyone out, and eventually, no one wanted to try anymore. People thought you were stuck up. Like you thought you were better than everyone else," I say.

Brooke's eyes narrow, but she stays silent. I think she felt she had to build walls around her so she didn't get hurt again, but did she realize it made her seem cold? I always knew she wasn't the ice queen everyone else thought she was. I saw her kindness, her fire, though I don't think she knows I saw those moments when her defenses thawed just enough to give me a peek.

"Allie and Kristie asked you more than once to hang out and you always said no," I continue.

"I thought... well, I thought it was a joke. I thought the minute I said yes, they would do something awful to me. I couldn't believe people like them would want to be friends with me. I let my guard down once and look at what happened. Besides, I didn't want to be friends with the girl who was devouring your face when—," Brooke cuts herself off quickly.

"I get that and I think to a point everyone else did too. I know Kristie and Allie felt bad about what happened and they were just trying to be nice," I say and watch all sorts of emotions pass over her face.

Brooke doesn't answer, and she's quiet the rest of the short walk. We pass through the arch leading into the resort. The place is huge with water slides and tanks full of marine life. There are beaches everywhere and crystal water surrounds us.

We both stop and admire the beautiful place. I've never been here before, and I'm pretty sure Brooke hasn't either. I wanted to take her to a place we could both experience for the first time together.

I glance over at Brooke and she's staring in awe of the beauty. She looks at me and I offer my hand. After a few seconds of hesitation, she gives in and takes it. We find a place to ditch our phones, clothes, and shoes before we go find something to do.

Seeing Brooke in just her red bikini makes my breath hitch in my throat. She has a slight tan and a lithe body. She's thin but also muscular and toned like she works out or something. She's curvy in all the right places, and I catch a small tattoo on her hip bone that makes me smile.

"What?" she asks when she sees me staring at her. Her gaze lingers on my body and it doesn't escape my notice.

"Nothing. Can we go do the slides?" I ask, grabbing her hand again. She smiles at me in a way that seems to say she thinks I'm cute. It's a start...

"Sure."

We immediately go to the Mayan Temple Pool so we can go down the Leap of Faith water slide. I follow Brooke into the water and it's warm. The sun is hot above us and I'm giddy with anticipation.

Brooke leans back in the water and back floats, closing her eyes to the sun. She looks radiant and relaxed. I walk so I'm next to her. She opens her eyes and gazes at me. She's got a small smile on her face and for once, there's not a look of wariness or hostility, just contentedness.

"I'm going down the slide. Do you want to come with me?" I ask. She stands up and nods. Her soaked hair drips down her back.

"Okay."

We walk to the stairs leading up to the slide. We have to wait in line for a bit, so I let Brooke go first and I stand behind her. The breeze catches her hair and blows the floral scent mixed with saltwater and chlorine into my face. It smells good. Brooke glances back at me as we walk up the stairs and gives me a small smile.

"Are you ready?" she asks when we get to the top. I smile and nod. She motions for me to go first, and I happily take my place sitting on the slide.

I cross my arms and legs and push myself off. The water carries me down the incline and I race through the shark tank. I look around, seeing a few sharks calmly swimming around me. I get shoved out the end and stand in the water with the biggest grin I've probably ever had

Brooke comes careening out right after me, and even with her hair wet and plastered to her face, she looks beautiful. I grab her hand and race off to the next slide called The Abyss. That one's a straight drop down fifty feet and through a waterfall. We land in The Cenote, which apparently is a lair for prehistoric fish.

We make our way through all the slides. I really like the ones that we go on together in a tube. She always sits in front of me and my heart races at her proximity. The Serpent Slide is especially fun. We're plunged into darkness, then we go through tubes underwater in pools filled with various marine life.

It's several hours later by the time we've gone down all the slides. We grab our things from the lockers. I'm sad to see Brooke cover herself back up in the sundress she brought. I put my shirt on and look at my phone. I have a few text messages.

I see one from Noah on the group message I have going with him, Allie, and Kristie.

Noah: Have you made Brooke fall in love with you yet?

Allie: Give the guy some time, Noah.

Kristie: He's going to need more than a few hours to make Brooke Jacobs fall in love with him. With his level of game or lack thereof, it might take years...

Me: Jesus Christ, guys.

I shake my head at my friends with a small smile. Brooke nudges my shoulder with hers as we walk. I put my phone away and grab her hand. This seems to be an okay level of intimacy.

"Your friends?" she asks.

"Yeah. How can you tell?" I reply.

"Your smile. I can't think of anyone else that could put a smile like that on your face," she says.

"I can think of one other person," I say, and watch her reaction intently. She gives me a small smile and her cheeks flood with color. Yes! I internally pump my fist in celebration. I'm slowly breaking down those walls she's built up.

We walk around hand in hand like a real couple looking for a place to have lunch. There's nothing stiff or forced about it. We find a little café where we can eat outside. The weather is perfectly warm but not stifling hot.

I pull out Brooke's chair, and she sits, thanking me politely. I sit across from her and we're shaded from the sun by a giant blue umbrella. We order our food and all is silent while we're waiting. Brooke sips at her soda. I'm finally about to break the silence when my phone rings. I pull it out and groan when I see it's my dad. We've been gone for less than twenty-four hours.

"Hello?" I answer in a clipped tone. I don't appreciate him disturbing our honeymoon, especially after the shit he said to Brooke at the wedding.

"Evan, I was just calling to see where you're at and how things are going," Dad says, and his voice is cold, almost bored.

"We're in the Bahamas and things are going great. We're currently having lunch," I reply, careful not to tell him exactly where. I'm sure he wouldn't approve even though I'm twenty-five.

"Good, good. And everything is okay with Mrs. Van Holsten?"

"Brooke? Yeah, Dad, she's fine. We're having a great time," I reply and hope what I said is true. I look up to Brooke in question and she gives me a small nod.

"I'll call again soon. We're going to need to speak about the next steps regarding the company now that you're married," Dad says.

"Sure, Dad. We can talk when I get back from my honeymoon," I say noncommittally.

As excited as I am to take over the company, it's not something I want to think about right now. I'm on vacation for the first time since graduating high school and I need to get to know my wife.

"Very well," Dad says, then hangs up.

"Goodbye to you too, Dad," I say to the dead line then set it down on the table.

Brooke looks at me with a pinched expression on her face. Her hands are in fists on top of the table. I grab one and rub circles on the top. She slowly relaxes enough for me to thread my fingers through hers.

"Everything will be okay," I say, and I hope I'm telling her the truth. I can't put anything past my father.

"I know," she replies, then our food comes and I'm forced to let her hand go.

We chat about mundane things like favorite colors and movies. I ask her about college and she's passionate as she tells me what her major was.

"I was supposed to start teaching in September, but now I'm not sure," she says.

"Why not?" I ask. She gives me a confused look.

"Honestly, I didn't think you were going to let me," she admits.

"Why on Earth would you think that? You spent years going to school for this."

"I didn't mean you, specifically. I didn't know anything about the man I was marrying except that he came from a wealthy family. I kinda figured I'd end up a trophy wife like my mom," Brooke explains.

"Well, I don't want that for you unless it's what you want. I'd say no since you bothered to go to college. Where is it you're supposed to teach? Did you tell them no already?" I ask.

"It's a school in the Bronx. I figured they would have the most need for a qualified teacher. Private schools and even public schools in Manhattan have tons of quality teachers. They don't need another. My parents aren't thrilled with my decision, and I assumed my husband wouldn't be either. I haven't told them no yet. I couldn't bring myself to do it."

"I think that's wonderful. We'll be home before September. We'll work out something so you can get there every day. My apartment is in Manhattan, but maybe we could move somewhere closer so the commute isn't so bad," I reply.

It would probably be a good idea to get a new place, anyway. One that isn't mine or hers, but ours. Brooke still hasn't said anything to all this, but her eyes are glazing over with tears. Shit. What did I say? I didn't mean to make her cry. I'm internally panicking so long, I forget to say something to make her feel better when the tears explode out of her eyes.

"What? What did I say?" I splutter.

"The exact right thing," she says, grabbing my hand again. I squeeze her hand and let myself relax as I smile at her. Eventually, her tears dry and we're able to eat.

After lunch, we drop our stuff back off at the lockers and go from pool to pool swimming or sunbathing on the beaches. It seems Brooke is getting more comfortable with me, and I'm glad for that.

Before dinner, we take the speedboat back to the yacht to shower and change. We have a reservation for some fancy restaurant so my t-shirt and board shorts won't cut it.

I walk Brooke to her room and rush to mine to get ready. I hope dinner is just as amazing as the rest of this day has been. I know now that her ice queen shtick is just that. She's let her guard down with me all day, allowing us to have fun and laugh together.

I want to decimate those walls she's got built so high, but I have to make sure I don't break her, or allow anything else to, once I take them down.

Nine

Brooke

It's been almost a week since we started our honeymoon. We've spent every day at the resort going through the water park. We've gone out on the Pieces of Eight tour and Evan reserved the whole boat, so it was just us. We took a tour of the harbor, then spent hours lazing about on Rose Island. We built a sandcastle together, and though the sandcastle looked like shit, the experience was marvelous.

Another day, we went to Exuma and swam with pigs then we went snorkeling. I've only been snorkeling one time before, but this was something else. The water is warm and crystal clear here so we were able to see all sorts of fish and reefs. Evan held my hand as we snorkeled, and it was sort of romantic.

Each day I spend with him, I feel the cracks in my walls grow and it scares me as much as it thrills me. Everything just feels easy with him. It always had when I let my guard down. Admittedly, it didn't happen too often in high school, but enough to know how dangerous he could be.

We ate breakfast together each morning and had dinner at a different restaurant each night. Sometimes it was in the resort and other times it was on one of the main islands.

We explored the outdoor markets, buying souvenirs for our friends and families. We explored the islands surrounding the resort and sometimes after long days spent at the beach, we'd go swimming together.

Honestly, I'm surprised I haven't heard from Willa yet. I want to call her and tell her everything that's going on, but I'm also scared about her reaction. She'll be mad I didn't tell her about the wedding and she'll be even more pissed I've been on my honeymoon for a week and I haven't told her every single detail. She might even be concerned that my husband is Evan.

Instead of being a big girl and dealing with it, I just decided to wait for Willa to call me. I'll deal with it then. God, I'm such a wuss.

I'm in my room on the yacht getting dressed for dinner. We're eating at some super fancy restaurant in the resort tonight that requires something a little nicer than my sundress and bathing suit.

I'm glad the personal shopper has included more formal-looking dresses, though I don't think an evening gown will be needed. I'm searching through my closet in a towel after my shower for something appropriate to wear when my phone starts ringing. I'm wondering if it's my mother while I search for it. God, I hope not.

The caller ID shows it's Willa, though. I smile seeing her name because she's been my best friend since the beginning of high school, but I'm also a coward and I know I'm in for some yelling.

"Hello?" I answer timidly.

"Don't you hello me, Brooke Marie Jacobs! How could you not tell me you got married! And it was over a week ago! What the hell?" Willa shrieks through the speakerphone I've got her on while I continue to sift through garment bags.

"I'm sorry and if you want to get technical, it's Brooke Marie Van Holsten now," I quip. I'm afraid to tell her the truth after the NDA my darling father-in-law made me sign, but I'm pretty sure Evan told his friends the truth.

"Sorry? You're sorry? Oh, for the love of God—," she breathes in a deep breath then starts again, though she's no calmer than she was before. "I wasn't even invited. I was supposed to be your God damn maid of honor, Brooklyn!"

56

"Not my name. Willa, if I tell you the truth, you need to promise you won't tell anyone," I say.

"What the hell are you talking about?"

"I had to sign an NDA and I'm not supposed to tell people the truth," I explain.

"Okay, you need to start at the beginning," Willa says.

So, I tell her about my dad approaching me about the wedding and my reasons for going through with it. I tell her all about the wedding and how I didn't know I was marrying Evan until I was at the altar. I tell her all about the NDA Mr. Van Holsten made everyone who knew the truth sign, and his conversation with me while dancing.

"That guy is seriously scary," Willa says when I finished explaining.

"Tell me about it," I reply, sitting on the little beige ottoman in my closet.

"So Evan Van Holsten, huh? You're actually married to Prince Playboy Jerkface himself?" she asks, reminding me of what she used to call him in high school.

I sigh because I think I've been unfair to him, and perhaps he wasn't as much of a jerk or playboy in school as I thought he was. He's been incredibly sweet this entire time. I've actually had fun with him every day for the last week. He's never once been a playboy jerkface. He hasn't even looked at all the beautiful women constantly staring at him. Instead, his eyes are always on me. Maybe I was just seeing what I wanted to see because I wanted to blame him and everyone else at that party for what happened.

"Has it been as awful as I imagine it is?" Willa asks when I don't respond right away.

"Actually, he's really down to Earth and sweet. We're at Atlantis Resort in Paradise Island in the Bahamas. He's never been to a water park before and he was so happy going down the water slides. He even said I could keep my job in the Bronx. I just feel like maybe we were unfair to him in school," I explain and I hear Willa scoff through the phone.

"Did you forget that it was at his party that his friends exposed you to the entire ninth grade class and he just stared? Did you forget he beat up,—oh what was his name? The scrawny kid with glasses that used to have a thing for you."

"Lester James?" I ask, thinking back. Yeah, Evan beat the crap out of that kid. He came back to school a few days later with a black eye and a broken nose.

"Lester, yes! That was not so sweet of him. Also, all those girls who used to pine for him that he left broken-hearted? I'm sure he did the hit it and quit it thing. Taking what he wanted and giving nothing in return," Willa says.

I remember that too. Somehow though, none of that seems in line with the Evan I'm discovering now. I'm wondering if we had him and his friends pegged all wrong, and every jerk thing he did had some sort of explanation we never cared to learn.

"I don't know, Willa. Even if that's who he was in high school, he's different now," I reply.

"He's not pressuring you into anything, is he? I know he's your husband, but if it's all for looks, you don't have to sleep with him unless you want to."

"No, he even provided me with my own room on the yacht. He kissed me a few times at the wedding, but I think that was mostly for show. Since we've been alone, he hasn't touched me and in public, he just holds my hand. That's for the possible paparazzi though," I respond.

"Good. He needs to keep his princely hands off you," Willa says fiercely, and I smile at her loyalty.

"You know he's still friends with Noah, Kristie, and Allie?" I ask, suddenly wanting to share my gossip.

"No way! Noah was a total stud muffin in high school despite his asshole ways. Is he still the hottest thing since the sun?" Willa asks and I giggle.

"I don't know. I haven't seen him yet. We're supposed to be visiting him in Florida when our time here ends. I'll let you know," I say.

"You better. Is he still dating Kendra because we all know she's the one who pulled off your top?"

"I don't know. I didn't ask," I respond and I shudder at the thought of seeing her two-faced ass again.

"Kristie, though? How does that make you feel?" Willa asks.

"I don't know. Evan's my husband, but he's not really mine, you know? He said they broke up sophomore year and I remember that. He said it was because his heart always belonged to someone else and I could swear he meant me, but that's ridiculous, isn't it? I think I was reading way too much into it all. Besides, if it were me, why was he making out with Kristie at the party?" I confide.

"Hmm. I can see it. You're hot, but guys are dumb, so who knows why he decided to mack on Kristie instead of you. I'm happy things happened the way they did, only for the fact that we became friends because of it," Willa says seriously.

"Oh, shut up! But I'm glad you were there. I have to get ready for dinner. I'll call you later," I say rolling my eyes though Willa can't see.

"Best believe I'll be calling you every day for updates, bitch. Ta ta for now. Love you," Willa says drawing out the last word then I hear the click of her hanging up.

"Love you too," I sigh into the empty line.

I stand up and toss my phone onto the ottoman and go back to searching through my closet. I finally decide on a red dress that looks like it's from the fifties. It's got a fitted waist, then flares from there and drops to my knees. I pair it with some red pumps and I curl the ends of my hair with a flatiron.

I apparently have a decent jewelry selection in this massive closet too, so I find some simple ruby studs and a matching necklace to go with the outfit. I put on some makeup, but it's light compared to the wedding. I end it all with some red lipstick that matches the dress.

I walk out to the deck of the yacht and look at the calm, still water. I find I have not hated the week I've been married to Evan, and that surprises me. Back in school, I wanted to hate every minute I had to be in the same room as him. I wanted to hate every second I was forced into conversation with him, though that wasn't often. I never really did hate any of our interactions, though. Secretly, and I never told anyone the truth, my heart beat just a little faster every time he looked at me. Now, I look forward to doing stuff with him and I don't feel the need to lie to myself.

I turn when I hear footsteps approaching me and I see the man himself in khaki slacks and a pale blue dress shirt with the first button undone, letting me see a peek of his tanned chest, and his sleeves are rolled up to his elbows.

"Ready to go?" he asks. I nod and follow him back to the speedboat that will take us to the island again.

We don't speak during the boat ride, but only because it's hard to hear over the engine and the water hitting the boat. Evan helps me out and we walk up the dock, passing by the pristine beaches.

The evening is warm but cooler than the days have been. At some point during our walk to the restaurant, Evan grabs my hand and it sends a flare of heat through my body. Then I remember this is all for show. Still, I let my hand stay in his strong, calloused, warm one.

We arrive at a place called *Casa D'Angelo*. We're seated at one of the square tables covered with a nice white tablecloth sitting almost directly underneath the painted circular fresco on the ceiling. It's stunning and takes my breath away.

There's a lamp in the middle of the table, making it seem quite romantic. I open the wine menu and glance through it without actually seeing anything. I look up over the top, staring at Evan's perfect face while he looks through it too.

A waiter comes up to us asking what we'll be having to drink. Evan looks at me expectantly, but I just shrug. I don't drink much and I have no idea what kind of wine is good.

"We'll just have whatever you think is best," Evan says, and the waiter nods before leaving.

I look through the menu. It seems the restaurant is Italian food with Caribbean flavors mixed in and now that I'm here, I'm beyond excited to try it.

The waiter brings by some sort of white wine and he pours us both half a glass. After taking our food orders, he leaves and I tentatively take a sip. It's the most amazing wine I've ever had, including the wine from our wedding, which I'm sure was some expensive stuff knowing Mr. Van Holsten.

"So, last week, when you talked to your friends, did you tell them that this marriage was arranged?" I ask, whispering the last word.

"I did. I don't lie to my friends. Besides, they knew something was up with it," Evan responds.

"Why? They couldn't believe you'd marry me of your own free will," I say like it's a joke, but deep down I desperately want to know the answer. I don't even know why. I'm not supposed to care what Evan thinks of me. Except I do.

"No. I mean, they were a little surprised *you* agreed to marry me, but mostly because they weren't invited," Evan says.

"They were surprised I agreed to marry you? Not the other way around?" I ask. Evan shifts uncomfortably.

"They know you didn't like any of us in high school, and you had good reasons. I can be charming, but they don't think I'll ever be charming enough to make you fall for me," he replies with a shy smile.

"Oh," I say. I can't let him know that I fell for him long ago.

"Why do you ask?" Evan asks, changing the subject.

"Well, Willa called today furious I didn't tell her I was getting married and complaining about how she was supposed to be my maid of honor and all that. I told her the truth. I know it's breaking the NDA, but I can't lie to my best friend either," I say in a rush of words. Evan nods.

"I get it. I don't expect you to lie to your best friend since I don't lie to mine. As long as we don't tell too many people, we'll be fine. I trust my friends and I'm sure Willa won't tell anyone either," he says and I let out the breath I didn't know I was holding.

"Thank you for understanding," I say and sip on my wine.

Evan gives me one of his dazzling smiles, but it's not the smile he used at our wedding when getting photographed, and it's not the smile I've seen when he gets pictures taken at events and things. This smile is almost shy and I've only ever seen it directed at me.

It reminds me of something, like a memory that I can't quite place. It leaves me with deja vu and I think hard, trying to recall where I've seen the adorable smile before. Then it hits me.

Our sophomore year of high school just started a few weeks ago and I'm sitting on the bleachers in front of the track alone, nibbling at my lunch. Willa's not at school today, and I can't stand to eat in the dining room when she's not with me. It's just a little too pathetic to eat alone.

I'm sipping my water when I see the prince himself run out of the locker room and onto the track. I look around for Noah or any of his other friends, but he's alone. I roll my eyes because I will never admit how attractive I find him still or how much my heart likes his. Not after what happened last year.

Evan doesn't seem to see me sitting there when he starts his laps. That's just fine. I can stare at his perfect body without him noticing my ogling. When he comes around the corner near where I'm seated, he glances up. I stare at him, frozen. He gives me a shy smile I've never seen before and waves a bit before rounding the next corner. I don't wave back.

I realize I'm staring when Zack Lochlan drops next to me, making me jump and nearly drop my lunch all over the bleachers. I shudder from his close proximity. He's part of the reason I even have to eat alone. He ruined my high school experience in one night, making it difficult to trust anyone. All anyone ever knows about me is that I'm the girl who flashed the entire class. The story's changed so many times that it's no longer remembered as a joke, but something I deliberately did to get into the "in" crowd. As if.

"Isn't he a little out of your league?" Zack asks, giving me a cruel smirk.

His smile reminds me of Evan's, but Zack's looks malevolent where Evan's is genuine. Zack's eyes are the same as Evan's and so is his hair color, but despite my dislike for Evan, I know he's basically good on the inside. When I look at Zack, I see the opposite. It's green and grotesque.

My face grows red in a blush so prominent it makes my whole body flush with heat. He's one of the few who knows I liked Evan last year.

"You like him still, don't you? Too bad Kristie's his future," Zack continues.

I don't reply because I've made it a point not to talk to him or any of the people he associates with, including Evan. I stare straight ahead, not looking at Zack's too handsome face.

"They'll stay together, you know. They're endgame," he says, shoving his arm around my shoulders. I cringe at the contact.

"He's too far up the social food chain for someone like you anyway, my little ice

62

princess. Me, though. I'd take you out of pity," Zack whispers into my ear.

Every particle of my body wants to rebel, run away or throw up, or both, but Zack seems like he could be dangerous and someone who's used to getting his way. His cologne is strong, and it makes me nauseous and dizzy.

Before I can do anything, Zack's ripped away from my side and I'm breathing in fresh air once again. I stare wide-eyed at Evan holding Zack by the front of his shirt.

"What the fuck are you doing?" Evan says with a deadly look in his eye.

"Nothing. Brooke and I were just having a friendly conversation," Zack responds, holding his hands up.

"Get the fuck out of here and don't bother Brooke again," Evan says and shoves Zack away from him.

Zack leaves without another word, but he gives me a smile that makes my skin crawl.

"Sorry about him," Evan says, sitting next to me, but not too close. He's always careful not to be too near me now. His exquisite cologne replaces Zack's, and it makes me want to lean into him.

"Thank you," I squeak out. I haven't spoken to Evan since he invited me to the party last year, but I can't bring myself to show him my normal level of coldness. He helped me.

Evan's girlfriend, Kristie, and her best friend Allie have asked me to sit with them or hang out, but I know it's only because they want to lull me into a false sense of security the way Kendra did. The minute I let my guard down with any of them, Evan included, I will be humiliated or traumatized, or both. No, thank you. I'll stick with Willa. I know she's genuine. How could Evan and his posse ever be genuine, given their parents are the richest people in America?

"No problem," Evan replies, then gets up. He looks back at the seat he just vacated somewhat longingly like he doesn't want to leave. It seems like he wants to say more, but he doesn't. Instead, he gives me that shy smile one more time before heading back to the track to finish his run.

I get out of there as fast as I can, no longer hungry after my run-in with Zack. That smile Evan gave will stay with me as long as I live. I can't have him, but he'll probably always give me butterflies which is totally unacceptable so I stamp *the feelings down so far they no longer exist.*

Ten

Brooke

I haven't thought about that day for a long time and remembering it now, Evan was actually pretty sweet.

"Are you okay?" Evan asks, concern evident on his face.

"Uh, yeah. I was just remembering something," I say slowly.

"What?"

"Just at the beginning of sophomore year. You came to my rescue when Zack Lochlan was bothering me. I'd forgotten you were so nice to me," I say, peering at Evan through a fresh lens.

"Zack's such a dick. I don't know why Noah is still friends with him," Evan responds with a disgusted look on his face. Interesting.

Before I can say anything, the waiter brings by our food. It smells absolutely divine and everything else is forgotten as I grab my fork and dig in.

Once the fusion hits my taste buds, I close my eyes and let out of soft moan of appreciation. The food is spectacular. When I open my eyes, Evan's looking at me.

"Sorry. This food is to die for," I respond after swallowing my bite. Evan shakes his head and takes a forkful of the food.

"I see now why this food elicited sex noises from you," Evan replies with a shit-eating grin. My cheeks heat.

"Those are not my sex noises!" I splutter and Evan's smile grows larger.

I roll my eyes and return to my meal, conscious not to make any more noises, sexual or otherwise. Evan and I fall into easy conversation.

"Would either of you be interested in dessert tonight?" the waiter asks after taking our dinner plates away. Evan looks at me questioningly. I shake my head.

"No, thank you. Just the check please," Evan says with a smile.

Evan is so kind to all the staff on the yacht and any waiters or workers of any kind we've met. It's not like I expected him to be a jerk to them or anything, but I'm just happy he's nice. It makes being married to him that much easier.

He must catch me staring at him because he gives me a questioning smile.

"What?" he asks.

"Nothing. I just—you're not so bad," I stutter then flush.

"Thanks... I think," Evan replies, getting up from the table after the check is paid. He holds his hand out for me and I take it gingerly. I feel its warmth and callouses.

Once we're out of the restaurant and back in the breezy, ocean-scent-filled night, Evan shifts until his fingers are threaded through mine. I feel the callouses again and I have to ask.

"Where do the callouses come from? They usually indicate some kind of manual labor," I ask.

"My father owns some construction companies and over the years I've tried to do every job at every level of each company. I spent the month before our wedding learning whatever the construction guys would teach me. I think it's important for me to know every facet of every business that will hopefully someday be under my control," Evan explains.

"And marrying me was the only way your dad would let you inherit the business?" I ask.

"He said he wanted whoever took over to have someone backing him, that by being married I'll look more stable to the board, I guess. He said he had someone in mind that would be suitable to him if I was really serious about taking over. I was—I mean—I am, so I agreed to marry whoever. I never dreamed in a million years it would be you," Evan says, looking at the ground as we walk.

"You've dreamed about being married to me then?" I tease to lighten the mood, but it electrifies when I catch a look at Evan's penetrating gaze.

"Only in my wildest ones," he says, and his voice has dropped and sounds husky. The sound is doing things to me that I am not prepared for.

I can't think of one thing to say. I'm caught up in his beautiful eyes and I only now realize we've stopped walking. Evan's in front of me, still holding my hand. The look in his eyes is smoldering and I'm fighting for breath.

Evan steps closer to me, and I let him. I'm so caught up in the moment that I'm frozen, but I don't think I really want to move, anyway. I'm trying desperately to restart my breathing, but all I can smell is his cologne. It smells heavenly and I close my eyes to breathe in the intoxicating scent. So different from the memory of Zack's.

When I open my eyes, Evan's hand is coming up to move a stray hair out of my face. His warm fingers caress my forehead and ear as he tucks the strand safely out of the way, leaving a path of fire along my face. My breathing hitches.

Evan looks down at my lips and then focuses his heat-filled eyes back on mine. He's asking for permission to kiss me. Before I really know what I'm doing, I nod just the slightest bit and that's all he needs.

His lips crash against mine, and it's even more dazzling than the kiss at the altar. My arms wind around his neck of their own accord pulling him closer to me. Evan's arms snake around my waist until I'm flush with his body. Warmth radiates through every part of me that touches him.

After a few seconds or a lifetime, I honestly couldn't tell which, Evan pulls away and rests his forehead on mine. I'm breathing hard, letting my hands rest on his shoulders.

"I've been wanting to do that for years," Evan whispers.

"You kissed me at the wedding," I whisper back because I can't believe for a second he liked me in school the way I liked him, the way I fought not to after that stupid party.

"That was different. It was for show, to let the world know our marriage wasn't fake. This... this is real and just for us," Evan says, taking his forehead from mine.

I still can't form a coherent sentence when Evan grabs my hand again and leads me to the speedboat to take us home.

Evan doesn't let my hand go as he walks me to my room. I wonder if he's going to want to come in. Part of me wants to be spontaneous and invite him in, but the other part, the bigger part, is too scared of what all of this means.

We stop in front of my door and just stand there awkwardly like we just had our first date. I guess in a way this was our first date and not just the end of our first week being married.

"I had a nice time today," I say like I would if it were just a date.

"I did too. I was thinking tomorrow we could go to the Dolphin Cay and swim with the dolphins," Evan replies with an innocent smile.

"That sounds great."

"Listen, I don't want to push you into anything you don't want to do. I know you have some preconceived notions about me, and I'm partly to blame for them. High school was not kind to everyone and I know I should have done more for you, to defend you the night of the party. I saw you at your most vulnerable and all I could do was stare. It's one of my greatest regrets, but there's nothing I can do now but make it up to you. I was hoping that maybe we could give this a try. We could do the whole dating thing and see if there's anything real here. I like you and I'd want to do this even if we weren't already married. I'll let you decide if we try dating or not and how fast or slow we go. Just know that I'm here and I'm more than willing to receive whatever it is you're willing to give... even if that's just friendship. Goodnight, Brooke," Evan says with a smile.

Before I can respond, he kisses me quickly then takes off towards his bedroom door. I'm standing here at mine dumbfounded by his admissions, so I haven't even opened the door yet. Evan gives me one last look and a kind smile before he disappears.

I finally catch my breath and head into my room. I go to the bathroom and take off my makeup and jewelry. Then, I go change into the little silk pajama shorts and tank-top that seem to be all I own these days. When I lay down in bed, my phone dings with a message.

Evan: Goodnight, beautiful. Sleep well. I look forward to our day tomorrow.

I smile at the words and it's crazy how much this feels like the beginning of a relationship. I haven't dated a lot, but none have ended like this. I choose to flirt a little instead of just being polite.

Me: Goodnight, Ev. Dream of me tonight.

Evan: Always.

I laugh at his response before putting my phone to charge and nestling under my covers. Day seven and this man is already putting serious gouges in my walls. How am I ever going to keep them from crumbling? They'll break and I'll be left vulnerable. I might not survive him breaking me again. Somehow, I'm not as scared of it as I should be.

Eleven

Evan

I wake up in the morning feeling more excited about the day ahead with Brooke than I've ever felt about anything else. She didn't quite give me an answer on if she wants to try this dating thing or not, but she didn't say no either and that's a damn good start.

I dress in board shorts and a t-shirt again before heading toward the dining room for breakfast. Eggs, bacon, and pancakes are already on the table and waiting for us when I arrive. Brooke isn't here yet, so I sit down and start stirring some cream in my coffee while I wait.

Just as I'm sipping on the coffee, Brooke enters wearing another sundress with a purple swimsuit underneath. Her blonde hair is pulled up into a messy bun on the top of her head that reminds me of Allie.

I smile at her as she sits next to me. She smiles shyly back while getting herself some coffee. She pours in the cream like there's no tomorrow, and I imagine the drink is more cream than coffee now.

I want to pull her onto my lap and kiss her like we have nowhere to be today, but I don't. I respect her space and the fact that she hasn't given me an answer yet. Instead, I opt for something a bit safer.

"Good morning. How did you sleep?" I ask.

"Wonderful. I had an interesting dream," Brooke replies, giving me a flirty look that hasn't been there before.

"Oh, really? Did it feature a ridiculously handsome man?" I ask with a flirty smile of my own. Brooke shrugs.

"Hm. Can't remember now."

I smile at her and bite down on a piece of bacon.

After breakfast, we go back to the resort. Today is the day we go to Dolphin Cay. We're doing the Ultimate Trainer Experience. We'll spend six hours learning how they take care of all the sea animals they have at the resort. It looked like a lot of fun while I was doing research, and I hope Brooke doesn't mind.

"What are we doing today exactly?" Brooke asks once we reach the resort. I take her hand and pull her closer to me.

"We're training dolphins," I say and explain further everything that's part of the package. Brooke's eyes light up.

"That sounds like so much fun," she squeals, skipping a few steps. Seeing her so happy and excited does something weird to my heart, and I can't help my smile.

We file in with the others in the group as the trainer explains everything she's doing and why. I'm only half paying attention. Mostly, I'm staring at Brooke, making sure she's having a good time.

The student in her, the one that loves learning about anything and everything, is listening raptly and I can almost see her taking notes in her mind. She probably wishes she had a notebook to take notes in. I should have had the foresight to bring one for her.

We feed the animals next. Several kinds need to eat right now. The nurse sharks are bigger than I thought, and we feed those as the trainers explain their feeding behaviors. I'm not a huge fan of sharks. Don't really have a reason, they just freak me out.

"You don't want to feed them?" Brooke asks when I don't get any closer to the tank. I know nurse sharks are relatively harmless compared to other shark species, but still, no thanks.

"Nah, go ahead. I'll watch from here," I say, struggling to suppress a cringe. Brooke smiles widely and her eyes light up.

"Are you scared of sharks?" she asks playfully.

"No," I say with a scowl.

"Okay then, come on," Brooke replies in a tone that suggests she does not believe me.

"Fine, jeez. I don't like sharks," I relent, and Brooke laughs lightly.

"Don't worry. I'll protect you," she says, kissing me quickly, then she goes back to feeding the sharks. I roll my eyes at her.

I relax when we finally leave the sharks to feed the Cownose stingrays. We stand in waist-high water hand-feeding them. They're soft against my legs as they swim around us, waiting for the food.

Once they're all fed, we receive snorkeling gear that we can take with us when we leave and we snorkel with the stingrays and the other tropical fish in Seagrapes Lagoon. I realize too late that sharks are in here too, but Brooke grabs my hand and my heartbeat slows enough for me to enjoy myself despite the sharks, who don't bother us, anyway.

By the time we're done snorkeling, it's lunchtime and we eat with a marine specialist. I sit quietly eating while Brooke and the specialist, Annie, talk back and forth.

I watch Brooke the whole time, marveling at how animated she is talking with Annie. I don't think Brooke is super passionate about marine life in general, but any chance for her to gain knowledge she might pass onto her future students who could become passionate about it is something she'll want to take advantage of.

After lunch, we take a tour of the facilities and the animal hospital that's on the island. We learn all about animal care and diagnostics. There are several families with children and I can see their eyes light up the same way Brooke's do. I can tell this is an excellent program they've got going on. One I think we should donate to. Van Holsten Conglomerate has several philanthropic endeavors we're a part of. I don't see why this couldn't be one of them.

We eat dinner at the resort, then head back to the yacht. It was a busy day compared to the relatively lazy days we've had the past week. Brooke and I go our separate ways to shower and change.

Once I've done that, I head back to the sitting area with the fire pit. It's a gas pit filled with blue polished stones. I turn it on and sit back against the couch, looking out towards the setting sun.

Brooke joins me after ten minutes and she hesitates only a few seconds before sitting close next to me. I put my arm around her shoulders and pull her the few inches left between us. She lets out a breath and lays her head on my shoulder. I can feel her body relax as we settle in.

In silence, we watch the sky become a mural of pink, orange, and purple until the sun disappears below the horizon. The stars twinkle into view and the crescent moon offers little natural night.

I look down to see Brooke's eyes have closed. There's a halo of light around her head from the inside of the yacht. Her skin is sun-kissed from being outside all week and her freshly washed hair is floating around her as it slowly dries.

"What are you staring at?" Brooke asks lazily, opening one eye.

"My beautiful wife," I reply with a smile. She returns it and snuggles closer into me, pulling her legs up onto the small couch. I readjust until we're both comfortable and we lay there in silence.

* * *

I wake up slowly, wondering where the hell I am. When I go to lift my head, I flinch with the pain from the crick in my neck. I blink until the blurriness has left my eyes and look around. Brooke is still laying in my arms, breathing evenly and obviously still fast asleep.

It's probably the middle of the night still as nothing is indicating the sun will be rising anytime soon. It's warm outside, but there's no way I'll be able to go back to sleep on this tiny couch without bugging Brooke.

Instead, I shift so I can pick up my sleeping beauty. She moves a little at the motion but doesn't wake up. I smirk down at her and carry her to her room. One of the yacht staff is luckily walking by and he sees me.

"Do you need help, sir?" the man asks. I smile at him and motion to Brooke's bedroom door with my head.

73

"Just open her door for me, please," I reply.

"Of course, sir."

The man opens the door, then leaves when I give him the go-ahead. Brooke's room looms before me. It's dark, but the floor plan is the same as mine. I make my way to her oversized bed by feel and lay her down. I flip on the bedside lamp so I can see.

The yacht housekeepers made her bed sometime during the day, and I've already laid her down on the duvet. I search around for another blanket to cover her up with and spot one on the sitting room sofa. It's just a throw blanket, but it will do for the rest of the night.

Once Brooke is all set, I lean down, catching the scent of her jasmine shampoo, and kiss her forehead lightly. She moves a little to get comfortable, but still, she doesn't wake. I laugh a little at how deep she must sleep.

I turn the lamp off and tiptoe out of the room. I shut the door as quietly as I can before heading to my room. Once there, I strip off my shirt and fall onto my bed face first, not bothering to put covers over myself. I fall asleep in seconds until the morning sun shines through the portholes and right into my eyes.

Twelve

Evan

The next week zooms by so much more quickly than I hoped. Every day, Brooke and I are back at the resort doing one thing or another. We swam with the dolphins and stingrays in Dolphin Cay the day after our dolphin training adventure. Sometimes we're busy the whole day exploring or having fun and other days, we laze about the beach or on the yacht.

We've spent the last two weeks talking about anything and everything, which is something I've always wanted to do. I've always been intrigued by Brooke's quietness and I wanted to get inside her head, to know what she's thinking. She kept those secrets every day for eleven unbearable years. It's no surprise that knowing what she thinks or how she sees things just makes me like her that much more.

Every day I spend with Brooke, I fall just a little further for the girl I thought was so unattainable. She still might be, but at least in some vague sense of the word, she's mine. I just have to work a little harder so she *wants* to be mine. I'm already hers. Honestly, I was hers long before either of us knew what that really meant.

On our last day here at the resort, we decide to redo whatever we enjoyed doing the most. We walk hand in hand through the resort's entrance. Brooke's skin is silky smooth and warm against mine. I wonder if the callouses on my hands bother her. Would she prefer hands as smooth as hers? Most guys in our social circle probably have hands like that, except Noah. He has callouses too, but those are from the multitude of instruments the guy plays, not hard labor.

Brooke's voice pulls me out of my ridiculous musings. I didn't hear what she said, and she knows it. I catch her amused smile and give a sheepish one of my own.

"You didn't hear me, did you?" she asks.

"No, I didn't. My mind was elsewhere. I'm sorry," I reply. A short laugh from Brooke has me smiling again.

"I was just asking what we're doing now that our time here is ending," Brooke says.

"If you don't have any objections, Noah wants us to go visit him in Florida before we head back to the city."

Brooke noticeably pales. It must be nerves about seeing Noah again, or maybe Kendra. She knows now none of us had anything to do with the pool house incident, but still.

"Don't worry. You'll love Noah once you get to know him. He seems like too much sometimes when you first meet him, but he's a good guy. I promise," I say quickly to quell her nerves.

Brooke nods and offers me a weak smile. She grips my hand tighter, perhaps for support, and that makes me smile. I like that in the short three weeks we've been married, I am a comfort to her now. It's a definite change from her dislike and wariness of my character.

"He's still dating Kendra?" Brooke asks. I make a noise in my throat.

"Unfortunately. Noah doesn't see what everyone else does. Kristie's tried to tell him over and over again what a snake she is, but he won't listen. He will have to find it out on his own. I just hope that when he does, it doesn't crush him too much. The guy's loyal and loves fiercely. He deserves someone worthy of being loved that way, and it is definitely not Kendra," I unload.

I've never told anyone besides Allie and Kristie how I feel about Noah's girlfriend. I never really liked her, but what can you say when your friend is head over heels for someone? They see what they want to see and they won't listen to you. I thought she would have shown her true colors by now. It's been almost thirteen years that they've been together. She's good at hiding and only showing what she wants to show.

"Tell me how you really feel," Brooke giggles with an amused expression.

"Sorry. Allie and Kristie know how I feel about her, of course, but like me, they can't say anything to Noah. It's just a waiting game at this point," I explain.

"Don't worry. I'm on your side. I don't like Kendra either or Zack. Is Noah still friends with him?" she asks.

"Another unfortunate thing," I sigh.

"Why is he friends with Zack? The guy is a creep."

"Kendra doesn't really have friends or not ones that actually like her, except Zack. They grew up together, way closer than any of us did. They were next-door neighbors. Wherever Kendra goes, so does Zack. I think they're closer because whether we like it or not, there are circles within the circles in our society. Noah, Kristie, Allie, and I are in one circle and Kendra and Zack are in another and no matter how close those circles get to overlapping, there's still an invisible barrier blocking them from colliding completely. Since our circles are so close, it's just easier to be friends and since Zack is wherever Kendra is, Noah didn't really have a choice but to befriend him." I flinch when I explain.

I don't mean to sound entitled, but that's how it is. Brooke is quiet, and I wonder what she's thinking. Did I offend her in some way? It was not my intention, but the world we both grew up and continue to live in is not always kind. It can be ruthless, vindictive, and cruel, but that doesn't mean we have to be. Most of the people I know aren't, but Kendra and Zack embody everything wrong with the wealthy.

"Never mind any of that, though. Kendra or no, we could have a really great time. It's important you like my friends. I don't have any siblings so they're the closest thing I have," I say and I hope I'm not pressuring her into anything she's uncomfortable with.

"That sounds like it could be fun. With everything you told me, I'm excited to meet them. I mean again, or whatever," Brooke says tripping over her words with her face scrunching like she's trying to figure out if what she said makes sense. It's adorable.

"After we get home and settled, you could introduce me to Willa. I've never really talked to her unless you count the insults she unleashed on me under her breath," I say smiling at Brooke.

"Willa did that? I'm so sorry," she groans.

"It's probably nothing we didn't deserve. She was just being a good friend to you. I could never fault her for that," I say and grab Brooke's hand, pulling her closer to me.

We spend our last day going through the water slides again. I don't know if Brooke actually wants to or if she's just humoring me, but I love her more for it. I've always loved her. I pined for the girl I ruined my chance with too early for a shot. Now's my chance, and I won't let it go up in smoke like last time. We've already wasted so many years. I won't waste a single second more.

Brooke picks the café for lunch. We've eaten here a few times in the last three weeks. It must be one of her favorites. I pay special attention to what she orders to store that knowledge for later.

For our last night in the Bahamas, we're going to another five-star restaurant that requires fancy dress. Brooke and I just got back to the yacht to change. We're walking hand in hand so I can deposit her in her room.

When we're in front of her door, she winds her arms around my back to pull me closer to her and she kisses me softly before resting her head against my chest. We stand there silently for a second. I'm afraid to say anything or move for fear of breaking this moment. It's not often Brooke initiates any of the little intimacy we've shown each other in two weeks. It's fine. I'm down to take things as slowly as she needs. All the same, it's nice I'm not the only one feeling things.

"I'll see you soon," Brooke murmurs into my chest before stepping out of my grasp. She rushes into her room, but I catch a glimpse of her red face before the door shuts. Is she embarrassed?

I'm as confused as ever when I walk into my room. I turn on the shower and I'm about to get in when my phone rings. I race to the bed where I left it and answer without looking.

"Hello?"

"Hey, Ev. You still coming to visit me?" Noah asks.

"Yeah, we'll be there tomorrow sometime in the afternoon," I reply.

"Good. I'm excited to meet this wife of yours."

"It's Brooke. You know Brooke," I say with a roll of my eyes.

"Yeah, but I don't *know* Brooke, you know?"

"Fair enough. I think Willa's the only one that truly knows her and maybe her sisters. I'm getting there, though. Kendra know we're coming?" I ask.

"Yeah, I told her. She says she's excited to see Brooke again. You're staying at my parent's house, right? They want to see you, but they won't be home for a couple of days. I think they're in Nice or something," Noah says.

"If it's no problem, we'll stay with you," I reply.

"Cool, cool. See you tomorrow," Noah says before hanging up.

I look at my phone shaking my head then I toss it back onto my bed so I can quickly shower before dinner.

Twenty minutes later, I knock on Brooke's door. She opens it and her perfume hits me. It's one of the few things she brought that was actually hers before the wedding. It smells like lilacs. I smile but quickly lose it when I see what she's wearing.

Brooke's dress is royal blue and lands nearly to the floor. The neckline swoops down between her breasts, stopping at her belly button, but there's this nude color, sheer stuff to give some sense of modesty.

I painfully swallow the sudden desire I feel for her, and she smiles at me brightly. She steps forward and I touch her back, which is bare to the top of her ass. Her skin is hot to the touch. Is she trying to kill me? Because God damn!

"Is this okay?" she asks, but she knows damn well it's more than okay.

"You look exquisite, Brooke," I reply and my breath is husky. Does she hear it? Does she know the kind of dirty things racing through my mind right now?

"You look good too," she says, blushing again.

I look down at my fitted black suit. It's something I wear often, but I'm glad she thinks I'm attractive too. That thought sends an electric zip down to my toes. I smile as we walk towards the exit.

At the restaurant, we sit across from each other sharing a bottle of wine. It's good, but I can't think of anything other than this beautiful woman in front of me. We chat about some unimportant things while waiting for the main course to arrive.

"I've really enjoyed our honeymoon. Thank you," Brooke says politely, and I wish she wouldn't. I was hoping we were past the politeness, although she was never really polite to me. It was more of a barely restrained dislike. Still, I thought she was getting more comfortable with me.

"Don't do that," I say. Brooke's eyes grow wide for a second.

"Do what?"

"Act like we're strangers. I know we weren't friends before, but we've known each other a long time and I don't want to backslide into acquaintances. If we weren't already married, I'd say you're my girlfriend. I want you to be comfortable with me. I care about you. I always have. Please, don't push me back to where I was three weeks ago," I explain.

Brooke's cheeks heat again, and I wonder if she even realizes what she's doing. Is she just trying to protect her heart? A rush of shame courses through me that she has to.

"You're right. I'm sorry. I'm fighting a lot of years' worth of protecting myself from hurt. The only person I've really let in besides my sisters is Willa. I'm trying to let my guard down with you because, despite everything, I do trust you. It's just going to take some time. Everything about this honeymoon has been wonderful and you've been great. I'm glad we agreed to try this relationship for real. Just be patient with me, please," Brooke says softly.

"I understand. Just please don't hide from me," I say because I want to know everything about her. I don't want her to hide even the worst parts of herself from me.

"Okay. I'll show you every ugly part of me," Brooke jokes, but there's a shred of anxiety in her slight laugh.

"No part of you could ever be ugly," I tell her dead serious.

For the next several hours, we do rapid-fire questions. All the little things we never got to find out about each other and Brooke's answers make me smile.

"*Dazed and Confused* is seriously your favorite movie? It's like I don't even know you!" I manage through my laughter.

"I love all those eighties movies. There's nothing better. *Fast Times at Ridgemont High, Pretty in Pink, Sixteen Candles*. Why? What's your favorite movie?" she laughs.

"Um, I don't know. I like a lot of movies. *Star Wars*, if I had to pick," I reply with a smile.

"I never pegged you for a nerd," Brooke teases.

"Nothing nerdy about *Star Wars*, baby. It was very advanced for its time. Besides, I didn't peg you for a pothead with *Dazed and Confused* as your favorite," I tease back.

"You just don't know much about me, I guess. I light up every day. This honeymoon has been the exception because I wasn't able to bring my stash. Just wait until we get home. Our new house will smell like nothing but marijuana," Brooke says seriously.

I falter a little because though I'm like ninety-five percent sure she's joking, there's still a lot I don't know about her.

"Your student's parents might object to that kind of behavior," I reply just as seriously. She shrugs but doesn't reply and I'm left wondering.

"I called the school yesterday and accepted the job position. I'll be able to set up my classroom in a few weeks. They set up a tour and everything. Will you come with me? I know your dad isn't going to like me working there, but maybe you'd feel more comfortable if you could see where I'll be," Brooke says instead.

"That's wonderful. Of course, I'll come. I'll help you set up your classroom too if you'd like," I reply and I can almost feel her excitement.

"I'm really glad you didn't make me give up on my dream," Brooke says softly, looking at her hands in her lap.

"I would never. It's important to you so it's important to me," I reply, reaching across the table and lifting her chin so she's looking at me. "You're important to me."

Dinner continues with harmless chatter. Nothing serious. We head back to the yacht well into the night and we sit cuddling together, looking at the stars by the fire pit again. It's a good way to end our time here.

We sip on wine and talk into the night. Our flight to Florida is early, but it's no bother. We can sleep on the plane. After our week with Noah, it will be the start of the rest of our lives. I hope once we go back to real life, she'll still want to pursue a relationship with me.

I know nothing would ever stop me from wanting to be with her. I'm already hopelessly in love with my wife.

Thirteen

Brooke

To say I'm nervous about seeing Evan's high school friend again is an understatement. Sure, I realized they weren't the jerks I thought they were, but that didn't quell the nerves. For some reason, Noah is still dating Kendra, and she was a tormentor of mine.

But whatever… I can do this. I'm married to Evan now, even though we've just started to explore a real relationship. That counts for something, right? Kendra is just going to have to deal with her shit because I won't let her ruin what's left of my honeymoon.

We touched down in Orlando a few minutes ago, and now we're exiting the plane. We've been on the yacht for nearly three weeks and it felt more like home than anywhere else recently. The weather here is kinda like the Bahamas, but I feel homesick for the yacht already. Everything about last night had been perfect.

Evan grabs my hand and brings it to his mouth. He kisses my fingers and smiles at me. My nerves relax at the adorable look on his face and we walk together to the car. It zips through the Orlando traffic until we're on the outskirts of the city.

Noah still lives with his parents, so we pull up to a mansion nearly the size of the Van Holsten's. When we stop at the giant fence that lines the property, Evan buzzes. A voice that probably belongs to a security guard, asks who's there, and Evan drops his name. Not long after, the gate opens with a creek, and the driver heads down the long driveway.

The driver stops at the front of the house where a large, tattooed man is waiting for us. Evan gets out of the car and holds his hand out for me. Together, we walk up to the man. As we draw closer, I recognize him as Noah Whittier, though he didn't have any tattoos the last time I saw him at graduation.

If Evan was the prince of Kingswood Prep, then Noah was a duke. He has always been Evan's right-hand man, his best friend.

Noah is much taller than I remember. He's several inches taller than Evan. Tattoos fill his visible arms and I can see some peeking out of his t-shirt collar, so I imagine they dot his chest and back too. He's got a thin hoop in his nose and a bar in his eyebrow.

Where Evan is wearing slacks and a button-down shirt, Noah's wearing a black *Mötley Crüe* t-shirt and gray jeans. His brown hair is getting long. It reaches past his ears now. He's a handsome man, always has been. He's almost as drop-dead sexy as Evan. All the body modifications give him a sexy bad boy look.

Noah smiles at us widely and he goes straight to Evan for a bear hug. Evan lets my hand go so he can fully embrace his best friend.

"Yo, Van Holsten! I'm glad you came to visit. Least you could do for not fucking inviting me to your nuptials," Noah says as he pulls back. He tosses me an amused glance. I give him a small smile in return.

"I already told you. Anyway, Noah, this is my wife. You remember Brooke," Evan politely introduces me. I go to extend my hand to give Noah a handshake, but apparently, that's not how this guy does things.

Instead, he pulls me into a hug just as big and tight as the one he gave his brother from another mother, and I feel choked up at being welcomed this way.

"It's good to see you again, Brooke," Noah says warmly when he finally releases me. His brown/green hazel eyes twinkle when he looks at me and I can't help my smile.

"You too," I mumble and return to Evan's side. He grabs my hand again just in time because my worst nightmare just walked out of the house.

Kendra Berretti in all her tall, model-like perfection struts out the front door and takes her place beside Noah. He puts his arm around her shoulders and pulls her close. She flips her brown hair off her shoulder and her shit brown eyes pierce mine.

"Hey, babe. They're here," Noah says, and he's completely oblivious to the poisonous look Kendra's giving me.

I'll give the bitch this, she's good at playing the sweet and innocent for the benefit of Noah and Evan, even though he doesn't like her. Evan doesn't realize how awful she actually is. He sees surface stuff. Neither of them sees the looks dripping in venom she's giving me.

Now that I think about it, I can see how she puts on a carefully crafted facade for Noah because if he's anything like Evan, and I imagine he is for them to be best friends, he wouldn't put up with her the way he has for over a decade.

"Oh Brooke, is that you? I saw you guys got married. How sweet of you to visit us while on your honeymoon," Kendra says in a sickly sweet voice. I can hear the undercurrents, though. *"Really? You married Evan? Hell must have frozen over."*

"Kendra. Long time no see. I heard you and Noah were still *dating*," I reply, emphasizing the word. It probably eats her up inside that he hasn't even popped the question after so long.

I guessed right because her fake smile slips just long enough for me to see I zeroed in on a big issue. The boys are oblivious to this double conversation we're having.

"Yes, we're very happy. We started dating the night of that pool party before ninth grade. You remember that, don't you?" Kendra says with a cruel smile that lets me know for the first time with any real certainty that she was the one that undid my top.

Evan stiffens next to me. I know what happened at the party is a big regret for him. I don't feel the normal level of embarrassment over it I used to feel, at least. Evan's silently seething that she brought it up, though. Apparently,

Noah caught onto his change of mood.

"Babe, why would you bring that up?" he asks, looking at her with disappointment.

"Oh, right, I completely forgot what happened to you that night. So sorry I brought it up, Brookey," Kendra says with mock shock, then turns around and goes inside.

Brookey? Fucking really? I shake my head and glance at Noah. He's giving me an apologetic look. I just shrug and flash him a smile. For however long we're here, I won't let my guard down. Kendra's the kind of person to find any weakness and exploit it. Not this time, bitch.

Noah shakes his head and invites us inside. The foyer is huge and leads to a large staircase that flares at the end dramatically. Noah gives us a tour of the giant home before finally showing us to the room we'll be staying in.

It's large and almost gaudy, but it'll be fine. Evan and I will share a room and a bed for the first time, so we'll see how that goes. I don't even mind. It's the next logical step in our relationship.

Noah's the only one in the house that knows our marriage was arranged and we want to keep it that way. Knowing Kendra, she would use that information for some nefarious purpose. Evan swore his friends to secrecy the way I did with Willa.

"I can sleep on the couch if that would make you feel more comfortable," Evan offers, glancing at the uncomfortable-looking two-seater sofa.

I laugh, picturing Evan's tall frame squeezing into the couch. I get a confused look from him while I try to stem my laughter.

"Don't be ridiculous. We're both adults and we're married, after all. We can share this giant king-sized bed," I reply, motioning to it.

"Thank you," Evan breathes out and rockets onto the bed. It deflates a bit from his weight, and I can tell the bed at least will be comfy.

Evan and I take turns in the bathroom, changing our clothes into bathing suits. I have a rush of panic as I change into my black bikini. The last time I was in a pool with Kendra was my most embarrassing moment.

Evan notices how tense I am when I exit the bathroom and places his hands on my shoulders. He rubs a bit and looks me in the eye.

"What's wrong," he asks. I blow out my breath.

"That night at your party when I flashed the entire freshman class—" I start.

"I told you, Noah and I had nothing to do with that," Evan says and I nod.

"I know that, but I'm almost positive Kendra is the one that untied my top. She and Zack were pretending to be my friends that night, encouraging me that you were happy I was there, then to go find you. They guessed I had a crush on you. I mean, it wasn't so far a leap. Every girl in our grade was in love with you. When I ran out after seeing you with Kristie, I wanted to leave, but they encouraged me to stay and go for a swim first. Kendra jumped in with me and when I came up, my top was floating away. She was the only one close enough to do it. I always sort of thought it was her, and then all I heard was laughing and you staring. I was mortified, and Willa was the only one to help me. Nothing happened, and you stayed friends with Kendra and Zack. Then Noah started dating her. I assumed, even though you obviously had nothing to do with it, that you thought it was funny, just like the rest of them. I thought you were all the same, and when Allie and Kristie did try to talk to me, I assumed they were just setting me up for embarrassment the way Kendra and Zack did," I finish in a hopefully coherent babble.

Evan's hands drop from my shoulders and he walks away, pacing around with his hand running through his hair. It's something he does when he's irritated. I'm about to say more, but he crushes me to his chest in a rib-breaking hug.

"I'm so sorry. I can't believe that bitch. I knew she was a snake, and we all had our suspicions she was the one that did it, but I had no way to confirm," he hisses.

"You don't have to apologize for them," I whisper.

"As soon as you and Willa ran out of there, I asked who did it and demanded answers. As you can guess, they were all tight-lipped about it. No one knew who did it, and Kendra played dumb. Zack inferred you were looking to shed your goody-two-shoes act before high school. Not that I believed him. Aside from my own guilt for not helping right away, things would have been different had I known it was them. I'm so fucking sorry, Brooke. I brought you here too, just to see my friend, and you knew you'd have to see your tormentor," Evan says into my hair. I pull back and smile at him.

"You can't take responsibility for the actions of others and I'm sorry I made you bear them all these years," I say then lean up to kiss him softly. After the kiss, Evan rests his forehead against mine and sighs.

"I liked you too, by the way. That's why I invited you. Zack and Kendra got into my head earlier that night saying it was obvious you liked Noah and you only accepted my invitation to get close to him. Then they pushed me towards Kristie. She was safe as we'd been friends our entire lives. Then after it all happened and you wouldn't talk to any of us, I figured we were doomed before we ever got started," Evan confesses.

"All those wasted years," I sigh. Evan smirks, stepping back to take my hand in his.

"For the record, I stared at you because my stupid fourteen-year-old body had never seen real boobs before and yours were perfect," Evan says with a laugh. I shove his arm and he pulls me to him again, kissing me deeply.

"They still are," he whispers into my ear.

I flush with the sudden desire to keep his perfect body in this room all to myself. I don't though and kiss him again once before pulling away to open the door. Evan drapes his arm around my shoulders and kisses my temple as we walk through the long hallways towards the pool outside.

I look up at him and smile at his utter perfection, not only in his looks but in his personality. How had I been so wrong all these years about him? He's shaken my walls so much these last three weeks, I'm afraid they're irreparable. I knew this was possible, and I wanted to fight it, but Evan took all the fight out of me. I'm already falling and I can't stop it now. All I can do now is trust Evan to catch me before I hit the ground.

Fourteen

Evan

Noah and Kendra are already by the pool. Seeing that two-faced bitch makes my blood boil after Brooke told me what really happened that night. I should have fucking guessed it was her. Who else would it have been if not Kendra and Zack? I'll have to talk to Noah. He really needs to dump this girl. I can't imagine she loves him. Not the way he deserves, at least.

As bad as it is to say, she might only be with him for his money and status. He's the oldest of two boys, so he's set to inherit his father's company when the time is right. Since Kendra and Zack come from the lower echelon of our society, I can see her wanting to reach for more. Unfortunately, it would at the expense of the only brother I have ever known.

For the week Brooke and I are here, I will do everything in my power to find something tangible to take to Noah. It will break his heart, and mine will hurt for him, but it will be better for him and my wife in the long run if Kendra's out of the picture.

Brooke stiffens in my arms when she sees Kendra lounging in a pool chair with sunglasses on. The smile on her face is venomous when she catches Brooke in her bikini. She looks amazing in it. We've both tanned a lot from being in the sun for the last three weeks.

"Oh, Brookey. Nice bathing suit. Let's go swimming," Kendra says with her cruel smile.

"Brooke and I are going to sit for a while," I say, directing her to some other pool chairs farther away from Kendra. I feel Brooke relax against me. I will make this week as easy on her as possible.

I sit in a chair and open my legs for Brooke. She happily sits in between pressing her back against my chest. I wrap my arms around her to hold her close. I can feel her heart racing, but eventually, it slows.

"Do you always let your husband make decisions for you, Brooke?" Kendra sneers.

"Why, yes, Kendra. Don't you know that it's a woman's job to listen and obey her husband at all times?" Brooke replies sounding like a fifties housewife. I stifle my laughter at her sarcasm by pushing my face into Brooke's neck.

Instead of answering, Kendra rolls her eyes and looks back at her phone. Noah's loud laughter sounds around us, making both me and Brooke laugh with him.

After some conversation and catching up with Noah, he decides it's time to get into the pool. Instead of going in like a normal fucking person, he cannonballs into the deep end from the diving board, getting the three of us soaked from the splash. Kendra lets loose a shrill scream, then stalks into the house without a word.

As soon as she's inside, Brooke, Noah, and I burst into laughter. Brooke seems a little less nervous now that Kendra isn't here. She gets up from the chair to take her place on the diving board.

"There's no way your splash will be bigger than mine," Noah says with a smile.

Brooke flashes him one in return, then dives cleanly into the pool, barely causing a splash at all. She gives me a brilliant smile when she surfaces and swims towards Noah. I laugh and jump in after her from the side of the pool. I swim under her and grab her around the waist, surfacing with a kiss on her cheek.

"You guys are just adorable together," Noah says in a feminine voice and a flip of his wrist. I punch his arm, getting a laugh and a return punch.

I haven't seen Noah in way too long, and it feels good to be here with him again. It feels even better because he likes Brooke and I can tell she's comfortable in his presence, which is more than I could have ever asked from her. Kendra's malevolent voice stops the laughing abruptly.

"Look who came to see our friends."

Brooke's body stiffens again when she looks over, and I inwardly groan. Zack Lochlan stands next to Kendra in nothing but board shorts and aviators with a glass of some amber liquid. He probably raided some of Mr. Whittier's good stuff.

"Hey, bro. What are you doing here? I thought you were going back to New York to see your mom," Noah says jovially. He's not at all bothered by his friend's presence, but Noah doesn't know what Zack did.

"I heard Evan and his new wife were visiting, and I couldn't pass up seeing them again after so long. What's it been, Ev? Three years? And Brooke. Look at you! It's been too long," Zack says with a smile as fake as everything else about him. I tighten my grip on Brooke's waist in response to his words.

"Yeah, man. Too long," I reply stiffly.

"I saw in the papers you guys got married a few weeks ago. Congrats. I didn't know you were even on each other's radar. You barely spoke in high school," Zack says, coming to step up to the side of the pool looking down on us.

"We recently found each other again after attending a function. We regretted all the time we wasted, so we got married," I reply.

"Kinda sucks no one was invited, though. I'd have thought Noah would have been your best man. Are the rumors true? Do you have a bun in the oven?" Zack asks, directing that last question at Brooke.

"No, I am not pregnant. People can get married quickly simply because they love each other and can't wait to start their lives together without a baby in the picture," Brooke says coldly.

Noah looks back and forth between us and Kendra and Zack. He doesn't say anything. He's probably nervous about letting the truth out. He's not great at keeping secrets.

"Don't have to be so defensive, Princess," Zack says, lifting his hands in surrender.

I'm ready to jump out of the pool and wring Zack's neck for calling Brooke princess, but before I can, the back door flies open again. This time, I'm happy to see who runs through. Kristie launches herself into the pool at full speed, still completely dressed, and gives Noah a hug and a wet kiss on the cheek. She turns her gaze on Brooke and me with an enormous smile.

Brooke seems unsure, but Kristie hugs both of us like she's been friends with Brooke for a lifetime. Allie stays poolside beside Zack, too reserved to jump straight into the pool in her clothes. She's wearing a nice blue sundress and her red hair is flying in the breeze. She smiles down at us and I can tell she's happy for me.

Noah climbs out of the pool and throws his enormous arms around Allie, soaking her almost as much as if she'd jumped into the pool. She squeals, trying to maneuver out of Noah's arms, but he doesn't give. He showers Allie's cheeks in kisses.

"I missed you, Sweets. I'm glad you could make it," Noah says, finally letting Allie go. She glares in his direction, but I don't miss the small smile and the affectionate look she's giving him, anyway.

Brooke and I make our way out of the pool, and I walk over to Allie. I kiss her cheek but avoid a hug so I don't get her any wetter.

"Oh, come here. Noah already soaked me," Allie says, pulling me into a hug.

Brooke stands beside me with a smile on her face. She doesn't look nervous or jealous in the slightest.

"Hi, Brooke," Allie says once she releases me. I step back beside Brooke and take her hand.

"It's good to see you again, Allie," Brooke replies with a slight wave and a small smile. Kristie climbs out of the pool, throwing her arms around me and Noah.

"Well, the fun's here now. So let's get this party started!" she yells walking into the house, presumably to change. Allie follows her silently.

"You invited them too?" Kendra says, and it's clear she's not enthused.

Kendra's "friends" with Kristie and Allie, officially, because it's good practice to befriend children of the "Big Four" when you're a status jumping bitch, but it's clear she doesn't much care for them. The feeling is mutual, so it's not like Allie or Kris care in the slightest. Kendra probably doesn't like how affectionate Noah is with them. Then again, Noah's a pretty affectionate guy with anyone he cares about.

"Of course. They haven't seen me or Evan in several years since they're all the way in L.A. I figured it would be a good time for them to visit. We can hang out for a week," Noah says, unconcerned by Kendra's tone.

"Great," Kendra says blandly.

Kristie and Allie emerge from the house in their bikinis with several bottles of liquor and a Bluetooth speaker. Allie queues up some music, and it thumps through the space. Kristie sets seven shot glasses out and fills them to the brim with tequila.

"Shots!" she yells and we clink the glasses together.

"Ugh," Brooke says in disgust once she's downed hers.

"Tequila not your thing, Princess?" Zack asks. I want to punch him every time he uses the stupid nickname.

"Not really. I don't drink much," Brooke replies quietly.

"Well, we're going to change that tonight," Kristie says, pouring another round.

Brooke smiles at me, and although Kendra and Zack are probably her mortal enemies, she looks content. It seems like she trusts me about Kristie, Allie, and Noah because she's let them in with open arms.

After our third shot, I pull Brooke a little ways away so we can dance to whatever is playing. I'm starting a buzz and feeling great. All my best friends that I've missed are here, and so is Brooke.

She laughs when I spin her out and back to me. We sway together with her back to my chest and I nibble at her neck. She squeals a little, and it makes me laugh.

"My turn!" Noah calls, trying to cut in. I nearly growl at him, but Kristie and Allie come up instead.

"No! Our turn!" They pull Brooke from my arms and the three of them dance together like they've been friends all their lives.

"I meant it's my turn to dance with Ev. Dance with Brooke. I don't care," Noah replies, grabbing my hips and dancing behind me. I laugh and swat him away.

Kendra is left on the sidelines, and she looks practically murderous. Poisonous bitch. Noah must realize because he pulls her to him. They dance a little, leaving Zack by himself. He sips slowly at the bourbon Kristie and Allie brought. He's glaring at Noah and looking longingly at Kendra.

Fifteen

Brooke

Kristie thrusts another shot of tequila at me. It creates a warm path all the way down my throat as I shoot it back. My body feels like it's heating from the inside out and my head is beyond fuzzy. My eyes are tracking much slower than normal and I feel giggly.

I've been dancing with Kristie and Allie almost exclusively all night instead of Evan, but it feels wonderful. I can't remember the last time I let loose like this. Maybe I never had. I don't drink much at all, and I definitely don't party. Not even in college.

Kristie seems like a partier, but I like her. Allie is reserved but so nice. I want to kick myself for pushing their friendship advances away in the past. Willa would enjoy this. Aw Willa. I miss her. I should invite her since all of Evan's friends showed up. I'm going to call her.

I step into the house, away from the music, and I sway a little as I head towards the bathroom. I sit on the toilet breaking the seal. Or is that only for beer? Shit, I don't even know. I pull out my phone and press Willa's contact information.

"Hola chica?" Willa answers.

"Willafred! Hi!" I yell into the phone.

"That's not my name, *Brooklyn*. Are you drunk?" Willa asks, sounding

95

amused.

"Thaas not my name either, but yes! I've had lots of shots of tequila. I'm gooood," I reply. I hear soft laughter.

"Where are you?" she asks.

"Noah Whittier's house. Allie and Kristie came, and oh my God, Willa, they are so cool. I don't know why we weren't friends with them before. But Kendra and Zack are here too. Zack keeps calling me Princess and every time he does, Evan gets a murderous look on his face. I'm waiting for a beat down," I explain.

"Sounds like a party," Willa says.

"Come and stay here. All of Ev's friends are here. I want you to be here too," I say.

"I don't know, Brooke. You know rich pricks aren't really my scene."

"Please, Willa. Pretty please. I miss you and I need to see my best friend. Come down. You'll really like Kristie and Allie. Probably Noah, too. He's really cool and still the stud muffin you said he was. He's got a nose ring and an eyebrow ring. He's even got his nipples pierced! And tattoos up the ass! Not literally, I don't think. I don't actually know, but I don't think I'm going to check. Oh! You could try to steal him from that bitch Kendra," I beg.

"I don't have the money for a plane ticket, Brooke," Willa says.

"Don't worry about it. I'm married to American royalty, remember? I'm going to book a plane ticket for you."

"You don't have to do that."

"I want to. It's happening, babe. You don't have a choice. I'll tell you the details. Be here tomorrow ready to have fun and wreak some havoc on Kendra and Zack," I say, and I won't take no for an answer.

"Fine, Jesus. Being married is making you a real bossy bitch. I'll see you tomorrow. Don't go too crazy tonight," Willa replies.

"I love you, Willa. See you tomorrow."

"Love you too," Willa says, then hangs up the phone.

I finish peeing and wash my hands. I leave the bathroom to find Zack hanging out near it. Eww. He's so fucking gross. He's so close to me, I can smell his cologne. It smells the same as the one he wore in high school, and it suffocates me with the nausea-inducing scent.

"Have fun in there?" he asks with a nasty smile.

"I was just peeing," I respond.

I try to walk away with some dignity, but I'm too drunk. I sway, and Zack's slimy hand catches my elbow. They aren't literally slimy, but he makes me cringe every time he touches me. I'm way too close to his face and I startle when I see the Caribbean eyes Evan has. It's like looking into the clear blue waters and seeing the dark sand at the bottom.

"Has anyone ever told you that you kinda look like Evan?" I ask, squinting at Zack. He pulls his hand from my arm with a deep frown.

"Be careful. It would be a shame if something happened to you tonight," Zack says. I scowl at him.

"I'll be fine," I say, stalking away.

I walk outside and my eyes find Evan immediately. He's talking to Noah with a smile on his face. The minute I'm outside, his eyes find mine. He smiles at me and it makes my insides turn to mush. I think I want to tell him I love him. Sober me would never want to do that. She's too fucking stubborn to admit I was basically a bitch for fucking ever. But, I'm drunk Brooke right now, and drunk me can admit I've loved Evan Van Holsten for a long time and he deserves to know.

Another upbeat song comes on and immediately I feel Kristie grind against my backside. Normally it would make me extremely uncomfortable since I barely know the girl, but tonight, I'm too drunk to care about that either. I back my booty up against her and laugh when she wraps her arms around my chest.

"Fuck, Kris. Get off my wife!" Evan shouts from the other side of the pool.

"No! This blonde beauty is mine tonight!" Kristie shouts back, leaving me in a puddle of giggles while she still holds me so I don't fall over.

"I didn't know you swung that way, Kristie," Kendra says sounding super judgmental.

"What fucking business would it be of yours if I did?" Kristie asks in a nasty tone.

"What? It didn't work out with Evan so you've got to steal his wife?" Kendra replies.

"Whatever, witch," Kristie says, letting me go and stalking off into the house.

I'm pretty sure Kristie is not hung up on Evan, nor is she really attracted to me. I'd take it as a compliment if she was because Kris is fucking gorgeous. We're just having fun and as usual, Kendra has to ruin it because hardly anyone is paying attention to her. God, she's such a diva.

"You okay?" Evan asks, coming up behind me and wrapping his arms around my waist.

"Mhm. I feel great actually," I say, and I may be slurring. Evan gives me an amused look and kisses my cheek.

"That's because your obviously a closet alcoholic," he jokes.

"I like your friends. How was I not friends with them before?" I ask.

Instead of answering me, Evan just chuckles and pulls me close as we sway with the music that is not meant for swaying. I'm feeling pretty sleepy, so I rest my head against Evan's cheek.

"Are you ready for bed?" Evan asks.

"Mhm," I reply, but I can't think anymore. Too sleepy.

Evan shifts so he's holding my hand, then walks me towards the sliding doors leading to the house.

"We're heading to bed," Evan says to Noah.

"Don't rock the house too much with your newlywed sex," Zack says with a laugh. Everything about him makes me cringe.

Evan doesn't grace Zack with a reply or a second glance before leading me into the house. Evan's muscular arms around my body make me feel all the things. Maybe we should have sex tonight. We've been married for almost a month and we should consummate it. Why not tonight? We're sharing a room and a bed.

When Evan shoves open the door to our room, I attack. Like literally, I attack the guy with my face. I kiss him like he's the air I breathe. It takes him a minute before he's kissing me back. He's not wearing a shirt, so I grab at the board shorts strings.

When it becomes apparent what I want, Evan pulls away and holds my shoulders. He gives me a sweet smile and I don't think he's drunk at all.

"As much as I'd love to have sex with you, I don't want to do that tonight when you're drunk off your ass. I want it to be something special that you'll remember and not regret in the morning," Evan says gently.

I pout, but in the back of my alcohol-addled brain, I'm thankful that this beautiful man respects me enough to want to wait.

"Fine," I say and sit hard on the bed. I lay back and close my eyes. I feel myself falling into the sweet escape of sleep.

"Let's get you changed," I hear Evan say rummaging through a closet. He must find what he's looking for because he comes back to the bed and pulls me into a sitting position.

Evan pulls a silk tank top over my bathing suit top, then pulls the strings of the bikini until he can slide it out from under my shirt. He slips the little shorts on and pulls the bottoms off the same way. Changing my clothes for me without ever revealing my naked body to him before I'm ready, though I was ready for him to see all that like five minutes ago, just proves how wonderful this man is.

After I'm changed, he picks me up and pulls the covers back on the bed. He tucks me in snuggly and I turn to my side. I'm almost on the cusp of sleep when the bed dips and Evan draws closer to me. He wraps his arms around my body and pulls me flush against his bare chest.

"I told Willa I would book her a plane ticket. I want her to come too," I say.

"I'll take care of it," Ev replies.

He's warm and comforting as I drift off. The last thing I hear before the alcohol-fueled sleep takes me completely is Evan whispering in my ear.

"I should have been all your first and you should have been mine. That's how it would have happened if Kendra and Zack didn't get in the middle of our happily ever after."

I want to respond and tell him nothing and no one before him matters to me, but I'm too far gone and I fall asleep instead, dreaming of the downright naughty things I can only hope Evan will do to me once we finally make love.

Sixteen

Evan

I wake in the morning with Brooke's head on my shoulder, her arm slung across my stomach, and her leg thrown over mine. Who knew she was such a cuddler? She was very much on the opposite side of the bed when I went to sleep last night. I wanted to be closer, but this was the first time we've shared a bed and I didn't want her to think I was taking advantage of her trashed state. Still, sometime in the night, she gravitated to me. I look down at her sleeping face. She looks tranquil with her hair splayed across the pillow behind her.

I glance at the alarm clock situated on the bedside table next to me. It's six in the morning. I know I won't go back to sleep, so I might as well get up. I can guarantee none of the girls will be up for several more hours yet after drinking a cask of liquor to themselves. Noah, maybe. We used to work out this early in high school and college for lacrosse.

I extricate myself from Brooke's heavy limbs. I'm wearing basketball shorts so I find a t-shirt in the dark and grab some socks and my sneakers. I slip out of the room quietly, trying my best not to wake up Sleeping Beauty in there. I lean against the wall to put on my socks and shoes when Noah rounds the corner.

"Hey, I was coming to find you. Wanna go to the gym?" Noah asks quietly.

"Yeah. I can't go back to sleep. I just need to make a call," I reply.

I call the only airline we use when flying commercial and book a ticket for a few hours from now from New York to Orlando. Once it's booked, I find Willa's contact information. I added it to my phone last night from Brooke's before I fell asleep. I didn't know if Brooke was going to remember she talked to Willa.

Me: Hi, Willa. This is Evan Van Holsten. Brooke said she wanted you to come down to Florida. I booked a flight out of JFK for noon your time. Just go to customer service and give them your name and they'll give you your ticket. I'm sending a car to pick you up and drop you at Noah Whittier's house. Brooke's very excited to see you. Have a safe flight.

Willa: Thanks, dude. I told her I didn't need you guys booking me a ticket, but it seems important to her that I come. Thanks for doing that. She sounded pretty drunk last night. I didn't know if she remembered.

Me: She mentioned it right before she passed out. Even if she doesn't remember it, it'll be a nice surprise. She misses you.

Willa: See you in a few hours. Thanks, Prince Playboy Jerkface.

Me: You really called me that?

Willa: Sure did. Be honored you had a badass nickname in high school. We aren't all so lucky.

Me: I don't know. I've heard Brooke call you Willafred. Seems pretty badass to me.

Willa: Ugh. I don't even count that as a nickname. And anyway, it's still not as badass a Prince Playboy Jerkface.

I laugh at her dumb nickname for me as I let Noah lead me down the hall to the home gym. It's not really a "home gym" because it's set up better than most of the expensive chain gyms in the city. Our houses have always been like that though, so nothing new to me. My apartment in Manhattan even has a gym in one of the spare rooms.

I walk into the sterile-looking space. There are tons of different machines and free weights on the other side. The room's walls are mirrors, so you check your form.

Noah starts some heavy metal. It's the kind of music he always works out to. We start our circuits on the machines. I get lost in the workout and the music I only listen to when I'm working out with Noah. We don't talk when we're doing this. It's one of the few times Noah's got his damn mouth shut.

The door to the gym opens. I don't know how much time has passed. I expect it to be one of the girls looking for us, but it's just Zack. Every time I see the fucker, my blood boils for what he did to my girl. I keep my cool. Now is not the time for confrontation.

"You gonna work out with us?" Noah asks between grunts as he lifts some weights.

"Nah. I'm not in the mood right now. I just came to find you," Zack replies.

"Then shut up and let us finish," Noah says. He's pretty serious about his workouts.

We finish our circuits and we're both covered in sweat. I'm panting from the exertion. I haven't worked out at all since before the wedding.

"You're going a little slow today, Van Holsten," Noah says, punching my stomach as he walks past me to down a bottle of water.

"Fuck off. I spent my honeymoon with my wife, not in a gym," I reply punching out towards him, but he dances away from me.

"He was doing a different kind of exercise with Brooke. I bet she's great in the sack," Zack says with a smile. I scowl at him.

"Don't fucking talk about my wife that way," I snap. I imagine she is great in bed, but I haven't been able to test that theory out for myself yet. Even if I had, Lochlan shouldn't be talking about it.

"Oh, I get it. You're not one to kiss and tell. You don't have to say anything. I can imagine all on my own."

"Don't," I say, walking past him out the door.

"Dude, don't talk about Brooke that way. Ev's not fucking around. He will lay your ass out," Noah says.

I don't hear Zack's reply as I walk away. Probably a good thing. Everything he says pisses me the fuck off. I try to open the door to my room quietly in case Brooke's still asleep. She's sitting up in the bed when I walk in, though. Her hair is mussed in the sexiest way. The makeup around her eyes makes her look like a raccoon, but I think it's adorable.

"Morning, baby. How are you feeling?" I ask, leaning towards her and giving her a quick kiss. She gives me a content smile.

"Okay. I have a headache, though. I saw the Tylenol you left on the nightstand. Thank you," Brooke replies.

I sit down on the edge of the bed. I don't want to get too close to her until I shower. Brooke scoots closer to me anyway and puts her head on my shoulder. She doesn't seem to mind I'm all sweaty.

"I made the arrangements for Willa. She'll be here later. I texted her and let her know when her flight was," I say.

"You did that for me?" she asks.

"Of course. You said you wanted her here last night. It's your honeymoon too. Your best friend should be here since mine are," I reply.

"Thank you," she says.

"I need to shower before breakfast. It looks like you could use one too. Do you want to go first?" I ask.

"You can. I need a second."

"Okay. I'll only be a few minutes," I say. I get up from the bed and kiss

Brooke's forehead before I go to the bathroom.

I shower quickly, even though I know the hot water won't run out here. I walk back out with just a towel and I watch as Brooke's eyes track each movement my body makes. I know she wants me as badly as I want her based on her actions last night when she tried to get me naked.

"Are you trying to undress me with your eyes? All you gotta do is ask," I say with a smile as I search through the closet. One of the house employees must have emptied our bags yesterday.

I glance back up and see Brooke blushing slightly. My smile widens at embarrassing her. She sticks her tongue out at me as she slips into the bathroom. I laugh and shake my head as I find the shorts and t-shirt I was looking for. I'm dressed long before Brooke comes out of the bathroom.

When the bathroom door opens, a cloud of steam blocks my view. She walks out of it looking gorgeous all wet in nothing but a towel. She smiles when she sees me staring at her.

"Are you trying to undress me with your eyes? All you gotta do is ask," she says with a wicked smile.

"Will you really drop it if I ask?" I challenge.

"Of course," she replies.

"Drop it then," I say sure she's not going to. Fuck if I was expecting her to do exactly that. I really underestimate what my wife will and won't do.

The towel drops to the floor in a heap at her feet. I start at her feet and work my way up her perfectly tanned legs. I stop for a second on the tattoo she's got on her hip, but I don't spend much time there. Up and up, until I reach those perfect boobs I've seen once before. They're even more perfect than they were eleven years ago.

Water is dripping from her hair down her collar bones. I can feel myself hardening. How is this perfect woman mine? I take slow steps toward her in case she wants to tell me to stop. She doesn't. She just looks at me.

When I'm in front of her, I drop to my knees. My face is directly in front of her belly button. I inspect the tattoo she has more closely for the first time. I'm curious what she decided to put on her body permanently.

I put a hand on each hip. Goosebumps rise on Brooke's skin where I touch it with my warm hands. My fingers caress the small turtle on her hip. It's done in a tribal design. It's just a black outline. I move my thumb over it a few times before asking,

"When did you get this?"

"My sophomore year in college. Willa's got a matching one," Brooke responds. Her voice is breathy.

I lean my face closer and kiss the small turtle. Brooke lets out a shaky breath and threads her fingers in my hair. Her nails in my scalp cause a groan to escape my lips. I rub my nose over her hipbone. I can almost wrap my hands around her hips. My thumbs stay on her stomach while my other eight fingers splay across her back. She's so warm.

I look up towards Brooke's face. Her eyes are closed, and her head is tilted back towards the ceiling. I smile against her and trail small kisses up her stomach, between her perfect tits, on her collarbone, then her neck until I reach her mouth.

I kiss her ravenously like she's the last meal I'm ever going to eat. She grabs my hair and pulls me closer, deepening the kiss as far as it will go. Moans escape her mouth as my hands travel down from her shoulders until they are full of her ass.

I pull her up and her legs wrap around my hips. I feel the warmth of her and I know she feels how hard she's made me. I grind into her, releasing louder moans from her lips. Brooke pulls at my shirt and breaks the kiss only long enough to tear it off of me. She throws it clear across the room like it's something vile.

I walk back towards the unmade bed, but as soon as my shins hit the frame, a loud knock at the door stops us. I sigh heavily and lay my forehead against hers. She laughs lightly.

"What?" I snap loud enough for the fucker that interrupted us.

"Breakfast is ready. We're waiting. Kendra sent me up to get you. She doesn't like it when she has to wait on guests," Zack says through the door. I bristle just hearing his voice. Why the fuck should we care what Kendra likes?

"We'll be out soon," I yell.

Brooke still has her arms around my neck. She laughs when we hear Zack's receding steps. The mood is officially ruined, so I let Brooke slide down my body until she's on her feet. I'm pleased to find that after the moment has passed, Brooke still doesn't look embarrassed or self-conscious. She actually has a cute scowl on her face.

"Fucking Zack. He's a cock-blocking asshole," she mutters as she walks to the closet.

She's rummaging through it until she finds some jean shorts and a lime green tank top. She finds some gray Converse and a bra and panties. She brings it all to the bed and starts dressing. She's grumbling the entire time about what a fucking creep Zack is. And of course, it would be him to ruin what was sure to be the best sex of her life.

I find my shirt and put it back on, then I walk back over to Brooke. I wrap my arms around her shoulders once she's dressed and kiss the side of her neck.

"We'll finish that later and you're damn right, it's going to be the best sex of your life," I say. She doesn't even blush. She must lose all nervousness when she's sexually frustrated. I love this side of her even more than the self-conscious side.

She leans her head against my chest and looks up at me. She gives me a devilish smile.

"You better finish what you started. You can't leave your wife hanging like that. Happy wife, happy life and all that," she says before walking back to the bathroom so she can brush her hair.

"I wouldn't dare do anything to make you unhappy. I'll always satisfy all your needs," I say following her in. I watch her as I lean in the doorway while she brushes her hair quickly and puts it into a braid down her back. She applies a little mascara, then she's ready to go.

Brooke smiles at me before kissing me quickly. She grabs my hand and we leave the room. I look back at the bed longingly. All the things we could have done. I sigh and Brooke sniggers. She must know what I'm thinking.

"With any luck, we have a lifetime to do everything you want to do," she says as we walk down the hall towards the dining room.

Seventeen

Brooke

Everyone is already at the table digging into their breakfast when we arrive in the dining room. Zack and Noah both give Evan a look like they knew exactly what we were doing, but where Noah's comes across as joking and sincere, Zack's look just comes across as creepy as everything else he does.

I sit down between Allie and Evan. She gives me a small smile while Kristie wags her eyebrows at me. They probably know Evan and I haven't had sex yet. We would have if fucking Zack and Kendra weren't such cock-blocking twat waffles. God, I hate them.

I'm glad Ev and I didn't sleep together last night because I want to remember it but sooner rather than later would be better. Maybe tonight? Just thinking of his powerful hands around my waist this morning has me dampening my clean underwear. I shift my legs to get rid of the ache.

Evan notices and squeezes my thigh with the hand I was just thinking about. He gives me a knowing smirk. I smile at him and squeeze my thighs tighter together, trying to squish his fingers. He lets out a light laugh and moves his arm until it's draped around my chair. He loudly pulls it towards him until our legs are touching.

"You guys are adorable," Allie whispers to me with a smile.

"Thanks. I kinda like him," I reply.

"More like nauseating. So, what's the plan for today?" Kristie asks loudly to get everyone's attention.

"Willa will be here in a few hours. When she gets here, we'll have an even number of players to have a friendly little game of lacrosse," Noah announces.

Willa played lacrosse in high school and college on the women's varsity team. Sometimes they would play with the boys in friendly scrimmages. She's an excellent player. I only know the rules of the sport because I was at every single one of her games.

"I want Willa," Evan says.

"Fine. I'll play with Zack," Noah replies.

"You act like it's a bad thing," Zack complains, folding his arms in front of him in a pout. Noah just shrugs, causing Evan to smile.

"What do we do until then?" Allie asks.

"Game room? We could play *Mario Kart*," Noah suggests.

"That game is how friendships are broken and enemies are made," Kristie says.

"That's why it's perfect. Shows you who your true friends are," Noah replies.

"Fine. I kick ass at *Mario Kart* anyway," Kris says taking a giant bite of a pancake.

I pick up a banana and start eating it mindlessly, blocking out the rest of the conversation. I feel Evan shift beside me and I look down. He's trying to fix his shorts to hide his massive hard-on. I look up at him with a questioning expression.

He smiles and leans in until his lips are touching my ear. His warm breath on my skin sets my body on fire. It seems like every little thing he does is going to turn me on until he scratches that damn itch he created earlier.

"The first day of our honeymoon, you were eating a banana, and it had me thinking of your lips on my dick. Now every time you eat one, I imagine what it would be like to fuck your mouth," Evan explains.

His words cause me to shiver and do some shifting of my own. Apparently, I'm not the only one in desperate need of some itch scratching. Evan drops a light kiss on my neck directly below my ear, making goosebumps erupt all over my body.

"Are you guys going to participate in the group activities or be all over each other like the rest of us aren't here," Noah asks, bringing my attention back to the group.

I blush violently, causing Evan to laugh. All his friends have various looks of amusement while Kendra's face is pinched in an unattractive way.

"What part of honeymoon don't you understand?" Evan asks, kissing my temple.

I laugh with the rest of the group before we get up and head to the game room for what I'm sure will be a violent game of *Mario Kart*. The game room is giant with a pool table on one side, an air hockey table, a ping pong table, and a TV screen the size of a wall with black leather couches in front of it.

"There are four controllers. Who's playing?" Noah asks, grabbing them to pass out.

"I don't play video games," Kendra says.

"I know, baby. I wasn't talking to you," he replies.

"Zack, watch my shows with me," she commands, leaving the room. Zack follows without complaint. I'm relieved they left. Having them around is a real downer.

I grab one of the controllers from Noah's hands and sit down on the soft couch. Evan joins me on one side and Kris on the other.

"I'll take over for whoever loses the worst," Allie says, sitting next to Kristie.

Noah jump sits on the couch next to Evan, causing the whole thing to shake violently. He presses some buttons on his controller to get to the screen where we all join and pick our characters.

Jesus, I don't remember the last time I played video games. It must have been middle school sometime. I have sisters and Willa's not into video games. She prefers physical activity.

"Who should I be?" I ask.

"Princess Peach is mine!" Kristie yells, clicking the blonde character in pink with a ferocity that is not warranted.

"Okay, Kris. Jeez," I say with a laugh. "I guess I'll be this guy."

I pick the green dinosaur dude. My screen says his name is Yoshi. Noah picks Mario. I do know who he is. Ev picks a skinnier version of Mario in green. It says his name is Luigi.

We pick our racing vehicles, then we're waiting for the countdown. I don't know what buttons to press, so I'm in last place before I even start going. I finally figure out which one makes the car go and I'm racing alone. I hit every fucking banana peel there is, even though I try to avoid them.

By the end of the race, everyone is waiting for me to finish for like a solid two minutes. Allie giggles at me. I shake my head and hand her the controller in defeat.

"You kinda suck," Evan says with a smile.

"It's been a few years. Give me a break," I reply with a laugh.

We play several more rounds and I get better each time, but either Noah or Evan always wins. It's a bloody battle between the two of them. It involves a lot of yelling, shit-talking, and arm punches. It's pretty amusing though.

We stop playing when Kendra comes in, complaining about how Noah's ignoring her. He relents and we eat a late lunch. We're seated back at the table, but now there are little sandwiches instead of pancakes.

"Willa will be landing soon. I'm sending a driver to get her," Evan says to make conversation.

"Can we go pick her up?" I ask.

"Okay. You and I can go get her."

"Shit. Let's all go," Noah says.

"Willa the Charity Case is coming here to our house?" Kendra asks.

"Don't call her that," I say defensively, giving Kendra a dirty look.

"Not cool, babe. She's pretty awesome," Noah says.

"You barely know her, Noah! Besides, she hates all of us. Why would she come here?"

"She's Brooke's best friend. She's giving us the benefit of the doubt," Evan jumps in.

"I will not be a part of the welcoming committee," Kendra says, standing from the table. Zack follows her out of the dining room.

"Well, that's settled. I'll grab my car and we can go," Noah says, slapping his thighs. He seems unaffected by Kendra's tantrum. He must be used to it. Weird Zack always goes with her, no questions asked. I'm not complaining though.

We follow Noah to the giant garage full of different kinds of cars. He grabs some keys and walks to a red seven-seater SUV. Allie and Kristie climb into the third row, I sit in the second row in one of the bucket seats, while Evan sits shotgun.

We pull up to the parking garage of Orlando International just as Willa's flight should be landing. We file out of the car and head inside the bustling building. Evan grabs my hand and pulls me closer to him. I narrowly avoid being trampled by some guy too busy looking down at his phone.

Evan and I stand right near baggage claim so Willa will see us. Noah, Allie, and Kris hang back a bit. I'm so excited to see her, my body is practically vibrating. Evan must notice because he squeezes my hand and smiles at me.

I see the top of Willa's head long before she sees us. She's looking at something in her hand so she doesn't notice me waving. Her short black hair is in a pixie cut like always.

"Willafred!" I shout, knowing it's going to piss her off. Her head snaps up, and she glares until her eyes meet mine. She gives me the finger and all the while I'm smiling like a kid on Christmas.

"Not my name, *Brooklyn*," Willa says when she's close enough that she's not screaming at me. People assume for some reason that my name is Brooklyn and I go by Brooke for short. It used to piss me off, so when I call Willa by my nickname for her, she'll call me Brooklyn out of spite. It's become an inside joke.

"Not my name either," I say, pulling her into a tight hug. She's several inches taller than me, so my arms go around the middle of her torso. She pulls me closer to her and lays her face on the top of my head.

"I missed you so much," I say when we pull back from each other.

"Missed you too," she replies, then catches Evan's eye.

"'Sup Prince Playboy Jerkface?" Willa says, nodding at him. I choke on my spit. I cannot believe she called Ev that to his face!

"Willa. It's nice to see you again," Evan replies with a smile. He doesn't seem to mind the horrible name.

"Prince Playboy Jerkface? You seriously called him that in high school? Oh, my God. That's too fucking good," Noah says, barely containing his laughter.

"That's the only way we referred to him, Stud Muffin," Willa replies.

"Ha! My nickname is a hell of a lot better and more accurate than yours, Ev!"

"Neither name fits you guys. They obviously knew nothing about either of you," Kristie starts, pushing her way forward. "You need to come up with better nicknames for these guys while you're here. Don't worry, I'll help. I know all their dirty and embarrassing secrets," she finishes, throwing an arm around Willa's shoulders. I expect Willa to throw her off. She's not big into people touching her, but she doesn't. She just smiles and laughs lightly at Kristie.

"My sisters called you Mr. Hottypants at the wedding," I say to Evan.

"How about that, Noah? I like that one better than Prince Playboy Jerkface. From now on, you may all refer to me as Mr. Hottypants," Evan declares, throwing his arms up in triumph before dropping one down around my shoulders.

"Fuck that noise!" Noah yells, and we're getting a lot of people looking at us with all the shouting.

"It's good to see you again, Willa. I'm glad you could come," Allie says in greeting.

"Wait! Before we go further, Evan, I need to know why you beat up Lester James," Willa says stopping us all in our tracks when we just started moving towards the exit.

"What?" Evan asks.

"Skinny dude with glasses. He came back to school with black eyes and told everyone it was you. I need to know why," Willa explains with dramatic slowness.

"Why do you need to know?" Evan asks, rubbing a hand down the back of his neck.

"You're married to my best friend, and she seems pretty happy, but there are some questionable things you did in high school and I need to know why to decide if you're good enough for my girl."

"At the end of our Freshman year, Lester was telling everyone he and Brooke had sex during Spring Break. That he allowed her to blow him. I knew it wasn't true but he wouldn't stop talking about it so I decked him. He fucking deserved it!"

"Right. Let's get this bitch moving then. I have a mansion to see," Willa says like his explanation is good enough.

I didn't know that, and now I'm grateful to Evan for sticking up for me like that when he had no reason to. Fuck Lester for spreading rumors about me!

We walk as a group towards Noah's car. Willa sits next to me in the other bucket seat. Noah drives way too fast through the Orlando traffic back towards his house.

"You fucking rich pricks. Who needs a house this big?" Willa asks when we stop at the gates. Instead of being offended, they all just shrug.

"It's my parent's house. Do you want to ask them?" Noah says good-naturedly.

"I might. Are Kendra and Zack here?" Willa asks. I know she wanted to use more appropriate nicknames for them, but I told her Noah doesn't appreciate it. Willa's brash and she doesn't give a fuck, but she's not cruel. She'll hold back for Noah's benefit.

"They didn't want to welcome you, but we're glad you're here. I know things went bad in school, but we were never a part of that whole pool incident. Brooke's forgiven us and it would be cool if you would too. We're family now whether you want to be or not," Noah says, turning around to look in the back seat once the car is parked in the garage.

"Water under the bridge. As long as Brooke is cool with you guys, so am I," Willa replies.

"Good, because with you here, we have an even number of players to play lacrosse," Noah says, excitement lighting up his eyes.

"Sick. What are the teams?"

114

"Evan called you. I'm with Zack," Noah responds.

"Great. Let's do this shit," Willa says, and I recognize the look in her eyes. She's ready to lay Zack the fuck out on the field. It will be an interesting game to watch.

Eighteen

Brooke

Allie and Kristie show Willa to the room she'll be staying in while Noah and Evan go searching through the ridiculous amounts of lacrosse equipment Noah's got in the house.

I walk through the confusing ass hallways trying to find mine and Evan's room. He's usually always with me. I know our room is on the left side of the hallway, so after searching for-fucking-ever, I end up just opening doors until I find a room that looks familiar.

Most of the rooms I try are dark and empty. The bedding doesn't look like ours, so I just close it and go on to the next one. I open the next door on the left side of the hallway, and instead of an empty room, I see a bare ass flexing with each thrust forward. The woman in front of him lets out loud moans and screams his name.

I put my hand to my mouth to stifle my shriek of surprise and hold back my vomit. I still let out enough noise for Zack to turn around, though. He looks shocked at first, but then a dirty smile slithers into place.

"Like what you see, Princess?" he asks.

I look in front of him to see who he's plowing, but it can only be one person. Sure enough, on all fours with her shapely ass in the air, is Kendra. She looks over her shoulder at me with a glare so potent, I could have died

116

from it.

"Shut up, Zack!" she yells as she tries to cover herself up.

I slam the door and haul ass away from the two of them as fast as I can. I'm grateful to the Converse I'm wearing since they let me run without hindrance. Whatever I needed from our bedroom is completely forgotten as I try to get back to where Noah and Evan are.

I burst into the equipment room like the house is on fire. Both men look up, surprised at the sudden interruption. Evan smiles upon seeing me, but when he notices my distress, the smile vanishes, and concern takes its place.

"What's wrong, Brooke?" he asks, dropping a lacrosse stick and stalking towards me.

Evan puts both hands on my cheeks and makes me look at him. I gaze into his beautiful eyes and feel my heart rate steadily drop. I'm still worried about what Kendra's going to do to keep her secret, but I'm safe when Evan's here.

"I need to talk to you," I say, glancing at Noah.

"Okay," he says, leading me out of the room and far away from his friend. He looks around and pulls me into a dark closet. He turns on the light and bars the door with his body.

"What happened?" he asks.

I look into Evan's concerned eyes, and I laugh. It turns almost hysterical because when I do think about it, I'm kinda scared of Kendra. She'll do anything to protect her secret.

"Brooke? You're scaring me. Please tell me what's going on," Evan begs. His grip on my arms grows a little stronger.

"I just walked in on Zack fucking someone," I say, and my laughter stops abruptly.

"Like one of the staff?" he asks.

"It was Kendra. She was on all fours and Zack was going to town on her doggy style," I explain.

"What? Really? Zack and Kendra? They're carrying on an affair?"

"Well, I don't know about that. It could have just been this one time, but the way Zack follows her around like a puppy makes it seem like more."

"Zack never dates, or at least I've never seen him with anyone. Noah thought it was weird, but it's probably because he's with Kendra. They've always been super close and no one really thought much about it since they're best friends, but I'm almost positive Zack's in love with her. Kendra's probably in love with him too. I bet my left arm she's only with Noah because of who his parents are," Evan explains.

"Poor Noah. I always knew Kendra was a two-faced bitch, but this is a whole different kind of low. Noah doesn't deserve to be blindsided like this."

"This is perfect. Now I have something concrete to take to Noah. He'll be done with her and she and Zack will be out of our lives forever," he says, looking happy.

"It'll break Noah's heart," I say, wrapping my arms around Evan's waist and putting my face on his chest.

"I know, but he should find out now rather than years down the line when they're married and have kids. Besides, if Noah ever found out I knew and didn't say anything, he'd be even more pissed and hurt that I kept it from him."

I nod against his chest. It's the right thing to do. I would want to know if it were happening to me. I peer up at Evan. I can't see him ever cheating on me. He hasn't said it yet, but I'm almost certain he loves me.

"We just need to find a good time to tell him," I say.

"I'll figure it out."

We leave the closet and Evan makes his way back to the equipment room. He gives me directions to the kitchen. I'm hoping to find Willa, Kristie, and Allie in there. They're supposed to be gathering snacks and drinks for the game.

I keep looking over my shoulder, waiting for Kendra to pop out like the witch she is. I can see the entrance to the kitchen and I let out the breath I was holding. I'm in the clear... or not.

I get pulled to the side into a shadowy alcove. It's like a fucking mob movie. I half expect to have a knife pressed to my throat while the threats roll in, but Kendra just pulls me in and steps back. She's trying to kill me with her glare rather than an actual weapon.

"You need to keep your fucking mouth shut," she hisses.

"Why would I do that?" I ask. Behind Kendra's glare is actual fear. She knows I hold her future in my hands. That knowledge gives me a boost of confidence and erases any fear I had.

"I'll make your life hell if you tell. You won't be able to get away from me. I'll be there waiting to ruin your life. I'll wait for any little scandal. Don't fuck with me, Brooke. I already ruined your high school reputation. I could do it again. Mr. Van Holsten doesn't like scandal," Kendra threatens.

"You do what you have to do, Kendra. Noah deserves better than a gold-digging bitch. Your family has money. If you're in love with Zack, just be with him," I say.

"You have no idea what you're talking about!" she shrieks and stalks away from me without any more threats.

I chuckle a little and continue making my way to the kitchen. The three girls are in there raiding the fridge, much to the dismay of the cook.

"I can make any snack you want, Miss," the plump woman says as she watches Willa and Kristie putting together a cheese tray with crackers and various fruits.

"It's no problem. We've got this," Kristie replies, waving off the woman.

"You're making a mess, Kris," I say, leaning against the counter and popping a grape into my mouth. Kristie swats my hand away.

"Hands off. This is for the game," she says. I rub my stinging hand and scowl at her.

"Jesus, okay."

It doesn't take much longer for everyone else to filter into the kitchen. Zack gives me an amused and challenging expression while Kendra's is back to a glare of absolute hate.

"Are we ready to play the most epic fucking game we've ever played in our lives?" Noah asks, raising his arms.

Kendra rolls her eyes, but the rest of us shout to build Noah up. He throws Willa a lacrosse stick and a helmet.

"No pads?" she asks.

"Why? Can't play without them?" Zack jokes.

119

"I'm good. Are you?" Willa challenges back.

"Fuck yeah. Let's go," he responds.

We follow the four players out with the food trays Kris put together. Allie grabs a box of beer and a box of fruity wine coolers. In the backyard past the pool, tennis courts, and basketball courts is a lacrosse field with two nets on either side.

There are several tables and chairs situated on the sidelines. Noah must have had some staff set them up for us. We place the food and drinks on it while the players get their helmets on and separate into teams.

"No goalies. One midfielder, one attacker each. Let's go!" he calls out to us. Noah tosses the ball to me. I stare at it with confusion.

"What do you want me to do with this?" I ask.

"Throw it up for us, then get the hell off the field as fast as you can," he responds.

I walk to the middle of the field where Evan and Noah are standing face to face with smiles on their faces. I wonder how long it's been since they've played.

I toss it up and run away almost as fast as I ran away from the room Kendra and Zack were fucking in earlier. I'm back on the sidelines getting handed a wine cooler by Allie when I turn to see Evan has the ball. His focus is on Zack. God help that man.

Nineteen

Evan

⁂

I have the ball in the pocket of my crosse as I sidestep Noah. He's following behind me at a run, but I'm faster despite not exercising much for the last month. Zack's in front of me, falling back to defend the goal. He's got both hands on his crosse, ready to body-check me. Not today, motherfucker.

Zack runs towards me as I get closer to the goal. Noah is trying to come at me from the side while Zack comes from the front, but I twist backward then step to the side to avoid both of them. I thrust all my weight into shooting the ball towards the net. It flies in the dead-center just as Noah takes me down to the ground with his crosse and body weight.

I roll onto my back with a grunt and take Noah's outstretched hand. He pulls me up as Willa cheers for my shot back in the midfield. I walk to my side of the field and switch positions with Willa.

We switch up positions pretty much after every goal. Noah scores on me, and I score on him, but Willa scores the other three goals. By halftime, we're at five-four, us winning.

I rip my helmet off, and my face is dripping with sweat. Brooke hands me a bottle of water. I down the thing in a few seconds and grab some cheese and crackers off the table.

"You guys are doing amazing!" she gushes as she throws her arms around me and kisses me despite the sweat.

"When's the last time you played?" Noah asks.

"I don't know. College?" I respond.

"Bullshit! How are you winning?"

"I have the better teammate," I say. Zack glares at me but doesn't say anything.

"Fuck yeah you do!" Willa shouts as she takes a water bottle out of Brooke's outstretched hand.

We're back on the field after halftime. Willa's playing midfielder while I play attacker. Zack's attacker now, too. He gets the ball Kristie tossed for us and steps around me before I can check him. He's running full speed towards Willa. It seems like he's intending to take her out, and I push myself to tackle him before he can hurt her. I can't get to him in time though.

Willa plants her legs and has both hands on her crosse. She's got a wicked smile behind her helmet and I slow just a little. She's got this.

Zack's in front of her now, and he can see her trying to check him with her stick. He goes to sidestep around her to get the goal that will put us tied, but Willa does some sort of fancy footwork we definitely didn't learn at practice, so his sidestep is essentially useless. She's still in front of him, and Zack doesn't even realize until she bashes him in the chest so hard he flies back.

The ball falls from the pocket and I scoop it up and run it back down the field towards Noah without even checking to see if Zack is okay. It's not very sportsmanlike, but this dude screwed with my girl and he's fucking over his "best friend" by screwing Kendra. Zack Lochlan is a royal fucking douchebag.

I score on Noah easily, then we run back over to where Zack is still wheezing on the ground. Willa's looking down at him. She's taken off her helmet, and she's pissed. I didn't even do anything to her, and I'm a little scared.

"That's for fucking with Brooke at the pool house. I know you and your little plaything were the masterminds behind that "prank". It ruined a lot of things for her, asshole. But, no, you guys feel so shitty about your own lives, you can't help fuck with other people's. There are consequences, fuckhead. Here's the beginning of yours: being laid the fuck out by a girl," Willa says, spitting near Zack's head and stalking away with her helmet and crosse still in her hands.

I glance over to the girls on the sidelines and they look as shocked as I am. The hand Noah had outstretched to help Zack up is pulled away at the last second and Zack falls back to the ground.

"Is it true? Did you and Kendra have something to do with Brooke's incident?" he asks. The scowl on his face makes him look ten times more dangerous than normal.

"That bitch is crazy! We didn't do shit!" Zack yells, getting up from the ground himself.

"We know you did. Did you enjoy fucking with mine and Brooke's lives like that? What did we ever do to you? I liked her, and she liked me. We could have been together for years if not for you," I say, evenly.

We're speaking loud enough that I'm sure all the girls can hear. They stay planted where they are, but they're staring, waiting for more.

"Why does it matter now? The prince of Kingswood Prep got what he wanted, as always. You and the princess are married now, and you'll have your royal little children. You have your happily ever after," Zack spits at me, but I don't miss the glance he shoots at Kendra.

"It fucking matters because Brooke had to go through so much shit in high school because of what you guys did and the rumors *you* spread afterward. Do you know what we had to go through for her to trust me again after all that? Why are you such an asshole all the time?" I ask, itching to push him.

"Oh, boohoo. She lived and so did you. The endgame was the same either way. So sad for you that it wasn't as easy as everything else in your life. Why am I the asshole when you guys have everything you could ever want and it's never enough? I'll never get my happy ending and it's because of the children of the "Big Four". We're all just fucking peasants to you, there to do your bidding," he replies.

"What the fuck? We've always been friends, not enemies. You know we don't care about the money," Noah says.

"Yeah, because you have it. It's never even a thought because the money is always there. You're going to take over a company that will make even more money. You don't have to worry about your future the way the rest of us do," Zack replies, throwing his hands up in the air.

"You act like your family is poor. They aren't. We all went to the same fucking schools," Noah says.

"We only went to the same schools and ran in similar circles because my deadbeat dad decided his bastard son needed to attend something better than public school. Not that he would actually claim me or let anyone know he's my father. My mom and I only have money and status because Dad gives it to us. Once he decides to be less than gracious, we'll be out on our ass. We. Are. Not. The. Same!" Zack explodes.

"You said you didn't know who your dad was," Noah prods.

"Well, I found out right around ninth grade when he got me into Kingswood Prep!"

Brooke looks between Zack and me, analyzing. She scrutinizes us both as her gaze swings back and forth. For a second, I wonder what she's doing, but then I compare myself to Zack the way Brooke is doing.

We have the same build, but he's shorter. Not by much, though. The same hair color but different styles. We have the same weird eye color. I never noticed it before because we have different-shaped eyes. Zack's mom is Asian, so his complexion is darker than mine.

"Richard Van Holsten's your dad, isn't he?" I say.

Everyone's eyes snap to mine except Brooke's, who nods like I confirmed something she's known a long time. Kendra doesn't look surprised either. Of course, Zack would tell her. Especially if they're together.

Zack opens his mouth to say something, but closes it and shakes his head. He stalks off the field and away from everyone. He slows long enough to gaze at Kendra. She gives him a sad, sympathetic look, and it's the most genuine look I've ever seen cross her face. She must actually love him because she never looks at Noah that way.

Kendra looks between Zack's retreating figure and Noah. She's debating on what to do. If she rushes to Zack, she might show her hand, and if she doesn't? Well, that's just shitty for someone who's supposed to love him.

"You should go see if he's all right," Noah tells Kendra tightly.

Because of the big heart he has, he's worried about his friend. He's also noticeably irritated with Kendra and Zack for what they did to Brooke, even though it's history.

Kendra doesn't say anything, but she runs after Zack until she catches up with him. I wait for her to throw her arms around him, but she doesn't even touch him. At least not in view of everyone else. She'll wait until they are alone to comfort him.

We pack up the snacks, drinks, and lacrosse equipment and head back to the house. It's silent for a bit. No one says anything, not even Kristie. I expected her to be in "I told ya so" mode, but she's as somber as the rest of us.

"I don't even know what the fuck that was," Noah finally says when we get to the back sliding doors.

"That was confirmation of suspicions most of us have had for years. It doesn't feel as good to be right as it usually does," Kristie replies.

There it is. She just couldn't help herself. It was toned down, at least. It didn't have the fanfare and confetti cannons I might have expected.

"I have a brother," I say. I really can't believe it. I've been an only child my whole life. I always wanted a brother, but not Zack fucking Lochlan.

"Yeah, that's fucking wild. Now that I think about it, though, you have a lot of similarities," Kristie starts, and when she sees my death glare, amends, "In looks, not personality, shit!"

"I'm sorry, Brooke," Noah says softly.

"It's not your fault, Noah. You didn't know. They did what they did, and it sucks, but I'm over it. I got what I wanted in the end," she responds looking at me with such... love? Is it too much to hope for?

"Yeah, but it took an arranged marriage for that to happen. You wouldn't even be together right now if not for that," Willa points out.

"Maybe. We'll never know now." Brooke shrugs.

"Still, it shouldn't have happened," Noah says, depositing the stuff on the kitchen counters.

125

"Water under the bridge. Seriously," she says, grasping Noah's arm and squeezing.

Noah pulls Brooke into his arms and crushes her into a typical Noah-style bear hug. We've all suffered bruised ribs from them, but they're comforting as fuck. At first, Brooke stiffens but quickly melts into Noah's arms. He releases her after like a minute which is thirty seconds too long in my opinion, but I don't say anything.

"What's for dinner? That game left me starving," Willa says breaking any moments we may have been having.

"I dunno. Wanna go out somewhere?" Noah asks.

"Texas Roadhouse!" Kristie and Allie yell in deep voices.

"Should we ask if Kendra and Zack want to come?" I ask.

"Nah. Let them stay. I'm still kinda pissed at them and dinner should be fun. Let's have Joshua drive. I wanna drink," Noah replies.

"We should shower and change before we go," I say, catching a whiff of my shirt.

Drinking sounds good anyway. Finding out I have a brother is not exactly life-changing for me. I won't be pursuing a brotherly relationship with Zack. Sharing blood doesn't change how I feel about the guy. He was a dick this morning, and he's still a dick now. A dick who's been fucking Kendra right under Noah's nose.

"Agreed. Let's meet back up in a half an hour," Willa says, already walking away.

A half an hour isn't enough time to do any of the things I want to do with Brooke, but she follows Willa to her room instead of coming back to ours, so I guess that point is moot.

"See you soon, babe," Brooke says sweetly, fluttering her lashes at me. She knows what she's doing.

I scowl at her and smack her ass as I walk past. She squeaks a little in surprise, but then gives me a devilish smile that makes my dick twitch. Well played, Brooke, well played.

Twenty

Brooke

I sit on the toilet in the bathroom as Willa showers off the sweat from the game. I have to raise my voice to be heard over the jet-like showerhead.

"Thank you for what you did to Zack," I say.

"Of course, chica. He deserved it after all these years of getting off scot-free. I can't believe he's Evan's brother," she replies. I'm dying to tell her what I saw earlier. I know she'll help Evan and I plan exactly when and how to tell Noah.

"I think I always noticed the similarities between them. But, hey, I saw something earlier you might be interested in knowing," I start as nonchalantly as possible.

"What did you see? Does Noah have a giant golden toilet he takes all his shits on? I would totally expect that in the houses of the "Big Four"."

"What? No! I saw Kendra and Zack fucking earlier," I finish.

Willa throws her head out from behind the wall of the shower. One of her boobs pops out with it but she's unconcerned. She's always been that way about modesty and nudity.

"No fucking way! Were you like creeping on them? You aren't getting any, so you have to watch others getting down?" she teases.

I pick up a bar of soap off the counter and chuck it at her. She pulls herself back into the shower just in time and it narrowly misses her face.

"I was not creeping. I was looking for our room earlier and I can't remember where it is. I was opening each door on the left side of the hall, trying to find it. In one of them was Zack plowing Kendra doggy style," I explain.

"Let's pause on that for a minute. Are you telling me you and Evan still haven't done the nasty?"

"Seriously? That's what you got out of the conversation?" I ask, giving her a dirty look.

"Why do you keep avoiding the question?"

"Fine! No, we haven't had sex yet. I tried to undress him last night, but I was plastered. He wanted me to remember it and, you know, not take advantage of me in my inebriated state. We would have this morning, but Zack interrupted and I've been wound up all fucking day, and everything he says and does makes it worse. I'm more sexually frustrated than I've ever been in my life!" I vent.

"Probably tonight, then. Try not to drink too much so he'll take care of you. I bet he'll rock your world. He seems like he knows what he's doing," Willa says, going back into the shower to rinse out her hair.

"Why are we talking about this? Why does my discovery not faze you?" I demand.

"It makes sense. It's probably more than just sex. I bet there are feelings involved. Honestly, them as a couple makes more sense than Noah and Kendra," she says. I nod, agreeing.

"Evan's going to tell Noah. Hopefully soon."

"Maybe he should wait until closer to the end of the week right before you leave," Willa says.

"But what if Noah needs his friends?" I ask.

"Evan knows him the best. He'll know when the right time is," Willa says, exiting the shower with nothing on.

I throw a towel at her, and she catches it cleanly before running it over her short hair. She wraps it around her body and goes out to the main room.

"Where did all my clothes go?" Willa shrieks.

"The staff probably put your stuff in the closets." I roll my eyes.

"Why are they touching my shit?"

"It's their job, Willa," I say.

She grumbles but goes to the closet to look through her clothes. She picks out some super skinny black jeans and a gold sparkly halter top. She pairs it with some black heels and dark eye makeup. She blow-dries and uses some product to make her pixie cut spiky. She looks gorgeous.

It has me looking down at my own outfit. It's pretty plain. I should probably go change. What if we do something else tonight?

"I need to change," I say as we walk out of her room.

"Why didn't you do that instead of waiting for me?" Willa complains.

"I didn't think I had to until I saw you looking sexy as hell," I grumble as we reach my door. I go to open it and then hesitate.

"Evan might be changing," I say, turning back to Willa. She rolls her eyes dramatically.

"I'll wait out here. No funny business. We'll all be waiting for you."

I step into the room to see Evan shirtless. He turns and gives me a panty-dropping smile. The sooner he's able to fuck my brains out, the happier I'll be.

"Hey, I'm almost done," he says pulling his undershirt over his head then buttoning up another one.

"I just need to change and put some more makeup on then we can go," I respond walking over to the closet careful not to touch him. That would definitely make us late.

I stare at my wardrobe, not even knowing what's really in here. I decide to go for a look similar to Willa's. I pull out some dark blue skinny jeans and a navy and white striped sleeveless top that's a little longer in the back than the front. I find some navy high heels that buckle at my ankle and throw them on with some simple diamond jewelry. I fix my makeup and hair real quick and I'm out. Evan's sitting on a loveseat, waiting patiently.

"You look stunning," he says, standing from the couch and crossing the room to me.

"You all right?" I ask. Finding out Zack's related to him must have been quite the blow. Not surprising Mr. Van Holsten had an affair, though. Seems on par.

"I'm good. Learning this changes nothing," he replies, then kisses my cheek and takes my hand as we leave the room.

"'Bout damn time. I was waiting out here forever," Willa complains.

"You could have gone to find the others," I say, rolling my eyes. It was less than ten minutes.

We meet up with the rest of the group in the entryway below the staircase. Kendra and Zack come in from the side. Kendra has a scowl on her face as her gaze glances over us all.

Noah's changed into some gray jeans and a black button-up shirt folded to the elbows to showcase his tattoos. The top button is undone, letting his white undershirt peek out. He looks much like Evan, except Evan wears blue jeans and a light blue button-up shirt.

Kristie is wearing sparkly black leggings with a tight silver top that stops just below her ass. Chunky bracelets clink together from her wrists, and a chunky necklace completes her look. She's got on knee-high black stiletto boots and her hair is loosely curled and full-bodied. Allie's dressed more like me, with blue jeans and a nice flowy white top with a purple cardigan. She wears ankle-high black high-heeled boots and her red hair is pinned back in a half-up, half-down style.

"Where are you going?" Kendra asks, directing her question at Noah.

"Out to dinner," he replies stiffly.

"You didn't think to invite us?"

"I thought about it but decided against it."

"Well, we're coming," she says. Noah shrugs like he doesn't care either way.

"Whatever. We aren't waiting for you to change."

"Good thing I look this good all the time," she replies, stalking towards the front door. Zack sighs behind her and makes a point not to make eye contact with Evan.

We get into the waiting limo and head for Texas Roadhouse. I'm sure Kendra is expecting somewhere fancier, but I love Texas and from their inside joke, it seems Allie and Kris love it too.

"Why are we eating at this hillbilly hick restaurant?" Kendra asks with a disgusted look on her face, as predicted, when we pull up.

"This is where we decided to eat. If you don't like it, you can go somewhere else," Kristie says, and I'm surprised by the lack of swear words.

Kendra huffs but doesn't say anything. People look at us strangely when we exit the limo. People in a limo probably don't eat here often but we aren't snobs… well, most of us aren't.

I walk in with Evan, my hand clasped in his. I look back at Kendra, who's looking at the floor littered with peanut shells in disgust. She clings to Zack's arm. What is she expecting? Him to pick her up and carry her to the table? She's such a freaking drama queen.

We order waters and various alcoholic beverages. There's a Kenny Chesney blue something or another that comes in a fishbowl glass. It is to die for.

The girls and I go to town on some right away while the boys get boring beers in frosted mugs. Kendra opts for a glass of Rosé. I internally roll my eyes at her lame prissy drink choice.

Our server brings three baskets of the to-die-for rolls with her when she drops off our drinks. Almost everyone rushes to grab some. Noah seriously grabs his fork and tries to stab at Evan's hand just to get a roll like there aren't more if we want them. I can't really blame him. These rolls are amazing.

"I don't eat carbs past six p.m.," Kendra announces like anyone asked or cared.

"More carby deliciousness for us then," Kristie says, shoving a roll covered in cinnamon butter into her mouth then chews it obnoxiously. Kendra's nose screws up in disgust. Kris adds to it by opening her mouth, showing the whole table her chewed-up food.

Never mind that four out of eight of us are the children of the richest people in America, or that the other three come from pretty affluent families. Right now anything goes and we can relax as if we're normal. It's been nice to see everyone so relaxed because usually, we have to attend stuffy functions and act the part of prim, proper, formal individuals. Our parents would just die if they saw us now.

Twenty-One

Evan

Besides Kendra's pinched face during dinner, we had a great time. Not that I like him any better, but even Zack wasn't that bad. He stayed quiet, but at least he wasn't an asshole or creepy with my wife. He seems to like to zero in on Brooke for that shit.

We all had more drinks than we intended, but it went well with the steaks and prime ribs everyone ordered. Again, Kendra was the only one who ordered a salad. Typical.

"We should go to a club!" Kristie shouts when we get outside. The sun has gone down, but the night is still warm.

"I'm not trying to get trashed again. I'm still hungover from last night. My liver!" Brooke says, pressing her hands to her stomach.

"Stop being a pussy! This is a vacation. We're supposed to be having fun."

"If you can't have fun without alcohol, you need to reevaluate your life," Brooke says.

"I don't *need* it to have a good time, but it helps. It's not like I'm asking you to get down with some coke," Kristie says as we slide into the limo.

"You know what? Let's do it. We can dance."

"Club it is!" Noah shouts and tells Joshua where to go next.

We pull up in front of a sleek-looking building with the name in cursive

133

neon. There's a long line of people and I can hear the music thumping even from inside the car. Lights strobe from the open door where security stands, checking IDs and letting people in.

Willa and Brooke head to the back of the line, but Kendra stops them.

"I don't stand in line," she says as if her name is enough to get her in alone. It's not. She'll be name-dropping Noah, which none of us like doing. Nevertheless, we follow her to the front of the line where the big ass bouncer looks at us down his nose.

"Back of the line, sweetheart," the guy says to Kendra.

"Do you know who we are?" she asks. I roll my eyes. Of course, he doesn't.

"Do I care?"

"This is Evan Van Holsten, Noah Whittier, Allie Stinfield, and Kristie Cleaston. You may have heard of their families. They basically run America," Kendra responds, sounding ten times snootier than normal.

"And the rest of you?"

"I'm Noah's girlfriend," she replies. I clear my throat. I know she "forgot" Brooke and Willa on purpose.

"Oh, right, Evan's wife and best friend," she finishes barely motioning at the girls.

"Come right in. Sorry about all this," a small man in a smart suit says coming out from behind the bouncer. He's got a clipboard in his hands and glasses perched on his nose.

We follow him silently through the loud club. Hundreds of people are dancing around to some music with good dancing beats. Up in the mezzanine are private booths. The small man leads us to the biggest of them.

"Please order whatever you'd like. It's on the house."

"You don't have to do that. We can pay," I say, taking out my wallet.

"No, no. I insist Mr. Van Holsten. It's an honor to have so many people of your caliber at our club. I'm sorry about the confusion with security. And may I say, congratulations to you and your new bride," he insists.

"Thanks," I reply before the man darts away.

I want to snap at Kendra for what she did. We all work hard to not use our name and money to advance ourselves beyond what we've actually earned. But it doesn't really matter now. We're already here.

A server comes by for our drink orders, then we make our way to the dance floor after downing one mixed drink and a shot of vodka.

"Dance with me, Sweets," Noah says to Allie, grabbing her hand without a look back at Kendra.

He's pissed at her now, but he's still going to be heartbroken when he finds out about her affair. I plan on telling him soon. Maybe now would be a good time when he's mad at her already.

I grab Brooke's hand and follow him and Allie onto the dance floor. She pushes her ass into my groin and starts swaying her hips. After this back and forth all day, this simple action has me wanting to take her to the bathroom and fuck her against the door. I resist because that wouldn't be a very good way to consummate our marriage.

I sway with Brooke and grab her hips with my hands. I lift her shirt enough that I'm touching bare skin. She's warm and soft, and I bury my face in her fragrant neck. She smells like her jasmine shampoo. I may or may not smell it every time I take a shower.

Brooke twists her hands into my hair. It's barely long enough in the back for her to do that, but she does. I pepper small kisses from her ear down to the base of her neck. She breaks out in goosebumps and a small sigh escapes her lips. I can only just hear it over the loud music.

I twist her around abruptly and her hands come up to my chest in surprise. I grab her hips again, my hands resting barely higher than her ass. I could grab a handful again like I did this morning, but I refrain since we're in public. We haven't really had this conversation. The small touches and bits of intimacy between us have been easier, but sometimes it's still stilted.

Brooke pushes herself as close to me as she can get. Her perfect tits smoosh against my chest and her lips crash into mine. It makes my heart race that she wants me... all of me, even when she's sober. That much was apparent this morning.

"If we don't stop now, I'm going to take you to the bathroom and fuck you," I whisper into her ear. Her breath comes out in a pant.

"Maybe I want you to," she challenges.

"I don't want to do that now. Maybe after I've had you every which way I can think of in the bedroom, we can venture to sex in public."

She groans in frustration and leads me back off the dance floor towards our table. We pass by a dark alcove on our way, and I recognize the dark hair and sparkly leggings I see. Kristie must have found herself some poor person to be her plaything tonight, though I don't see them.

"Be safe, Kris," I say loud enough for her to hear.

Kristie's body turns fast at my words, and she has a dirty smirk. Instead of a man behind her, it's Willa in her shimmery top and pixie haircut. I'm a little surprised to see Kristie's tongue down Willa's throat, but it's not really all that unexpected. Willa's not really small by anyone's estimation, but Kris towers over her a bit with her sky-high stilettos.

Kristie loves and hates everyone equally. She's into having fun with anyone and everyone. She's not really picky as long as they're up for a good time. Willa's actually a lot like Kristie. They're both brash and have an "I don't give a fuck about your feelings" attitude. They tell the truth even when it hurts. Good thing I haven't told her about Kendra and Zack yet. She would have let all the beans spill.

"Get the fuck out of here, Ev. I've got business to attend to," Kristie says, putting her hand into my face to shove me back.

"Have fun tonight," Brooke says with a giggle as we walk back to our booth.

Noah and Allie are already there, talking quietly with their drinks in hand. I always thought they'd make a cute couple. They compliment each other well. Noah's loud and makes jokes all the time while Allie is quiet but full of love.

They're just friends, though. They love each other the way I love them and vice versa. They'll both find their right people because even if they seem good together on paper, it would never work. Allie needs to be with someone fun and spontaneous the way Noah is but reserved too. Noah is anything but reserved. He lays it all out on the table all the time kinda like Kris.

"Did you see Willa and Kris? Because we caught full sight of that," Noah asks when we slide in next to them.

"Yeah, we saw," Brooke giggles, taking a sip of her fresh daiquiri.

"Good for them," Allie says with a kind smile.

"Where did Kendra and Zack get up to?" Noah asks, scanning the room.

I exchange a look with Brooke, which Allie zeroes in on. I shake my head slightly so she doesn't bring it up, and she nods with understanding. I'll tell her and Kris later so we can decide how best to break the news to Noah.

"Dunno. It's getting late. Should we head home?" I say.

"Yeah. Let's go gather everyone," Noah says, somewhat perturbed. It seems his anger with Kendra is diminishing. Noah leaves the table to find his girlfriend just as Willa and Kendra slip in.

"Spill it," Allie says, narrowing her eyes at me. It's not often she's this authoritarian.

"Spill what?" I evade.

"I saw the look you two exchanged when he mentioned Zack and Kendra. What do you know?"

I exchange another look with Brooke and she gives me the smallest of nods. Now's as good a time as any. I let out a deep breath and look around me to make sure no one is eavesdropping.

"Brooke caught Zack and Kendra fucking in Zack's room today. I don't know if it was a one-time thing or not," I say. Allie looks shocked, but Kristie's eyes harden.

"Ten bucks it's been going on since high school," she says.

"Kristie! Our friend is going to be hurting. However long it's been going on, she's cheating on him with his friend!" Allie says.

"Zack was her friend first. Seems they're closer than we all thought. I can't believe I didn't see it before," Kristie says, slapping her forehead with the heel of her hand.

"When are we going to tell him?" Allie asks, looking back at me.

"Maybe tomorrow?"

"We should tell him tonight. He'll be mad if we sit on this information for any longer than we already have," she says.

"Okay. We'll pull him aside when we get home. It's probably best if it's just us four," I say. Everyone at the table speaks in unison.

"Agreed."

Twenty-Two

Evan

We leave the club with everyone in tow. The closer we get to the house, the more nervous I become. I don't want to hurt Noah, but I have to. It should only be Kris, Allie, and me. He doesn't need an audience when his life falls apart.

We all sort of pool at the entry of the house. Willa and Brooke give me sympathetic looks, then Brooke squeezes my arm and kisses my cheek before leaving for our room.

"I'm going to bed," Kendra says to no one in particular, then walks away. When she gets to the base of the stairs, she looks back at Noah, who still hasn't moved.

"Are you coming?" she asks.

"I'll be up later."

"Ugh, fine," Kendra huffs then stalks up the stairs, her heels clinking against the marble steps.

"I'm going to bed too," Zack says, following behind Kendra at a much slower pace.

"Can we talk to you?" I ask Noah once everyone else is gone.

"Sure. What's up?"

I lead him towards the game room we were in earlier and I sit heavily on the leather couch. Noah plops down next to me, and Kristie and Allie snuggle in close to Noah for the comfort he's sure to need.

"Dude, what's going on?" Noah asks, wondering why I brought him all the way here.

"Brooke saw something earlier, and we thought you should know," I start. Noah looks at me expectantly. "Um, this is difficult—"

"She saw Zack plowing Kendra earlier," Kristie interrupts me.

"Jesus, Kris. That was blunt," Allie says, scowling at her best friend.

"Evan was pussyfooting around it," Kristie replies in her defense, crossing her arms over her chest.

"Noah. Are you all right?" Allie asks softly, putting her hand on his cheek and turning his face so he's looking at her.

Noah opens his mouth to speak, but instead of words, a sob comes out. Tears spill over onto his cheek in a torrent. I can count on one hand how many times I've seen Noah cry. It's never been like this. Allie pulls Noah's large body to her and lays his head on her chest. She strokes his hair back and kisses his forehead. It looks sort of intimate, but it's just a friendly gesture.

"You can talk to us," she whispers.

Kristie leans against Noah's back with her arms around his chest and her hand resting on Allie's back. I move until I'm kneeling in front of him and take his hands in mine. We sit like that for an immeasurable amount of time while Noah cries. He doesn't need words quite yet. He just needs us.

"What the hell is going on?"

We all turn towards the door to see Kendra in a long silk robe tied around her middle. Her arms are crossed and her scowl is more prominent than usual. Hearing her voice, Noah jumps up, leaving Allie and Kristie falling towards each other and me to fall on my ass to get out of his way.

He crosses the room until he's right in front of Kendra. I follow him slowly, ready to pull him away just in case. Noah's breathing heavily as he glares at his girlfriend hard enough to kill her; if looks could do such a thing.

"How long?" he grits out.

"What are you talking about?" she asks, looking bored.

"How long have you and Zack been fucking behind my back?!"

Kendra drops her bored expression, and in its place is shock. Her arms drop to her sides and she takes a step forward.

"Noah—"

"Answer the fucking question, Kendra!" Noah yells, taking a step back for every one she takes forward.

"I—You don't understand," she offers weakly. She has no good defense.

"You're damn right I don't understand! If you want to be with him, why aren't you? Why be with me?"

"It's not that simple, Noah."

"Yeah, it really is that fucking simple."

"What's going on in here," Zack says, coming into the room behind Kendra. "I heard yelling."

Wrong move, brother. Noah's eyes flash on his and in an instant, Noah punches him in the jaw. Zack falls back against the wall as Noah rains punch after punch down on him. Kendra's screaming for him to stop. After a few good punches that leave Zack's nose broken and bloody, I pull my best friend off.

Noah's panting with the exertion and his knuckles are in the same state as Zack's nose. I glance towards the door and see Brooke and Willa in their pajamas peering in. They knew what was happening in here tonight, but they probably didn't expect a fight.

"How long have you been fucking my girlfriend, Zack," Noah spits at him. Zack's holding his nose with his shirt to stem the bleeding.

"Thirteen years," he answers with a shrug, though he turns his steely glare in Brooke's direction.

Apparently, Zack is not going the apologetic route. Noah stumbles back at the answer and Kristie and Allie try their best to keep him vertical despite the half a foot and hundred-pound difference.

"The entire time?" Noah says, and some of his anger has given way to hurt again. "Why?"

"Family expectation, Noah. You of all people should understand that," Kendra says evenly.

"I understand expectation, but I would never do something like this."

"I did what my family expected of me. They want me to marry well. Evan was always too hung up on Brooke to notice me, but you were there. Second best in my parent's eyes, but still a viable option," Kendra says coldly.

"I loved you, Kendra. You were going to be my forever," Noah says.

"Then why haven't you proposed?"

"It just never felt like the right time. Maybe this is why. You really are a snake in the grass like everyone's been trying to tell me."

Kendra shrugs like she doesn't even care she lost Noah but looks back at Brooke, fury on her face.

"You're dead, cunt. You ruin everything! You ruined any chance any of us had at Evan since he's been in love with you since middle school. Then you come out as his wife, despite the fact I know you haven't spoken pretty much the entirety of the last thirteen years. I don't know how you tricked him into marrying you, but you did. Then when I catch the next best thing, you find a way to fuck that up too!"

I'm about to yell at Kendra and back up my wife, but Brooke doesn't need saving or protecting. She can fight her own battles.

"I didn't have to trick Evan into marrying me. He loves me and I love him. I didn't fuck anything up for you, you did that by playing Noah. You could have been happy. If Zack's who you're in love with, you've had him this entire time. Instead, you chose to be a pawn in your parent's game. We all have a choice and you chose wrong. Money is more important to you than happiness so don't come crying to me saying I ruined it," Brooke says then looks at me.

Aren't we also pawns in our parent's games of expectation? The only difference is being the pawns worked out for both of us because we wanted each other, anyway. I'd choose Brooke every time, even if doing so took everything else from my life. She's the only thing I need. That's the difference between us and Kendra.

"I want you out of my house and out of my life. Leave us all alone. Brooke is my family now, and so is Willa. Lay a hand on either of them or us and I'll show you the full influence of the Whittier family you were so hell-bent on using to advance yourself. We're done. You and Zack have a nice fucking life," Noah says quietly, turning his back on Kendra.

"You'll be seeing me again," she says to me with a deadly glare.

"For your sake, you better hope not," I threaten.

Kendra huffs, throws her hair over her shoulder, then stalks out of the room with her head held high. Zack turns his glares on each of us before following her. In truth, I kinda feel bad for him. He's probably been in love with Kendra his whole life, and he's had to stand by while she fully intended to marry someone else.

Still, Zack could have left and chosen not to be a part of this. He could have chosen not to hurt the only friend he had. But he didn't. He kept this secret relationship with another man's girlfriend. Perhaps he was hoping Kendra could be his sugar momma since Dad could choose to cut him off at any time.

Noah steps back and falls onto the couch heavily once they are no longer in the room. He leans his head back and closes his eyes in exhaustion.

"What do you need from us, Noah?" Allie asks in a whisper.

"I think I just need to be alone. Can you make sure they leave, please? I don't want to see them again," Noah replies without looking at us,

"Of course." Allie steps closer and drops a kiss on Noah's forehead.

"Love you, Sweets," Noah mumbles.

"Love you too, Noah."

Kristie squeezes Noah's hand and the three of us leave while Noah wanders to who knows where.

We plant ourselves by the front door, waiting for Kendra and Zack to depart. She gives us nasty glares as she passes carrying suitcase after suitcase.

"I hope you're happy. You just hurt your best friend," she spits.

"Extremely happy. 'Bout time he dropped the dead weight," Kris replies with a genial smile.

"This isn't the last you'll see me," Kendra promises, then stomps out the door. Zack follows slowly but looks back at us with sad eyes.

"I do care about Noah. This isn't really how I wanted this to play out. I've been in love with Kendra since we met. You should understand that. I know you've loved Brooke since you were ten, but I've loved Kendra since we were in diapers. I couldn't let her go, but her dad doesn't want her to marry a bastard with no real family name," he says, looking down at the ground with his swollen and bruised face.

"I get it, but it doesn't make it right. Maybe now you two can be happy," I say, and I really want that to be true for them. Everyone deserves happiness and love, no matter how awful they are.

"Yeah, maybe, but I won't ever be the Van Holsten heir. It doesn't matter that I'm a few months older than you. I'll always be a nobody and girls like Kendra? They just don't end up with the nobody," he replies then slides into the waiting car.

I stare off after them a while longer, hating my dad for what he did to Zack and his mom. The least he could have done was claim Zack. Then all this hurt could have been avoided. But my dad is nothing if not a selfish, vindictive ass.

When the car is out of sight, the three of us relax. That's over and done with. Now Noah can heal and be happy again. We'll help him through this one day at a time.

Twenty-Three

Noah

I wail on the punching bag strung from the ceiling with a chain with my bare hands. The canvas material and my never-ending, hard punches are causing my knuckles to split and bleed. I don't even care. I don't feel a fucking thing except for the hurt in my heart.

My punches get faster and sloppier as the anger and hurt I feel reach a fever pitch then I drop to my ass trying to claw away the tears that are escaping. What in the actual fuck? I don't cry... ever. Not that I think men can't cry, I just don't. My life has never been so fucked up that I've felt the need to cry. Now though, my tears drain from my eyes, creating Niagara fucking Falls off my chin onto the floor.

I scream out my frustration, and I wonder if anyone hears me. I'm not too far from the room Evan is sharing with Brooke. Thinking of them makes my heart hurt more. I was never envious of him. Sure, he's been in love with Brooke longer than I've known Kendra, but for thirteen years, I got my girl. Evan and Brooke were estranged, leaving him pining.

I realized how in love they were with each other the minute they stepped out of their car. Even with all the shit that went down. Even with the arranged marriage. Even with the universe telling them time and time again that this wasn't going to happen, they're so fucking in love it made me equal

145

parts happy and sick to look at.

One look at them and I realized how much my relationship with Kendra was lacking. She's been annoying me more and more lately, and her shitty fucking attitude with my friends pissed me the fuck off. I pushed her away this week because of it, and for a split second, I thought I was the one that pushed her into Zack's arms.

That's not the fucking truth though, is it? She's been with him the entire thirteen years of our relationship. Our first time together where I thought we lost our virginity at the same time was probably a lie as much as the rest. She probably did that with Zack. Fucking asshole.

I grab my head and thrust it between my legs and sob for everything I lost. Half my brain says fuck that bitch and Zack, but the other half sorta misses them already. They were both pretty constant in my life, always here, even when my best friends couldn't be. Now I feel more alone than I've ever felt in my life.

I was gonna marry Kendra. I've had a ring picked out for years since we graduated from college, but it never felt like the right time. Maybe a part of me always knew she wasn't the one. Now that I look back, her stupid affair with Zack was pretty fucking obvious. He followed her around like a puppy. I didn't think anything of it because they were friends. I figured it's fine. I'm best friends with two girls, and though Kendra didn't like them, she didn't give me shit for it.

My heart breaks for the girl I gave it to, knowing hers was never mine. It always belonged to Zack. It almost drowns me in sorrow. I struggle to suck in enough breath. I don't like feeling like I'm dying. Back to anger. I can deal with that.

As soon as I give in to it, my anger explodes like an atomic bomb when I think of her explanations. Expectation? Bull fucking shit. No one knows more about expectations than the children of the "Big Four". Our whole lives have been: act this way, don't act that way, this will be your job in life, you get no say, be with someone "appropriate", do as your told, you have a family legacy to uphold.

I've been rebelling against those expectations my whole life. Tattoos up the ass on nearly every visible surface, nose ring, eyebrow ring. My parents hate them all. They hate I wear band t-shirts and practice music instead of learning anything about what my dad does for a living. Music's always been my passion, but I have to push it back to second best just to live up to my family's expectations.

I do it even though my little brother, Abel, is more than willing to take my place running the family business. It doesn't have to be me, but because I was born a few pesky years earlier, it falls on my shoulders. But at least if I live up to those expectations, I don't hurt anyone but me. Not the way Kendra living up to hers broke my heart. I'd never do that. I'd give my parents the finger with a shouted 'fuck you' before I hurt another person in the name of expectations.

"Fuck!" I shout into the empty room.

"You all right?" Evan asks, leaning against the door frame.

I look up at my best friend. He'd never hurt anyone this way just to get ahead. His whole life he's actually wanted to take over his dad's business. His dad treats that like shit, but Evan would never break anybody to get there. If his dad would have claimed Zack as heir, Evan wouldn't fuck him over to run the business.

"I don't think so. I'm balancing between being pissed off enough to set the world on fire and sad enough that I'm going to drown in it," I answer and my voice cracks on the last word.

Ev pushes off the doorframe and takes a seat next to me. He grabs my hand and squeezes in a ridiculously comforting way. Platonic affection from your best dude friend should be more widely accepted because his touch feels like he's lending me some of his strength and broadcasting all his love for me.

"It's okay to not be okay for a little while. I'll be here for you as long as you need. Just don't lose too much more to Kendra. She's not worth it. You'll be happy again with someone who deserves your love," he says softly.

I know he's right. He's not trying to be heartless or mean. He just doesn't want me to continue drowning longer than I should.

"Thanks." My tears are finally drying on my face, making it feel tight.

We sit together in companionable silence for a little longer before Evan pushes himself up and helps me to my feet. He claps my shoulder and squeezes.

"Night, dude. I gotta go see my wife."

Evan leaves the room with one last concern-filled expression and I stand here for a few minutes staring after him but seeing nothing. Soft hands grab mine and rub circles in the area between my thumb and pointer finger. I look down, startled to see my Sweets staring at my knuckles with a pinched expression.

"What's up, Sweets?" I ask, my throat feeling like sandpaper.

"I just wanted to make sure you're okay. What happened to your hands?" she asks in her soft, sweet voice.

"My punching bag got a beating. I didn't wrap my hands or put on gloves."

Sweets nods and drags me over to the first aid kit on the far wall as if I weigh no more than a child. She pushes me down to sit on a bench and her face comes directly to mine. I study the stunning woman in front of me. Her long red hair lays down her shoulders, touching her ribs. Her ocean-blue eyes study the contents of the kit before coming up to meet mine. She's so beautiful.

"This is going to sting," she says, bringing an antiseptic wipe to my knuckles. I hiss in pain when the cold wipe hits my wounds.

"Sorry," she apologizes but keeps the cleaning and stinging going.

"Why couldn't I just love you, Sweets?" I ask and my voice breaks as I'm swallowed by sadness again. She gives me a kind smile.

"You do love me, Noah. You're just not in love with me. We're friends, family, really. We aren't meant to be together, but we'll both find someone out there worthy of all the love we have to give. You're a special man with a heart full of the best kind of love life has to offer. Anyone that gets even a fraction of the love you give is lucky. The girl you find will receive more than anyone else, and you'll light her life up so bright everyone before her will disappear into the past where they belong. Don't shut yourself off from finding her just because a bitch like Kendra was dumb enough to hurt you and throw your love back in your face," she says kissing my forehead softly.

"Whoa, Sweets, what's with the swears?" I joke with a smile. She makes me feel more normal than I've felt since Kendra walked out of my house.

"What can I say? Kendra brings out the worst in me," she replies with a light laugh.

We sit in silence while Allie puts antibacterial cream on my hands. She rubs it in gently and I feel somewhat peaceful.

"I love you, Sweets," I say, resting my head against her warm chest. She wraps her arms around my head and kisses the top of it.

"I love you too, Noah. I'll be here for you, always, cheering you on. Do what makes you happy. Maybe it's time to shuck off the pesky expectations our parents set forth."

"Will you shuck them off too?" I ask, pulling back, hazel eyes burning into ocean blue ones.

"I'm not as brave as you yet. Maybe someday I will be."

Sweets squeezes my hands one more time before turning around and walking out of the gym. I think she's right. I need to be happy and this life is not making me happy. I've been fantasizing about moving away and producing or writing music or playing music for as long as I can remember. I think maybe I'm going to do just that.

Fuck expectation. All it's ever done is crush people under its immense weight. I won't be another casualty.

Twenty-Four

Brooke

Willa and I sit in the middle of my bed waiting for Evan to get back. They're just downstairs. I don't expect to hear much now that Kendra and Zack left. My heart hurts for the gentle giant who's breaking somewhere in this house, but at least we're rid of Kendra.

The door opens softly and Evan walks in. He flops down on the bed next to us, laying his head near my leg. I stroke his soft hair and his eyes close.

"How's Noah?" I ask.

"As well as expected," he answers.

"At least the bitch and her boyfriend are gone," Willa says, standing from the bed. "I'm going to bed. Catch ya in the morning."

"Night," Evan and I say as our door closes, leaving us alone.

"Come here," Ev says, pulling my face down gently by the ends of my hair.

He kisses me sweetly, and I shift until my face is lying on his chest. He strokes my hair the way I was stroking his just a minute ago and kisses my forehead every once in a while as we lay there in silence.

"I love you, Brooke. I've been in love with you for damn near half my life. I loved you the whole time you hated me. There was never going to be anyone else for me," he whispers into my hair.

I smile and sit up so my chin is resting on his chest, but I can look into his eyes. In them, I see the truth in his words.

"I didn't hate you, Evan. You've been my dream guy for half my life, even when I wanted to hate you so much it hurt. I couldn't, though. I love you and I always have. The minute I saw your face the first time when we were ten at that stupid gala ten-year-olds should not have been invited to, you were it for me."

"I honestly didn't know if you told Kendra you loved me for her benefit or if it was the truth," he whispers.

"Nothing about this marriage has been fake, Evan. If we hadn't been pushed together, I wouldn't have married you but not because I didn't love you. Sure, I didn't like you too much at the beginning but I've always loved you. I just didn't want to be swept up into this world more than I had to be after everything that happened and you're at the top of it. Then we got married, and it felt like everything was as it should be. I couldn't help liking you as much as I loved you. I'm happier than I ever thought I would be," I reply, kissing his perfectly sculpted chest.

Evan brings my hand up to his lips and kisses it softly before folding it back to his chest and closes his eyes. We lay like that long enough for both of us to fall asleep. Sideways on the bed on top of the covers, we sleep wrapped up in each other after both a mentally and emotionally draining night.

All thoughts of sexual tension and frustration have gone for now. It's enough for us to be totally transparent about our feelings for each other. We never have before and it wasted too much time, but maybe this is exactly how we were supposed to get here. We'll never know what could have been. All we have is the now, and the now is pretty perfect.

* * *

Someone jumps on the bed shaking me violently like there's an earthquake. I startle awake and sit up quickly, banging my head against something hard. What the hell? I grab my head as the pain radiates out and squint my eyes against the bright light.

Willa's face is right in front of mine with a silly grin. She's holding her head too, but now that I know it was her that woke me up, I don't care. It's her fault. I glare at her and she moves back to sit on her haunches.

"Good morning, chica," she says.

I reach for a pillow and throw it at her hard enough she falls off the bed backward with a loud bang. She scrambles up and gives me a glare of her own. She torpedoes the pillow at me and I fall back, landing on Evan's chest. His breath whooshes out and he lays back groaning.

"I'm sorry," I say, touching his chest and face to make sure he's all right. He is, of course. I'm not that heavy.

"What the fuck, Willa? Why are you in here? We could have been naked!" I scream at her, looking for another pillow to throw at her face.

"Whatever. Not like I haven't seen all your goodies before," she responds.

"But you haven't seen, nor will you ever see, Evan's!"

"You can stop looking at my wife's goodies," Evan says, sitting up on his elbows when his breath has come back.

"She was mine way before she was yours," Willa says, glaring at Evan.

"You sure about that?" Evan challenges with a smirk.

"You both suck. Hurry up so we can eat. Everyone's at the table waiting for you. Noah said we're going to Disney World today and I can't wait to get started on that. I've never been," Willa says, dancing to the door.

She exits the room, leaving the door wide open. I groan at how annoying my best friend is and jump off the tall bed. I slam the door and hope she can hear. I turn back to Evan still on his elbows smiling at me. I laugh and walk towards the bathroom to shower all of last night's shit off.

I step into the steaming waterfall, and instantly my muscles relax. I probably won't even need coffee today since Willa gave me a shot of 'wake the fuck up bitch' when I came face to face with her minutes ago.

I'm washing the shampoo out of my hair when hands on my hips have me glancing over my shoulder. It's Evan. Who else would it be? Well... I wouldn't put it past Willa to get in with me, but the hands are too big in any case.

I spin in Evan's arms and throw mine around his neck. He stares at me for half a beat before he leans down to kiss me. It starts out tender but grows in intensity. As the kiss intensifies, his hands drop until they're grasping handfuls of my ass. He pushes me until my back hits the water-slicked tiles.

I wrap my legs around his hips, and his erection presses against me, making me whimper. This has been a long time coming. It's every wet dream I've had. What I was thinking about every time I was with someone else, which honestly wasn't all that often.

Evan's lips drop from my mouth to my neck. He nips at the sensitive skin there, then soothes it with butterfly light kisses. I squirm against him to create the friction he's not giving me. He chuckles lightly in my ear. His breath sends my body skittering with goosebumps even in this now stifling shower.

He brings his mouth back to mine, kissing me once, twice, three times before pulling back and waiting. I open my eyes and look into his. So much love shines in them and under the love, lust. I smile and press one gentle kiss to his mouth.

"Is this how you want our first time to be or do you want to wait?" His words catch on the steam and float to my ears.

"I just want you. Any way I can have you," I whisper back. He smiles once before going back to my neck.

"I'm already yours every way you want me," he says as he slowly enters me.

I gasp as he fills me fuller than I've ever been before. It doesn't hurt though. It's a spectacular feeling. With one last thrust, he's fully inside, and he pauses long enough for me to get used to it.

When I nod against his cheek, he pulls out and thrusts back in, leaving me breathless. My breath mingles with his as he swallows all my sounds and I swallow his.

I can't even measure the amount of time we made love in the shower. The hot water never falters, of course, so it could have been hours or only minutes. Either way, it was perfect. He lets me slide back down to my feet, kissing me the entire way.

I put conditioner in my hair and let Evan wash my body. I wash him then we get out with smiles and sore muscles but in the most delicious way possible.

We dress quickly and hold hands the entire way to the dining room. Like everyone knew what we had just done, they lift their heads with dirty smiles and twinkling eyes. I expect to be called out, but everyone surprisingly holds their words if not their leers.

"Are we really going to Disney World today?" I ask, grabbing for a banana and unpeeling it slowly.

"Sure, why not?" Noah replies, shoving a large piece of waffle into his mouth.

"I'm down if you all are," I say with a shrug.

"I need me some Disney magic," he says, and though he has a smile on his face, it's not as bright as it normally is. He's sad and heartbroken. It seems almost wrong to be as happy as I am when he's hurting.

"We'll leave after breakfast. It'll be hot. Wear tennis shoes and bring sunblock if you need it," Noah says to the table.

All through breakfast, we murmur our plans and the excitement builds. I've been to Disney World before, but most of them haven't. I know Evan is probably bursting to get there like a child would.

Staff clears the table as we all stand. I'm already wearing a racerback tank, jean shorts, and Nikes, so I'm ready to go. Evan grabs my hand as we exit with our group of friends.

"Let's roll," Noah says, grabbing a hat and putting it on backward as he heads out the door to the garage will of us in tow.

He leads us to the same SUV we were in yesterday and we clamber in. Obvious excitement fills the car as we drive towards the happiest place on earth.

Twenty-Five

Evan

Of course, Disney World is busy as shit. We're waiting in line to pay for parking, but inside, I'm jumping up and down like a little kid. Much like the water slides in the Bahamas, I'm ridiculously excited to be here.

Dad would probably flip his shit if he realized half the things we were doing on our honeymoon. He'd think it's not proper enough, but it's our time, so he can go suck it. Besides, it might be a good distraction for Noah after all the shit that went down yesterday.

When we've finally parked, little trolley things pick us up and we pile in so it can take us to the entrance and ticket booth. My first stop is going to be a gift shop so Brooke and I can get those "I'm his, I'm hers" shirts with Mickey's hands. I want to be the cliché honeymooners.

I pay for the tickets and we head through the entrance in groups of two. I see a gift shop immediately and pull Brooke in. I find the shirts I'm looking for and throw a tank top one at her. She holds it out to read and laughs.

"Really?" she asks.

"Fuck, yeah! I need everyone in this park to know you're mine."

"Pretty sure the world knows, Evan. We were plastered all over the front page three weeks ago and holding steady on page four now," she says, shaking her head with amusement.

She throws the shirt back to me so I can pay. I shove her towards a bathroom to change. Allie, Willa, and Kris follow her in because it seems girls can't go to the bathroom alone.

Noah and I sit outside waiting awkwardly, but we aren't the only guys doing it, so whatever. I bump my best friend with my shoulder.

"How are you holding up?" Dumb question, but I need to know.

"Last night was rough. I didn't really sleep. I've been sharing a bed for a long time and it was sort of lonely. Today, I just want to forget she was ever in my life. Let's have fun and laugh. Make me forget," he says, and it almost sounds like a plea.

"We're going to have the best day. You have to be happy here. It's the happiest place on earth according to the commercials," I say, nudging his shoulder with mine again.

"They wouldn't dare lie," he says with a smile much smaller than normal. I'll take it.

The girls emerge from the endless bathroom at that moment. Noah and I push off the wall and head towards them. I grab Brooke's hand and we walk. Kris and Willa are holding hands today too. More than just sex, then. Hmm.

"Be my date today, Sweets?" Noah requests, holding his hand out after he sees the other couples.

"Always, Noah," she replies, grabbing his hand with a smile.

I smile back at them as we head further into the park. I made a vow to go on every single ride in this place. Today we'll be in Magic Kingdom and Hollywood Studios. Tomorrow we'll go to Animal Kingdom and Epcot. Who can say no to food and alcohol from around the world?

The morning and part of the afternoon fly by, waiting in line and going on the rides. Laughs and smiles fill the time, and even Noah looks like he's enjoying himself. I hope this is acting as a salve to his broken heart.

We stop a lot to wait up for Kristie and Willa while they make out in whatever corner they can without too much PDA.

We stop for lunch to eat at *50s Prime Time Café.* The food is good, and the themed restaurant is fun. Good thing we got the park hopper so we can go between parks until we hit the floor from exhaustion.

For dinner, we go to *Be Our Guest Restaurant,* located back in the Magic Kingdom park. The restaurant is in the Beast's castle and is seriously cool as fuck.

By the time the sun has gone down, we make our way to the main streets to watch the parade. Tons of kids are with their parents on the edge of the street with these light-up things that spin.

I stand with my arms around Brooke's waist and pull her snuggly to my chest. Watching the kids all around me, I whisper into her ear.

"Do you want kids?"

"Yeah, someday. I just want to do it differently than our parents did," she whispers back and I know she has a small smile on her face.

"Me too."

I imagine little girls with Brooke's blonde hair and icy blue eyes, or little boys with my uncommon hazel and brown hair. The thought makes me smile. I want to do everything differently from my father. I want our child free of the expectations that crush Noah and Allie right now. I want them to be free at the same time they're taken care of. I want them to be able to pursue their dreams and not worry about losing their security.

I barely see the parade as I daydream about the future with Brooke. I've done it a thousand times over the years, but now that she's resting comfortably in my arms, it's real for the first time.

It's pretty late when we get back to Noah's house, and even though we just spent all day together, we go to the game room to watch a movie. We watch some random Disney one on Disney + in honor of our day.

Brooke falls asleep almost immediately and slowly so does Willa. Then Noah and Allie with their heads together, leaving only Kris and I awake as the end credits roll.

"Should we all just sleep here tonight?" Kristie asks with a smile.

"I can carry Brooke to bed, but Noah's too heavy for me," I answer.

Kristie laughs imagining it and shrugs as she snuggles close to Willa.

"Thanks for being so nice to Brooke and Willa. It means a lot to me," I say after some silence.

"You love her, so I do too."

"That's not always true. Noah loves Kendra, and you didn't love her," I point out.

"Noah didn't really love her. He only thought he did. It's different with Brooke. Anyone can see you two are head over heels for each other. Good job making your wife fall in love with you, Ev."

"Apparently, she's loved me for as long as I've loved her. All I had to do was get her to like me too. I'm so happy, Kris. You have no idea," I say with a smile as I move some hair out of Brooke's face.

"I can see it, Ev. I can even fucking smell it on you. You're relaxed in a way you've never been before, and you look at Brooke like she's your whole world. You've never looked at anyone the way you look at her, but it's more now that everything's fallen into place," Kristie explains.

"The last month has legit been the best time of my life. I love you guys, but this is something else."

"I know, Ev. I mean, I *don't* know, but maybe someday I will," she says putting her face in Willa's hair.

"Is she possibly that happiness," I ask, motioning to the girl.

"Probably not, but I can be happy with her for now. We have fun and that's where I'm at at the moment. I have time to find my forever," Kris responds.

"Be careful with your heart and hers," I warn. That's all I need in life. My best friend fucking over Brooke's best friend.

Kristie flashes me the finger, then hunkers down and closes her eyes. I laugh lightly and pull Brooke's sleeping body closer to me and fall into sleep.

Twenty-Six

Brooke

We spend the rest of the week going to various theme parks in the area or just chilling together at Noah's house. His parents and his brother, Abel, never came home while we were here, so it's been comfortable with just us. As someone that's only had one friend consistently for almost thirteen years, it amazes me how fast Evan's friends became mine. Like they were mine all along.

Allie and Kristie are going home tonight too, on a commercial flight and Willa's coming back to New York with Evan and me on the Van Holsten private jet. We have about twelve hours until we go back to real life. I'm both ready and not ready at the same time.

This last month has been so far removed from real life, I don't even know what to expect anymore. Everything will change. Evan and I will be looking for an apartment and I'll be getting ready to start my teaching job. Evan will start his actual training with his dad and our lives start. Like the last seven years were nothing, life truly begins now that we'll be home and together.

The six of us hang around the game room having an air hockey tournament for a few hours. Then we play some more *Mario Kart.* I thought Noah was good at it, but he has nothing on Willa. She's deceptively good at a lot of things you wouldn't expect. We have lunch together and then chill by the pool until it's late enough we need to get our stuff together.

It shouldn't come as a surprise that all our shit's packed up already by Noah's staff. All our stuff is put into the back of Noah's SUV. He's driving us all to the airport, then coming back to an empty house. I wonder if he's going to be okay. He's had us all week to distract him from his heartbreak. Now it'll be coming back full force. Poor guy.

In front of the airport, the six of us stand in a group getting ready to say our goodbyes. Allie and Kristie's plane takes off soon, so they're the first to go. Allie gives Evan and me hugs and cheek kisses.

"I'll come to visit as soon as I can. Get settled. I love you guys," she says, then walks into Noah's waiting embrace.

"I'm going to miss you more than normal, Sweets," Noah says into Allie's hair.

"I'll be around if you need to talk, Noah. Call me anytime. I'll always answer," she replies.

Kristie comes in, hugging both Evan and me at the same time with one arm around each of our necks. She kisses both our cheeks, then makes her way to Noah.

"Holy fuck, what am I? Chopped liver?" she says with a laugh as she tugs Noah down to her level so she can go high on the hug. His deep laughs rumble and I hope he never stops laughing.

"You're my best friend too, babe. I love you, Kris," Noah says.

"Love you too, big guy. Call me whenever. Though I guess when you call Allie, I'll be right there," she replies.

While Evan and I share our goodbyes with Noah, Kristie pulls Willa towards her and kisses her deeply for a long time. Willa blushes and I smile. No one makes Willa blush. I hold back my laughter while Evan and Noah do a bro hug, just like the one they shared when we got to Florida.

"I'll miss you, Brooke. I got you. Call me if you ever need anything or just if Ev is pissing you the fuck off and you need someone to vent to. Someone to agree with you when you say Evan's acting like a dipshit," he says kissing the crown of my head. I step back from him with a laugh.

"I'll miss you too. We'll see you as soon as we can."

160

"What happens now?" Evan asks as everyone hangs around. We need to go, but no one moves.

"It's time for me to be brave and move on. I found a place I want to buy on the beach a few hours from here. I'm going to get a job doing something with music like I've wanted to do all along. If my parents cut me off, so be it. I don't want to be unhappy anymore. Fuck their expectations. I need to live my life the way I want to," Noah replies, shoving his hands into the pockets of his grey jeans. He has a *Queen* shirt on today.

"Good for you. Let us know where you'll be living," Evan replies, clapping Noah on the shoulder with a smile.

Noah nods with a small smile, and I think this is a step in the right direction for him. We all deserve to be happy.

Finally, we separate. Evan, Willa, and I head to the jet and settle in for the several hours of flight we have ahead of us.

"You guys are pretentious assholes, you know," Willa says as she gets comfortable in one of the light-colored leather seats.

"Don't hate," Evan replies, throwing a small travel pillow in her direction.

It's late by the time we get back to Manhattan. The driver drops Willa off at her apartment, then takes us to Evan's. I still lived with my parents, and I'm definitely not taking my husband there. We talked about finding a new apartment together, but I suppose we'll have to live somewhere while we look. I don't know if I'm ready to see Evan's bachelor pad, though.

We pull up to a modern-looking building and our driver pulls into the parking garage. Evan helps me out of the car while the driver deals with our bags. Evan leads me to an elevator where he pulls out a plain-looking credit card. He swipes it across a sensor and the elevator ascends.

The doors open to the foyer of a grey, black, and white pristine apartment. Evan leads me in further. The whole living room area is filled with presents. They must be from our wedding. I don't know how we ended up with so many because there weren't all that many guests. Maybe people sent them after the fact when they saw a Van Holsten got married in the paper.

"So this is my place. We can stay here while we look for something closer to the school you'll be teaching at," Evan says, gesturing to the apartment.

He scratches the back of his neck like he's nervous. It's adorable.

"I appreciate you being open to finding somewhere else to live. This place is amazing," I say. He just shrugs.

"It's just an apartment. I'm not that attached to it. It's not something that was built for me. I just wanted to get out of my parents' house, so this is where I've been living since I graduated from college."

"Do you want to show me around?" I ask.

"Uh, sure."

Evan takes my hand in his and escorts me through each room. The master is huge with a king-size bed. There are no decorations and looks like a typical men's apartment. I'm happy to find no woman paraphernalia anywhere.

When the tour is finished, we go back to the living room. Evan's housekeeper/cook comes out from somewhere to introduce herself. She's an older lady, maybe in her fifties. She's skinny and short. She's got graying hair, green eyes, and what I would imagine is a kind, grandmotherly smile.

"It's so nice to meet you, Brooke. Evan's told me so much about you, but I never thought you guys would get married," she says grasping my hand in her small one.

"He used to talk about me?" I ask, surprised. I'm sure Ev hasn't seen her since the wedding.

"Oh yes, dear. He used to tell me all about the girl he'd fallen in love with when he was ten and how you were the one that got away. How he'd never be happy with anyone else, but he could blame no one but himself for letting you slip through his fingers," she says, smiling kindly at Evan.

"Geez, Mrs. G. Just tell her all my secrets," Evan complains, but there's a loving smile on his face.

"Well, don't get drunk and mope around. You have friends to tell these secrets to, but you chose to tell me," she scolds. I snigger. I like her already. "Anyway, I just wanted to say welcome and let me know if you need anything."

"Thank you, Mrs. Gibbons. It's been a pleasure meeting you," I say. Evan mentions her a lot in conversation. She seems to be a big presence in his life.

"Oh, Mrs. Gibbons is too formal. Call me Mae or Mrs. G. I didn't touch the gifts because I thought you'd like to go through them yourselves. I'm going to unpack your bags and I'll put away the gifts tomorrow. I'm going to go home after I unpack your stuff," she says, patting my arm.

"Thanks, Mrs. G. We'll see you tomorrow. Tell Harry I said hi," Evan says kissing the older lady on the top of the head. She smiles at him as a mother might before swatting his arm and walking towards the bedrooms.

Evan and I sit down on the floor with our backs to the couch while we go through all the bags. We got pretty typical stuff. Fancy china, silver silverware and utensils. I assume that will not be for everyday use and instead when we host dinner with his parents or mine.

We got various kitchen stuff like a pressure cooker, Crock-Pot, and a juicer. Evan probably has all that already, but the sentiment is nice. We got several cards full of cash as if we need more. We got bottles of expensive wine and champagne. Someone did get us a large wall canvas of our first kiss picture. Literally, the first kiss we ever shared and it will be on display in our home for posterity. I smile at it. We look as in love there as we actually are now. I guess if you want to get technical; we were in love when the picture was taken. We just really didn't know it.

It takes us hours to go through everything, but we leave it nicely for Mrs. G. She left several hours ago, so it's just Evan and me in the house. We get undressed and get into bed. We make love for the first time since we've been home. It's just as unforgettable as every other time we've had sex.

Afterward, we lay with our legs tangled together, looking at apartments or houses for sale at the halfway point between Manhattan and the Bronx. We settle on a few and Evan promises me we'll go look at them tomorrow. I still have a few weeks to go before school starts. I called the school last week to confirm when I could come set up my classroom and they said sometime this week.

Evan says he can go back to work whenever he wants, but he needs to have a conversation with his dad first. I guess now that we're married and Evan's done what he was supposed to, official training for Ev to take over after Mr. Van Holsten retires can begin.

Everything seems like it's falling into place for both of us. Evan's living his dream of taking over the family business, I get to teach at the school I wanted, and we're happily married. Our lives seem perfect. I just hope it stays that way.

There was another time I thought everything was perfect, and it changed the course of my life. Evan and I just made it back to each other. I couldn't stand if anything tore us apart now that we've gotten everything we ever wanted.

Twenty-Seven

Evan

Dad's been pestering me to come to the house for our official meeting to start my successor training since I stepped off the plane. Before the wedding, I would have jumped on the chance to get started and I'm still excited, but somehow it's not the most important thing to me. I want to spend more time with Brooke. I want to look for houses together. I want to go with her to take a tour of the school she'll be teaching at. I want to help her set up her classroom. The small moments that make up life have become important. I don't want to sit on the sidelines and watch the moments fly away. I want to live them.

So I ignore my dad's summonses and spend the next couple of days house hunting with Brooke. We go on tours of dozens of places at the halfway point between Manhattan, where I'll be working, and the Bronx, where Brooke'll be working. It ends up being a really fun experience going from house to house deciding what we like about the places and what we don't.

On the third day, we finally find a place we love. It's on the top floor of a really nice apartment building with good security and a doorman. Just like my apartment now, it requires a keycard to get the elevator to even go to the top floor. The elevators open directly into the place. The actual apartment has floor-to-ceiling windows overlooking the city at the end of the living room. It had a large modern kitchen and a separate family room.

There are six bedrooms and four bathrooms, as well as an in-home gym that looks a lot like a condensed version of the one at the Whittier mansion. Brooke falls in love with the place as soon as we step through the door. I can see how her face and eyes light up as we walk through each room. This is it. Our new home.

I buy it as soon as we finish the tour. I'll have the movers move our stuff to this place as soon as possible. It should be ready for us to stay here by tomorrow. Brooke is pretty much bouncing from excitement in the car as we travel back to my apartment.

"I never thought I would be this excited to buy a home," Brooke says as she leans against me when I pull her to me. I smile against her temple. "When we got married, I was so sure I was going to be miserable. So sure that everything we had to do together would be horrible. I mean, that was before I knew it was you I was marrying, but still. I never expected to be this happy, to feel so much like we're a team," Brooke continues with a sigh.

"We are a team, Brooke. There's no one else I ever wanted to do all this stuff with," I reply and I feel her relax further into my side. She fits there perfectly like we were made to be together.

"I finally feel ready to start my life. It feels like everything is exactly how it always should have been. I feel invincible like I can take on anything," she says.

"You can and I'll be here to support you. Did you find out exactly when you can go see your classroom?" I ask.

"Tomorrow. Can you come with me or do you have to get started working with your dad?"

"He keeps calling, but I'm making myself free this week. Finding us a home is something we need to do, and going with you to set up your classroom is something I *want* to do. Dad can wait," I say, nuzzling my nose into her hair. It's my favorite smell in the world.

"Your dad doesn't like to be kept waiting," Brooke says seriously.

"Tough shit for him then," I reply, not worried at all.

Evan

* * *

The next morning, the movers are here bright and early to pack our stuff and get it to the new apartment. That's just as well because Brooke's been up since the ass crack of dawn too wound up to go back to sleep. We're going to tour the school today and figure out how she wants to set up and decorate her classroom.

Brooke practically vibrates the entire car ride over to the school. We pull up to a brick building that looks like it could use some love. The playground equipment is outdated and falling apart. We walk through the doors and I can see the interior needs a fresh coat of paint and the floors need to be repaired. It makes me sad that schools like this in the poorer parts of New York aren't taken care of. I get there's no money in the budget, but why? Why do these schools need less than others?

As we walk through the halls to the principal's office, I'm taking mental notes of everything the school needs. I wonder how the music department is faring? The instruments probably need to be replaced. Do they even have a music department? The Van Holsten family will be making a sizable donation to this school so they can get all the repairs they need, as well as anything else, like textbooks or whatever. I'll talk to the principal before we leave.

Brooke knocks softly on the door labeled "Principle" and we wait a second before we hear a muffled "Come in!". Brooke opens the door slowly and we see an older woman sitting in a chair with papers all around her. She's got glasses on her forehead and she's wearing a t-shirt and jeans. Might as well be casual when you can before school starts.

"Miss Jacobs, I'm so pleased to meet you. I'm Principle White," Mrs. White says, extending her hand for Brooke.

"Pleased to meet you, Principle White. This is my husband, Evan Van Holsten. We got married only about a month ago, so I'm actually Mrs. Van Holsten now," Brooke says as she shakes the woman's hand.

"My apologies, Mrs. Van Holsten. I didn't know. Please, have a seat," Mrs. White says, motioning to the empty chairs in front of her desk.

167

"It's nothing," Brooke says, waving off the apologies.

"So, school starts on the first Monday of September. I'll show you your classroom in just a moment. You can set it up however you like. I'll get you the curriculum we must follow but within that, you can plan your lessons however you see fit. Class sizes are usually bigger here. About thirty-five kids. Most supplies for the classroom you'll have to purchase yourself. You might create a list of supplies you'll need the students to buy so they'll have what they need for your class. Other than that, I have everything I need from you. I just have some paperwork for you to sign, then I can show you to your classroom," Mrs. White explains.

Brooke's students won't be buying any supplies. I'll purchase all of them. These kid's parents probably struggle enough to put food on the table without having to worry about supplies the schools should be able to provide.

Once Brooke signs her papers, Mrs. White leads us down a few hallways until we come to a near-empty classroom. There are tables and chairs pushed towards the back and a dirty-looking whiteboard at the front. Despite the peeling paint and old furniture, Brooke absolutely beams at this room that now belongs to her.

"Mrs. White, could I please have a word?" I ask. She nods, looking somewhat suspicious. Brooke's absolutely oblivious as she looks around the room.

"How can I help you, Mr. Van Holsten?" Mrs. White asks. I wonder what she thinks I want to speak to her about.

"I was hoping you'd be able to tell me about the things this school might need," I say. Mrs. White's face goes blank then furious.

"Excuse me?"

"Do you have a music department? School sports or other after-school activities? How are your textbooks faring? How is your library?" I ask.

"Mr. Van Holsten, I understand someone from your family might be used to a higher caliber environment, but unfortunately we just don't have that kind of budget. We do what we can to teach each student. I assure you, your wife will be safe here. The kids are not all hoodlums," she replies. I smile at her defensiveness. Good. It means she cares about this school and the students.

"You misunderstand me, Mrs. White. I only ask because I'd like to help in the areas you're lacking because the money in the budget has to go elsewhere. If there's no music department or sports or after-school activities, I'd like to help with funding to provide those to the students. My best friend is a wonderfully talented musician, and we would never have known if it wasn't for the school music program. I know how important after-school activities can be to keep kids out of trouble. It looks like some areas of the school could use some updating or repairs. I'd really like to help," I explain.

Mrs. White stares at me for a minute with a blank face again. Her anger has dissipated, at least.

"Why are you doing this, Mr. Van Holsten?" she asks warily.

"Ideally, I'd like to help all the schools and underprivileged children, but even my money only extends so far. If you choose to accept my help, your school will just be lucky since my wife happens to be working here. It's not fair, but it is the way the world works. Will you accept my help?"

"Of course, I will accept whatever you're willing to donate. I just want it to be known your wife won't get any special treatment because of it," she drawls.

"I wouldn't dream of it. We don't need any legs up. I really just want to help where I can. Please, come up with a list of anything and everything that's lacking or things you'd like to change or add and send the list to my email. I'll help. I'd like to get most of it done before school starts, so the sooner that list makes it to me, the better," I say writing my email down on one of my business cards.

"Thank you, Mr. Van Holsten. I hope your wife is happy working here," Mrs. White says.

"I expect she will be. It looks like it's a great environment," I reply with a smile. Mrs. White gives me a small one in return before turning and walking back towards her office.

I reenter Brooke's classroom. She's going through what will be her desk and making a list of her own of what this classroom needs.

"What were you and Mrs. White talking about?" she asks, not looking up from the paper in front of her.

"Nothing important," I say, sitting on one of the tables. There are pretty decent drawings scratched into the surface. I'm impressed. Brooke gives me a snort in response.

"We can go shopping for anything you need, then go to lunch," I suggest after a silent moment.

"Sounds good. Let me just finish my list."

"Maybe we can go shopping for the new house too. New bedding and décor or whatever," I say. I throw my arm around Brooke's shoulders as we walk out of the school.

Brooke smiles at me as she slides into the black town car that's waiting for us. She gives the driver instructions on where she wants to go and we spend the rest of the day shopping for school, for the house, and spending as much time together before real life begins again.

Twenty-Eight

Evan

Mrs. White sent me her list later the same day. As I suspected, the school needed new instruments, textbooks, regular books for the library as well as new computer lab equipment, and several repairs through various parts of the school.

I immediately get to work on it all from my laptop while lying in bed with Brooke as she reads a book she bought today. The movers were able to get everything over here, and Brooke decorated a bit with the things we bought.

It's comfortable to be laying next to Brooke in bed. She's in those racy silk pajamas she wore all through our honeymoon, me in my boxers. We're together, but doing our own thing. We don't have to speak, we barely touch beyond occasional hand-holding yet it's perfect. This is not what I imagined when I thought of how our lives would be, but I guess these are just some of those small moments that make up life.

"I'm going to see my dad tomorrow. He's really insisting on the meeting. Will you be okay?" I say as I shut my laptop and place it on the bedside table. Brooke looks up from her book and smiles at me.

"Yes, dear. I will be fine. I have a curriculum to go over and lesson plans to get started on," she says.

The next morning, I get up bright and early, shower, dress, and kiss a still sleeping Brooke on her forehead before heading towards my childhood home. I enter the same study Dad's always in. This is where my life changed forever four months ago. I can't even be mad.

"Evan, thanks for finally making time for me," Dad says, looking anything but thankful.

"Sorry, Dad. I had a wife to spend time with and some stuff to settle," I say, plopping down into the chair opposite him with none of the apprehension I had before. I already did what he asked of me. I married who he wanted. Now my dream of taking over the family business begins. Bonus that I actually love my wife and it's no hardship. The opposite, in fact.

"I understand you bought a new apartment. Why did you choose that area?"

"Brooke starts work at a school in the Bronx in two weeks. We decided it would be good to get a place between there and here," I explain. Of course, he knows exactly where we live.

"Is that what all the charges are for? The school she works at?" he asks, seemingly not impressed.

"We toured the school together, and it needed some things. I want to make the school my wife's working in as nice as possible. Besides, it's good for optics and will come with a nice tax break," I say. They aren't the real reasons I did what I did, but these are the reasons Dad will understand.

"Very well. Are you okay with Mrs. Van Holsten working?" he asks. I don't care, but he probably does.

"She went to college for this, Dad. What kind of husband would I be to take that away from her? She'll make a fantastic teacher. It's another good thing for optics. Giving back to those who are underprivileged. Better than her staying home spending money," I say with a sigh.

"I see. As long as she realizes being by your side is the most important thing in her life. It's her job to support you first and foremost. Her teaching career will come second."

I don't grace Dad with an answer, which is just as well, he doesn't really want one. What he says is the law, as evidenced by my arranged marriage. I won't argue with him, but I also won't be bringing the message back to

Brooke.

"Other than that, how are you and Mrs. Van Holsten getting along?" Dad asks. The way he won't call Brooke by her name annoys me.

"Her name is Brooke and we're good. In love, even," I say, though Dad doesn't care about that.

"In love? Really? You've known the girl for a month," he says, actually surprised and not calm and composed like normal.

"I met Brooke when I was ten, Dad. I liked her throughout high school. This was a long time coming and honestly, we should probably thank you. If it weren't for the forced marriage, we might not have found our way back to each other," I say with actual sincerity. My dad's eyebrows climb higher and I know he was not expecting this at all.

"Well, good for you, son," he says with a light cough. It makes me want to smile, but I hold it back and wait for him to get to the reason I'm actually here.

"I think we can start on your training, then. You will shadow and work with me. You've already done everything else you can in the company, so now you'll see what I do. After I feel like your trained enough, you'll become my number two until I actually retire," Dad explains getting right down to business.

"Sounds great, Dad. I look forward to working with you and learning all you have to teach me," I say with a smile.

And I am excited. This is everything I've worked for and now after everything, I'm here. It's happening, and I got a beautiful wife out of it. I ended up on the winning side of it all. How did I get so lucky? I'd say it's too good to be true, but it is true.

"You can go now. I'll see you tomorrow at the office. Eight sharp," Dad says, dismissing me. He probably doesn't want me to infect him with my happiness. God forbid he be happy.

"One more thing, Dad," I say, pausing after I stand. He looks up expectantly. "You remember Zack Lochlan, right?"

Dad gives me a blank stare. He raises his eyebrows at me. It's a silent gesture for me to get on with it.

"I found out he's my brother a few weeks ago. Does Mom know you have another child?" I ask.

"I don't see how it's any of your business."

"Why didn't you claim him? Technically, this should be his job."

"Again, not your business. Would you rather I give him this job? After all you've done for it?"

I don't want that, but I wouldn't fight Zack for it either. It does technically belong to him as the firstborn son of Richard Van Holsten.

"Just thought it was interesting. I always wanted a brother," I reply with a smile.

I did want one, but not Zack. We won't be chummy, but I got the glare from my dad I was trying to get. Worth it.

After exiting the study, I go in search of my mom. We've texted a little, but I haven't actually seen her since we got back. She's in the drawing-room sitting at her white grand piano. Listening to her play is one of my fondest childhood memories.

"Hey, Mom," I say, sitting down next to her and playing a harmony.

Her eyes are closed, but she smiles when she hears my voice. She leans her head against my shoulder and we play together until the song finishes.

"That was wonderful," she says softly when the last note has disappeared into the air.

"I'm not that good, Mom," I say with a smile.

She taught me to play, but music's never been my thing. Not the way it's Noah's. He can play circles around me in any instrument on the planet. That might be an exaggeration, but I'm confident he could pick up any instrument and learn to play it decently within half an hour.

"You're plenty good. Thanks for stopping by. I feel like I haven't seen you in ages," she says, turning slightly to get a good look at me. "You look good, Evan. Marriage suits you."

"Only marriage to Brooke. How have you been, Mom?" I reply with a smile.

"You and Brooke are doing well then?" she asks.

"I've loved Brooke since I was ten, Mom, so yeah, it's going wonderful," I say with a smile.

"Ever the dramatic one, Evan," she says with an eye roll and a smile.

"I'm not even being dramatic. It's just the truth. I'd like you to get to know her. I think you'll love her."

"I'd like that, Evan. You seem happy. Does she love you too?"

"She does. Honestly, I might have to thank Dad. We wouldn't have gotten together without his bullshit marriage stipulation, but it worked out. I'm happier than I've ever been," I say.

"Maybe I can come to see your new place this week. I could come for dinner, maybe. Does Mrs. Gibbons still work for you?"

"She does. Come tomorrow. Bring Dad if you must," I say with a light laugh. Mom laughs too and lightly backhands my shoulder.

"I've got to get going. I just wanted to stop in. I love you, Mom," I say kissing her forehead before standing from the piano bench.

"I love you too, Evan. See you tomorrow," she responds, starting a new song as I walk away.

Brooke seems equal parts excited and nervous to have my mom and possibly my dad over for dinner tomorrow. She talked to her mom while I was gone and has planned for them to come later this week.

Seems like it's going to be a week of getting to know the family we found ourselves in. Everything's going so well. Should I be waiting for the other shoe to drop or can life really be this good?

Twenty-Nine

Brooke

I've been running around the house like a chicken with my head cut off all day trying to get ready for Evan's parents to come over. I don't really like Mr. Van Holsten, and I'm nervous to meet Mrs. Van Holsten. Evan says she's a sweetheart and I don't doubt it, but I think it takes a special sort of lady to be married to a man like Richard.

Mrs. Gibbons has been cooking all day. Whatever it is, it smells delicious. She wouldn't let me help, so I've been setting up the formal dining room with the new china and silverware we got for our wedding. The house is pristine, mostly because we haven't lived here long and Mrs. G cleans all the time.

We still have several hours to go before Evan's parents get here and the wait is slowly killing me. I'm jittery from nerves and I can't focus on any one task unrelated to getting ready for this dreadful dinner.

I'm sitting in the library pulling book after book down, trying to find one to interest me enough when my phone rings. I glance at the display to see it's Willa. I smile as I bend down to answer it.

"'Sup, bitch."

"That is no way to answer a phone call, Mrs. Van Holsten," Willa says, but her voice is lit with amusement.

"It's the way I answer when it's you."

"Whatever. What's up, Brooklyn," she says.

"Not my name, Willafred. Evan's parents are coming over for dinner tonight. It's the first time I've seen them since the wedding. I'm so fucking nervous, I feel like I'm going to puke," I reply, grimacing at the unwelcome rolling in my stomach.

"Just show Dick who's boss. You'll be fine." I let out a strangled laugh.

"He could probably have me killed, Willa."

"Good ol' Dick wouldn't do that. He picked you to marry his only son. He must think you're good enough for the family."

"Not his only son, remember? Besides, he also told me not to make waves," I point out.

"No one wants to think about Zack and you don't make waves, Brooke. He probably did thorough research on your ass to make sure. He wouldn't have wanted anyone like me. Besides, Evan will be right there. That boy's got it bad for you."

Thinking of Evan makes me smile. Yeah, he does have it bad for me, but I have it bad for him too. Evan loves me and he won't let anything horrible happen to me. We'll be fine. This dinner won't be any worse than any typical dinner with the in-laws. I let out a noisy breath and I can feel the tension leaving my shoulders.

"Thanks for talking me down, Willafred."

"Not my name," she starts with a laugh. "Call me after dinner and tell me all the juicy details. Bye-bye, bitch."

I shake my head with a laugh as I set the phone back down. When I right myself, strong arms thread around my waist, and warm breath crawls over my neck. Feather-light kisses trail from the back of my ear to my collarbone. I sigh and relax into Evan's embrace.

"I thought I'd find you somewhere nervously pacing, trying to keep yourself busy in the hours before my parents get here," he whispers between kisses. I shiver as goosebumps raise on my skin.

"I was not!" I want it to be an indignant shout, but it just comes out a breathy whisper as Evan continues his gentle assault of my neck.

"You were too. Maybe Willa's call distracted you enough to stop your obsessing."

"What makes you an expert on my habits?" I ask with a scowl.

"I watched you for four years, Brooke. I couldn't talk to you, so I sat and observed. I could tell when you were nervous about tests because the studying you were supposed to be doing couldn't hold your attention. When something at home bothered you, you'd pace up and down the walkways of the school muttering under your breath like a crazy person. I always thought it was cute. I imagine you're doing both today. You're in here trying to find a book to read to occupy the hours left, but nothing will hold your attention. You've been walking miles around this house. You've probably been muttering too. Mrs. G probably thinks I married a lunatic," he explains in those huskily whispered words of his.

I'm surprised at how observant he'd been in school, but I really shouldn't be. His assault on my neck and his low words distract me enough that I want to tear off his clothes and push him down to the floor. We probably can't do that right here with Mrs. G in the house, but I could take him to the bedroom. That should be an adequate distraction until it's time for us to get ready.

Evan's hands are already trailing down my arms towards my stomach and lower until he reaches into my leggings. I nearly combust the moment his calloused fingers touch me. I shake and my breaths turn to embarrassing pants.

"Let's go to our room," Evan whispers into my ear. I nod when my words fail me.

Evan picks me up and throws me over his shoulder like a caveman. He slaps my ass hard. The crack from it sounds around the house and I giggle against his back as he races to our room.

Once inside, he throws me onto the bed and the down comforter fluffs around me on impact. It's like falling onto a bed of clouds. I giggle again and stare up at Evan as he tears off his tie. He throws it across the room and nearly rips the buttons off his shirt in a struggle to be free.

I sit up on my arms watching him undress in a haste. Each piece of clothing flies to a different part of the room. When he's as naked as the day he was born in all that brilliance, he turns his attention to me.

Evan rips my leggings off, taking my underwear with them. They end up on the dresser. Before I have a chance to do or say anything, he plunges long fingers inside me, leaving me to fall against the bed again with a moan. Jesus, he knows what he's doing.

When I explode with my first orgasm, Evan pulls my tank over my head gentler than anything he's done prior, then fits himself into me until we both let out gasped moans and I forget what I was worried about.

Afterward, we lay tangled together, my head on his chest. Evan's rubbing circles into the small of my back. I glance at the clock on the wall and groan when I see the time. I need to get ready, but I'd rather lay here in Evan's arms for the rest of my life. It took so long to get here; I don't want to leave.

With one last groan, I extricate myself from my husband and head for the shower. Evan crashes it, of course, leading to more funny business, which I'm not complaining about. Then he leaves me to get ready in peace.

Evan's dressed and out the door before I even step out of the shower. I wrap myself in a fluffy towel and head into my walk-in closet. I push dresses this way and that, looking for something appropriate for tonight yet comfortable because it's my God damn house, and I'd rather be eating in sweatpants on the couch while watching a movie. Alas, the Van Holstens don't work that way... at least mommy and daddy Van Holsten don't.

I pull on my undergarments and head to my vanity to put some makeup and jewelry on. I blow out my hair quickly, which leaves it straight down my back. Good enough. With only twenty minutes left until our guests arrive, I slip into my dress and shoes then walk my way to the formal dining room.

Evan is there sitting in his seat staring at his phone. He's sporting a scowl so whatever it is is bothering him. I take my seat next to him, placing my hand on his thigh. The touch has him looking up. When his eyes meet mine, he smiles sweetly and puts his phone away.

The doorbell rings and I can hear Mrs. G shuffling around to answer it. There's some muffled conversation, then my in-laws enter the dining room.

Evan stands and strides to his mom with a smile that tells me he adores her. He kisses her on the cheek and pulls her into a long embrace.

"Mom, since you were never properly introduced, this is Brooke. Brooke, this is my mom, Trish," Evan introduces us.

"I remember you from Evan's school. My my, what a beautiful woman you've grown to be. I hope my son is being good to you. I know I taught him better if he's being an ass," Trish whispers with a contagious smile.

"Trish!" Richard barks, presumably at her curse or simply because she was talking. Trish's smile falters and she looks at the floor. I choose to ignore his scowl and poor attitude.

"Your son has been absolutely wonderful. He's a good man. His momma raised him well," I say, trying to sound upbeat. The smile returns to Trish's face, and she squeezes my hand as I lead her to her seat.

Mr. Van Holsten takes the chair next to her, directly across from his son. Once we're all seated, Evan places a hand in mine under the table. The silence is awkward as Mrs. G serves us our food. Everyone but Richard murmurs their thanks to our wonderful cook/housekeeper. His flippant attitude towards her pisses me off.

"So Brooke, what are your plans now that you've settled," Trish asks.

"I start teaching at an elementary school in the Bronx next week. I'm really excited," I respond with a smile. Richard grunts but says nothing, which surprises me. Evan must have told him where I'd be working.

The dinner continues on that way. Trish asks about our honeymoon and questions about me in general. I answer genuinely and it becomes a three-sided conversation, leaving Richard out of it. He neither participates nor seems to care what we're talking about, but he's been staring at me intently this entire time. It's unnerving, but I try my best to ignore it.

When it's time for them to leave, we stand by the front door. Evan has his arm around my shoulder. Richard looks at us funny. Does he wish we never fell in love? Would he rather this be a marriage of convenience? When Trish congratulates me on my job once more, Richard finally speaks.

"We'll play your teaching by ear. If it seems to interfere with your family duties, we will have to rethink your career choice. Trish is quite busy helping me run an empire without a job. I'm just afraid you won't be able to do both. I chose you to marry my son to help him with his running of the family business, not for him to bankroll your work with underprivileged children."

I stand there gaping at him, but before I can even think of something to respond with, Richard pulls Trish along out the door. Trish manages a small smile and a wave before the door closes, cutting off my view.

When the shock wears off, I'm pissed. No, I'm fucking livid! More upset than I think I've ever been. Even madder than when my parents informed me of my impending nuptials. I storm off in the direction of the bedroom, ignoring Evan's pleas for me to wait. I slam the door then lean against it, trying to catch my breath. I'm not mad at Evan. He can't control his dad, and I'm positive he would have defended me given the chance. Even so, I can't see him right now. He doesn't deserve my anger.

My fear of Richard Van Holsten is quickly being replaced by my severe anger and dislike. I should have known a man capable of marrying off his only child to a stranger would be horrible, but it still surprised me. Our marriage worked out, but not because Richard planned it that way. He would have been fine with a loveless marriage for his son.

My parents forced this marriage on me too, but they never wanted me to be unhappy. Honestly, at this point, I should thank them because I married the man of my dreams.

Eventually, after giving me time to cool off, Evan nudges his way in the door and sits next to me. He pulls me into his arms and whispers into my ear,

"I won't let him take away your dream. He made me jump through hoops to reach mine and I won't let him do the same to you."

Evan's promise makes me smile. I love this man so much it terrifies me. Being a part of his family and world terrifies me, but I know we can get through anything as long as we're together.

Thirty

Brooke

Two Months Later

The air is turning chilly now that winter's approaching. It's almost five in the evening and Evan's probably wondering where I am. I stayed late in my classroom grading papers and getting my lesson plan for next week done. I always try to give Evan my undivided attention at home if I can swing it, and he tries to do the same for me.

The last few months since our lives together began, we've been learning more about each other, how to live together, basically just learning how to navigate our new lives. It's been equal parts amazing and frustrating. I love the man, but he doesn't pick up his damn clothes off the floor. I try to do some things around the house. Mrs. G is just one woman, an amazing woman, but I can't make myself make her do everything.

I see Trish every few weeks. We go to lunch or whatever with my mom and sisters. She's a really wonderful lady, and I can't figure out how she married Richard. I wonder if there's was an arranged marriage, a marriage of convenience, the way mine was. That would explain so much.

My relationship with my mom and dad is improving too. Now that Mom has married me off to a suitable family, she's relaxed and we've been working on becoming friends. She gets along great with Trish, and my sisters constantly tease me about Evan. Whatever, I'm happy.

Everything at school's been going great. I love my kids and I feel like I'm making a difference in their lives. Our donation has gone a long way and is so appreciated. Evan's been shadowing his dad the last few months since our wedding, and he's busy a lot. Sometimes working late.

He's probably not quite home yet. I usually get home before he does, but I send Ev a quick text to let him know I'll be there soon. I don't want him to worry. I should take the black town car with a driver that's specifically employed to drive me around, but I feel like walking a bit tonight. I can see it following me out of the corner of my eye and smile a little. My driver, John, doesn't let me out of his sight. He's probably terrified of my father-in-law, and rightly so.

I turn the corner down into a dilapidated neighborhood. It's probably not a good idea for me to be walking down a street like this in my designer clothes and bags, but one of my students lives down this way, and she's been having a rough go of it. I try to walk past her house every evening just to make sure she's okay.

I pass my student's house, and everything is fine. She sees me from the front window and runs out the door, stopping on her porch.

"Hi, Mrs. Van Holsten!" she yells with a smile. Yes, she's okay. I let out my breath.

"Hi, Tylee. Just checking in. You all good?" I ask.

She nods and runs back into the house when her mother calls her for dinner. I think her dad is finally out of the picture. Thank fuck. From what little I could gather, he's an abusive asshole, at least to Tylee's mom.

I walk further down the street and just as I'm about to leave it to get into the car with John; I see a little girl. She can't be older than four, and she's crying in a corner. I rush to her and my heart nearly breaks. She's so tiny. Maybe she's younger than I thought. Her hair, the same color as mine, is tangled and dirty. She has streaks of dirt all over her body and she's not wearing any shoes. She doesn't have a coat either. She just has on a ratty *Frozen* nightgown. She's shaking from the chill in the air.

"Oh my God, honey, are you okay?" I ask, wanting to comfort her, but she flinches at my near touch. The girl is cradling her arm to her stomach. Something must be wrong with it. I look around and see no one on the street.

"Where are your parents?" I ask, taking off my coat to drape it over her trembling little body. She's so skinny. The girl doesn't answer me, but she can't have had proper supervision to be looking this bad. It doesn't look like she's eaten or bathed in weeks.

I pick her up and bring her to my chest. I wrap her up in my warm coat and take her to the car. John rushes out to open the door for me. He looks as concerned for this little girl as I am. John blasts the heat as soon as he's back in the driver's seat and I cradle the girl to my chest, careful not to jostle her arm.

"Where to, Mrs. Van Holsten?" John asks, but he's already pulling into traffic.

"The hospital, please. I think her arm is broken. She needs to get checked out," I say. I get a curt nod from John and he speeds to get there.

"What's your name?" I ask the girl. I expect her not to answer me, but she does.

"Summer," she replies in a voice as small and trembling as she is. I smile at her, hoping it has some sort of calming effect.

"That's a beautiful name. It's my favorite time of the year. My name is Brooke. I'll take care of you, Summer. You're safe with me,"

Summer nods but whimpers at the motion. Thankfully, we've just pulled up to the hospital and John opens my door for me. He offers to take Summer, but she cowers away from him. I smile at him and walk through the waiting doors. It's not like Summer weighs a ton, anyway. Nurses rush to me the minute I'm inside the doors and they see the girl cradled against me.

"What happened?" one asks.

"I don't know. I found her like this on the street. She won't answer any of my questions," I reply, trying to hand Summer over to the nurse.

"No!" Summer yells and clings to me despite her broken arm. The nurse nods and motions for me to follow.

"Do you know her name?" the nurse asks.

"Summer. That's all I got out of her. I think her arm's broken," I reply.

We stop at a room in the ER, and the nurse takes me to an empty bay. I try to put Summer down on the bed, but she won't let me. I sigh and sit down with her in my lap. A different nurse brings me a hospital gown and asks me to try to get it on Summer.

As gently as I possibly can, I lift the grimy nightgown over her head. I can count every rib and vertebrae. Her little body is filled with ugly black and blue bruises. I hold back my tears as I put the animal print hospital gown on her. I tie the back and Summer falls against my chest as if that much movement exhausted her. Who did this to this sweet girl?

A doctor comes in and examines Summer while she's in my arms. He asks me questions and I give him what answers I can. He nods at my lack of them seeming to understand. Someone comes in and puts an IV into Summer's hand on the side that's not broken, then we get taken for x-rays. She finally lets me put her down after explaining I need to so they can get a picture of her arm to make it better.

They do full-body scans on her, then they let me take her back to her room. I lay with her in the bed while we wait for the doctors to come back. At some point, a nurse gives Summer something for the pain and she drifts off to sleep.

A different doctor and a woman I've never seen before motion for me to come out of the room. I glance at Summer, but she's sound asleep. I wriggle my way out from under her and exit the room. A nurse goes in after me to clean her up.

"Mrs. Van Holsten, my name is Dr. Adams. I'm a Peds doctor and I will be taking over Summer's case. We'll be getting her moved to the Pediatric ward here soon. This is Tina Rodriguez. She's a social worker and she'll be taking on Summer's case as well," Dr. Adams says.

"Hello, I'm Brooke Van Holsten," I respond, shaking Tina's hand.

"I understand you found Summer in the street," Tina says, and I nod, giving her the exact location.

"Dr. Adams, can you tell me exactly what's wrong with Summer?" Tina

185

asks, ready to take notes on her tablet. I'd like to know, too.

"She does indeed have a broken arm, as Mrs. Van Holsten thought, but the full-body x-rays show she has several healed broken bones. A lot of them were not properly set, or possibly not set at all. She's dehydrated and malnourished. She should weigh twenty pounds more than she does. She's about four years old. If I had to guess, she's been severely abused her entire life. Some breaks go back to infancy. She's lucky to have gotten out of where ever she lived," Dr. Adams explains.

My hand flies to my mouth, and I feel sick to my stomach. Who could do that to a child? I look back at Summer's sleeping body and my heart breaks for all she went through.

"What will happen to her?" I ask Tina.

"She'll go into foster care while we try to locate her parents. Since her parents are probably the abusers, she likely won't go back. How long will she need to stay here?" Tina says turning back to the doctor.

"She needs to stay at least a few days. We will go ahead and set and cast the arm, get her hydrated, and fed. Then she can be discharged," Dr. Adams says before taking his leave when he's paged.

"Is it possible for me to take her home?" I ask.

I can't imagine letting that sweet girl go to another home where she might be treated the same. I'd have to ask Evan, of course, but I think he would say yes. She's so scared of everybody else. I don't want to do that to her.

"Are you a foster parent?" Tina asks.

"Well, no, but we could apply. Maybe fast-track it. My husband is Evan Van Holsten. I'm not trying to throw our name around, but I just can't let Summer go to someone who might hurt her more. She'll be safe and well taken care of with us," I say.

Tina stares into my eyes for a second, perhaps trying to see if I'm telling the truth. I sure hope the paperwork can be fast-tracked. Money talks, after all. After an eternity, Tina nods.

"I'll see what I can do. Can you stay with her while she's in the hospital? We'll get the rest figured out so you can take her home when she's released. I'm really glad you found her."

"I'll stay with her as long as she's here. I can't imagine what that poor girl went through," I say noticing my cheeks are wet with my tears. I didn't even realize I was crying. Tina gives me a sympathetic smile.

"I'll be back with some paperwork for you and Mr. Van Holsten to fill out to get the foster stuff situated. We can forgo the home study. I'm sure you have adequate accommodations for Summer," Tina says before shaking my hand and leaving me alone.

I walk back into Summer's room and sit in the chair beside her bed. My phone buzzes and I see Evan's name and a picture from our honeymoon pop up.

"Hello?"

"Hey, babe. Where are you?" Evan asks and I hear a door in the background shut. He must have just gotten home.

"I'm at the hospital," I reply.

"What? Are you okay?" he asks, sounding concerned.

"I'm fine. I found a little girl with a broken arm on my way home from school. Evan, it's bad. Can you come to the hospital, please?" I say. I'll explain the rest to him when he gets here.

"Of course. I'll be right there," he says.

"We're in room twenty-one oh three."

It doesn't take more than fifteen minutes for Evan to stride into the room. He takes in Summer with sad eyes. He kneels in between my legs and takes my hands in his.

"Why are you here with her? Where are her parents?" he asks quietly so as not to disturb Summer.

"She's been badly abused, Evan. Since she was a baby. Whoever her parents are, they did this to her. She's dehydrated, malnourished, and has a broken arm. She has several other breaks that never received medical attention. She was freezing in a dirty nightgown when I found her. I can't leave her, Evan. I can't let her go into foster care. What if she goes to a home worse than the one she escaped from? I'm pretty much the only one she lets touch her," I answer with tears streaming down my face.

Evan nods and looks at Summer for a long time before she stirs and cries out for me. I stand at once and lay in bed with her cradling her body against mine.

"I'm here, Summer. Did you see your cast? I had them make it purple. I hope that's okay," I say.

Summer's hair is still dirty and I wish they would let me bathe her. She's at least been given a sponge bath, so she's cleaner than when I found her.

"Brooke, it hurts," Summer says pathetically. I look up at Evan with pleading eyes. He nods and walks out of the room to get someone.

A nurse and Evan come back in and she gives Summer some more pain meds. It's about time, anyway. Summer stares at Evan with a look of pure fright on her face.

"Don't worry, Summer. This is my husband, Evan. He's a nice man and he would never hurt you. He's like me," I try to soothe her.

"Hi, Summer," Evan says, getting back to his knees on the opposite side of the bed. He gives her a small smile.

"Hi," Summer replies, though she's hesitant.

"Are they taking good care of you?" he asks. Summer nods her head a little and gives Evan a smile she's only given me so far.

Kids have not been at the forefront of our minds yet with our unconventional start, but it melts my heart to see Evan interact with this little girl. He would make a wonderful dad.

"Do you think you'd like to come home with Brooke and me when they let you out of here?" Evan asks Summer and my eyes dart to his. He gives me a small smile, then returns his attention to the little girl in front of him.

I hadn't really talked to Evan yet about bringing her home, even though I already asked the social worker. I shouldn't be surprised, though. Evan's always given me whatever I want.

"Yes," Summer replies in a hesitant voice.

"Okay, we'll make that happen. Tell me your favorite color and cartoon character and I'll get a room set up for you at our house," Evan says.

"I like *Frozen* and my favorite color is purple. How did you know, Brooke?" Summer says weakly. I smile because this is the most she's said since I met her, and oh my God, it makes my heart soar.

"Lucky guess, sweetheart," I say with a smile.

"You will come home to a purple *Frozen* bedroom," Evan says, getting up from the floor. I look at him with a smile that I hope conveys how much I adore him.

"I love you," I say, and Evan gives me a breathtaking smile.

"I love you too. I'm going to find that social worker and get our fostering stuff all set up. Then I'll go get the things Summer needs. How old is she?" Evan says.

"She's four, but she weighs about twenty pounds less than she should. Maybe some 3T clothes," I reply. Evan nods, kissing me on the head, then exits the room.

"He's nice," Summer comments.

"Yes, he is a very nice man," I reply looking after my husband.

I look back at Summer, and she smiles at me. I'm already attached to this little girl and I can't imagine giving her to anyone else, or worse, back to her parents. I want her to be mine, but Evan's only agreed to have her temporarily.

Whatever happens, I'm determined to show Summer that people can be kind, that she's loved. I want her to have a happy childhood where she doesn't have to worry about starvation and beatings. I know we can be that for her. I just hope Evan agrees.

Thirty-One

Evan

I leave Brooke and the little girl, Summer, in the room and search for the social worker I was told about. I can see how attached Summer is to Brooke and vice versa. It would break Brooke's heart to leave that little girl to an uncertain future. She's already been through so much in her four years. She deserves to have a happy life.

All of those reasons are why I'm going to make this happen for Brooke. We haven't really talked about kids yet beyond the fact that we want them one day, so I don't know that I'm quite ready for a child. Even though we're married, Brooke and I have only been together for a few months and a month of that we were just trying to get used to being together. I love Brooke more than anything and I always have, but we had to go through a lot. Are we really ready to throw a kid into the mix? Isn't that supposed to make marriage harder? It probably won't be forever anyway, just until the social workers can find a suitable home.

I find Tina Rodriguez sitting in an uncomfortable plastic chair in a waiting room on a tablet. A nurse points her out to me and I go sit next to her.

"Ms. Rodriguez, my name is Evan Van Holsten. You spoke with my wife, Brooke, earlier about fostering Summer," I say when Tina looks up.

"Mr. Van Holsten. It's nice to meet you. Yes, I understand you are not foster parents or currently in the foster system but would like to house Summer for the time being. I have the foster paperwork here. Brooke filled out her portion already. It just needs your information and signature, then I can get it expedited. We'll skip the home study," Tina explains, all business.

"Okay, wow. This is fast," I say taking the paperwork from her.

"Is this something you want?" Tina asks with a brow raised.

"Yes. It's just fast and not something I expected when I got home from work today," I laugh.

"Summer is very lucky Brooke found her. She might not have survived the night outside."

"She's a cute girl and I'm sure she'll fit in nicely with our new family," I say.

"How long have you and Brooke been married?" Tina asks.

"Four months, but we've known each other since elementary school," I answer, hoping our short marriage won't hurt our chances of taking in Summer. I hand back the filled-out paperwork and Tina stands.

"Summer has to stay here for a few days. By the time she's discharged, you should be good to take her home. Are you okay to get the things you need for her?" Tina says.

"Of course. I'm going to get a bedroom set up for her at our apartment and some clothes and toys," I say getting up from the hard chairs. Tina nods at me before walking away.

I leave the hospital making a mental list of everything a child might need. I like kids, but I don't really know much about them. I call my friends. Though they might not be much help, I want to tell them our news.

I slide into my town car and let the driver know where we're going. I pull my phone out and connect a video call to Noah, Allie, and Kristie. They answer one by one.

"What's up, Ev?" Kris asks.

"I've got some big news," I reply, and Allie's face lights up.

"Brooke's pregnant!" she shouts.

"Oh, damn. You knocked up your wife?" Noah asks with a chuckle.

"No, Brooke isn't pregnant. It involves a kid though," I say and explain how Brooke found Summer and her horrid past.

"Oh my God, that's so sad. That poor baby," Allie says, and I can see her eyes glaze with tears.

"And you don't know the sorry fuckers that hurt her?" Noah asks, pissed.

"No, she was alone when Brooke found her. She's only four, so she doesn't know much. We got paperwork going to bring her home with us when she's discharged in a few days," I say.

"You're bringing the kid home?" Kris asks.

"Summer is very attached to Brooke. She barely lets anyone touch her, especially men. Brooke can't stand not knowing where she'd go. Besides, we're more than capable of taking care of her. We have space and money. We'd provide her with a safe, loving home," I explain liking the idea more and more.

"You guys are doing a good thing," Allie says with a small smile.

"I need to get a room set up. I don't know what to buy," I say.

"Did you call us for advice? Because none of us know jack shit about kids, including you and Brooke," Kristie says.

"I know. I'll probably have Mrs. G do the shopping. I need to get some purple paint," I say.

"Send us pictures of the room and Summer," Allie says.

"Will do."

Allie and Kristie hang up, leaving only Noah on the line.

"You okay?" I ask. Noah sighs and scrubs his hand over his face. He knows exactly what I'm talking about.

"I think so. I think I'm sadder about how the relationship ended and less that it ended. I should have been honest with myself earlier. I just—I don't know how to do this again. She's been here since I was fourteen. I don't really know who I am without her, ya know?" Noah replies.

"Kendra was never going to be the one for you. She hid it well, but she was a toxic person. You would have never been truly happy with her as your wife. There's a reason you didn't propose. You'll find the girl for you. You just need to be open to it. She'll probably drop in when you least expect it," I say with a smile.

"I think I'm gonna be by myself for a bit. It's only been three months and I need to mourn. Kendra keeps trying to call me. Zack too," Noah says with a sigh.

"Did you take the calls?"

"Fuck no. I have nothing to say to either of them," Noah replies, his voice rising.

"Good."

"So, a kid? We're really there? My best friend is married with a kid. Where did the time go?" Noah says, sighing again.

"We are twenty-five. It was bound to happen sooner or later. Summer's probably not staying with us forever. Just until she can find a good family to take her in," I say.

"You and Brooke are pretty good people. Why couldn't it be you permanently?"

"We haven't really talked about it. We're taking it one step at a time. Right now, we're just trying to get the foster paperwork through so we're legally her guardians."

"Mhm. Go shopping. I'll talk to you later," Noah says, hanging up after I say goodbye.

Mrs. G is still at the house when I return, though she's getting ready to leave.

"I'm finished up here, Evan," Mrs. G says, patting my arm. She's been with me since I moved out. She's like another mother to me.

"Before you go, I was wondering if you could help me with something," I say stopping her before she can leave.

"Anything, dear," she says with a kind smile.

"We're having a four-year-old girl stay with us for a while. She'll be coming home from the hospital in a couple of days and I need to have a room ready for her. Could you help me make a list of all the things I need to buy?" I ask.

Mrs. G smiles kindly at me. She brings me to the kitchen table and we sit, making a list. It's a long list. I already know I need to hire painters for tomorrow.

"Thanks, Mrs. G," I say before she leaves.

"Of course, dear. I can't wait to meet her. It's a wonderful thing you're doing for her."

Mrs. G leaves and I sit on the couch, resting my head on the back of it. I'm exhausted and ready for bed. Brooke won't be home tonight, probably. I'm alone and I don't like it like I used to. I don't want to sit here by myself, so I decide to go to the store. I don't usually do a lot of shopping myself. Our family has always had people for it, and I still do.

I walk into the mall, bustling with people, and head straight for a JC Penney. Mrs. G said they have a good Disney section. An associate helps me pick a twin-sized frame, mattress, dressers, and a nightstand which will be delivered tomorrow. The set is a cream color and looks kinda princessy.

After that, I'm pointed in the direction of the bedding section. I find a purple *Frozen* bed set. It's got two girls and a snowman on it. It comes with sheets, pillowcases, and a comforter. I grab some fluffy pillows and the two *Frozen* princess dolls.

I have to ask a woman to help me pick some clothes for her. I end up with a ton of jeans, leggings, shirts of the short and long sleeve variety, socks, *Frozen* underwear, jackets, winter coats, dresses, skirts, tennis shoes, sandals, and boots.

Another lady helps me with wall decorations and a floor rug. I walk out of the store with a metric shit ton of bags and a hope that I have everything. I've scheduled the painters to come in the morning and the furniture to get delivered and set up in the afternoon. Mrs. G will help me set up the room so everything will be done when Summer gets home the day after tomorrow.

I send pictures of everything to Brooke, and she seems happy with it. I spend the rest of the night hanging up shirts, dresses, and jackets in the bigger of the spare room's closet with child-sized hangers I didn't even know they made. It makes me wonder how in over our heads we'll be in trying to raise a child.

Thirty-Two

Brooke

Summer had a rough night. She wouldn't sleep unless I laid in bed with her. I didn't sleep much, but I did set up a substitute for my class so I could take a week off to stay with Summer in the hospital and get her set up at home.

Evan texted me pictures of all the things he bought for Summer and it melted my heart. I don't know that he's ever really gone shopping by himself, but he did for her. If I wasn't in love with Ev before, I definitely am now. He's got such a kind heart. How didn't I see it before?

Dr. Adams comes in to check on Summer, but she's still asleep. He motions for me to follow him out into the hall. Evan is striding up the corridor towards us with coffee in his hand. Thank the good Lord. He smiles as he kisses my temple, then hands me my coffee.

"I just wanted to update you on Summer," Dr. Adams starts. "She's doing much better now that she's been attached to an IV for almost a day and is getting regular meals. She should be good to go home tomorrow, but she will need to come back in six weeks to get the cast taken off. In the meantime, she should eat high-calorie and well-rounded meals to gain some weight. Have her drink plenty of water. Set her up with a pediatrician and get an appointment within the next few weeks. We gave her all her vaccines, but she needs to get evaluated to see if she's hitting her milestones. Monitor her over the next few weeks so you can answer the pediatrician's questions."

"So, she'll be discharged tomorrow?" Evan asks.

"As long as nothing happens during the night, she should be good to go by tomorrow afternoon. She'll still be in a five-point harness car seat, so make sure you have one installed. We'll need to see it before she leaves. The fire department can do it for you," Dr. Adams replies.

"Is Ms. Rodriguez here?" Evan asks.

"She'll be by to talk to you next. Have a good day," Dr. Adams says before walking away.

Evan runs his hands up and down my arms while I lean against his chest. It rumbles when he speaks.

"I brought you some clothes to change into."

"Thank you," I reply. Evan drops a kiss on the top of my head and pulls me closer to him.

"Are you ready to become a mother?" he asks. I laugh lightly.

"I'm not her mom. She's not ours. We're just taking care of her," I say with a sigh.

"Do you want her to be ours?"

I lean away and look at the sleeping girl in the room. She's peaceful and untroubled when she sleeps. My heart squeezes at the sight of her.

"More than anything," I whisper.

"Let's tell Tina then," Evan says. Speak of the devil. Tina walks up to us, giving us a happy greeting.

"So, the foster paperwork is all set. Summer can go home with you. We don't know her last name, so I put yours on her paperwork. I hope that's okay," Tina says.

"Of course. What would the process be if we wanted to adopt her?" I ask.

"Well, we will do what we can to find her parents. We'll have to terminate their parental rights so you can adopt her. The process could take time. In the meantime, she'll stay with you as her legal guardians. I'll make a note that your ultimate goal is to adopt Summer," Tina says.

She hands us a folder with all the paperwork we'll need for Summer and makes notes on her tablet. Tina says goodbye and Evan looks at his watch.

"The painters will be at the house soon. I better go. Summer's furniture will be there later in the afternoon. I'll come back after everything's set up. I'll get a car seat installed in both our cars. I love you. Tell Summer I said hi," Evan says kissing me.

"I love you too," I reply before he leaves.

I sit down beside Summer and lay back. She's still sleeping, so I'm left to my thoughts. I need some advice and I want to call my mom, but I don't know how much help she'd really be even though our relationship has been better lately. Besides, she might tell Evan's dad before we're ready to tell him. I'm sure he'll have something to say, but he shouldn't oppose it. He's big on family... at least as far as the general public is concerned. This could be good for optics.

I decide to text Willa instead. She's not a mom, but she is my best friend and she might be able to help me.

Me: Hey, I have some news.

Willa: Hit me with it, chica.

Me: Evan and I are fostering a little girl named Summer. Hopefully, we'll adopt her.

Willa: WTF!

Me: I found her in the street, freezing. It's under terrible circumstances, but I'm excited. Is that weird? I figured Evan and I would have kids one day, but something about this just feels right. Ya know?

Willa: I really don't know, but if you're happy then so am I. I'll come to meet the kid when you're all set up at home. Love ya. See you soon.

Summer wakes up as I exit out of my message screen. She tweaks her casted arm and winces from the pain. She doesn't cry out though, which makes me both admire her for her strength and mourn all that she must have gone through to get it.

"Morning, Summer. You get to come home tomorrow. Evan wanted me to tell you hi, and that your *Frozen* room is almost finished," I say with a smile. Summer returns it with a toothy grin. I need to make her a dentist appointment too.

Nurses and techs come in to take Summer for more tests. While I have some downtime, I make an appointment with the best pediatrician in the city and a children's dentist. Also, an eye exam, just in case. I don't think she's ever had any of this checked before. As a last-minute thought, I also schedule an appointment with a therapist who specializes in abused children. It would probably help Summer out.

I feel accomplished by the time Summer gets back. I've been getting pictures all day of Evan's progress with the bedroom. The pictures of him setting up toys, hanging decorations, or attempting to put things together all with big smiles like he's the happiest he's ever been are killing me they're so cute. I'm a little jealous I don't get to be there to decorate it, but I'm right where I need to be.

Summer and I talk all day to get to know each other. She doesn't know her last name or her birthday. She could only tell me it's coming up in December. I guess we could just pick a day and give her the best birthday party she's ever had.

I relay what little I could get from Summer about her home life to Tina, but she doesn't like talking about it. I can't really blame her, and it reaffirms the need for the therapist appointment I made. She should talk to someone, even if it isn't me.

Evan comes by with lunch and a kid's meal for Summer. She's still wary of Evan, but less than with other men. She doesn't even like the male nurses that come in and only mildly tolerates Dr. Adams.

"Hey Summer, I brought you some chicken nuggets. I hope you like those," Evan says as he sits in the chair on the opposite side of the bed.

Summer shrugs but takes the food. She struggles to open the box with her cast. Evan reaches for it slowly so he doesn't spook her. He opens the nuggets and empties the fries onto the top part of the box. He pokes the straw in her juice and puts it on the table we pushed in front of her.

"Do you like ketchup?" he asks.

"Yes," Summer replies in a small voice.

Evan squeezes out some ketchup for Summer next to the nuggets. When she's all set, he hands me my food and digs into his own. I'm staring in astonishment at this man. Seeing him interact with Summer makes my ovaries want to explode.

"What?" Evan asks after swallowing a bite of his burger.

"Nothing," I reply. Evan gives me a lop-sided smile that makes him look younger, and it warms my heart.

We eat our first meal as a family in relative quiet, but after a few minutes, Evan asks Summer questions. They're different from the ones I asked. They're harmless and non-intrusive. They make her smile rather than making her feel sad. I can tell Summer is getting comfortable with Evan based on her answers.

I feel more content and happy than I have in a long time as I sit eating my greasy fast food while watching Evan and Summer talk to each other.

Thirty-Three

Evan

I stayed with Summer and Brooke all day yesterday, talking, playing games, and eating. I can see how afraid of men Summer is and I'm happy she seems comfortable enough with me. She comes home with us later today and I can't wait for her to see her room. It feels like a weird thing to be excited about, but I am. I want to see her eyes light up. I want to give her everything she was missing wherever she came from, and I don't just mean material things.

I want Summer to feel loved and safe. I want her to feel happy and comfortable. I can't believe how fast she wormed her way into my heart. I barely interacted with her before yesterday, but somehow it's like she never belonged anywhere else.

Dr. Adams walks into the room with a smile on his face and a clipboard in his hands. He hands us some papers to sign.

"Okay, Miss Summer, you get to go home today. Are you ready?" Dr. Adams asks. She nods but doesn't ever talk to the doctor.

"Have you made those appointments?" he asks, turning his attention to us.

"Yes. I made one for the pediatrician, the dentist, eye doctor, and a therapist," Brooke replies.

"Great. Therapy is a good idea. Hopefully, we won't see you back here again. Good luck, guys. Bye, Summer," Dr. Adams says, tapping his clipboard on the little table.

Summer flinches from the noise and grabs Brooke's hand. Brooke squeezes it as Dr. Adams exits the room. The tension leaves Summer's shoulders when he's gone. Tina comes in next just to let us know we're good to go. She gives us the court dates for Summer's stuff. It seems they opened a court case on her behalf. Tina gives us a business card that she's written her cell phone number on in case we need anything and promises to call if they hear from Summer's parents.

The nurses come in a little later to get Summer unhooked from her IV. I brought clothes for her. As soon as we get the go-ahead, Brooke takes her into the bathroom to change. Summer comes out freshly showered in some jeans that are a little loose still despite the small size, a long sleeve sweater, brown fuzzy boots, and a purple coat. Brooke sits down to brush her shoulder-length hair and braids it real quick.

We're finally ready to go home. Brooke takes Summer's hand as we walk out of the hospital. John, Brooke's driver, picks us up. There's a purple car seat in the back waiting for Summer. Brooke clips her in like she's been doing it for years and we're finally on our way home. The closer we get, the more nervous I feel. We're going to need to tell our parents eventually, but I think Summer would be scared of my dad.

Summer is asleep when we reach our apartment. I unbuckle her gently and pick her up to carry her upstairs. I lay her down on the couch and drape a blanket over her so she can nap some more. All that walking probably made her tired.

Mrs. G has just made us lunch. She sets it on the table and we sit to eat, then pokes her head around to look at the little bundle asleep on our massive sectional.

"That's her?" she asks.

"Yep. Her name is Summer," I answer.

"She's so tiny. I can't wait to say hi."

Thirty minutes later, Summer stirs on the couch. Brooke walks over there so she sees a friendly face. The two of them walk back to the table. Mrs. G puts a peanut butter and jelly sandwich in front of Summer.

"Hello, Summer. My name is Mrs. G. If you need anything, you just ask. Okay, sweetie?"

Summer doesn't respond, but she nods as she takes small bites of her sandwich. Mrs. G smiles at the little girl but doesn't push her for a response. She turns and goes about cleaning the kitchen.

"Are you ready to see your room?" I ask when Summer pushes her half-eaten sandwich away from her.

Summer nods enthusiastically and awkwardly jumps off the chair. She grabs my hand and I take her to her room. Brooke trails behind us with a smile on her face. I turn to her and flash her one of my own.

"Okay, Summer. This one is yours. It's right next to mine and Brooke's," I say and push open the door.

Summer runs in and spins around, trying to take everything in. The walls are purple with *Frozen* wall hangings and decals. The closet is full of clothes. The princess bed is made with the bedspread I got. There's a bedside table next to it with a lamp with the snowman on the shade and a large dresser with a mirror on it to match the bed frame. There's a light blue rug in the middle of the room.

On the other side is a little table with four chairs. It's got the snowman on it and a reindeer, a guy, and two girls on each of the chairs. On top is a tea set and behind it is a toy box full of *Frozen* dolls, *Barbies*, and baby dolls. All the clothes and accessories are in coded bins on some organizational shelf. Mrs. G did all that.

"This is all mine?" Summer asks, sitting down on a chair at her table.

"Yep. You can play in here whenever you want. Everything in here belongs to you," I say, taking a seat in the little chair across from her.

I'm afraid I'm going to break the thing, but it's surprisingly sturdy and doesn't even bend. Summer takes the kettle and pours three cups of invisible tea, then pats the chair next to her. Brooke takes the hint with a smile and sits in between us. Summer gives each of us a cup and we drink our tea.

We spend most of the day playing with Summer's various toys until Mrs.

G calls us to get ready for dinner. I invited my parents and Brooke's family over tonight to join us. Might as well just pull off the band-aide. We'll be dining in the formal dining room this evening. My dad expects us to be formally dressed whenever he comes for dinner. It's annoying, but just another thing I'm used to.

Everyone will be here in an hour, so Brooke retires to our bedroom to get ready. Mrs. G helps me bathe Summer without getting her cast wet and pick out a dress, tights, and shoes for her to wear. I get dressed in my suit quickly after a shower while Mrs. G dresses Summer. She looks adorable in her light blue dress. I sit down on the floor with her in my lap, trying to brush her hair gently. I don't want to hurt her. Every time I hit a knot with the brush, I flinch, but Summer doesn't even acknowledge it.

"You going to do her hair?" Brooke asks from the doorway. When Summer sees her, she jumps up from my lap and races to her.

"You look like a princess," Summer says, gazing up at Brooke with an awestruck expression.

Brooke is wearing a floor-length icy blue dress similar to Summer's that matches her eyes almost exactly. It's got those quarter-length long sleeves that stop at the elbow. It's simple but elegant enough to appease my father. Her hair is braided down to the side.

"Your hair looks like Elsa's. Can you do mine like that?" Summer asks Brooke.

"That's what I was going for. Let's do yours," Brooke replies with a smile and guides Summer to her table. Brooke brushes Summer's hair faster than I did, but I'm happy with my attempt.

The doorbell rings just as Brooke is finishing Summer's hair. I take a deep breath and walk out. Mrs. G answers the door to my mom and dad. Brooke's family is standing behind them, waiting. They walk in without an invitation. My father looks around the place appraising it like it's a museum. He acts like he's never been here before. It hasn't changed much in two months. I let my frustration go and greet them all.

"Mr. and Mrs. Jacobs, it's great to see you again. I haven't seen you since the wedding. Rebekah, Natalie," I say kissing each of the women on the cheek. Natalie's face is bright red when I pull away, and I'm sure Brooke would have gotten a kick out of that. Brooke's had several lunches with her mom, sisters, and my mom, but I've been too busy with work.

"Hi, Mom," I say, hugging her. My dad only offers a stiff handshake in greeting.

"Where's Brooke?" Mrs. Jacobs asks.

"She'll be right out. We have some news to share with you," I reply and Mrs. Jacobs's eyes light up. She probably thinks Brooke's pregnant like my friends did.

Brooke takes that moment to come out with Summer. She's wrapped up against Brooke's leg and positioned behind her. She's been pretty comfortable with us and getting warmer to Mrs. G, but all these strangers scare her. I can't blame the poor girl.

Everyone's eyes zero in on Summer with confusion coloring their faces. I clear my throat to get the attention back on me.

"This is the news we wanted to share. Everyone, this is Summer. We're fostering her with the intention of adopting if we're lucky. She just got home today from the hospital. Summer?" I say. Summer darts from Brooke's side to mine. I bend to one knee to be on her level and introduce her to each person.

"This is Rebekah and Natalie. These are Brooke's sisters. This is Mr. and Mrs. Jacobs, Brooke's parents. Then over here we have my mom and dad, Mr. and Mrs. Van Holsten," I say as I point to each person. Mrs. Jacobs surprises me by leaning down and shaking Summer's hand with a smile far more maternal and kind than I would have expected out of her.

"Pleasure to meet you, Summer. You can call me Nana if you'd like," she says.

"Auntie Rebekah and Auntie Natalie work for us," Rebekah says, leaning down to do the same. Summer takes their hands hesitantly but gives them little smiles after looking to Brooke and me for approval.

My mom goes to introduce herself, but my father stops her with a firm hold on her arm and a slight shake of his head. My mom sighs but only offers Summer a small smile instead. My father says nothing. He just appraises her as if she were a horse he's trying to decide is worth buying.

Brooke sweeps Summer into her arms, and she buries her head in Brooke's neck.

"Let's go eat," Brooke says, giving my dad a withering look and disappearing into the dining room without another word.

The food is already on the table when we sit down. Mrs. G pours wine for each of the adults and water for the minors. We serve our food and sit in awkward silence for a minute.

"So, how did you meet Summer?" Mrs. Jacobs asks, giving Summer a kind smile which is surprisingly returned.

Brooke tells everyone about finding her in the street and bringing her to the hospital, our conversation with Tina, and our reasoning for deciding to keep Summer if everything goes right.

"Do you have a problem having biological children? Harold, you assured me your daughter had no problems with fertility," my dad says.

Mr. Jacobs chokes on his wine, and Mrs. Jacobs pats his back until he can breathe. Brooke is sending a glare fit for death at my dad again. It seems her anger outweighs her fear of him. I knew it was happening when he threatened her job two months ago.

"To answer your question, Mr. Van Holsten, no, I don't have a problem with my reproductive organs. The doctor checked before Evan and I got married, as was stipulated in whatever contract you had my parents sign for you. I'm not opposed to having our own children and we probably will someday, but Summer sort of fell into our laps and she needs a safe home. Evan and I have more than enough space and money so I don't see why we can't be her family," Brooke says evenly.

My dad stares at Brooke but only gives her a noncommittal grunt. He's letting it go for now, but I'll be hearing it later.

"Well, I think it's lovely what you're doing," Mom says with a kind smile in Brooke's direction.

"Thank you, Trish," Brooke responds politely. My mom squeaks a little, and I glance over to see my dad's hand on her thigh. I glare at him, but he's ignoring me.

Richard Van Holsten does whatever the hell he wants when he wants to do it. It pisses me the fuck off that he thinks he can lord over everyone in the family.

Thirty-Four

Evan

For the rest of dinner, we stay away from speaking about Summer. Brooke's parents ask how school is going for her. My mom doesn't speak again. She looks down at her plate and won't meet anyone's eyes. It makes me furious my dad treats her that way, but I don't say anything right now.

Natalie plays with Summer quietly, and my dad is constantly looking at her with disgust when she doesn't hold her fork right. She's a freaking four-year-old who grew up in an abusive home. Of course, she doesn't hold her fucking fork right.

"I have to go potty," Summer says.

"That is not appropriate language for the dinner table, young lady," my dad snaps before anyone else can answer. Summer's lip trembles from the harsh tone.

"This is my home, Mr. Van Holsten, and this is my daughter. I'd appreciate it if you didn't try to tell her what she can and can't say at my dinner table," Brooke says, standing and picking Summer up to take her to the bathroom.

My dad glares at Brooke's back as she walks out of the room. Shit. He doesn't like a woman who talks back. He probably thought Brooke would never be that person. She was pretty quiet growing up, but not because she couldn't stand up for herself. He really doesn't know Brooke at all.

"She's not your daughter and she never will be," Dad says, throwing his napkin on his plate and standing. "Trish, we're leaving."

"But—" Mom starts.

"We're leaving," Dad snaps. He grabs my mom's hand and practically drags her out of the house. My front door slams shut, making Mrs. Jacobs jump.

"I'm really sorry about my parents," I say.

"No need to apologize, dear," Mrs. Jacobs says with a small smile.

"Did your parents leave?" Brooke asks, setting Summer back down in her chair.

"Yes," I reply.

Brooke's family stays a bit longer playing with Summer. She wanted to show Natalie and Rebekah her room and all her toys. Around nine, they finally leave and we put Summer to bed. She was a little scared about sleeping on her own, but she fell asleep after two stories and a promise to keep the nightlight on.

I strip off my clothes, putting on some pajama pants with an exhausted sigh in case Summer comes in and gets into bed. Brooke takes a little longer to clean off her makeup and change, but she joins me before too long. We both lay there staring at the ceiling. It's been a tiring few days.

"Your dad is an asshole," Brooke states. I laugh, and she looks at me sternly for a second before bursting into laughter.

"I know. I'm sorry he talked to you that way tonight and a few months ago. Hell, at our wedding, too," I say. Brooke shrugs.

"He is who he is. After our wedding, I didn't expect him to be a good father-in-law. It's his way or the highway. I can let him have his way with most things, but not this," she replies.

"I'll talk to him soon," I say with a sigh.

Brooke switches her lights off and lays her head on my chest. Her arms hang around my hips. I wrap my arm around her shoulder and kiss her forehead.

"I love you," she says with a sigh.

"Not regretting marrying me yet?" I ask. She laughs a little.

"Not yet. There's nothing your dad can do that will make me regret being with you. I already wasted so much time being angry at you for something you didn't do. I can't spend more time being mad at you because of your dad. You aren't him, and he alone is responsible for his actions. Just make sure you don't become him. I won't let you push me around the way he does to your mom," Brooke says.

"I know. I don't know why she stays. I'm twenty-five, so there are no kids to stay for. She's probably worried about what kind of life she'd have. My dad wouldn't give her much in a divorce," I say with a sigh.

"She'll get the strength to leave one day."

"I love you," I say. I feel her smile against my chest.

"I know."

We get a few hours of sleep in before I hear footsteps across the hardwood of our bedroom. I open my eyes and glance at Summer's little body, stopping at my side of the bed.

"You all right?" I ask.

"Can I sleep with you?" she replies, glancing around the room like she's afraid.

"Sure," I say, throwing the blankets back for her to get in with us.

She moves to the middle of the bed and snuggles next to Brooke, who throws an arm around Summer and pulls her close to her until she's safely tucked against her.

Summer hits me a few times during the night with her cast and I have some bruises I didn't have when I went to bed last night, but looking at them and knowing where they came from makes me smile.

* * *

Weeks pass by quickly. Brooke and I go back to work while Summer stays with Mrs. G during the day. I give her a raise for her added babysitting duties, but Summer loves her, and she's so uncomfortable with strangers I couldn't justify a nanny. Mrs. G assures me she doesn't mind spending her day with Summer.

Summer has been adjusting well. Sometimes she acts up then flinches and cowers like she's expecting some physical punishment but we use only stern words to reinforce acceptable behavior. Brooke's been doing a ridiculous amount of research, so we handle her tantrums correctly.

We take Summer to her doctor's appointment and we're pleased to find that she's hitting all her milestones. Though she is still a little underweight, she's gained a few pounds since living in our home.

The dentist said her teeth are decent, but some cavities need fixing. He opts to put her to sleep to get everything fixed at once. He doesn't want to scare her further by buzzing around in her mouth while she's awake. We get that scheduled for next week.

The eye doctor says she has perfect vision but to bring her once a year for a checkup in case it changes. Summer also had her first appointment with her therapist. They do play therapy and according to the doctor, she's doing well.

Tina comes by once a week. She checked the place out the first time she came and found it suitable. She offered a check to help with the expenses, but we declined it. We don't need it. Tina watches us interact with Summer and watches how Summer interacts with us. Summer's talking a lot more now that's she's comfortable with us and Tina.

"Everything's going great here with Summer. I'll write up my report for the court, so they know. We still haven't been able to locate her parents, but we'll keep trying. We might not be able to proceed with adoption until we find them, but it'll be a bit before that's an option anyway," Tina tells us before she leaves.

"Thank you, Tina. We'll see you next week," Brooke says as we walk Tina to the door.

"So, your birthday is coming up. What kind of party do you want?" Brooke asks after Tina leaves.

"*Frozen!*" Summer yells as she runs in circles around us. Brooke laughs.

"I don't know why I even asked. Okay, time for bed, little lady," she says, picking up Summer and taking her to her room.

I follow and set up beside Summer so I can read her a few bedtime stories. Brooke leaves us alone to go shower. I help Summer into her nightgown.

It's still hard for her to dress herself with the cast. It'll be a few more weeks before it gets taken off.

When Summer's changed, she snuggles up next to me and we read some fairytales about princes and princesses. Right before she falls asleep, Summer kisses my cheek.

"I love you, Daddy," she mumbles, then I hear her soft snores.

I kiss her forehead and extricate myself before my heart bursts from her declaration. I rush to our room as Brooke's getting out of the shower.

"What's wrong?" she asks when she sees me skidding to a stop.

"Summer called me daddy! She said she loves me!" I almost yell. Brooke gives me a face.

"No fair!"

"She loves me more than you," I declare, walking towards her and pulling to my chest. "Don't worry, though. I love you mostest," I say snuggling into Brooke's neck. She leans it back and moans a little.

I kiss down to her collarbone, then gently tug her towel off until it drops to the floor. I walk forward until Brooke's legs hit the bed, and she drops onto it.

"I love every inch of you," I murmur as I kiss further down. Brooke lets out more soft noises that go straight to my groin.

Thirty-Five

Brooke

It's two weeks into December. We bought a tree, a fake one since I'm allergic to real ones. The three of us had a blast buying decorations for the house since it's our first Christmas together.

Thanksgiving had been okay. We went to my parent's house because Evan still hasn't talked to his family after that disastrous dinner when we introduced Summer to them. Whatever. As far as I'm concerned, they can stay away. They make Summer nervous. Well, not Trish, but unfortunately where she is, so is Richard. We do have to go over to their house for a Christmas party the week before Christmas. Ugh. Kill me now. At least Summer and I get to go shopping for dresses.

So, our house is decorated for Christmas, but we decorated the family room for Summer's *Frozen* birthday party. My family is coming. We invited Evan's, but they declined or Richard declined on behalf of them both. Willa, Noah, Kristie, and Allie came just for the party to meet Summer. It made me happy they were willing to show up to a birthday party for a five-year-old they hadn't yet met.

Good thing we have several more bedrooms than we need so we can accommodate all our friends visiting. Everyone got here two days ago. I was worried about how Summer was going to react having all these people she doesn't know in the house, but she warmed up to them all right away, especially Noah.

Summer took one look at the tattooed giant with shaggy hair and piercings and ran to him like he was a teddy bear. She wrapped her arms around his legs until Noah picked her up, hugging her. He's the first man she hasn't cowered from upon first meeting. Maybe she knows he's good people.

In any case, Noah and Summer have been inseparable ever since they got here. She likes the girls well enough and plays with them when they agree, but she's got Noah wrapped around her little finger. Maybe Noah needs a friend as much as Summer does because he does everything she asks. He's taken to reading her bedtime stories. His deep voice changes for each character, getting higher for the girls. Evan and I laugh about it every time he reads to her.

I'm thankful for Kris, Allie, Willa, and Mrs. G's help with setting up all the decorations and getting all the food ready. I found some fun games to play online, but there won't be any kids here. Maybe we should be sending Summer to a daycare a few times a week to interact with other kids her age. She doesn't start school until next year, so daycare is kinda the only option. I'm just nervous about all the stories I've seen of abuse. Summer doesn't need more of that, and I trust Mrs. G with our lives.

"Summer will be fine not having kids here. You know Noah's already her best friend," Willa says, motioning to Noah and Summer sitting at the table. It's like she can read my mind.

Noah's wearing a princess tiara and clip-on earrings while drinking his imaginary tea. He looks ridiculous with sleeves of ink on both arms and the princess getup. I take my phone out of my back pocket and snap a picture of him sipping the cup with his pinky raised.

I send the picture to the group text I'm a part of with all of them. As soon as I send it, I hear laughter throughout the house. I watch Noah put his tea down to pull his phone out of his front pocket. He looks at the picture and gives me a dirty look and the finger.

Kristie: I'm so making this your contact picture in my phone!

Allie: Ooh me too. The tiara really brings out your eyes.

Evan: Pretty pretty princess.

Noah: Fuck you guys! You're just jealous Summer loves me more than you.

Willa and I laugh and shake our heads. I put my phone away and we go back trying to hang the birthday banner. We're struggling when Noah comes up behind us sans princess clothes.

"Need help?" he asks.

"Please," I reply and let him take my end of the banner. Between him and Willa, they get it pretty straight.

"How's it going with Kris?" Noah asks Willa while they empty chips into bowls together. Willa shrugs.

"We're just having fun whenever we see each other. It's nothing serious," she replies.

"Do you want it to be?"

"I don't think I want to be tied down. I mean, I live here and Kristie lives in California. I think what we're doing suits us both just fine."

"Fair enough," Noah replies.

I'm glad Willa is getting along with Evan's friends. They really are great people, and we've gotten close since the whole honeymoon debacle. Since shedding the poison, everyone's been happy... except Noah.

He still looks kinda sad sometimes, but I don't think it's really Kendra he misses. He's sexy and funny. He has a kind heart, and he's great with kids. Noah's a catch and any girl would be lucky to have him.

Evan comes up behind me and puts his arms around my waist. He kisses my neck.

"Your family is here," he whispers into my ear. His warm breath on my neck leaves goosebumps on my skin.

Mom, Dad, Rebekah, and Natalie walk into the room. My sisters go over to Summer and immediately start having a tea party with her.

"Mom, Dad, you remember Noah Whittier?" I introduce.

"Yes, your Clarence's boy, aren't you?" Dad says, thrusting his hand towards Noah.

"Yes, sir," Noah replies, shaking his hand.

Allie and Kristie wander over, and I introduce them to my parents as well. Since Evan's parents aren't coming, it seems like everyone invited is here. I decide to start the games, which Summer insists we all play with her. I explain the rules of musical chairs but we're using square decorative pillows instead of actual chairs since the small ones are too small for adults and we only have four, anyway.

Everyone else has to play, so that leaves Mrs. G stopping and starting the music. I created a playlist of *Frozen* songs for Summer to listen to. I've probably heard *Let It Go* a million times over the last month. I'm much more partial to Kristoff's power ballad from the second movie.

Summer won musical chairs, but Allie won pin the tail on the donkey. We do presents next. She opens each one up like a madwoman, and I realize that this is probably the first birthday party she's ever had. No one skimped on presents. Each is more expensive than the last. Not that that matters, but it's expected.

Mrs. G baked Summer's cake from scratch and decorated it. She put an Elsa doll in the middle and the cake's the skirt. She used icing to draw on the top part of her dress. Summer loves the cake and is thrilled she gets to keep the doll afterward when it's all cleaned up. She blows out her five candles, then we cut the cake and give pieces to everyone. The cake's fantastic. Better than a bakery.

When it's finally bedtime, Summer's gone. She's been going all day from sugar and excitement. Now she's finally crashed. I hope she sleeps well. My family leaves not long after Summer goes to bed, then it's just the six of us. We sit down at the kitchen table where we eat most of our meals and play *Cards Against Humanity*.

"You guys staying for the Christmas party?" Evan asks, half an hour and four beers into our game.

"Classes are over for this semester, so I'm free," Kristie replies.

"I got nothin' goin' on," Noah says.

"Do you mind us staying here for another few weeks?" Allie asks.

"I'd love it if you did. I have another week of school left, but after that, we can hang out. You and Kris could come shopping with me. Oh, stay for Christmas, too," I say, getting excited.

"I'll be at the party," Willa says.

"Perfect. I'll need all the help I can get. Mr. Van Holsten's not thrilled with me since we took in Summer," I say.

"He was always going to find a reason to dislike you," Noah says.

"Why? I mean, he chose me as Evan's wife. It's not like we had any say in it," I reply, confused.

"It was a business deal. He didn't expect you to defy him," Noah says with a shrug.

"My dad's a little vindictive if you haven't noticed. He usually gets his way," Evan says.

"Y'all are too rich," Willa comments.

"Yeah, we are," Allie replies with a laugh.

"We definitely don't have rainbows and butterflies coming out our asses like everyone seems to think," Kris says.

We laugh until we're crying. It seems like such a stupid thing to be complaining about, but it really isn't all rainbow and butterflies. Expectation can be crippling. I know Allie, Noah, Kris, and Evan's shoulders are constantly bowed under it. Being married to Evan, I'm feeling the effects, too.

Thirty-Six

Evan

I haven't seen or talked to my dad since we introduced Summer to them. He's been working from home so he can avoid me at the office. He's acting like a child throwing a tantrum because he didn't get his way. Well, he won't be getting his way this time.

Though Tina's office is still having trouble finding Summer's parents, eventually the courts will allow us to adopt her and we will. She's become this shining star in our lives for the last month and a half. She's even got Noah, Kris, and Allie under her spell. She's family. There's nowhere else she belongs.

Now, the seven of us are piled into a limo on our way to my family's estate. I'm glad my friends could stay for this. My family's Christmas party isn't anywhere near as big as Helen Stinfield's Christmas Soiree. Allie's mom goes all out for it every year. Still, my family doesn't do anything half-assed, so it'll be big.

A valet opens the door for us once we reach the house. We shuffle out and walk up the front steps in pairs. Kris and Willa, Allie and Noah, then Brooke, Summer, and I. My mom is waiting to greet us by the front door. She looks around for my dad before she kneels a bit to say hi to Summer. It irks me she has to look over her damn shoulder just to say hello to my daughter. God, my dad is a fucking prick.

Christmas music echoes throughout the house, getting louder the closer we get to the ballroom. Summer looks around in amazement at the Christmas decorations that were vomited everywhere in the place.

"Dance with me, Sweets," Noah says, grabbing Allie's hand and pulling her onto the dance floor.

Kristie and Willa disappear, and I see them resurface at the refreshment table with champagne in their hands. I return my attention to Brooke. She's a little stiff and I know it's because she's waiting for the inevitable confrontation with my dad. There always seems to be one when we see him.

One minute Summer seems relaxed, the next she goes rigid. She whimpers then grabs my legs and hides behind them. She has a death grip on my knees and I know something is wrong. I look to Brooke, who's as confused as I am.

"Summer, honey? Are you okay?" Brooke asks, kneeling to her level. Instead of answering, she whimpers again.

I reach down and pull her into my arms. She buries her face in my neck the way she used to do with Brooke when she first came home with us. I shoot Brooke an alarmed look. She comes closer and puts her head on Summer's back.

"Baby, what's wrong?" Brooke asks desperately.

"Evan, Brooke, I'd like to introduce you to Mr. and Mrs. Kessel," Dad says, coming up to us with an out-of-character smile.

I look up and see a man and a woman walking behind my dad. They look twitchy as fuck with sunken faces and stringy hair. They are not the type of people my dad usually associates with. When the woman sees Summer, she runs towards her and attempts to rip her out of my arms.

"Summer! We've been searching for you everywhere!"

Summer's light whimpers turn into a cry when the woman's hands touch her. It's like the touch burned her. I tightened my grip on Summer and stepped away from the junkie.

"Who the fuck are you?" I ask harshly.

"Evan! That is no way to speak to our guests. It just so happens Mr. and

Mrs. Kessel are Summer's parents. They've been looking for her for a month and a half. Summer can finally return to where she belongs," Dad says.

Mr. Kessel looks at me evenly. He has a dangerous look in his eye. He's the one that hurt Summer, I'm sure of it. Who knows in which ways he hurt her more than just physically.

Summer still has her face buried in my neck. She's shaking uncontrollably and I pull her tighter to me. Mrs. Kessel doesn't look at Summer the way she should if she were really a concerned mother. It's more like she's a paycheck.

"In that case, you can get the fuck out. We have custody of Summer for now and we will not be handing her over until or unless the courts order us to. I wouldn't hold your breath for that either. We have x-rays of all the abuse you inflicted," Brooke seethes.

"This is my home. You will not speak to my guests that way. You may be Mrs. Van Holsten, but you have none of the power that comes with the name," Dad says coldly to Brooke.

"But I do. Don't worry, Dad. If you insist that Mr. and Mrs. Kessel stay, then we'll leave," I say cutting off Brooke's reply. I grab her hand and walk away back toward the front door. Noah and Allie catch up with us.

"You leaving?" Noah asks.

"It seems my father's spent the last month and a half looking for Summer's parents. They're here and they terrify Summer," I reply.

When Summer hears Noah's voice, she reaches out for him and he takes her into a gentle but firm hug. She rests her head on Noah's shoulder and looks at me. Her little cheeks are wet with tears.

"Can you take her to the car? I have something else to say to Mr. and Mrs. Kessel," I say.

"No problem," Noah says. He grabs Allie's hand as they exit out the front door while Brooke and I make our way back to the scum that birthed Summer.

"Have you decided to give her back to us?" Mr. Kessel says. His voice is grating and cold.

"Not a chance. I know you haven't been looking for Summer because her social worker has been searching for you. There's been no missing child report on her or anything. I can only imagine you want her back because my dad has offered you an exorbitant amount of money to take her home. I can tell you right now that won't be happening," I say.

"Will you be offering us more to get out of the picture?" Mrs. Kessel asks.

"No. I won't be offering you shit. We have all the evidence of the abuse Summer's suffered since she was born at your hands. The courts will terminate your parental rights, then we will adopt Summer. She will never have to see you again, nor will you ever lay hands on our daughter," I reply.

"She's our daughter," Mr. Kessel says.

"You lost the right to call her that the first time you laid hands on her," I bite out.

"Do yourselves a favor and leave Summer alone," Brooke says.

"We'll see you in court," Mr. Kessel says.

"Yes, you will," I reply, then grab Brooke's hand and we storm out of the place.

Kristie and Willa are waiting for us outside the limo. Noah and Allie are inside with Summer. I'm breathing heavily by the time we reach them. Noah opens the door and sticks his head out.

"Can we please go kick some ass?" Noah asks. I want to. God, I want to show them what it feels like, but it's not the smart play right now.

"No. I don't want to risk anything going wrong for court," I reply with a sigh. Noah huffs, but he gets it.

We pile into the limo to head home. Everyone is quiet. Brooke has Summer on her lap. Her head rests on Brooke's chest while she runs her hands through Summer's hair, murmuring a lullaby.

When we get home, Brooke gets Summer ready for bed and, after reading her a story, lays with her long after she's fallen asleep. I leave them be. They both need the comfort. Instead, I sit in the living room with Allie, Kristie, Willa, and Noah. We're sipping on scotch as we curse Summer's parents.

"Your dad really found them. He would send Summer back to them, knowing what they did to her?" Willa asks.

"He really did. I didn't think taking in Summer would be a big deal to him. On the outside, he's really big into family and the optics of taking in a child that needs a home look good. I should have known better though. He's serious about bloodlines," I reply with a sigh.

"What will you do? If you and Brooke don't do what he wants, he might not let you take over the business," Allie says. She knows my dad well.

"I know. I thought of that, but I won't let Summer go back to them. She's my daughter now. She belongs with us," I say.

"We'll have your back then. I know it's your dream to take over Van Holsten Conglomerate, but you'll be okay if you don't. You have enough experience and work ethic to start your own business and build it better than anything Dick did," Kris says.

"Thank you."

I'm always touched when my friends have my back and give me compliments like this. I shouldn't be. We're family. Always have been, always will be. They will have my back long after my "blood" has let me down and thrown me to the side.

Thirty-Seven

Brooke

I've been fuming for days since that stupid Christmas party. I would say I can't believe Mr. Van Holsten did that, but I really fucking can. Evan's just as pissed off at his dad as I am. He hasn't been going to work at the office since the party, but I'm putting it behind me now.

I woke up stupid early, almost as excited about Christmas morning as I was when I was little, and still believed in Santa. It's our first Christmas as a family and I'm sure Summer's first real one, so I'm more excited than ever. I've been sitting on my bed bugging the shit out of Evan, waiting for Summer to wake up. I thought she'd be up at the ass crack of dawn like most children, but maybe she's never had anything to be excited about.

I'm practically vibrating on the bed when Evan throws a pillow at my head. I throw it back, missing him by several inches, causing him to laugh at my failed attempt. I'm a really shitty aim.

"Either go back to sleep or just wake everyone up," he complains.

"Fine! Put some clothes on so we can go wake Summer," I say bounding out of bed. I grab my silk bathrobe and put it over my less than modest nightgown. Noah doesn't need to see everything I've got going on.

Evan pulls on some plaid pajama pants and a black hoodie, then we leave the room and tiptoe down the hall. I peek in Summer's room and she's still fast asleep. As excited as I am for her to see her presents, I don't have the heart to wake her up. I love watching her sleep. She just looks so peaceful.

Before I decide to shut the door and let her rest, Noah clambers down the hall towards us in gray sweatpants that leave nothing to the imagination and a black Metallica t-shirt. He's bright-eyed and bushy-tailed as he yells,

"Merry fucking Christmas, bitches!"

The rest of our house guests poke their heads out their doors with various looks of hatred on their faces at being woken up that way. Kristie slams her door with a huff so even if Summer slept through Noah's greeting, she's definitely up now.

Summer's confused at first, but she perks up and looks around excitedly when she realized what today is. She jumps out of bed and launches herself at Evan.

"Can we open presents now?" she asks, vibrating with excitement like I was.

"We sure will, baby. We just have to wait for everyone else," I reply.

We don't have to wait long before Willa and Kristie emerge from one room, both in sweatpants and t-shirts with their hair in messy buns. Allie comes out last in her signature yoga pants and a racerback tank with a matching messy bun. She wears black-rimmed glasses this morning instead of her normal contacts. Maybe I should have corralled my hair like they did. I didn't and now it's just a rat's nest. Oh well.

Now that we're ready, Evan lets Summer down and she leads us to the family room where we have the Christmas tree set up. I can see her eyes light up as soon as she zeroes in on the dollhouse we set up for her. More dolls and all the doll accessories she'll ever need surround the house. She runs up to it and picks up one of the dolls. She rocks it in her arms, then looks back at us.

"This is all mine?"

"All yours, baby, but maybe other people might want to play with you. Make sure you're sharing," Evan responds as he sits on the floor near her.

We let Summer play with her presents from Santa for a bit as we settle in in a semicircle around the tree. All our friends are watching her play with her toys with similar looks of love and affection. How quickly she's captured all our hearts.

"Who's playing Santa?" Noah finally asks.

"Go for it," I say, and he passes out gifts one by one to all of us.

"We should try to spend Christmas together every year. Maybe switch places. Like maybe next year, we can go to Noah's place, and the year after, ours. My mom would have a heart attack if we continually missed her Christmas Soiree," Allie says as she rips open the wrapping paper to her gift.

"That sounds like a good plan, Sweets. Holidays are for family and you guys are mine," Noah replies with a somewhat sad smile that breaks my heart.

"Noah's place next year, then. Let's rock Christmas in Florida. No damn snow or cold ass weather," Kris rejoices.

It's a good hour and a half before we're finished unwrapping presents and picking up all the garbage those gifts created. It'll be time for us to get ready soon as I have plans for dinner. It won't be extravagant like I imagine anything the "Big Four" would put on, but still, we were brought up a certain way, so formal dinner and formal clothes. It's all we know.

Mrs. G has the week off until after New Year's and seeing as none of us can cook since it wasn't something we ever learned, I'll be ordering a full Christmas dinner from one of the nice restaurants in Manhattan. Noah and Evan are picking it up while the girls get ready. My mom, dad, and sisters will be over soon.

I spend the next several hours getting ready with the girls. Willa complains about having to get dressed up again so soon after the Van Holsten Christmas Party but grudgingly dresses, anyway. Willa was a scholarship student at Kingswood Prep, so she understands our world, but she's not really from it.

The rest of the girls leave the room, but my phone rings. I grab it off my bed and see that it's Tina calling. Maybe she just wants to wish us a happy holiday.

"Merry Christmas," I say in answer.

"Merry Christmas, Brooke. I wish I had better news to give you today. I wanted to let you know that since we located Summer's parents, they set a

224

court hearing in a few weeks. The judge will hear testimony from everyone and decide. Unfortunately, with them found, it might take longer for their parental rights to be terminated so the adoption won't be going forward as soon as we hoped."

I sit down on the bed, my legs suddenly feeling weak. I'm kinda freaking out that Summer's entire life will be determined by a judge that may be swayed by Mr. and Mrs. Kessel's manipulation, but I have to put trust in the system. We have irrefutable evidence that they abused Summer.

"Thank you for letting me know," I manage.

"I'll text you all the court information. Time, place, courtroom, that sort of thing. I'll be there and so will your lawyer. I have to be confident everything will go okay."

After a few more reassurances from Tina, I hang up the phone and sit on my bed so long Evan comes looking for me. I barely notice when he walks into the room until he's kneeling in front of me, taking my icy hands into his warm ones.

"Brooke, what's wrong?"

I explain everything Tina told me until his expression mirrors mine. We both knew this was possible, but suddenly it feels like everything is changing. It would be bad enough to lose Summer at this point. She's ours. But to lose her to those monsters we met days ago who don't give two shits about her is just too much to bear.

The doorbell breaks us out of our reverie. Evan stands and pulls me to my feet. He envelops me in the most comforting hug I think I've ever received. It makes me feel safe. Nothing bad will happen as long as Evan's arms are the ones that hold me.

"Everything will be okay. Let's not let this ruin our holiday," Evan says as he takes my hand in his. I nod and try to put everything to the back of my mind.

Noah's answering the door, Summer on one hip, when we finally leave our room. He wears a simple black suit which looks identical to the ones Evan and my father are wearing. Evan leads everyone to the dining room while Willa and I bring out what we've plated. There's silence in the dining room while we pass dishes around and silverware clinks against the kaolin of our fine china. Once everyone's plates are filled and we dig in, groans of appreciation fill the air.

We fill dinner with conversation, laughter, and fun. It's different from any Christmas I've ever had, and I think it's because I've never had so many friends. Willa usually spends the holiday with her family. Spending the day watching Summer and that wonder that only happens to children on Christmas is enough to make me fall in love with the holiday all over again.

Evan catches my eye from across the room as we sip on wine towards the end of the night. Everyone is engaged in animated conversation with each other, but sometimes we catch these breaks where we lock eyes. In them, I see a love like nothing I've ever experienced before and fills my heart with happiness.

I've forgotten Tina's phone call mostly and when I do remember and start to worry, Evan's love-filled looks are enough to reassure me everything is going to be fine. It has to be.

* * *

Now that the holidays are over, I'm back at school. I've been nervously counting down days until we have our court hearing with Summer's parents. The rights were supposed to get terminated at this hearing since we couldn't find them after some due diligence, but now that they're here, I don't know how long we'll have to wait.

It's entirely possible Mr. and Mrs. Kessel could get Summer back. That absolutely cannot happen. They could kill her next time. I'd run away with Summer before I let her go home with them. I know that's not the right approach for foster parents, but fuck that. I was in the hospital with Summer. She was lucky she didn't have to spend more time there.

"Ready?" Evan asks, putting his arms around my shoulder and kissing my temple. I lean against him, willing some of his strength to seep into me.

"Not really, but we don't have a choice," I reply, trying to mentally prepare myself to walk into the courtroom.

Mr. and Mrs. Kessel are there. They don't look any better today than they did a few weeks ago. They look like fucking meth heads. Mr. Kessel gives me a creepy sneer, and I see several missing teeth. I take a deep breath and sit on the opposite side of them. Our lawyer sits with us and Tina's just behind. She gives us a small smile and a nod. All that's missing is two thumbs up, but she doesn't go that far.

A douchy-looking guy is sitting next to the Kessels. He's wearing a super-expensive three-piece suit. He gives us a superior smile. It seems like Mr. Van Holsten hired a lawyer for the Kessels, too. This just got that much harder. Fuck!

The judge comes in and our hearing starts. He listens to Mr. and Mrs. Kessel talk about how they've been looking for Summer for the last few months, and when they finally reunited with her at the party a few weeks ago, we wouldn't even let them touch her. They cry and ham up their fucking sob story. Their lawyer is saying all the right things to make them seem like parents of the year in a bad situation. It's making my blood boil. The only thing keeping me in my God damned seat is Evan's steady hand on my thigh.

"There were no missing person's cases for anyone matching Summer's description. Mrs. Van Holsten found her freezing, dehydrated, malnourished, and with a broken arm on the street in November. She was dirty and clearly not being taken care of. Dr. Adams was Summer's doctor when Mrs. Van Holsten brought her to the hospital. X-rays confirmed several broken bones that were not set at all dating back to Summer's infancy. Everything Dr. Adams saw points to years of systemic abuse. It could only have happened at the hands of Mr. and Mrs. Kessel. It would be ill-advised to release Summer into their care," our lawyer argues when it's finally our turn.

"Mr. and Mrs. Kessel have had a babysitter regularly since Summer was a baby. After each one of the injuries, the babysitter informed them that Summer is a clumsy child and she fell. Their babysitter was a registered nurse, so she took care of any injuries at home. She also informed the Kessels that Summer was a picky child when it came to food and would not eat. She also refused to bathe."

"Then why were the broken bones never set. A nurse would know that a hospital and doctor are required for setting broken bones, and she would also know that the bones were broken in the first place. Summer was almost five before she escaped the Kessel's care. What about all those years of injuries? Could they not tell Summer hadn't been eating as much as she should have? There are too many factors here that point to abuse and neglect at the hands of her parents. In the months that Summer's been in the Van Holsten's home, she's had no problem eating whatever they make, nor do they have issues getting her to bathe. It seems like the Kessels have neat little excuses for everything without actually taking responsibility for the reprehensible state Summer was found in.

"Mr. and Mrs. Van Holsten want to adopt Summer. They understand that the court may need to give the Kessel's time to work a case plan, but Summer's wishes should be taken into account. She was terrified when she saw them. We can do a supervised visit with a social worker. She can note Summer's reactions. Also, Summer's been seeing a therapist who can tell us exactly what she's been saying about her home life and what it's like now that she's been staying with Mr. and Mrs. Van Holsten," our lawyer argues.

"Very well. Let there be a supervised visit with Summer and her parents. I want a full evaluation of Mr. and Mrs. Kessel by a psychologist. A full evaluation of Summer by her therapist as well. I understand the State is also bringing criminal charges against Mr. and Mrs. Kessel for child endangerment and injury to child. It's a separate proceeding but will be taken into consideration. We will set the next hearing three weeks from now to give time for the evaluations," the judge says. He bangs his gavel and stands to leave. Everyone rises.

I get another sneer from Mr. Kessel as we leave the courtroom. Tina stands with us by the front doors. She squeezes my arm and gives me another smile.

"I know this isn't ideal, but Summer's therapist will help us and if the Kessels actually do their evaluation, it can't be helpful to them and if they don't, that's just another nail in their coffin. Everything will be fine."

"I'm afraid with my father bankrolling this, it won't be. I'm sorry to be that person, but money talks and I'm sure my father has some powerful people in his pocket. If he makes it his mission to get Summer out of our lives, he'll make it happen," Evan says, sighing heavily as he looks outside at the gently falling snow.

"We just need to see how it all plays out. We can only do what we can do," Tina says.

In the car, I lean heavily against Evan. He wraps his arms around my shoulders and kisses my forehead.

"I'm so scared for Summer to see her parents without us there. I know they can't do anything to her with the social workers present, but she's going to be so scared," I say, and I feel tears wet my cheeks. I angrily swipe them away.

"I know, baby. I'm scared too," Evan replies.

I sigh at my lack of power in this situation. I only relax when we get home and Summer comes bounding towards me when we walk into the house.

"Hi, Mommy," she yells as she launches herself into my arms. It's not the first time she's called me mom, but it still makes my heart happy every time I hear it.

"Hey, baby. Did you have fun with Mrs. G?" I ask.

"We baked cookies!"

"We should eat them with some milk. We can watch *Frozen* while we do," I suggest.

"Yes! Daddy let's watch *Frozen*!" Summer shouts looking at Evan. It's got to mean something about her life that she's so quick to call us mom and dad after only being with us two months.

"I'll go get it set up while you and Mommy get the cookies and milk," Evan says, going into the living room.

Fifteen minutes later, we're all seated snacking on our cookies while we watch Anna sing about building a snowman. I look at Evan over Summer's head. She's snuggled between us. I catch Evan's eye and he smiles.

"I love you," I mouth silently. Ev gives me a brilliant smile.

"I love you," he mouths back.

This right here is everything to me. I can't lose it. Especially not because of my father-in-law. If he wants a fight, I'll give him one.

Thirty-Eight

Evan

By the end of January, our worst fears are coming to fruition. The hearing started great. Summer's therapist's account was damning to the Kessels, and they never showed up for their own evaluation. Surprise, surprise. Dr. Adams testified. Tina testified. The social workers at the supervised visits testified that the visit did not go well.

Summer was too terrified to leave their sides and, as expected, the Kessels were not patient with her at all, which ended up with a lot of yelling and tears from Summer. Everything was going our way. Even if Summer's parents, and I use that term as loosely as possible, did do their evaluation, there was no way they'd ever get Summer back.

The end is where everything goes to shit, and mine and Brooke's worlds are shattered. The lawyer my dad hired for the Kessels gets up and tells the court we're liars. Our lawyer argues, asking what we ever lied about. Their lawyer pulls out some documentation and hands it to ours. He studies it before looking back at us with wide eyes.

"It says here that you and Mrs. Van Holsten aren't married."

"What? How the fuck is that possible?" I whisper shout.

"It seems your wedding was all for show. Someone didn't get the marriage license recorded with the state. You and Brooke aren't legally married, Evan.

231

You never were."

Brooke looks at me wide-eyed. Does she think I knew? No, she can't possibly think that. I've wanted nothing more than for her to be mine since we met.

"I don't really see how that's our fault. We had nothing to do with the marriage licenses. We assumed my dad's people filed them," I say.

"That's another thing. Somehow, they found out that your marriage was arranged, which invalidated your licenses, anyway. It's not putting you in a good light."

"As you can see, your honor, the Van Holstens have done nothing but lie. Their parents arranged this marriage as a part of a business deal. Sure, they knew each other from school, but according to the reports we have, they did not get along. Then we find out they were never actually married but put they were on all their paperwork. How can you send Summer to live permanently with a family that believes in arranged marriages and lies about being married? What assurances do we have that they won't marry Summer off to the first person that provides business alliances to line their pockets? As everyone knows, Van Holsten Conglomerate holds money in the highest regard and does everything in its name. You cannot, in good conscience, allow them to have Summer any longer than they have. It's always best if foster parents are married, and the fact that they lied on their paperwork shows you how trustworthy they are. Given the amount of money they have access to, how do we know they didn't pay off everyone that testified on their behalf today? In fact, I have proof from various bank accounts that they did just that."

What? This is a bunch of bullshit! My father probably made it look like we paid off these people. Unfortunately, I don't think it matters how vehemently we deny the allegations. The proof is in the bank statements. I sit heavily in my chair and glance at Brooke. It's almost too painful to see the tears falling freely down her face and the shattered look in her eyes. I have failed this woman. She had everything she wanted. And just like that, it's taken away because of my father.

After a lot of back and forth, the judge finally orders that any custody we have of Summer be immediately terminated and that although the state will retain custody of her, she will be on an extended home visit with the Kessels while they work their case plan to get her back permanently. We have to have Summer packed up and ready for Tina to pick up by five tonight.

The minute we're outside the courtroom, Brooke breaks down. She loses all the strength she kept while in front of the judge. Her knees buckle alarmingly and she's sobbing against my chest as I hold her as tightly as I possibly can to keep her heart from leaving her body. It must be threatening to leave in millions of pieces if it matches mine.

I bring her to a bench where we sit together for an immeasurable amount of time, crying together and holding each other. At some point, Tina comes and sits with us. She whispers things, reassuring us that they'll work hard to keep Summer out of the Kessels home permanently, and she's sorry things turned out the way they did. She knows we didn't do anything wrong, but until we can prove it, we're basically fucked.

After several attempts to get Brooke to walk outside, I finally pick her up and carry her to John and the waiting car. She hides her face in my neck and warm tears stream steadily down into the collar of my shirt. We sit in silence the whole way home.

Brooke schools her features enough as we enter the house. Summer greets us the same way she always does; with shouts of happiness and hugs. I can tell how much effort it's taking Brooke not to break down immediately after seeing our baby. It's taking Herculean strength for me.

"Summer, baby. We need to talk. Let's go sit on the couch," Brooke says in a wobbly voice.

The three of us sit together on the couch we've spent so many nights watching Disney movies, primarily *Frozen* on. Brooke pulls Summer onto her lap and nuzzles her face into blonde hair, so much like her own.

"What's wrong, Mommy? Are you crying?"

"You know we went to talk to a judge about keeping you forever, right?" I ask. Summer nods. "Well, some things came up, and they made the decision that you couldn't stay here. Tina is going to pick you up soon and take you to your mom and dads. You have to stay with them for a little while," I finish nearly choking on my words.

"You're my Mommy and Daddy," she answers. Tears form on her eyelashes and it guts me. Take whatever's left of my heart and pulverize it into dust.

"I know, baby, and we love you so, so much, but we don't have a choice. You have to go live with the parents you had before," Brooke manages.

"I don't want to go! I'll be good. I'm sorry if I did anything wrong. Don't make me go back there!" Summer screams, the tears coming harder.

Brooke can't hold back hers anymore. She lets them free and so do I. We smoosh together in a hug I never want to end.

"You are a good girl. You never did anything wrong. We aren't sending you back because we want to. We have to. I'm so sorry, baby. I love you," Brooke sobs into Summer's hair. We cry together so long that Tina's knocking on the door before we've packed Summer's things. Mrs. G lets her in and they walk to the living room. When I glance up, I see both women have red eyes too.

Brooke pulls back from Summer and both have puffy eyes and snot-filled noses. I kiss Summer's forehead and excuse myself to gather her things. I find the purple luggage in her closet and slowly fill it with winter clothes to keep her warm as well as Summer's favorite dolls. I try to fit all her stuff in those suitcases, but it barely puts a dent in her bedroom.

I slowly roll the bags out and set them beside Tina. Brooke and Summer are still pressed so close together, they're almost one person. Tina gives me the smallest nod and I know it's time to say goodbye. God, I am not ready for this. How do I say goodbye to my heart?

Brooke catches my eye and stands with Summer. She just barely got her cast off. I hope they don't break any more bones. Brooke transfers Summer to me and I hug her so tight, kissing every inch of her face.

"Summer, I love you more than you know. You might have to go away right now, but I promise, we will do everything to get you back. Do you hear me? You will come home," I say. Summer weakly nods through her tears and gives my cheek a wet kiss. I give her back to Brooke.

"We'll get you home. Call Tina if you need anything. I love you so much, baby."

There are more tears by everyone in the house as Tina takes Summer's hand in hers and pulls the luggage with her free hand. Summer doesn't yell or scream or bargain. She's so much stronger than your average five-year-old. She walks with slumped shoulders and gives us one last longing look before the door closes, taking my heart with her.

Brooke breaks down, slumping to the floor as sobs wrack her body again. She must be physically and emotionally exhausted. I know I am. How are there still more tears? I carry her to our room and lay her in our bed. We cuddle together and mourn the loss of our daughter. We haven't even had time to process the fact that we aren't married. It doesn't really matter now, anyway. We're married in all the ways that matter.

When Brooke's finally exhausted herself enough to fall asleep, I quietly slip out of the room and head to Summer's. I sit on her perfectly made bed. It something Summer and Mrs. G do every morning before breakfast to start the day. Mrs. G always said you can't start the day unless you make your bed first.

I pull out my phone to connect a video call to Kris, Allie, and Noah. It's been less than a month since I saw them last and only a few days since we spoke, but I need their support more than I think I ever have before.

"'Sup, dude?" Noah answers, then when he gets a look at me he sits up straight. "Fuck. What's wrong?"

"Oh my God, Evan. Did something happen? You look terrible," Allie says upon answering.

"She's gone. They took her," I reply, my voice cracking, and I have to work hard not to shed more tears.

"Who took who?" Kristie asks, looking more concerned than I've ever seen her.

"The judge terminated any custody we had of Summer. She went back to the Kessels."

"What dumb fuck would do that?" Noah asks, looking enraged. I can tell he's pacing his house now.

"Apparently, Brooke and I were never married. The license wasn't recorded with the state so legally, our marriage doesn't exist. They also found evidence that we bribed all the witnesses we had today. Our bank accounts show massive transfers to the therapist, doctor, social workers. Everyone."

"Your dad?" Allie asks, trying to hold back her own tears.

In the short time they've known her, Summer wormed her way into their hearts too. They love her like family now. We don't quit on the family that matters.

"I think so," I reply.

"You need to go beat his fucking ass, Evan. He can't just mess with your life like this! He's sending a little girl into an unsafe situation because he can? He's a power-hungry dick. You can't let him get away with it!" Kristie shouts.

"No, I can't. I won't give up on Summer. I'm going to see my dad tomorrow. I'll do whatever it takes to get her back," I say.

"I'll get my dad to look into it. I know he's friends with your dad, but once I tell him what happened, there's no way he won't help. He's one of the best lawyers in the country. If anyone can find proof that your dad made these transfers, it's him," Kristie says.

"Thank you, Kris. I'll be in contact with you about that. Thanks for your support. I love you guys," I say with whatever smile I can manage. I think it comes out looking like more of a grimace.

"We're here for you, Ev. Whatever you need," Allie replies.

"Got your back, bro. Call us when you know more. Give my love to Brooke. I know she needs it," Noah says.

We exchange goodbyes, and by the end of the call; I feel my resolve coming back. It feels like my friends lent me their strength when I had none left, even from thousands of miles away. We'll get Summer back, then I'll deal with my dad. He's not a puppet master, and I'm not on fucking strings. He doesn't get to mess with my family without consequences. If he wants to go to war, then war is what he'll get.

Thirty-Nine

Evan

After a horrible night of me not being able to sleep and Brooke waking every hour on the hour crying, I go to my dad's place first thing in the morning. My resolve from last night hasn't waned. In fact, the more I think about the injustice of it all and the more I worry about Summer, the more pissed I get.

Right before I leave, I call Willa. I don't think Brooke's called her yet, and she deserves to know, but also I don't feel right about leaving Brooke by herself.

"What's shakin', Prince Playboy?" Willa answers and the stupid nickname still makes me smile just a little.

"Do you think you could come over and sit with Brooke for a few hours?"

"Sure. What happened?"

"They took Summer. She's back with those monsters. On top of everything else, we found out we were never legally married. I need to go talk to my dad because he did all of this, but Brooke's not in a good place right now," I explain.

"That dickhole! I'll be right there," Willa says before hanging up.

I lay in bed spooning with Brooke as she stares at the wall while I wait for Willa to show up. Once she does, she takes my place behind Brooke and something about having her best friend there makes her cry again.

I stop at the door looking at them together and I don't want to leave, but I know what I have to do. I don't know how I'm going to get Summer back, but I know something awful will happen if I don't.

I calm myself down on the car ride to my parent's house because I need a cool head if I have any chance in hell against my father. As soon as I hear my dad's voice telling me to come in when I knock on his study door, my anger races through my veins making me see red when I finally come face to face with the devil himself.

"Evan, my boy, I'm glad you came. We have much to discuss now that the nasty little business with the child is finished."

I want to strangle him. I want to fling myself across his desk and strangle the bastard as he begs for his life and his eyes show nothing but the fear I'm sure my little girl is facing every single second she spends away from us. Instead, I take a deep breath and sit in the same chair that set me on this path.

"My daughter is not nasty business," I reply dead calm.

"She's not your daughter. She's just some little girl Miss Jacobs found and brought home like a stray dog," dad says, flipping his hand as if brushing it all off his perfectly tailored suit. I don't miss how he calls Brooke by her maiden name again. Just dig the knife further into my heart, why don't you.

"She is a helpless little girl, and you actively worked to send her back to those monsters who abused her! How could you do something so heartless?"

"She may not belong with her parents, but she certainly doesn't belong with you. You have a reputation to uphold and I hoped Miss Jacobs would help you, but she is much too defiant to be married to a Van Holsten. I had nothing to do with the fact that the marriage license was never recorded, but it happened to be a good thing. Miss Jacobs is not who you need at your side. She insists on working at that school on the wrong side of the city, making you move to a less than ideal area. She doesn't listen, nor does she speak only when spoken to. She was the whole reason behind the child and I cannot have someone like that married to my son. So now that it's as if you never married at all, you can marry someone better. Someone unlike Miss Jacobs"

I'm speechless. Is he for real? Why would he think I'd ever agree to marry yet another person he picks for me when Brooke is it? She's my past, present, and future. There's nothing in this world that would make me marry anyone besides her. Part of me is tempted to take her ass to the courthouse and make it official and legal right now.

"Why the fuck do you think I would ever marry someone other than Brooke? She's my wife in every way that matters and I love her. Who do you even have in mind? Wasn't it hard enough getting one woman to agree to an arranged marriage? Where would you find another suitable match, as you put it last time?"

My dad's thin lips turn into a sneer as he presses a button on the phone he has near his computer monitor like he's in his office and his assistant's at his beck and call. I suppose the buzzer goes to the house staff somewhere. The door behind me opens and I don't bother to turn. My focus is on my father.

"Miss Berretti. Thank you for joining us," dad says, looking behind me.

I whip around and see Kendra standing there in a business casual black dress and a smug expression on her face. I haven't seen her since we sent her packing at Noah's house.

"What the fuck are you doing here, Kendra?" I ask.

"That's no way to speak to your future wife," my father says with a cruel smile.

"There's no way in hell I would ever marry her, even if I wasn't in love with Brooke," I reply, shaking my head. Dad's got to be off his fucking rocker if he thinks I'd ever tie myself to this bitch.

"You will marry Miss Berretti if you want to take over this company. The condition is the same. Since you and Miss Jacobs were never actually married and I find her unsuitable anyway, you will marry Kendra or lose the company."

"Fine! I don't want it if this is the cost. Brooke is more important than Van Holsten Conglomerate."

I never thought I'd see the day where I'd give up this company when I worked my whole life for it, but it's the easiest thing I've ever done. Going by the murderous expression on my dad's face, he must not have expected me to give it up that easily either. He grossly underestimates how important Brooke is to me. I turn on my heel and start towards the door. I don't need anything more from my dad.

"If you won't do it for the company, consider doing it for Summer," Dad says injecting even more venom into his smile like he's got me right where he wants me. And fuck, he does. I turn slowly and though I don't want to ask, I do.

"What do you mean?"

"I will get the girl away from the Kessels and back in Miss Jacob's care if you agree to marry Miss Berretti. Miss Jacobs can adopt the child and everyone will be happy."

"Except me," I whisper.

"There is no room in our lives for happiness, Evan. There is only expectation and responsibility. Take on yours and get that child away from harm and back into the arms of the woman you claim to love. I bet she's downright mourning the loss. She's laying in bed staring at the wall. She's been crying nonstop since the girl left, hasn't she? Getting the child back will ease all her sadness. You're telling me you don't love Miss Jacobs enough to do it?"

Fuck! I want nothing more than to tell my dad where to shove it all, but I know I probably won't be able to get Summer back on my own. Not if I have to go up against my dad. Even if I could swing it, it would take too much time and something horrible could happen to her in the meantime. My dad zeroed in on the one thing I would marry another for. I take a deep breath as I make the decision that will end my life and happiness.

"Fine, I'll marry Kendra. Before the wedding, I want proof that Summer is back with Brooke and will stay there. I also want assurances that no harm will come to either of them after this. I want them both to be taken care of, even though we were never actually married. After I do this, you leave us all alone. I'll take over your company and I'll work my hardest to erase you afterward," I say standing up straighter. Show no fear to the likes of this snake.

"Wonderful. The child will be back with Miss Jacobs by tomorrow afternoon. She can keep the house you live in and the wedding will be next week. Better go home and tell her. Miss Berretti will be wedding planning. See you soon, my son."

I shudder at Kendra's smug expression as I slip past, resisting the urge to shoulder-check her on the way out. She did say she'd make sure we regret what we did in Florida.

I sprint down the halls to get away from this vile house as fast as I can. Nothing good has ever happened at this stack of stones.

My head is spinning and my stomach is churning so violently, I retch the meager contents of my stomach all over the pristine driveway. I came here to go to war with my dad and instead; he won again. How does he always win? It's like he doesn't even try. Meanwhile, I can't think of any other way to get Summer home safely.

I dry heave some more and only when I stand up straight do I notice the tears in my eyes. Tears for my lost life, my lost love, my lost daughter. All at the hands of the man who was supposed to love me above all else.

Forty

Brooke

~~~ ❧ ~~~

Willa lays with me for a while taking Evan's place and we sit in silence. She doesn't ask me dumb questions like if I'm okay or anything. She knows I'm not. She just lends me her support and I love her for it.

I finally get up from the bed when my mother calls. Our relationship has been better lately since my marriage and short bout of parenthood. She loves Summer too. I debate for a second whether to answer, but she deserves to know what's going on.

"Hello?"

"Brooke, darling, I was planning on a visit with you and Summer. I wanted to take you girls for a spa day and some shopping. How does this weekend sound?"

I have to hold back a sob. I don't want to cry anymore. My eyes are puffy and red. My throat is sore and raspy. My stomach hurts and I just have no more tears. But hearing my mom so happy asking to spend time with us nearly pushes me over the edge.

"Mom?" I gasp with the plan to tell her everything, but my throat closes with the intensity of the emotions swirling in my stomach.

"Honey? What's wrong?" She sounds concerned.

"Everything!" I wail. "The court hearing didn't go well. They took

Summer. She's back with the Kessels and I'm worried sick about her. To top it all off, Evan and I aren't even married!"

"How are you not married?" Of course, that's what she focuses on.

I explain everything that happened in the court hearing and after. I told her Evan went to see his dad, but I don't know how much that will actually help. If Mr. Van Holsten wanted us away from Summer, there's no way we'll get her back easily.

"The marriage is no matter. You and Evan can just go make it official at the courthouse. That boy loves you, Brooke. There's just no one else he would marry. That part sounds like the least of your problems. Now, getting Summer back will be an issue. I'll speak to some lawyers. Has Evan asked Mr. Cleaston for help? I know he's friends with Richard, but surely he'd think this is a good cause," Mom says staying calm and unemotional.

"I'll call Kristie. Evan and I haven't really spoken since last night. Thanks, Mom."

I hang up with her. She wasn't exactly comforting, but not cold either. That's just my mom. I switch to a video call with Kristie. Willa and I wait patiently for her to answer. When she does, she looks unkempt and frazzled. Allie's in the frame too, looking sleep-deprived.

"Are you guys okay?" I ask.

"Are you?" Allie asks.

"Evan called us last night. We know what happened. We've been doing everything we can to help. I talked to my dad, and he agreed to help. We've been going over all the public documents and precedent. Any other documents about your case with Summer will be helpful. Can you send them so I can get them to my dad?" Kristie says, barely lifting her eyes to the screen.

"Sure. Can you tell your dad thank you, please? Evan's been with his dad all morning. I don't know if him being gone so long is a good thing or a bad thing," I respond.

"Any meeting, no matter the length, won't go well. Evan's smart, but Dick is a ruthless motherfucker. It's going to take hard work and possibly a sacrifice to get him to agree to anything he doesn't want. You can't strong-arm him or negotiate. Richard Van Holsten gets what he wants and fuck everyone else," Kristie says crushing whatever hope I had.

"I'm sorry if that sounds harsh. That's just what we know of him and what we learned from Mr. Cleaston when we told us how hard this is going to be. It *is* possible though and we will do everything we can to help you and Ev get Summer back," Allie says, trying to reassure me.

I manage a small smile for them. I really appreciate how much they're doing for us. Kristie's distracted again so I let them go, then it's just me and Willa while we wait for Evan to get back and give us the news. I can't bear to be hopeful anything will go our way.

Evan doesn't get back until well after lunch. Willa and I are now in the living room, staring blankly at the TV as it plays some reruns. I jump up when Evan enters. He looks worse than he did when he left, and that only means one thing. Something went horribly wrong and we're doomed.

"Willa, can you give us a few minutes?" Evan asks, his voice monotone. He sounds so emotionless.

"Of course."

"Evan, what's wrong? I assume you couldn't get Summer back. Don't worry, I just got off the phone with Kristie and Allie. They're working hard with Mr. Cleaston for some other recourse," I say as I step in front of him.

He looks down at me and his expression is filled with anger, but that's not the most prominent emotion. Profound sadness unlike anything I've ever seen is front and center. His hazel eyes look like they're frozen in grief worse than before. It's like his world is falling apart in front of him and he's just forced to sit there and watch. Something is very wrong, worse than just losing Summer.

I sit silently waiting for him to say whatever he has to say. Has he heard something about Summer? Is she hurt or in the hospital? I can't let myself think it's any worse than that. My poor heart can't take much more. When Evan finally speaks, his words are monotone still.

"I was able to get Summer back to you," he starts, and before he can go on, I cut him off with a squeal of happiness. I jump into his arms, kissing him with a smile on my face.

"That's wonderful news," I say.

When Evan's only move is to hold my waist so I don't fall and he has no expression other than sadness, I pull back until I'm standing on my own two feet again. He lets me go, but he keeps one of my hands firmly clasped in his. He stares at our intertwined hands instead of my face and my heart drops into my feet. What did he have to do to get her back? I thought Kristie was joking about a sacrifice, but maybe she wasn't.

"Go on," I say when Evan makes no move to continue. He sighs heavily, still not looking at anything but my wedding rings, which he twists back and forth.

"I had to agree to some things for my dad to get her back from the Kessels. I know we could have gotten her back eventually, but going around my dad would take too long and get too messy. Horrible things could happen to Summer in that time. I don't trust her parents."

I nod. At least Mr. Cleaston could help with the adoption so Summer's ours legally and permanently. That way this doesn't happen again. Maybe he could even help get Evan's dad arrested for his involvement in doctoring our accounts. I don't really know if that's an arrestable offense, but it should be. It fucked a lot of lives up and who's to say he hasn't done other illegal things in all his business dealings.

"My dad insisted that the condition of me taking over the business still stands. I need to get married before my next birthday."

"I'll take you to the courthouse today to make this official, Evan. I love you and I want to be married to you," I say with a smile. All this sounds like good news, so why does he look so devastated?

"My father no longer thinks you're a suitable option for marriage. He thinks you're too defiant and has brought too much trouble to our family," Evan deadpans finally looking me in the eye.

I ache for Evan. His dream is to take over that company, but I know he would choose me over it in a heartbeat. He loves me more than that. I step forward to wrap my arms around his waist in comfort. He lets me, but he's stiff for a second before melting into me. He buries his face in my neck and I feel his hot tears against my skin. Evan's every reaction has me so confused.

"I'm sorry you lost the business," I say.

As soon as the words are out of my mouth, Evan pulls back from me, creating a few feet of space between us. Just add to my confusion, why don't you?

"I didn't lose it, Brooke. I would have given it up in a heartbeat if it meant I got to keep you and make you my wife, but it's not just about us. It's about Summer and her safety. Her well-being is more important than my happiness. I love her as much as I love you, and you need her back to be happy. Without her, there would always be a piece of you missing. Seeing you so crushed has broken my heart. I'd give anything to take your pain from you and make you whole again, so that's what I did," he explains. He paces as he does, refusing to look at me.

My stomach drops at his implications, but I still can't fathom what he gave up to achieve everything he's saying. Why does it feel like the rug is about to be swept from under my feet?

"I can't marry you, Brooke. I can't even be with you or see you anymore. To get Summer safely back in your arms, I had to agree to marry someone else. My dad will ensure Summer stays with you forever. You can keep this house and the two of you will be taken care of so you don't need to worry about money or anything. You won't have to deal with my family anymore, so that's also a plus."

Evan's speaking, but all I can hear is a high-pitched ringing in my ears. My vision goes spotty and I stumble back until I crash onto the couch. Evan rushes forward until he's kneeling between my legs with his hands holding onto mine for dear life.

"Who?" I rasp out.

Who's the lucky woman that gets the man who holds my heart? Will she love him like I do? Will she cherish him? Will she be worthy of him? Does she deserve him more than I do? Has too much time gone by and we missed our chance to be together? Did the one misunderstanding that cost us thirteen years also cost us the rest of our lives? Were we only able to have this glimpse of what absolute happiness could be like so we know what we'll be missing?

"Who did your dad pick for you to marry, Evan?"

"To get Summer out of the Kessels clutches forever and to get her back into your arms, my dad demanded I marry Kendra," Evan whispers looking into my eyes. His eyes implore me to understand that this was not an easy choice, but one he was willing to make for his family.

"Kendra," I say as I lose all breath in my lungs. She just won the ultimate prize. She lost a duke but gained a prince destined to become king. And to answer all my earlier questions, no. She won't love him, and she definitely doesn't deserve him.

"I love you and Summer so much that I'll do it to ensure you're both safe and happy. It's the only way, Brooke. I hope you understand that and can forgive me one day," he answers.

"When do you marry her?"

"Next week. Summer will be returned to you tomorrow."

Evan pulls me to my feet and wraps me into a hug so tight it's like he's trying to fit a lifetime of embraces in this last hug. He pulls me up until my legs wrap around his waist and his lips crash to mine. He carries me to our room, never breaking our tear-laden kiss. One last chance to make love, one last chance to be together before he leaves my life forever.

Every movement, every kiss, every caress is slow and sensual. We know it's the last of everything, so we're both savoring every touch. The tears never cease and before either of us are ready, we're dressing again, preparing to say goodbye for the last time.

Evan packs a bag. He won't be back here. Movers will pick up the rest of his stuff sometime in the next week. Before I'm anywhere near ready, we're standing by the front door. When Evan leaves, it will be the end of my happily ever after. Evan cups my wet cheek with his hand and leans in to place a soft kiss on my lips.

"You'll always hold my heart, Brooke. It's always been you, and it will always be you. You're it for me. I love you. Please don't forget that," he says.

"I love you too, Evan. Thank you for bringing Summer home. I know what it's costing us," I say.

"You sacrifice for the wellbeing of your children. To bring her home, it was an easy choice. I'm just sorry I'm taking yours away from you," he replies, smiling grimly.

"I would have made the same choice. I'll be waiting for you in case our stars happen to align again," I tell him, giving him my own sad smile.

"I wish you wouldn't. I want you to be happy."

"Impossible without you. You're it for me too. I'll be happy enough to have Summer, but I won't give my heart to another," I reply, leaning close to steal another kiss. Evan gives me one last longing smile before walking away.

When he's out of sight, I shut the door and slide down it to the floor where I let out a wail and burst into tears. The wail is loud enough that Willa comes running. She doesn't ask questions. She just sits next to me, holding me to her while I cry into her hair. She comforts me as my world falls apart.

Forty-One

Evan

I drop my bag at the door of my near-empty apartment. Almost everything was taken to the house I shared with Brooke. At least there's a bed for me to sleep on this week until my life ends. At that point, it doesn't really matter where I live.

I'm so drained, physically and emotionally. I drop onto the bed with sheets that haven't been changed in months. I want to call my friends, but I know how upset they're going to be. The decision is taken out of my hands when my phone buzzes with Kristie's video call. I sigh but slide the green button. I'm about to greet her and Allie, but she steamrolls me before I can.

"What in the actual fuck, Evan?"

"Hello to you too," I grumble. Does she not think I'm more unhappy about this than she is?

"Who did you agree to marry?" Kris demands, and that has me blinking. She must have spoken to Brooke, but did she not tell Kristie and Allie?

Before I can answer, Noah's picture box pops up and I groan a little. This conversation will not go well.

"What up, fuckers? What did I miss?" Noah says with his feet kicked up on a lawn chair and the ocean behind him. I'm about to ruin his day.

"Evan just broke it off with Brooke," Kristie says accusingly.

249

"The fuck? Why?" Noah asks with a furrowed brow.

"My dad made it clear that I still needed to marry to take the business, but that Brooke was no longer a suitable option," I start.

"You chose the business over Brooke? Fucking really? Evan, you fucked up. Brooke deserves more than that. She's amazing. If you're going to care more about the business than her, maybe I'll marry her and show her the proper way to be treated," Noah replies.

I growl at him like an animal. Just the thought of Brooke marrying anyone, let alone Noah, has my skin crawling. I mean, I told her to do as much, but I couldn't stand her marrying my best friend. Seeing her all the time would kill me.

"I can't believe you did that," Allie whispers, a horrified expression on her face.

"Jesus Christ, guys. Give me more credit than that! I was happy to give up the business, but then my dad said if I marry who he wants, he'll get Summer back to Brooke forever. How could I say no? I'd do anything for them, and this is the only solution to take care of both girls. I'll give up my own happiness for that."

The four of us are silent as my friends process what I just told them. Instead of anger, their faces just show the sadness I'm sure they see in mine. They must realize how hard all this has been for me. Understanding and sympathy are all I see now.

"Who's your dad making you marry for Summer's safety?" Noah asks.

I almost chicken out telling him. Even though Kendra broke his heart, me marrying her is going to gut him. He still loves her, no matter how much he wishes he doesn't. I take a deep breath and let the name out on a sigh, waiting for the explosion.

"Kendra."

Kristie and Allie are the ones to explode with anger and questions, but I ignore them and focus only on Noah. He opens his mouth, but no words come out. Instead, he chokes on his breath and blurts,

"I have to go."

"Noah, wait!" I shout, but he's already hung up. Shit. I'd welcome his anger and yelling over hurting him this way. Let him be pissed, but don't let him regress in whatever healing he's managed.

"Kendra? Really?" Kristie asks, but her words no longer carry anger, just resignation.

"It was the only way. Have your dad keep working on it, though. I don't trust mine," I answer.

"Of course, Ev. When's the wedding?"

"Next week. I have about five days of freedom."

"Head up, babe. Maybe my dad will find something helpful before then," Kristie says gently.

"Yeah, maybe." I'm not hopeful.

"Take care, Evan. We love you," Allie says with a sad smile.

"Love you guys too," I say, then hang up.

I toss my phone away from me and stare at the ceiling of what was once my bedroom. I hate everything about this. When my phone rings again, I let my heart think for just a second that it's Brooke. Instead, it's an unknown number. I debate whether I should answer. I do.

"Hello?"

"Hello, fiancé. I was just calling to get your opinion on flowers. Should we do the classic rose or something else? I mean, you had roses with Brooke, and I want our wedding to be different and just... more. I'm thinking calla lilies. Pink ones. We should stay away from white."

"What the fuck are you calling me for, Kendra?"

"I just told you, silly. I'm calling to get opinions on flowers."

"Just because we're getting married doesn't mean you have the right to call me. We're not in a relationship. This is a business deal and nothing more. Now kindly fuck off!" I shout as I hang up.

I'm half tempted to throw the fucking thing at the wall, but then how would Brooke contact me? I close my eyes and try to dream of happier times.

* * *

For one wondrous minute, I forget where I am. I turn to my side and throw out my arm to bring Brooke closer to me, only for it to be met with nothing but air. When I open my eyes and look around, I'm reminded all over again what happened and where my life took such a shitty turn.

Looking on the bright side, today Summer goes home. She leaves the dangers of the Kessels behind and rejoins the one person in the world who loves her as much as I do. I can be happy about that. It's what my sacrifice was for.

I check my phone and see my dad's requested my presence in his office in the Van Holsten Conglomerate high rise. Might as well go make sure he holds up the end of his bargain. When I walk in, Kendra's once again there and I scowl at her self-satisfied smile. God, I fucking hate her.

"Why is she here?" I ask.

"She needs to learn how to be a proper wife to you, Evan. I think that was one mistake I made with Miss Jacobs. I never trained her how to conduct herself. I just assumed because of her family she would know. Since Miss Berretti comes from even lower stock than Miss Jacobs, I need to be sure she has what it takes before the wedding next week," Dad says waving his hand like what he said is as bland as the weather.

I glance back at Kendra and I see the hurt his words inflict on her before her nonchalant mask of not giving a fuck settles back. I feel bad for her for half a second, but then she gives me a malicious smile and I remember everything she's done.

"Speaking of the wedding. I need to be sure Summer is back home with Brooke like you said she would be," I say focusing my attention back on my father.

"That social worker, Ms. Rodriguez, should be picking her up any minute now. I've already had the paperwork filed with the court, and the hearing for the Kessel's parental rights to be terminated is scheduled for the day after your wedding to Miss Berretti. If you don't go through with it, the child will go back to her parents and there will be no second chances," Dad responds.

"I understand. I would request that I see Summer one last time before the wedding. I just want to say goodbye to her," I say.

Dad looks at me for a long time, considering my request. I can almost see the gears turning in his head as he decides whether or not this will serve his purposes.

"Very well. You may see her when Ms. Rodriguez drops her off with Miss Jacobs, but I insist Miss Berretti be there," Dad says, daring me to object.

"Can I ask why? Brooke and Kendra have bad blood between them," I say.

Kendra scoffs behind me but wisely says nothing. My dad glances between the two of us, looking bored as hell, but I know he's not. He's calculating.

"I don't care about petty squabbles between women. Miss Berretti is about to be your wife, and I want Miss Jacobs to know that it is over between the two of you. We can't leave her with any hope you might warm her bed again. Either take Miss Berretti with you or don't see Summer. Your choice, son."

I scowl harder, then I turn on my heel, flying towards the door. I grab ahold of Kendra's arm and pull her with me.

"We should get lunch before we go. It'll be a bit before Summer gets to Brooke's place anyway," Kendra says when I let her go. She rushes after me in her stilettos.

I want to say no, but I'm starving and she's got a point. Besides, we'll be married before long. I need to learn to talk to Kendra with something other than vitriol in my voice.

"Fine."

We go to some expensive restaurant Kendra picked. I can't help but pick out the differences between Brooke and Kendra. For starters, Brooke would have preferred some little mom-and-pop shop over a place like this. Kendra's not exactly rude to staff, but she's got this obvious air of superiority to her that Brooke's never had. It makes me miss her that much more.

"Look, Evan, I'm sorry about Brooke. I can tell you really love each other. I feel bad about what I did to you guys. I know Noah loved me, but it was never like you and Brooke," she says humanizing herself just a bit.

"What about Zack? Why did you agree to this?" I ask.

"Same reason I was with Noah all those years. Don't get me wrong, a part of me loved him, but not like I love Zack. He knows everything about me and loves the broken, fucked up, cruel parts of me. He's never asked me to change, but he also knows my family. Their expectations weigh heavy on me. Your dad fucked Zack over by not claiming him and my dad won't let me be with him, so he set this up with Mr. Van Holsten. I didn't really have a choice," she explains.

"You could say no and run away with Zack."

"Easy for you to say. You have all the money from your trust from your mom's family that your dad can't touch. You could break away from your dad and be fine when he cuts you off. Zack and I don't have that. If I disobey my family, I'll have nothing and Zack already has nothing. He can't leave his mom destitute either. When your dad decides enough is enough, she's on her ass," she says.

"You'll have each other," I argue. Kendra gets a dreamy look on her face like she'd love nothing more.

"In a perfect world, that would be enough. But we don't live in a perfect world. So here we are, forced to marry someone we don't love while the ones we do are forced to watch their happily ever afters go up in flames," she says on a sigh.

I still don't care for Kendra. She's caused a lot of hurt, but I at least understand her better than I did before. Maybe that's all we can hope for in this marriage: mutual understanding.

Forty-Two

Brooke

Willa's snuggled up behind me when I wake in the morning. After Mrs. G made us breakfast, I get a text from Tina letting me know when she'll be dropping off Summer. Despite everything, I'm beyond excited to have her home where she belongs. It's only been a day and a half that she's been gone, but it feels like a lifetime.

While we wait, I get a text from my sister. I feel like I haven't seen her since Christmas. She's been off to college, staying in the dorms despite being close to home. I guess she wants the complete experience.

Rebekah: Hey, Sissy. Mom told me what's been going on with Summer. I just wanted you to know I'm sorry.

Me: Thanks, Beks. I appreciate it. Summer should be coming home soon.

Rebekah: Oh, that's wonderful. I'm sure you and Evan are very happy to have her back. When are you making your marriage official?

Me: Evan's marrying someone else. To get Summer home, he has to cut ties with me.

Rebekah: What!? Mr. Van Holsten made him do it, didn't he?

Me: Yep.

Rebekah: I'm really sorry, Brooke. It's not fair he's doing this to you guys. I know it worked out for a little while and you were really happy, but I wanted to say thank you for not bailing when Mom and Dad arranged this marriage. I know you would have been fine on your own, so thanks for loving me enough not to subject me to Mr. Van Holsten.

Me: I'd do it again and again, even if it wasn't Evan. But it was, and at least I know what happiness and love feel like now. Even with everything I know now, I wouldn't give up the time I had with him.

Rebekah: Let me know if you need anything or if you just want to talk. I'm here. I love you, Sissy.

Me: Love you too, Beks.

The doorbell rings mid-afternoon. The room has been pretty silent, so the sudden noise makes me jump. It must be Summer and Tina, so I get up and answer the door before Mrs. G can get it. I flip the door open with a wide smile, but it drops quickly when I see who's actually at the door.

My heart races when I meet Evan's beautifully mixed hazel eyes, but his face is marred by his expression. Usually, when his eyes are on me, his face is filled with happiness and love. The love is there, but so is such sadness and anger. He doesn't really look like my Evan. I frown at the woman behind him instead of throwing myself at Evan.

"What's she doing here?" I ask, glaring at Kendra.

"I wanted to see Summer one last time and say goodbye. My dad wouldn't permit it if I didn't bring her. I'm sorry, baby. I didn't want to," Evan replies, looking so helpless. My heart breaks for him.

Evan's hands twitch like he wants to pull me into his chest and never let go, but with Kendra here, he can't. I reach for his hand and squeeze it. I give him a small, sad smile.

"I understand."

I step back to let them into the house. Kendra stands there awkwardly. The usual look of disgust isn't on her face. She looks sad too, and thoughtful. Mrs. G comes out from the kitchen and pulls Evan into a tight hug. He wastes no time hugging her back. He holds onto her like she's the only thing keeping him from drowning.

My heart breaks for Evan when I see his shoulders bouncing while his face is buried in Mrs. G's neck. She rubs his back in comfort. They embrace for a few long minutes until he pulls back, his eyes rimmed red and wet.

The doorbell rings again, and it has to be Summer and Tina. I flip the door open and Summer jumps into my arms, wrapping her skinny ones around my neck and nuzzling into my hair. I hold on to her so tight I might be preventing her from breathing, but I don't care.

"I missed you, Mommy," she sobs.

"I missed you too, baby. You're home now and I won't let you go again," I say looking at Evan over Summer's head.

He's gazing at her with love and when his eyes meet mine, I hope he can see how much I appreciate what he did. It wasn't an easy choice, but our little girl deserves this. Summer stretches to Evan's arms and he holds her as tightly as I did. His hold is more of a goodbye than a greeting. This might very well be the last time he sees her, and he did it all for us.

When the hugs are over, I get a good look at Summer. She's dirtier than she should be after only less than two days. It makes me wonder what kind of place the Kessels are living in. Did the social workers check their home to see if it's safe?

"We should give her a bath," Evan breathes, looking at Summer like he wants to memorize her every feature.

"Good idea. Kendra, you're welcome to wait in the living room," I say, barely looking at her.

I expect her to say something snarky, but she just bobs her head as she walks to the couch. I give Willa a look and she nods ever so slightly before following Kendra to the living room.

Evan picks up Summer and takes her to her bathroom while I go to her room and grab some pajamas and underwear. Evan already has the bath started, and he's helping her get undressed when I walk back in.

I survey every inch of her bare skin and I have to hold back my sobs when I see new purple bruises on her thighs and all along her back. What did they do? Use her as a fucking punching bag for the thirty hours she was in their home?

Evan glances at me after he's helped Summer into the tub and there's fire in his eyes. If he weren't such a level-headed guy, he'd be busting down the Kessels door and beating the shit out of them for hurting our little girl.

Instead, we both keep quiet and sit at the tub's edge while Summer plays with her toys. I let Evan wash her hair while I just sit and watch. The longer Summer plays, the more the fire in Evan's eyes goes out and regret takes its place.

"I love you, Brooke," he whispers as he stares at Summer.

"I love you too."

"I hate this. I just want to lock the three of us in this house and never leave," he sighs.

"I'd be okay with that. Sounds like a dream," I reply with a smile.

"I'm not ready to say goodbye."

"We could say 'see you again someday' instead," I offer. He finally smiles at that.

"That sounds better than goodbye."

"Yes, it does."

We help Summer out of the tub and dry her off, careful not to touch the bruising too much. Evan pulls the nightgown over her head and gently brushes the tangles out of her hair.

"Maybe you should take her to the doctor to make sure she doesn't have any internal bleeding. Those bruises look bad," Evan says when we enter Summer's room and she races across to the toys she left behind.

"Yeah, I'll take her to see Dr. Adams tomorrow. Do you think it'll be okay to text you what he says?" I ask.

"Probably not. I don't trust my dad not to monitor my phone, and I don't want to give him any reason to take Summer away again," he replies.

"I can let Kristie and Allie know. They can relay the information to you through a phone call. He can't expect you to cease contact with your best friends," I say.

"Thank you. I should probably get going. I don't know when I'll see you again," he says, hooking a finger in a belt loop and pulling me to him.

I collapse in his arms and cling to his waist. We stand like that for a while, breathing in the familiar scents of each other. Long before I'm ready, he lets me go and drops to Summer's level. When he calls, she comes to him and hugs him back like she knows he can't stay.

"See you again someday, Summer. I love you lots," he says into her hair.

"I love you too, Daddy. See you someday," she replies, kissing his cheek.

I walk Evan back into the living room where Kendra's waiting, texting rapidly on her phone. I assume she's talking to Zack. She stands when she notices us and walks to Evan's side. She doesn't attempt to touch him at all.

"I'm sorry for how this turned out, Brooke. I just want you to know I had nothing to do with it," Kendra says, surprising the fuck out of me.

Willa snorts behind me like she doesn't believe her. It's pretty hard to after how much she's lied and schemed, but she actually seems genuine. I give her the kindest smile I can manage.

"Thank you, Kendra."

Kendra moves out the door and waits in the hallway. Evan leans down to kiss me one last time. He rests his forehead on mine for too short a time then whispers 'see you again someday' before flying out the door.

Five days from now, the love of my life will be married to Kendra and I'll be alone but for Summer. I want to do what I can to get Evan back, but I don't have any time. The most I can hope for is that Kristie's dad can find anything to implicate Mr. Van Holsten in something illegal, and we can have him arrested before the wedding takes place. I don't have much hope. Nothing seems to want to go our way.

Forty-Three

Brooke

Days go by without speaking to Evan, and it becomes a sort of new routine for Summer and me. Willa finally went home when she was sure I was finished with my mental breakdowns, but she still calls every day, as do Allie and Kristie. I'm grateful for them all, and I'm glad I didn't lose them in the separation between Evan and me.

I try calling Noah every day to see if he's okay. Kris and Allie said he took the news about Evan's upcoming nuptials hard and that none of them have heard from him since. I'm worried too when all my calls to him go straight to voicemail. Instead, I send him texts to let him know that I'm thinking of him. He answers those, so at least I know he's okay.

Me: Noah, I'm just checking in to see if you're okay. If you feel anything like me, you're not, but let me know you aren't doing reckless shit.

Noah: I'm fine, Brooke. Physically, at least. I know it's not Evan's fault he's marrying Kendra, but it's too soon. If I want to stay Evan's best friend, I'll have to see Kendra all the time. It's hard enough thinking about her, let alone seeing her and knowing she only married him for the same reason she was going to marry me.

Me: I get it. I miss him already and I don't know what would be better. Seeing him every day with her or never seeing him again.

Noah: Marry me, Brooke. I already told Evan I would since he didn't appreciate you, but that's when I thought he was marrying Kendra for the business, not Summer. How is she, by the way?

Me: That's a shitty proposal, Noah. I'd need a better one if I'm going to say yes. She's got bruises all over. She's okay, though, and happy to be home.

Noah: Fuckers. I'm glad she's safe with you. Who would have thought how fucked up our lives would turn out just because of the families we were born to?

Me: Not all that glitters is gold, huh?

Noah: Not even a little. I'll be around if you need anything. Love you, Brooke.

Me: Call your friends. They're worried about you. Love you.

Noah: I'm not ready.

Me: Kristie and Allie, then, if not Evan.

Noah: Fine, mother. I'll shoot them a text.

Me: Good boy.

Noah: Ha!

I still wake up every morning expecting Evan to be there, but my bed remains empty except for the few nights Summer climbs in after a nightmare. I took her to see Dr. Adams the day after I saw Evan last. He was sad to see her again so soon and appalled at the state of her poor little body. He gave us good news, though. Those fuckers claiming to be her parents didn't hurt any of her internal organs, and the bruising will go away completely in a few weeks.

I texted Kristie and Allie to tell them the news, and at the same time, we went over anything Mr. Cleaston might have found. Unfortunately, there was not much. Evan and Kendra's wedding is the day after tomorrow. We don't have any time to find enough to stop the wedding and keep Summer safe. They did promise to relay the message of Summer's health to Evan, though. At least he could have that good news.

I'm miserable without Evan. I never knew happiness like I've known the last few months. I'm not ready to give that up. Summer provides me with a lot of joy, but having Evan is different. I keep my smile for Summer's benefit. I can tell she misses him too.

Tina's been to the house a few times in the days since Summer's been home. Part of it is to check to see how she's doing after the short stint in the Kessel's home. The other part is to go over court things and what to expect. It seems Mr. Van Holsten's been true to his word. He has the termination hearing scheduled for the Monday after Evan's wedding. There was enough

263

evidence provided to show that Mr. and Mrs. Kessel are not fit parents and that the extended home visit which lasted all of a day and a half had disastrous results. Their criminal trial is also going forward and is expected to end in their convictions and subsequent jail time. Summer will need someone to go to anyway, so they are allowing me to adopt her by myself once the termination goes ahead.

It's pretty much the only thing I have to be excited about since this is my life now. I go back to work next week. I haven't been at all last week because of all the life-changing SHIT that happened. I'm so tired of it all. Why can't my life go back to normal? My life in December is how I want it to be all the time.

Summer and I spend the night and most of the next morning binging on ice cream in front of the TV watching Disney +. Ice cream and Disney is the best thing for when the man you thought you married in an arranged marriage you didn't want and subsequently fell in love with… again after being separated for seven years gets for real married to the woman you can confidently call your arch-nemesis since you were fourteen even though parts of you feel kinda bad for her. God! When did my life become akin to a freaking Telenovela? I spent the later years of high school, all of college, and my early twenties drama-free, then Evan Van Holsten strolls back into my life lighting it on fire in the best way but brought his "Big Four" drama and bullshit with him. I'd take it all to have him back, though.

By mid-afternoon when there are less than twenty-four hours before Evan ties the knot and I've eaten absolutely nothing but junk despite Mrs. G making an actual lunch, the doorbell rings through the house. I wonder who the hell that is? Who's come to join in my misery? I lazily open the door, not even caring that one of my sweatpants legs is up to my knee and the other is down where it should be. I don't care that I'm wearing a tank without a bra that I'm pretty sure has multiple stains on it or that my hair looks like a rat's nest because I have neither washed it nor brushed it since I saw Evan last.

Kristie and Allie stand in front of me with suitcases like they're planning on staying for a bit. At first, I just stare at them. I can't comprehend that they're actually here. These women are Evan's friends. Why are they here at my house instead of supporting him on what's sure to be the worst day of his life? I break down into tears long before I can even attempt to answer any of those questions. Allie drops her bags to fold me into her arms as I cry on her shoulder. I'm just so happy they're here.

"Dude, you look like absolute shit," Kristie says, staring at me. I look down, seeing a chocolate stain on my shirt that kinda looks like Africa. Allie shoots her an unapproving look and hugs me harder.

"What are you guys doing here?" I ask through my sniffles.

"We're here to help you get Evan back," Allie says, squeezing my arm before letting me go when she's sure the tears have ceased.

"It seems like both you and Ev feel like the world is ending if you aren't together," Kris says.

"My world is ending! Evan's marrying fucking Kendra tomorrow," I reply, aware of how dramatic it sounds.

"Not if we can help it," Allie says as Summer comes running towards the girls, flinging herself into Allie's arms.

Once the hellos from Summer are through and Mrs. G has taken her into the kitchen to make cookies for our guests, I lead Allie and Kristie to Evan's study. It's still the same as he left it, minus the laptop he uses for work.

Instead of sitting at the sturdy mahogany desk, we sit in the plush loveseat. It only seats two people, but the three of us squish in. Kristie sits in the middle, grabbing her laptop out of the bag and pulling up everything they've been working on.

"Okay, so my dad hired a forensic accountant and a whole other team of people to comb through everything Mr. Van Holsten has touched since he took over the company from his dad a lifetime ago. The forensic guy could see clearly where he fucked with your accounts to make it look like you paid for those testimonies. They traced it back to him so that alone will at least bring charges against him, but he has enough money to get out of that. Enough people are in his pocket here, it'll be hard to nail him without more," Kristie explains.

"Okay, well, have you found more?" I ask, daring to hope that this will go our way.

"Not yet. We have about twenty-four hours to find enough evidence to get Dick arrested and stop the wedding," Kris says.

"Best get to work then," Allie declares, taking her tablet out to do her own research.

"Sandwiches and drinks while you work?" Mrs. G asks, carrying a tray with the snacks.

"Yes, please! You da best, Mrs. G!" Kristie cries as she snatches a sandwich from the tray set in front of us on a little table.

"Bring Evan home, dears," she says quietly in response before leaving us alone in the study.

I leave briefly to get my own laptop and Kristie gives me access to all the information we'll need to bring Mr. Van Holsten to his knees and get Evan back home where he belongs.

Forty-Four

Evan

Today is the day my life officially ends. Not more than two hours from now, I'll be marrying the woman who crushed my best friend's heart under her heel. I'll be marrying the woman who ruined Brooke's whole high school experience for shits and giggles. Where did my life go so wrong? I had everything set out for me to have a perfect life, and instead, it's just turned out to be a fucking nightmare.

I haven't heard from Noah since I told him I'd be marrying Kendra. I keep calling him, but he never answers. I talk to Allie and Kristie every day. They say they haven't heard from Noah either, but that he's texted Brooke. I wish I could fly out to his place in Florida so I could check on him and profusely apologize for all this.

He should be here standing next to me as my best man, but I know that's just a pipe dream. If the bride were Brooke, like it's supposed to be, he'd be here with his infectious smile and jokes at our expense. It's only been five days, but God, I miss my best friend.

I stand in the groom's room of the church they chose to have the wedding in, staring at myself in the floor-length mirror. I have dark circles under my eyes since I haven't been sleeping a wink without Brooke in the bed next to me. My three-piece black suit hangs against the door. Kendra insisted

I wear a vest since I didn't at my last wedding. Luckily for me, I haven't spoken to her much since that night we went to Brooke's house. Let's hope we can continue on that way until one of us dies.

An hour and a half later, my father comes into the room in his matching suit. I'm just finishing with my tie when he lets himself in. I see him in the mirror and I can't help my scowl at the self-satisfied look on his face.

"You look good, son," he says.

"I'm no son of yours," I hiss, turning to face him.

"Don't be dramatic, Evan. You are still my son and heir. You'll inherit my business with an obedient wife at your side. You'll build it up better than I did, just like you said you would. I did you a favor, and it's about time you learned to appreciate all I've done for you," Dad says.

"Yes, I do so appreciate you inserting yourself into all my major life's decisions," I deadpan.

"Don't act like you weren't thankful for your marriage to Miss Jacobs"

"I was, but then you took her and my daughter away from me," I seethe, growing angrier with each word out of his mouth.

"That child is not your daughter, and, unfortunately, Miss Jacobs chose her over you while also proving she didn't have what it takes to be a Van Holsten."

I don't respond. There's nothing I can say to this man to get him to understand that all he's done is fucked up and wrong. Sometimes, there's just no changing people.

"If you'll excuse me, *Dick*, I have a wedding to attend," I say shoulder checking my dad on the way out of the room.

I stride up the aisle toward the altar. Random guests and our families crowd each side of the aisle in the pews of the cathedral, looking at me curiously as I walk. I catch my mom's eye and she looks so sad and apologetic; it makes me want to cry. She never wanted this for me, and now it's happened twice.

I found out Mom and Dad's parents arranged their marriage, and that explains why she's with him. She didn't have a choice, and my dad turned out to be a fucking dick. They've never been in love because how could you

268

love a monster like that? She's been trapped in a loveless marriage for the last thirty years with no escape. Now, I'll follow in her footsteps.

I stand underneath the giant Jesus, but instead of freaking out about who my bride will be or why I'm even going through with this like I was at my last wedding, I'm just resigned. I know who's walking down that aisle and I know why I'm going through with this. It's no longer about something as trivial as taking over a company. It's about the welfare of those I love more than my own life.

At the back of the church, Zack sits looking miserable as hell. He watches as we pass, looking at Dad with a pained expression. I feel for the little boy he used to be just wanting his dad to acknowledge him. I was also that boy. I may be the heir and I may not be the bastard child of Richard Van Holsten, but he paid as much attention to me as he did to Zack.

Too soon for my liking, the flower girl and ring bearer make their way down the aisle. We have no wedding party, so after the little kids come barreling down, the *Wedding March* plays and I watch with little interest as Mr. Berretti and Kendra take their slow, measured steps towards me.

Zack stares at her with such longing and sadness. I understand the emotions and I genuinely feel for the man my dad fucked over worse than me. Neither of us can marry the person we love. He has to watch as she becomes permanently unattainable because I know our dad read Kendra and her father the same riot act he gave to Brooke at our reception. There will be no affairs by either of us. Kendra's dad won't let her mess this up by allowing her to fuck Zack behind my back. Not that I'd care even a little.

Mr. Berretti practically shoves Kendra's hands into mine, and I feel nothing. When her dad sits down, I see her throw a pained look towards Zack. I squeeze once and I hope she takes it as an acknowledgment that I understand how she feels. She wants this wedding to take place just as much as she doesn't. She's so torn between what she really wants and what she wants for the sake of her family and status.

The priest starts his spiel about love and unity and all that bullshit that doesn't apply to us in the slightest. I pull back Kendra's veil to see a satisfied smile on her face, and any sympathy I had for her evaporates. I grab her hand and pull it towards me in a way that no one could describe as gentle or kind and slide on the gaudy, huge ring she must have picked out. She puts mine on and it rests in the space where the one Brooke slid on my finger with shaky hands and words has been for months. Seeing it makes me want to puke all over Kendra's off-white dress. We each say the vows the priest wants us to repeat, but neither of us means any of the words.

"Is there any reason why these two should not be wed? Speak now or forever hold your peace," the priest asks in a loud voice speaking to all our guests. When no one objects, I know the next words are going to pronounce us husband and wife and I'll be forced to kiss this woman.

Just before the priest goes to speak those lawfully binding words, the heavy doors locking us in this church open with a screech, effectively silencing the priest. At the end of the aisle, three women stand staring at us. I smile widely when I find it's Brooke, Allie, and Kristie.

None of them are dressed for a wedding. Instead of gowns fit for the event, they each wear skin-tight jeans and tops as different as their personalities. Instead of strappy high heels, they wear heeled ankle-high boots. Instead of intricate up-dos, their hair is free with gentle curls. It's amazing how they contrast with the drastic differences in their hair color as well as the colors they choose to wear.

"I object to this wedding!" Brooke shouts to be heard as she strides confidently up the aisle towards us.

Kendra's expression changes from satisfied that she snagged THE billionaire's son to a scowl so deep I worry her face will be stuck like that.

"What are you doing here, Brooke? You gave him up for a child that's not even yours. Now you need to get lost so I can marry him. You lost me one son of the "Big Four", you won't lose me another," Kendra says with so much venom in her voice I'm surprised Brooke doesn't drop dead from it.

"He's mine, Kendra, and I'm not letting him go," she says staring straight into Kendra's eyes daring her to argue.

"What's the meaning of this, Richard? You assured me your son was free to marry," Mr. Berretti accuses.

"He is! Miss Jacobs, Miss Cleaston, Miss Stinfield, you need to get out. I can easily have Summer sent back to her parents if you continue to interrupt this wedding," Dad says, glaring at the girls.

Allie and Kristie stand behind Brooke, ready to back her up or provide protection if she needs it. It makes me smile and so happy they love her enough to protect her like that. Kristie and Allie shoot my dad smiles that say he's in trouble, he just doesn't know it yet.

"Here's the thing, Dick, she won't be going anywhere, and neither will I."

Forty-Five

Brooke

I stare at Mr. Van Holsten while Evan and Kendra stand behind me, still at the altar. Everything is so quiet in here, you could hear a pin drop. Dick is seething at me for ruining this wedding, and I smile at him. Not one to back down from anything, he walks straight up to me until we're basically nose to nose. He stands much taller than me, and I'm sure he's expecting me to cower away as most people would. He's formidable, but he's not as invincible as he thinks he is.

"You need to leave," he growls at me in a whisper no one else can hear.

"Nope. I learned some stuff about you, Dicky Boy!" I bellow. I want everyone to hear.

"Whatever you think you know, it won't be enough to damage me the way I will wreck you. The child will be gone, you will lose your job and any money you got from my son. I will ruin your entire family and anyone dumb enough to associate with you," he threatens.

Once upon a time just him speaking to me in this way regardless of the words would have had me wetting my pants, but now that I know what I know, he doesn't scare me. I'm going to ruin him. I give the asshole my most malicious smile and I hope he has the good sense to be scared, but I don't think he does.

"Your dear friend, Mr. Cleaston, didn't like how you've been handling your shit lately, so he was more than happy to help me compile a metric shit ton of evidence of every illegal thing you've done since you got off your momma's tit. I have it all, Dick, and I'm going to fucking bury you under it. You fucked with the wrong person," I say quieter now. Mr. Van Holsten's eyes flash for a second, but he's a master at not showing weakness.

The man has plenty of weaknesses and vices, though. Most of them are as illegal as his business dealings. It took us hours, and a lot of help from people smarter than us that Mr. Cleaston hired, to find what we were looking for, but once we did, it was all there staring us straight in the face.

A simple call to the FBI, who had apparently long suspected Mr. Van Holsten of insider trading as well as dozens of other illegal activities, were more than happy to talk to us. Upon seeing our evidence, which they were able to make sure was collected legally so it couldn't be thrown out when all this went to trial, they agreed that this was the best time to search his office at Van Holsten Conglomerate and his home with warrants.

Before Dick can make any more threats, the FBI, in full tactical gear, come slamming in the door guns trained on us. Dick glances at them and back at me. In his eyes, I see fear and a whole lot of anger. I smile at him in triumph.

"I'm stopping this wedding and I'm marrying your son as soon as humanly possible. After that, we're adopting Summer and giving her your name. Evan will take over your company, or what's left of it, and run it legally and legitimately. Summer will be his heir, and if she wants to, will take it over when it's her time. All your assets will be seized and Mrs. Van Holsten will be filing for divorce. Lucky for her, she gets to keep whatever isn't seized and you have no more control over her family's money or the trust they left Evan. We will be together and we'll be fine, but you? Your ass will be in prison for the rest of your life and maybe, just maybe, you'll regret inserting yourself where you don't fucking belong," I say loud enough for all to hear as my FBI contact slaps cuffs on Dick.

"Richard Van Holsten, you're under arrest for insider trading, tax evasion and fraud, gambling, money laundering for cartels in your smaller businesses, conspiracy to commit murder, and about a thousand other things.

You have the right to remain silent," the FBI guy says as he walks Mr. Van Holsten out of the church.

I watch for a second, satisfied justice has been served, and that I was in time to stop Evan from marrying Kendra. I'm about to turn around when I feel familiar arms wrap around my waist and pick me up. I kick out my legs with a laugh. Evan lets me down and I turn until I'm able to thread my arms around his neck and pull his face down for a kiss.

High-pitched screeching stops the kiss before it goes on too long and we break apart to look behind Evan. Kendra's head is thrown back as she yells. Angry tears are falling down her face and her expression is murderous.

"Why do you always ruin everything!" she yells, stomping her foot. She's like a second away from falling to the floor, kicking her arms and legs out in a toddleresque temper-tantrum.

"Don't touch things that aren't yours," I reply, giving her a sly grin that elicits more squeals before her dad takes her arm gruffly and pulls her towards the door.

I go to kiss Evan again, but Kristie and Allie run up to us, jumping in excitement that we were able to pull this off. I smile at them, as does Evan. He still looks a little shocked at all he learned, but happiness outweighs all of that.

"I love you," he says with that shy smile of his I love so much.

"I love you, too."

"We did it!" Kristie shouts.

Most of the guests have left the church, leaving the four of us and Evan's mom remaining. She hangs back until Evan breaks his embrace with us and pulls her in. She's crying and I hope they're happy tears. I hope what I said is what she wants. I can't imagine she wants to be married to that abusive piece of shit any longer.

"Let's go home. I have a daughter I want to see and for you to get to know," he says to his mom, wrapping one arm around her shoulders and the other around mine.

* * *

Instead of getting married at the courthouse as soon as possible, we decide to have the wedding we wished we had the first time around. Small and intimate with our friends in attendance and a part of the wedding party. It takes some planning so we'll be tying the knot for real this time in May.

In the meantime, our hearing for Summer goes ahead on Monday. They assigned a new judge to preside over our case. The Kessel's parental rights are terminated promptly, and we're able to file for adoption right away. Tina's still our caseworker and probably a lifelong friend. Everything seems to be falling into place as the months pass us by. We have a lot to look forward to and I'm ready for it all.

Now we're here. Today is my wedding day, and it's supposed to be one of the happiest days of your life. I can tell you right now, it's going to be one of mine. For me, my life is just now beginning. I only ever imagined marrying one person, and it's finally happening!

Forty-Six

Evan

Standing at the altar this time is worlds away from either of the other two times. I'm not nervous thinking I'm in Hell, nor am I simply resigned that this is how it has to be. Instead. I'm overjoyed and ridiculously happy. My heart feels like it wants to beat right out of my chest in the best possible way.

Noah is standing right behind me in a seriously smart suit. Kristie's behind him to give us an equal number on both sides. Willa's the maid of honor and Allie is the other bridesmaid. The four of them smile at me, genuinely happy too as we wait for Brooke.

As soon as I was able, I flew to Florida to check on Noah. He was kind of a mess but forgave me easily because that's what you do for your family when they deserve it. I don't know what more I can do for him. He's working through a lot of hurt, and I think my brief engagement to Kendra put him back in the process. I'll just be here for him. I think at the end of the day, that's what he needs the most.

Despite all that, he's happy for me and he's standing with me just like he was always meant to. Summer's sitting with my mom, who looks happier than I've ever seen her now that her divorce from my dad is going ahead. She adores Summer and vice versa.

Next week, we have our final court hearing for Summer's adoption, where she'll become ours permanently. I can't really decide if I'm more excited to make Brooke my wife or becoming Summer's dad officially.

My dad is in jail pending his trial. He pled not guilty to all charges, obviously. My dad won't go down without a nasty fight, but the judge agreed to remand him to custody without bail since he has the means to flee the country. I haven't seen or spoken to him since his arrest. I see him on TV all the time and get people asking about him, but I don't answer.

I've been spending all my time with my family or trying to pick up the pieces of Van Holsten Conglomerate. The FBI gave me the go-ahead to start business again, but we lost a lot of contacts and businesses. I didn't realize how many were just fronts for all the side hustles my dad had going on. Good thing a majority of our stuff is legal and most people are happy to do business with me. I'll get it back on track. This is everything I ever worked for and wanted, after all.

Pachelbel's Canon starts and I whip my head up to see Mr. Jacobs and Brooke walking down the aisle. Her dress looks a lot like the one she wore to our last wedding, but this time her hair is down with soft curls flowing in the soft breeze. We're getting married in a park outside of the city. It's a perfect day outside and the place is surrounded by beautiful flowers.

Mr. Jacobs places Brooke's hand in mine and she meets my eyes head-on this time with the most beautiful smile known to man. She gives her bouquet back to Willa and takes both my hands in hers. Our officiant does his thing and I'm barely listening, but this time it's because I'm lost in Brooke's blue eyes.

I come back down to Earth when Brooke places the ring we married with before on my finger. With a too-hard shove on my back, Noah gives me the twisted bands of Brooke's wedding set, which has since been soldered together, and I place it back on Brooke's finger. These are staying where they're at for the rest of our God damn lives. Nothing is tearing us apart again. No more weddings! I'm personally taking this license to get recorded with the state to ensure this marriage is fucking legal this time around.

"The bride and groom have written their own vows. Evan, you may go first."

Promises of Forever

I take a deep breath as I hold on to Brooke's hands like my life depends on it.

"Brooke, I've loved you for half my life and I promise to love you for the rest of it too. I'll love you through whatever life has thrown at us. We've already made it through enough to pull others apart, but I think in our case, it's made us stronger. I can't imagine my life without you. I almost had to, and it killed me. Now I'm making you officially mine and there's nothing anyone can do about it. Now, as I stand here in front of you and everyone we love, I'm promising you forever. I love you," I say itching to kiss Brooke's lips, which are turned up at the sides in a smile.

"Evan, we spent too much time apart because I blamed you for things not in your control. There is just nothing left that can tear us apart. My life began when I met you almost twenty years ago at that gala we shouldn't have been attending, and it ended for a while after that day in the pool house. I didn't realize it had until it began again the day I saw you standing in front of me at the altar. It ended and began a thousand times after that, but now I can say that it's beginning again for the last time as I stand here promising my forever to you too."

"You may now kiss the bride," the officiant says.

"Don't mind if I do," I whisper in Brooke's ear as I pull her close to me for a kiss even more dazzling than the last.

When I pull back, all I see is Brooke's megawatt smile that tells me there is nowhere else she'd rather be. Ditto, babe. This has been fifteen years in the making and we're finally here.

278

Epilogue

Noah

Standing beside Evan as he gets everything he wants, simultaneously makes me happy as shit for him while also inflicting little stabs to my heart. It's not that I really wanted to marry Kendra before I found out about her betrayal, or now that I know. Especially not after she was ready to fucking marry my best friend for a status boost, but I want love and happiness like Evan has with Brooke.

I'm not too proud to admit I'm kind of jealous of them. Happy for them, but also jealous. All my friends are telling me I'll find love and happiness too. I just need to open my heart and shit for it to happen, but I don't know if I'm ready for that. It ended really fucking shitty last time. What makes me think next time will be any different?

Kendra's been texting me on and off for the last few months since her failed wedding. For the most part, I ignore her. If I'm really pissed, I tell her to fuck off and go fuck Zack like she's been doing for the last thirteen years. Like always, she doesn't react to my outbursts. I guess that was one good thing about her. I can get mean sometimes when I'm mad. Call it a character flaw or whatever, but Kendra just ignored them because she knew I rarely meant it. Well, I mean every fucking word I say to her now.

Still, it doesn't stop her from texting and as we drew nearer to Brooke and Evan's real wedding, she's been texting more. She's texted me more today than she has in the last few months combined. She's bringing up some

279

painful fucking memories. Each time they squeeze at my heart, I take a shot of whiskey.

The wedding has an open bar and while I hang out with Summer, Kristie, and Sweets, Kendra's burying herself into my head with each little ping of my phone. Shot after shot leaves me drunk as shit when I finally call my car to take me back to Evan's place.

When my phone chirps again with another text for Kendra, I don't even think about the repercussions or how much of a bad fucking idea it is. I just hit the call button and do the one thing drunk people shouldn't fucking do. There is a reason you don't talk to your ex when you're wasted. It's because if they want you as badly as Kendra wants me, they'll fucking answer and it's all downhill from there.

"Noah? To what do I owe this pleasure?" she purrs into my ear like she hasn't been texting nonstop.

"I'm staying at my dad's hotel on fifth avenue. Come see me."

Ready for Book Two?

Noah's story is next! Forever is Our Today is book two in the Drops of Forever series. Get it now on Amazon or Barnes and Noble.

FOREVER IS OUR TODAY

A DROPS OF FOREVER NOVEL

HOPE RUIZ

Want to see more of Brooke, Evan, Allie, and Kristie? They'll be back in Forever is Our Today. It picks up right where Promises of Forever ends.

Each book in this series about the children of the "Big Four" is a standalone, but when you read them in order, the timelines and the things that happen to each character make more sense.

Noah

I'm standing behind my best friend in the entire world, my brother from another mother as he marries the woman of his dreams. Literally. Brooke had been the one for Evan since before high school. It was too bad Kendra and that fuckwit Zack got in the way of them being together sooner. So many wasted years.

Speaking of wasted years, how many had I wasted on Kendra? Too fucking many. Thirteen years, I spent with that manipulative witch and I didn't even realize what kind of person she was until Brooke caught Kendra and Zack, my other really good friend, fucking at my house when they were all visiting during Brooke and Evan's honeymoon.

All the most important people in my life were in my house at the same time in way too fucking long and that's when I find out the woman I was going to spend my life with had been fucking around with Zack nearly the entire time we'd been dating.

For thirteen solid years, they'd been carrying on an affair right under my dumbass nose. How had I not seen it? They'd been best friends since they were in diapers, and I was the dipshit that trusted them both. Kendra was only with me for my money and status. I was supposed to take over my father's company as the firstborn Whittier son. She wanted the fortune, the status that Zack, though somewhat rich, could never afford her.

She sunk her claws into me just as we were going into ninth grade and never let go. What a fucking idiot I am. Kristie, the other of my three best friends, knew what kind of snake Kendra was from the beginning. I'd heard all her comments but never listened to them. I thought Kristie was just being Kristie. She's brash and unapologetic.

For a minute there, I was genuinely pissed at Evan, Kristie, and Allie for not telling me about Kendra's toxic behavior, but I know why they didn't. Besides the fact that they didn't know how bad it truly was, I wouldn't have listened. I had blinders on where she was concerned, and it took Brooke to get me to see the truth finally.

So, I'm standing here as the best man for my best friend, watching him find the absolute happiness I always wanted and never really had. I'm smiling for him. I'm genuinely happy for him, but I'm not happy. I'm hurt and pissed still, even though it's been nine months.

Thirteen years with someone is too long to not still be sad after nine months. I'm not so much sad that our relationship is over. I'm fucking thrilled to be rid of someone so awful, but I'm sad for the end of my relationship. I'm sad I don't have someone to come home to anymore, no matter how unpleasant and high maintenance she was.

Most of all, I'm lonely. I've spent most of my adolescent and adult life always with someone, and now I'm alone. Like truly alone for the first time in… ever. I don't even live in the same city as my parents and little brother anymore.

After Kendra tore my fucking heart out of my chest and threw it into oncoming traffic, I was just done. I didn't want to take over my dad's company. I never really had, so I didn't. I noped the fuck out of that expectation, and my little brother was more than happy to take my place.

Of course, my dad threatened to cut me off if I left, but whatever, I made it work. I got a job producing music, which is something I always wanted to do but never pursued because of my responsibility to my family. The minute I inked myself up and refused to wear a suit, he knew the company life wasn't for me. My dad didn't cut me off or anything, but I don't want anything from them. I'll make my own way. Dad knew I was a lost cause long before this, anyway.

I moved several hours away from them, and now I rarely talk to my family at all. I just need some distance from that life. I am finally on my own for the first time in my life and though it's ridiculously lonely, it's also freeing as hell to have no expectations except for my own.

I came back to New York for Brooke and Evan's real wedding five months after I was here to spend the holidays with them. It's great since I wasn't invited to the first. I stand here and try to look as happy as I should feel, but I see Allie and Kristie's penetrating stares. I know they'll call me on my bullshit the minute there's time.

That time comes during the reception. We're sitting together as plates of food are placed in front of us. I try to dig in without meeting the stares of my other best friends, but it doesn't work.

"Noah, talk to us," Allie says, soft-spoken as always. She's the sweetest person in our group of friends.

"Don't be sad over that bitch you dumped. It's been nine months and we know for damn sure she's moved on. She was all up for marrying Evan," Kristie chimes in.

She's talking about the fact that when Evan's dad found out the marriage between Brooke and Evan wasn't legal, he wanted to get rid of Brooke. He arranged for Evan to marry Kendra instead because Mr. Van Holsten thought Kendra would be a better puppet.

The reminder stings a little, but it is what it is. Brooke, Kristie, and Allie were able to stop the wedding before it became legal while also getting Evan's dad arrested for all the illegal shit he'd done over the years.

I kinda wish Kris didn't bring it up because it fucked me up real bad when I heard that Evan would be marrying her, but Kristie is—well—Kristie. She's a spit-fire. The one that never does what anyone expects. She's outspoken and gives zero fucks about how her words come across. She's also the most real person I've ever met, and I love that about her.

"Kristie, don't. He's allowed to be sad," Allie chastises with a stern look on her face. She doesn't get mad often, but Allie can be just as formidable as Kristie just in her own way.

"Sorry. I know you're hurting Noah, but you're a wonderful guy. There's someone out there perfect for you. She's just waiting for you to find her," Kristie says with a kind smile.

"Whoa there Kristie, you almost sounded like Sweets being all genuine and shit," I joke because what else can I do? This is who I am. The jokester, the easy-go-lucky guy that always has a smile for everyone.

Kristie scowls at my teasing, but it quickly morphs into a satisfied smile. She nudges my shoulder as we eat our dinner.

"It will get better," Allie whispers and grabs my hand. She gives it a reassuring squeeze and I can't help but feel comforted in their presence. I'll be sad when they go back to L.A. tomorrow and I go back to Florida. I always feel at home wherever they are.

I dance with Allie throughout the night. Kristie's the only one with a date. She's seeing Brooke's best friend, Willa, on and off when they're in the same city. Allie's my date tonight, and that's perfect. Maybe this is all I need right now. My own company and the company of my best friends in the entire world. I know them well and I love them dearly.

Evan and Brooke come dancing up to me and Allie sometime during the night. I smile at the happy couple and it's not even forced. I wonder if they've noticed the difference. It's getting easier as the night goes on. Kendra's been texting me nonstop and every time she does, I take a drink or a shot.

"Sorry, I haven't been able to chill with you guys. Weddings are a little crazy, and this is the second one we've had in the last year," Evan apologizes.

"At least this one is significantly smaller and less public than our last one," Brooke says with a twinkling laugh.

"So where's the honeymoon this time?" I ask.

"No honeymoon this time around, but I think we'll take a family vacation in a few months after school's ended, and the adoption is finalized. Summer's never been to Disney World, and I have fond memories of the place. We'll come see you when we go," Evan replies with a smile.

"Sure. I'd love to see my niece. Speaking of which, where's my little princess?" I ask, looking around.

Summer comes bounding out of nowhere and jumps into my free arms. She's wearing a white dress that comes to her knees, and her blonde hair has escaped whatever was holding it together. If no one knew better, they would think Summer is Evan and Brooke's biological child, but she's not. They're getting ready to adopt her after Brooke found her wandering the streets alone. They couldn't find her family and Brooke couldn't stand the thought of the little four-year-old going into the foster care system, so she and Evan took her in. It was love at first sight in a way no one had experienced before. Trying to become foster parents and eventually adoptive parents to Summer was how they found out they weren't actually married, as they had thought. There was a bunch of other drama with Evan's dad, which is what led to his brief engagement to Kendra.

Summer is still kind of afraid of strangers, but when we met for the first time back in December for her fifth birthday party, we were instant friends. I guess my height and tattoos didn't scare this little girl. She's my favorite person in the world now.

I poke Summer in the ribs, and she giggles as she nuzzles into my neck. I can feel her yawn.

"Is someone tired?" I ask, poking her again.

"Not tired," Summer sighs, but then her breathing evens out and I know she's down.

"Sorry, Noah. I can take her," Brooke says, tearing herself away from Evan.

I gently shift Summer to Brooke's waiting arms and as soon as she's there, a content smile crosses Brooke's face. She looks so happy and an unexpected pang of jealousy hits me. I tamp it down because their gain is not my loss and I refuse to be anything but happy for them today.

"Summer really loves you," Evan comments as we walk over to the bar for a drink.

"I love her too," I say.

"How are you?" Evan asks. I think about giving him the same answer I gave him before. It was true but also only superficially what I'm feeling. I decide to give him a more genuine answer.

"Better than before. I'm lonely and I'm sad, but also I feel free for the first time and I'm going to explore that feeling. Who knows, maybe I'll date," I respond.

"Good, good. It's only a matter of time before all the girls in Florida realize you're single and are knocking down your door," Evan says with a laugh. I laugh with him, but it's not my normal laugh.

"Or maybe I'll take a stab at being single for a little while longer," I say because I don't think I'm ready to be dating anyone. Evan shrugs.

"Everything with be waiting for you when you're ready," he says and claps my shoulder.

"Thanks, Ev," I reply.

Despite all the words of encouragement from my friends, I'm still sad enough that Kendra's barrage causes me to drink too fucking much. There's an open bar at the wedding and I've been taking double shots of whiskey all night. By midnight, I'm wrecked. The good news is the alcohol did what it was meant to do. It made me forget why I'm sad and that I'm even sad in the first place. The bad news? As soon as the car came and picked me up, I do exactly what drunk ass people do. I call my fucking ex. Kendra's all too happy to answer when I call.

"Noah? To what do I owe this pleasure?" she purrs into my ear like she hasn't been texting me all night.

"I'm staying at my dad's hotel on fifth avenue. Come see me," I reply. I'm actually staying at Evan's place, but I won't bring Kendra there. I wonder if she understands. Even I can hear the slurring of my speech.

"Sure, baby. I'll be right there," she answers, then hangs up the phone.

I'm sure somewhere in the back of my mind, I know this is a shitty fucking idea. And somewhere I'm asking myself where the fuck Zack's at tonight, but the drunk part doesn't give two single fucks about the answers to either of those questions. I'm lonely and I'm sad. Kendra will make it better... or worse. Probably worse, but I'm too fucking drunk to care.

When I stumble out of my car to the front doors of the hotel, I see Kendra in a tan trench coat standing by the reception desk. I stalk over there and before I can think about what I'm doing; I grab her around the waist and pull her close to me. I crash my lips down to hers and she moans into my mouth, spurring me on.

I pull her to the elevator and smash the button for the penthouse suite. I didn't actually check-in, but the penthouse is always open to me since my dad owns the place. I continue to devour her mouth and neck with mine and I'm rewarded when I finally push her into the room and she slowly takes off the trench coat until it pools at her feet.

Underneath she's wearing a lacy black bra, a matching thong, and some sort of garter holding up black thigh-high tight things. She's wearing hooker heels and I can barely contain myself as I launch at her. The last thing I remember is pushing her onto the bed and the echoes of her giggles. Then everything goes black.

* * *

Three Months Later

Tom, my first and only friend I've made since moving away from my parents, stomps into my office at the music producing studio I work at.

"What's up?" I ask when he shuts the door behind him.

"I have a proposition for you," he says, sitting down in the chair across from me.

"Okay," I respond suspiciously.

"So, I know you just got out of a terrible relationship, but I've watched you mope around for like almost a year and I can tell you're lonely. My girlfriend has a roommate who also got out of a bad relationship too and has been moping around, same as you. We thought maybe you guys could go on a date. You know, get back out there," Tom says.

I stare at the guy. Is he fucking insane? I'm not ready for that kind of thing. Especially not with some chick who's probably still pining for the jack-off that dumped her.

"No," I say.

"Dude, come on. Her name is Avery, and she's cute," Tom says, holding out his phone for me to see.

I don't really care what she looks like. She could be a perfect ten, and it wouldn't change how I feel about dating right now. I look at the picture anyway and I see three girls. I recognize one as Holly, Tom's sometimes girlfriend. The other two I don't recognize.

"Which one's Avery?" I ask because though all three girls are beautiful, the one with black hair and pale green eyes catches my eye.

There's something alluring about her. I don't know if it's because she kinda reminds me of Kristie with her eyes or if it's because her smile is sweet like Allie's. She's got a sparkle in her eye like she's happy. I could use a little happiness in my life.

Tom points out of black-haired beauty I was hoping it would be. I shrug when he pulls his phone back.

"Okay," I say. Tom stares at me wide-eyed. He didn't expect me to say yes.

"You'll go?" he asks.

"Yeah, I'll go. How bad could one night out be?"

About the Author

Hope Ruiz lives in Mountain Home, Idaho with her husband and two kids. She enjoys reading, writing, and gardening. You can often find her at time reading a good book or hanging out with her family and friends.

You can connect with me on:

 https://www.facebook.com/hopemarie55

Also by Hope Ruiz

Hope Ruiz writes fiction, usually romance.

Simple Twist of Fate

Sisters Paige and Olivia Wells have normal but opposite lives until Fate sends them on an unbelievable journey through time to find their soulmates. First, they find themselves aboard the R.M.S. Titanic only days before it's destined to sink. They face an impossible choice; Try to stop it and risk changing the future or let it happen, even though they might perish too. When they travel again, they find themselves in 1941 with the bombing of Pearl Harbor looming on the horizon. Will they make the same choices as they did on the Titanic or will they choose differently? Trying to get home from this adventure they never wanted, they find themselves in ways they never expected.

What Lies Beyond

Jackson Myles died at the ripe old age of twenty-one. Follow him through his journey through the afterlife as he meets various people and deities to learn what his life meant. Flipping back and forth between the past and his present in the afterlife, learn what led to Jackson's tragically brief life.

Forever Is Our Today (Drops of Forever Book Two)

Noah

It's been a year since I got my heart broken into a million pieces by the woman I thought I'd spend my life with. Now, people are done with my pity party, so they set me up on a blind date. What's a few hours? I can handle this.

Avery

When my friends give me no choice but to go on a blind date with a stranger, I figure maybe it's my time to get back out there. What's the worst that can happen? Maybe a hurricane that demands a stay in place advisory and a weekend alone with that stranger.

This is book one in a series of standalone novels in the Drops of Forever series. You can read each book separately and the story will make sense, but if you read them in order each child of the "Big Four" gets their own story.

Made in the USA
Las Vegas, NV
06 August 2021